ABOUT THE EDITORS

LIZ GRZYB was born in the middle of a thunderstorm in Perth, Western Australia. She is the editor of the acclaimed paranormal romance anthologies *Scary Kisses* and *More Scary Kisses*, and of the webzine *Ticon4.com*. Forthcoming projects include co-editing *Damnation & Dames* with Amanda Pillar.

TALIE HELENE is a musician and writer, from Melbourne, Australia. She has poetry published in journals including *Voiceworks*, *Avant*, and *Inkshed*, and Mary Manning's *About Poetry* (Oxford University Press), and a co-authored short story "The Last Gig of Jimmy Rucker" (with Martin Livings) in *More Scary Kisses*. Talie was News Editor for the Australian Horror Writers' Association for four years (2006–2010), for which she received a Ditmar nomination. As a journalist she has been on staff at the UK's bible of extreme music, *Zero Tolerance* magazine, for five years; her column Waltzing Macabre was a regular in *Black: Australian Dark Culture* magazine. Talie has performed with many artists including The Tenth Stage, Wendy Rule, Sean Bowley, Saba Persian Orchestra, Maroondah Symphony, and Eden. She is currently developing a new audio arts anthology titled *The Unquiet Grave*. You can find out more at www.taliehelene.com

THE YEAR'S BEST AUSTRALIAN FANTASY & HORROR

~ 2010 ~

EDITED BY

LIZ GRZYB & TALIE HELENE

THE FIRST ANNUAL COLLECTION

THE YEAR'S BEST AUSTRALIAN FANTASY & HORROR
~ 2010 ~

EDITED BY
LIZ GRZYB & TALIE HELENE

T≋ Ticonderoga
ƥ≋ publications

for

Helen Grzyb [LG]

&

Olive Dean Egan [TH]

The Year's Best Fantasy & Horror 2010
edited by Liz Grzyb & Talie Helene

Published by Ticonderoga Publications

Copyright © 2011 Liz Grzyb & Talie Helene

Introduction copyright © 2011 Liz Grzyb & Talie Helene
"The Year in Fantasy" copyright © 2011 Liz Grzyb
"The Year in Horror" copyright © 2011 Talie Helene

Cover "The Fortress" by Yaroslav Gerzhedovich

Designed by Russell B. Farr
Typeset in Sabon and Poor Richard

A Cataloging-in-Publications entry for this title is available from The National Library of Australia.

ISBN   978-0-9807813-8-0 (hardcover)
       978-0-9807813-9-7 (trade paperback)
       978-1-921857-98-0 (ebook)

Ticonderoga Publications
PO Box 29 Greenwood
Western Australia 6924

www.ticonderogapublications.com

10 9 8 7 6 5 4 3 2 1

ACKNOWLEDGEMENTS

The editors would like to thank RJ Astruc, Peter M Ball, Alan Baxter, Jenny Blackford, Gitte Christensen, Matthew Chrulew, Bill Congreve, Rjurik Davidson, Felicity Dowker, Dale Elvy, Jason Fischer, Dirk Flinthart, Bob Franklin, Christopher Green, Paul Haines, Lisa L Hannett, Stephen Irwin, Gary Kemble, Pete Kempshall, Tessa Kum, Martin Livings, Maxine McArthur, Kirstyn McDermott, Andrew McKiernan, Ben Peek, Simon Petrie, Lezli Robyn, Angela Rega, Angela Slatter, Grant Stone, Kaaron Warren, Janeen Webb, Jonathan Strahan, Chuck McKenzie, Angela Challis and Russell B Farr.

Liz would like to thank Talie Helene, Helen Grzyb, Shane Cummings, Amanda Pillar, Kate Dunbar-Smith, Kate Williams, Andrew Williams, Matthew Williams, Debbie Wilson, Jacinta Rosielle, Ambre Hillier, Michael Hillier, Tasmar Dixon, Kylie Dainton, Mel Barndon, Mel Donald, Phil Ward, Ruza Foster, Lina Piscitelli, Nikki Irwin, Andrea Orlowsky, Angie Irwin, Fee Wort, Jane Hebiton, Lynne Keenan, Zoe Brooks, Jane McKenzie, Dionn Godhino, Clare MacFarlane, Anne Hodgson, Meredith Wright and Suad Majrouh.

Talie would like to thank Liz Grzyb, Jason Nahrung, Gillian Polack, Sharyn Liley, Ellen Gregory, Lee Battersby, Marty Young, Alisa Krasnostein, Tehani Wessely, Jack Dann, Stephen Dedman, Danny Lovecraft, Leigh Blackmore, Robert Hood, David Conyers, Robert Shearman, Lucy Sussex, Kim Wilkins, Fiona Trembath, Earl Livings, Barry Watts, Mary Mannning, Barry Dickens, Deborah Crabtree, Sonia van Maanenberg, David Wattie, Mark Evans, Lee Du-Caine, Lisa and Leon Macey, Calum Harvie, the HorrorScope team, Nyssa Pascoe, Peter Hurley and Barbara Crowe.

CONTENTS

INTRODUCTION: THE YEAR IN REVIEW

LIZ GRZYB & TALIE HELENE

THE YEAR IN FANTASY

2010 was a great year for Australian fantasy. The Worldcon held in Melbourne served as an impetus for many publishers, both large and small, to focus on Australian and New Zealander speculative fiction. Several hundred stories in all subgenres of fantasy were published in 2010, contained in Australasian and international magazines, webzines, anthologies and collections. These were complemented by a wide range of novels reaching from dark and urban fantasy, paranormal romance to high fantasy and steampunk.

It was fantastic to see Australians being published in a range of international publications such as Lezli Robyn in IDW's *Classics Mutilated* anthology, Peter M Ball appearing in *Apex* Magazine, and Jason Fischer in the *Writers of the Future* competition and anthology. Lisa L Hannett had a productive year, appearing in the *Tesseracts 14* anthology, joining Angela Slatter in having work published in Ann & Jeff VanderMeer's *Steampunk Reloaded* anthology, and selling a story to *Weird Tales* magazine alongside Aidan Doyle, among others.

Australians also featured prominently in worldwide awards, such as Shaun Tan's Oscar for *The Lost Thing* short film; Tansy Rayner Roberts' novella *Siren Beat* won the Washington SF Association's Small Press Award this year; and World Fantasy Awards went to Margo Lanagan for her novella "Sea Hearts", published in coeur de lion's *X6* anthology, and to Jonathan Strahan for his anthology editing work. Strahan was also nominated for his science fiction and fantasy anthology *Eclipse Three* from Night Shade Books.

Tansy Rayner Roberts continued her excellent year by winning an Australia Council grant to write her next novel, an urban fantasy called *Fury*.

RECOMMENDED NOVELS

The first two instalments of Trent Jamieson's Death Works series were published by Hachette Orbit this year, and are unmissable. *Death Most Definite* is the first, introducing anti-hero Steven de Selby and his family business Mortmax. They are responsible for simplifying Australian deaths and "pomping", processing their souls. *Managing Death*, the second in the series, is another gritty take on urban fantasy with a very Australian flavour.

Juliet Marillier's *Heart's Blood* is a wonderful high fantasy novel published by Pan Macmillan this year, that will become a classic. Loosely structured around my favourite fairytale *Beauty and the Beast*, *Heart's Blood* tells a tale of adventure and love, while exploring ideas about loyalty, mental illness, and how women can forge their own way in a patriarchal world.

Feisty characters, steamy romance, danger and magic in an Australian setting: what more could any paranormal/urban fantasy fan want? *Secret Ones* is the first novel in Nicole Murphy's *Dream of Asarlai* series from Harper Voyager about the Gadda, an almost-human race of magic users.

Power and Majesty is Tansy Rayner Roberts' first instalment in her Creature Court series released by Harper Voyager, telling of power struggles of a group of beings augmented with "animor", animal spirits. It is a page-turner of a novel which overlays compelling reality and relationships with the fantastic.

OTHER NOTABLE NOVELS

The big international publishers continued to play a large part in the Australian fantasy world this year, with Hachette and Harper Collins releasing many fantasy novels, as well as many titles from smaller publishers and independent press.

Some notable fantasy titles from Harper Collins include: Anita Bell's science fiction/fantasy novel *Diamond Eyes*; Trudi Canavan's first novel in the Traitor Spy series, *Ambassador's Mission*; Kylie Chan's first two novels in the Journey to Wudang series, *Hell to Heaven* and *Earth to Hell*. Sara Douglass concluded her DarkGlass Mountain trilogy with *The Infinity Gate*; Will Elliott released *Pilgrims*; Kim Falconer finished her Quantum Enchantment trilogy with *Strange Attractors*, and started her new trilogy Quantum Encryption with *Path of the Stray*. Traci Harding began her scifi/fantasy Triad of the Being series with *Being of the Field* and *Universe Parallel*; Glenda Larke continued her Watergivers series with *Stormlord Rising*; Duncan Lay continued his Dragon Sword Histories series with *The Risen Queen* and *The Radiant Child*. Bevan McGuinness began a new The Eleven Kingdoms series with *Slave of Sondelle*; Fiona McIntosh completed the Valisar trilogy with *King's Wrath*; Karen Miller released the second in her Fisherman's Children series, *The Reluctant Mage* and the third in the Rogue Agent series, *Wizard Squared*, under her nom de plume K E Mills. K J Taylor released books two and three of the Fallen Moon series, *Griffin's Flight* and *Griffin's War*; and Mary Victoria began her Chronicles of the Tree series with *Tymon's Flight*.

Notables from Hachette Group include: Sam Bowring's Broken Well trilogy books two and three, *Destiny's Rift* and *Soul's Reckoning*; Joel Shepherd's fourth book in his A Trial of Blood and Steel series, *Haven*; Nalini Singh's continuation of her Guild Hunter series with a reissue of *Angels' Blood* and *Archangel's Kiss*. Singh's Psy/Changeling series was previously published in the USA, but was first released in Australia this year, including *Slave To Sensation*, *Visions of Heat*, and *Caressed By Ice*.

Pan Macmillan released two novels from Juliet Marillier this year: the previously mentioned *Heart's Blood* and a continuation of the Sevenwaters series, *Seer of Sevenwaters*. Lara Morgan also continued her Twins of Saranthium series with *Betrayal*.

Random House published a couple of Australian young adult fantasy novels this year, Ben Chandler's *Quillblade*, and Michael Pryor's *Moment of Truth*.

Other publishers who brought out fantasy titles from Australian authors include Solaris Books who released three volumes of Rowena Cory Daniells' King Rolen's Kin series: *The King's Bastard*, *The Uncrowned King*, and *The Usurper*. Allen & Unwin brought out Deborah Kalin's *Shadow Bound* and Berkley Heat (Penguin) published Christina Phillips' paranormal romance *Forbidden*.

Australian independent presses have brought out some interesting books this year, such as Twelfth Planet Press publishing Peter M Ball's fantasy/horror novella *Bleed* and the fantasy and science fiction novelette duo *The Company Articles of Edward Teach* by Thoraiya Dyer and Matthew Chrulew's *The Angælien Apocalypse*. Anne Hamilton published *Many Coloured Realm* through Wombat Books, and Davenport Creative released Virginia Higgins' young adult novel *Faerytale*. Clouds of Magellan published G L Osborne's *Come Inside*, and Interactive Publications brought out Jess Webster's *The Secret Stealer: A Grand History of the Curse and its Accursees, Volume 267: James Winchester IV*. US small press Jupiter Gardens Press published Sylvia Kelso's *Source*.

Some notable self-published novels for the year are Reece Hauxby's *Justin Gale Deals With Death*, Andrea K. Höst's novels *The Silence of Medair* and *Champion Of The Rose*, and Robert N Stephenson's *Uttuku*.

ANTHOLOGIES

Independent presses brought out some great themed anthologies this year. For an overview of fantastic New Zealand speculative fiction taking a new look at the country and the world, you cannot go past Random Static's *A Foreign Country* edited by Anna Caro and Juliet Buchanan. From Australian independent presses we recommend: Ticonderoga Publications' *Belong* edited by Russell B Farr which takes a look at the search for home and belonging; Twelfth Planet Press' *Sprawl*, edited by Alisa Krasnostein, which reinvents Australian sub-urban fantasy; and *Baggage*, Eneit Press' final anthology, edited by Gillian Polack, exploring Australia's cultural baggage.

If you were to buy one anthology from the big publishing houses this year, it should be the aptly named *Legends of Australian Fantasy* edited by Jack Dann and Jonathan Strahan, published by HarperCollins. Between the covers lie stories from such greats as Isobelle Carmody, Juliet Marillier, Trudi Canavan and Kim Wilkins.

Jonathan Strahan has had a very busy year with fantasy anthologies. In addition to *Legends of Australian Fantasy*, he also edited *Swords and Dark Magic* with Lou Anders for Harper Eos, *Wings of Fire* with Marianne S Jablon for Nightshade Books, and *Subterranean Magazine Spring 2010* for Subterranean Press.

Other anthologies of note published this year include: Holly Black and Justine Larbalestier's *Zombies Vs Unicorns* from Allen & Unwin; *The Year's Best Australian SF & Fantasy*, edited by Bill Congreve (Mirrordanse Books); *The Phantom Queen Awakes* edited by Mark S Deniz and Amanda Pillar, published by Morrigan Books; Ticonderoga Publications' *Scary Kisses* edited by Liz Grzyb; Chris Lynch's *The Tangled Bank; Love, Wonder & Evolution* from Tangled Bank Press; new press Fablecroft Publications' young adult anthology *Worlds Next Door* and reprint anthology *Australis Imaginarium* edited by Tehani Wessely; and the Romance Writers of Australia yearly anthology *Little Gems: Topaz* which contains some urban fantasy and paranormal content amongst the romance stories.

COLLECTIONS

Again, it is the independent presses who made a strong showing in single-author collections in 2010. PS Publishing in the UK brought out Rjurik Davidson's *Library of Forgotten Books*, a collection of his novella-length works. Twelfth Planet Press brought out Marianne de Pierres' linked series of fantasy stories in the beautifully packaged *Glitter Rose*. Subterranean Press published Terry Dowling's *Amberjack: Tales of Fear & Wonder*, with a starred review from *Publishers Weekly*. Simon Petrie's *Rare Unsigned Copy: Tales Of Rocketry, Ineptitude, and Giant Mutant Vegetables* was published by Peggy Bright Books. Angela Slatter had two collections of shadowy fairy tales published: the excellent *The Girl With No Hands and other tales* from Ticonderoga Publications and the similarly delicious *Sourdough and other stories* from Tartarus Press in the UK.

Ticonderoga also published the darkly fantastic *Dead Sea Fruit* from Kaaron Warren.

MAGAZINES/EZINES

Those who like their short fiction in periodical form were blessed with many publications to choose from, in both print and webzine format: *Andromeda Spaceways In-flight Magazine* is available in both print and pdf format; *Aurealis Magazine* is available in print; *Orb Speculative Fiction*, a print magazine, released Issue #8, a Greatest Hits collection of 29 of their stories. *Antipodean SF, Moonlight Tuber, Semaphore Magazine* and *Ticon4.com* are all free webzines that published Australian fantasy this year.

PODCASTS

Podcasts seem to be the new big thing, with many new podcasts available discussing Australasian speculative fiction, including: Alisa Krasnostein, Tansy Rayner Roberts, and Alex Pierce's *Galactic Suburbia*; Kirstyn McDermott and Ian Mond's *The Writer and the Critic*; Ion Newcombe's *Antipodean SF Radio Show*; *The Terra Incognita Podcast* from Keith Stevenson; *The Bad Film Diaries Podcast* from Grant Watson; and Gary K Wolfe & Jonathan Strahan's *The Coode Street Podcast*.

OTHER MEDIA

2010 was definitely dominated by Shaun Tan, as his short film *The Lost Thing* was released to thunderous acclaim from all, including the Academy of Motion Picture Arts and Sciences. He also produced *The Bird King*, a picture book from Windy Hollow Books, and *Eric*, a small picture book telling an excerpted story from *Tales from Outer Suburbia*, from Allen & Unwin.

THE YEAR IN HORROR

Aussiecon 4 (Worldcon), held in Melbourne in September 2010, provided a focus for writers and publishers to connect with a fan base on a larger than usual scale, and the breadth of the horror stream curated by Kyla Ward was an excellent showcase of the genre. Notable events included the launch of *Macabre* with a rockstar reading line-up, the AHWA Nightmare Ball, and the panel discussion Directions in Australian Horror featuring Stuart Mayne, Honey Brown, Trent Jamieson, Bill Congreve, and Angela Slatter.

The Australian Horror Writers Association (AHWA) annual general meeting was held at Aussiecon 4. A new committee was elected, including Leigh Blackmore taking role of president, and Geoff Brown vice president. At this time, the *HorrorScope* webzine ended its partnership with the AHWA as official news provider. Chuck McKenzie launched *NecroScope* as a zombie review sub-site of *HorrorScope*.

The US Horror Writers Association announced a non-professional Supporting Membership with reduced rates. Supporting members are eligible to recommend works for the Bram Stoker Award, and receive discounted prices to the Stoker Award Weekend, receive the HWA's monthly newsletter and get limited access to the message board.

NOVELS

Van Badham's *Burnt Snow* (Pan Macmillan), the first in a YA trilogy about witches, follows the tribulations of a teen witch battling through Year 11 at a NSW Central Coast highschool. John Birmingham's post-apocalyptic adventure *After America* was published by Pan Macmillan Australia. Sue Bursztynski's *Wolf Born* (Woolshed Press) is a medieval romance about werewolves. David Conyers' Cthulhu mythos novella *The Eye of Infinity* was released as a chapbook on Halloween by US publisher Perilous Press. Terry Dowling's *Clowns At Midnight* (PS Publishing) follows a writer on retreat from a clown phobia, who discovers strange artifacts in rural New South Wales. Anna Dusk's debut novel *In-Human* (Transit Lounge) explored the erotic werewolf archetype using unconventional literary devices.

Kirsty Eagar's debut *Saltwater Vampires* (Penguin) is a YA riffing on vampires, surfer girls, and rock music. *Poison Kissed* (St. Martin's Press), third installment in the Shadowfae Chronicles by Erica Hayes, tells of a gang enforcer banshee who suspects her snake-shifter gang boss of her mother's murder. Trent Jamieson's *Death Most Definite* (Orbit), the first installment in the Death Works series, follows a psychopomp employed to dispatch zombies and demons, who must fight for his own survival. Brett McBean's The Garbage Man crime/horror series kicked off with *Dirty Laundry*.

Kirstyn McDermott's stunning debut novel *Madigan Mine* (Picador) entwines doomed romance with occult obsession and possession, and traverses Melbourne, Berlin and Ireland. Foz Meadows debut *Solace & Grief* (Ford Street) is an introspective YA vampire novel, with a vampire foster child coming into her powers. Tara Moss cat-walked into the realm of the paranormal with *The Blood Countess* (Pan Macmillan), the first Pandora English novel; an aspiring clairvoyant fashionista in New York takes on a vampire conspiracy in the cosmetics industry.

Jessica Shrivington found publication with the first book in The Violet Eden Chapters, *Embrace* (Lothian), a YA paranormal romance with avenging angels; Shrivington had outstanding Christmas sales. Robert N Stephenson's *Uttuku* (Altair), the first in the Dark Books series, tells of a writer battling suicide survivor guilt and a Mesopotamian demon. Kim Wilkins' debut novel, *The Infernal*, was published as a limited, signed and numbered hardcover edition by Ticonderoga Publications.

COLLECTIONS

A US edition of Leigh Blackmore's weird poetry collection was published by Rainfall Books with the revised title *Sharnoth's Spores and Other Seeds*. The collection was first published as *Spores from Sharnoth and Other Madnesses* by P'rea Press. P'rea Press also issued a numbered limited reprint, with an updated bibliography, and a foreword by noted critic ST Joshi. The U.S. and Australian editions feature some variations in the selection of poems. Red Blade Press published Bill Congreve's wonderful collection *Souls*

Along The Meridian. Well known stand-up comic Bob Franklin made a very successful transition into print storytelling, with his collection *Under Stones* (Affirm Press). Twelfth Planet Press published a boutique collection of stories by Marianne de Pierres, *Glitter Rose.* The edition is hardcover, limited edition, signed, and with interior illustrations.

A bumper year for Angela Slatter, as Ticonderoga Publications published *The Girl With No Hands,* and Tartarus Press published *Sourdough and Other Stories;* both to deserved critical acclaim. Ticonderoga Publications published Kaaron Warren's *Dead Sea Fruit,* a powerhouse collection of 27 of Warren's greatest hits.

ANTHOLOGIES

Allen & Unwin published a teen anthology *Zombies Vs Unicorns,* edited by Justine Larbalestier (zombies) & Holly Black (unicorns). The anthology included stories from Margo Lanagan, Scott Westerfeld, and Garth Nix.

Brimstone Press produced the massive anthology devoted exclusively to Australian horror, *Macabre: A Journey Through Australia's Darkest Fears.* Reading almost as three volumes in one—Classics (1836–1979), Modern Masters (1980–2000), and The New Era (first publications of stories by authors active since 2000)—this anthology is an essential cornerstone for any serious private collection of Australian horror. The anthology is prefaced with an introductory essay and boasts an array of authors too extensive to list here. While Brimstone will be sadly missed as the publishers move on to other endeavors, *Macabre* is such an excellent primer on uncanny fiction in Australia, that it is worthy of acquisition by academic libraries for use in coursework in the fields of cultural studies, literature, professional and creative writing. No higher compliment can be paid to editors Angela Challis and Dr Marty Young.

Cthulhu's Dark Cults: Ten Tales of Dark & Secretive Orders was released by Chaosium; edited by David Conyers, the anthology included fiction from David Witteveen, Penelope Love, Shane Jiraiya Cummings, and David Conyers. Dark Prints Press launched *An Eclectic Slice Of Life* edited by Craig Bezant, an anthology of the best stories and poems from the online magazine *Eclecticism,* divided into Dark Little Oddities, Fantastical Twists, and Obligatory Dramas. *Chinese Whisperings: The Yin & Yang Book* (Emergent Publishing), edited by Jodi Cleghorn and Paul Anderson, was an interesting experiment in gender voices—the male anthology half edited by Jodi, and the female edited by Paul. Benjamin Solah contributed an interesting piece engaging with paranoia about terrorism.

Eneit Press published an anthology that was sadly to be their last. *Baggage,* edited by Gillian Polack, is a beautiful swan song, with very personal interpretations of cultural baggage. The anthology is a true showcase of strong female voices in the speculative field. Morrigan Press published a concept anthology based on an album of the same title by industrial act The God Machine. *Scenes From The Second Storey* came in two different editions, one comprised exclusively of Australian authors. Horror had a strong showing here, with stories by David Conyers, Kirstyn McDermott, Felicity Dowker, Paul Haines, Andrew J McKiernan, Martin Livings, LJ Hayward, Robert Hood, Stephanie Campisi, and Kaaron Warren.

Dark Pages: Tales of Dark Speculative Fiction (Red Blade Press) was Brenton Tomlinson's first outing as anthology editor, and included tales from Marty Young, Felicity Dowker, Martin Livings and ex-pat Naomi Bell. *The Tangled Bank: Love, Wonder, & Evolution* marked the 150th anniversary of Darwin's *Origin of Species*, and featured a story from Christopher Green.

Tasmaniac Publications produced a rather macho Christmas themed anthology, *Festive Fear,* which included a number of antipodean authors such as Michael Radburn, Daniel I Russell, GN Braun, Steve Cameron, Matthew R Davis, and Scott Tyson.

Liz Grzyb made her editorial debut with *Scary Kisses* (Ticonderoga Publications) a whimsical paranormal romance anthology, which among the lighter moments included some gritty horror from Felicity Dowker and Martin Livings, gothic wit from Kyla Ward, and a bleak suicide letter from Ian Nichols. *Belong* (Ticonderoga Publications), edited by Russell B Farr, included one strong zombie story from Penelope Love. *Sprawl* (Twelfth Planet Press), edited by Alisa Krasnostein, explored the urban landscape and odd intersections of wilderness and suburb, and featured darker tales from Angela Slatter, Ben Peek, Pete Kempshall, Paul Haines, and Deborah Biancotti.

A number of Australian horror writers saw publication in significant overseas anthologies. Most notably Robert Hood's excellent tale *Wasting Matilda* appeared in *The Mammoth Book Of The Zombie Apocalypse*, edited by Stephen Jones, and Narrelle M Harris' zombie YA story *The Truth About Brains* appeared in Canadian anthology *Best New Zombie Tales: Volume 2*, edited by James Roy Daley. Stephen Dedman and Kaaron Warren both had fine ghost stories in *Haunted Legends*, edited by Ellen Datlow.

MAGAZINES

Andromeda Spaceways Inflight Magazine published six issues in 2010; of these, issues 46, 48, and 44 all sported horror content. Issue 44, edited by Felicity Dowker, featured a comic zombie flash from Chuck McKenzie. Issue 46, edited by Mark Farrugia, was very horror oriented, with stories from Christopher Green, Jason Fisher, Pete Kempshall, and Felicity Dowker, and a poem from Grant Stone. Issue 48, edited by Juliet Bathory, featured fiction from Mark Farrugia, Marty Young, Amanda Spedding and Mark Welker.

Aurealis magazine celebrated 20 years in print with issue 44 in September, which featured horror fiction from Christopher Green and Kirstyn McDermott. Issue 43 in June featured horror fiction from Bill Congreve, Felicity Dowker, and Geoffrey Maloney.

Eclecticism e-zine published four issues in 2010. Issue 11 was the ghost story themed issue, with fiction from Mark Smith-Briggs, Trost, Allan Wilson, and Lynley Stace. Issue 12, Obsession themed, featured stories from Mark Farrugia, Alice Godwin, Michael Clifton, Lana Harris, Simon James, Susan Adams, and Dam Frederick Hellmons. Issue 13 was appropriately themed Superstitions, and featured creative writing from Brett McBean, Sally Franechevich, Geoffrey Maloney, Simon James, Andrew J McKiernan, Martin Livings, and Shane Jiraiya Cummings. *Eclecticism 14: Freedom* included stories by Deborah Sheldon, Trost, Dianne Dean, Simon James, Shane Griffin, and poetry by Juliette Gillies.

The AHWA launched issue 4 of *Midnight Echo*, edited by Lee Battersby; this issue included fiction by Jason Crowe, Christopher Green, Lisa L Hannett, Patty Jansen, Geoffrey Maloney, Andrew Baker, and Steven J Stegbar, poetry by Jude Aquilina and Jenny Blackford, as well as illustrations from Justin Randall, Ian Van Gemert, and Harold Purnell.

Ben Payne launched *Moonlight Tuber,* featuring fiction from Gitte Christensen, Peter M Ball, Adam Browne, and Matthew Chrulew. Twelfth Planet Press released the final issue of YA zine *Shiny,* featuring fiction from Dirk Flinthart and a reprint of Deborah Biancotti's award-winning story "A Scar for Leida".

COMICS & GRAPHIC NOVELS

Black House Comics published the second volume of their zombie apocalypse After The World graphic novel series of novellas set in a shared world—*Gravesend* by Jason Fischer.

Dark Oz Productions published three issues of horror comic series *Decay,* edited by Darren Koziol. Stories by Darren Koziol, Dave Heinrich, Tanya Nicholls, Mark Hobby, Steve Colloff, Steve Carter, Antoinette Rydyr, Courtney Egan and Shane Jiraiya Cummings. U.S. publisher Asylum Press continued the retro *EEK!* comic series written and inked by Australian Jason Paulos, and distributed to newsagents in Australia by Black House Comics. *Five Wounds* (Allen & Unwin), written by Jonathan Walker and illustrated by Dan Hallett, is a graphic novel where five supernatural orphans come to terms with strange origins.

Rocky Wood had his first graphic novel released—*Horrors! Great Tales of Fear and Their Creators* (McFarland). Illustrated by Glenn Chadbourne, *Horrors!* explores the premise of genre masters (including Mary Wollstonecraft-Shelley, Bram Stoker, and Edgar Allan Poe) being haunted by their supernatural creations.

THEATRE

Dancing On Your Grave, a vaudevillian musical from director/choreographer Lea Anderson, graced the Perth International Arts Festival. Bare Elements Productions' horror-themed musical whodunit *Vincent Lyce's Final Curtain* directed by Simon J Robinson was revived for performances in Melbourne. PMD Productions presented the Australian premiere of Liz Lochhead's *Blood And Ice,* originally premiering in the UK in 1984. The play concerns the life and fiction of Mary Shelley. The Australian production was directed by Jennifer Innes in Melbourne.

Sydney-based repertory company Theatre of Blood performed Stephen Hopely's adaptation of Edgar Allan Poe's *The Tell-Tale*

Heart (Director: Masie Dubosarsky), an original black comedy penned by ensemble member Kyla Ward entitled *Chocolate Curses* (Director: Steven Hopley), and *The Torture Garden* (Director: Irving Gregory), a visceral classic of the Grand Guignol tradition written by Pierre Chaine and Andre de Lorde.

FILM & TV

Carmilla Hyde, directed by Dave de Vries won the Best International Feature award at the Swansea Bay Film Festival and Best Feature at the 2010 South Australian Screen Awards. It saw an indie cinema release in Australia including the Indie Gems Film Festival and Supanova Brisbane Directors Day, and international festivals in South Africa, Thailand, Ireland and the Heart of England International Film Festival. *The Dark Lurking* (2010), directed by Gregory Connors, toured Australia in conjunction with the Supanova pop culture expo. *Damned By Dawn* (2009) written and directed by Brett Anstey, was released in Australia in April, and in the U.S. on Blu-ray and DVD by Image Entertainment in November. A young woman Clare (Renee Willner) fights to save her family from a revenant known as "The Banshee" (Bridget Neval).

El Monstro Del Mar (2010), directed by Stuart Simpson, is a rockerbilly-styled exploitation horror film blurbed as 'three vixens versus the creature from the deep'. *The Horseman* (2008), directed by Steven Kastrissios, came out on DVD and Blu-Ray in March in the UK, had festival screenings at Sitges Film Festival, Fantasia Festival, and FrightFest, and saw limited theatrical run in the U.S. in June through Screen Media Ventures. *The Loved Ones* (2009), directed by Sean Byrne, had an Australian cinema release through Madman Entertainment in November 2010. Festival screenings included the Hong Kong International Film Festival, Dallas International Film Festival, SXSW Film Festival in Texas, and the San Francisco International Film Festival. *Needle* (2010), starring Ben Mendelsohn and directed by John V Soto, premiered at Cinefest OZ in August, and screened at the British Horror Film Festival and Screamfest Horror Film Festival in the USA.

Prey (2008), directed by George T Miller and staring Natalie Bassingthwaighte, had a U.S. DVD release in July 2010 through Xenon Pictures under the new title *The Outback*. *The Tunnel*, directed by Carlo Ledesma, is a documentary style horror film set in the subways of Sydney. The film won in the categories of Best Use Of Social Media, Viral Or Word of Mouth and Peoples Choice Award at the 17th Australian Interactive Media Industry Association awards. The film won in the category of Cross Platform Interactive in the 2010 Australian Directors Guild Awards. The film is notable for being made available legally via Bittorrent download, simultaneous with conventional modes of release. *Uninhabited* (2010), directed by Bill Bennett, premiered at the 2010 Cannes Film Festival and in Australia at the Melbourne International Film Festival. A couple holidaying on a coral island encounter a vengeful ghost.

Classic Australian horror film *Wake in Fright* (1971) directed by Ted Kotcheff was released by Madman Entertainment in a delux edition on DVD and Blu-ray. Starring Chips Rafferty, Jack Thompson, Donald Pleasance and John Meillon, the film is considered a landmark in Australian horror cinema, but has been previously only available from degraded prints. The package includes special features and a full-colour 32-page booklet contextualizing this piece of Oz horror history, which found some critical acclaim overseas in the 70s under the alternate title *Outback*.

Screening on TVS, the *Independent Inkwell* documentary by Max Rowan, explored indie publishing in Australia, and included interviews with Alan Baxter (Red Blade Press) and Keith Stevenson (coeur de lion Publishing). Pay television Channel W saw the first season of TV series *Spirited*, a paranormal romance between a divorced dentist and the ghost of a 1980s English rockstar.

THE YEAR IN THE INDUSTRY

In a new Literature Board initiative from the Australia Council for the Arts, the Tasmanian, NSW, Victorian, South Australian, and the ACT writers centres combined to form a national organization called Writing Australia, with writing centres from the remaining states participating as associate members. The goals of the new organisation include professional development and interstate promotion for mid-career writers, a program of residencies, a national conference, and linking to similar international programs.

The Aurealis Awards ceremony moved to Sydney; the awards' new administrator, SpecFaction NSW, signed publisher HarperVoyager as exclusive major sponsor.

The Australian Horror Writers Association's (AHWA) annual literary prize, the Australian Shadows Awards, introduced a prize pool of $750. Craig Bezant, Stephanie Gunn, and Jeff Ritchie comprise the preliminary judging panel, and Chuck McKenzie, Kaaron Warren, and Rocky Wood were the final judges. The 2010 Awards Director was Shane Jiraiya Cummings.

HarperCollins publishers announced that Eos Books, a US imprint, would be rebranded as Harper Voyager, to consolidate with the Voyager imprints in Australia/New Zealand and the UK.

The Speculative Fiction Writers of New Zealand organization was officially launched in April, and The Australian Science Fiction and Fantasy Writers Association became open to memberships in August.

The Specusphere webzine announced the launch of a new small press, leading with a *Myths and Legends* anthology.

Tehani Wessely launched Fablecroft Publishing, with the children's anthology *Worlds Next Door*, and the reprint anthology *Australis Imaginarium*.

Author Narrelle Harris launched the Melbourne Literary iPhone application, a virtual tour guide to literary locations, local authors, and books set in Melbourne.

E-Readers were marketed in a big way in Australia in 2010. Angus & Robertson and Borders introduced the Kobo platform.

Amazon's Kindle device became available in Australia. Google ebooks announced plans to open to the Australian territory. Sony also weighed in as a provider, and various reader applications became available for smart phones such as iPhone and Android, some with work arounds for territory restrictions in Australia.

OBITUARIES

Donald H(enry) Tuck, 89, Australia's first Hugo Award winner, editor of the first *Encyclopaedia of Science Fiction*. **Alinta Thornton**, writer, Clarion South graduate, whose first story was published at *TiconderogaOnline* in 2000. **Randolph Stow**, 74, Miles Franklin Award winner. **Patricia Wrightson**, 88, winner of the Ditmar and Hans Christian Andersen Awards. **Ruth Park** AM, 93, Miles Franklin Award-winning writer of *Swords and Crowns and Rings*, *Playing Beatie Bow*, and *The Muddle-Headed Wombat*. **Norman Hetherington**, 89, creator of iconic Australian TV show *Mr Squiggle and Friends*. **John Cleary**, 92, Ned Kelly Award-winning and winner of the Australian Crimewriters Lifetime Achievement Award. **Lynn Bayonas**, 66, TV writer and producer, produced the mini-series of Patricia Wrightson's *The Nargun and the Stars*.

THE YEAR'S BEST AUSTRALIAN FANTASY & HORROR

~ 2010 ~

THE FIRST ANNUAL
COLLECTION

AFTER THE JUMP

FELICITY DOWKER

Commercial Diver.

That's what I scribble on my tax return every year, in the box titled OCCUPATION. And, strictly speaking, it's the truth.

But it's not the whole truth; not even close.

If I told you I was a HAZMAT Diver, it would be more technically accurate, but would still only steer us further away from the reality of what I do. You see, the diving isn't important. It's the most basic essential facet of my work, but it's ultimately meaningless.

It's the people that matter. Their empty, broken bodies. Their stories. Their tragic faces. And the swampy mud of the riverbed; deep, rich and wet.

That mud is like decadent chocolate; the bodies mired in it, the fillings. Sometimes hard. Sometimes soft. Sometimes oozing. Always delicious—at least, the riverbed seems to think so. It holds fast to its prizes, refusing to release them without a struggle. Oh, the power of that dense mud, the incredible suction it exerts, the *sound* as its treasures are finally pulled loose . . .

Yeah. The name of what I do is one thing. The experience is quite another.

• • •

It's called the West Gate Bridge. It spans the Yarra River, a harsh slash of grey against the smoggy sky, connecting Melbourne's inner city to the Western suburbs. It's a cable-stayed box girder contraption, 2,583 metres long and 58 metres high. It carries four lanes of motor vehicle traffic in each direction.

But who gives a fuck, right?

I'm telling you the dry, boring shit only for the sake of context; so that when I tell you there is an average of one suicide on the bridge every three weeks, you can picture the distance those desperate souls need to walk to find the highest point to jump from. You can probably hear the endless roar of the traffic; maybe you can even smell the exhaust fumes, feel the *whoosh* as the cars go by and the *hummmm* as the bridge vibrates under their onslaught. And when the soon-to-be-corpse looks down from the great height of the West Gate to the filthy, churning Yarra below, I think perhaps you can feel your own head spin with vertigo and your heart clench with a sort of primal fear that screams without words or sound.

I know I can.

I've thought about it a lot. I wonder if the actuality is worse than my imaginings. I know, of course, that it must be; far, far worse.

I've heard it said that the only truly important question in life is whether or not to kill yourself. If so, then every ruined body I've retrieved from the bottom of the Yarra is the shell of a great philosopher, who solved the only real riddle in existence with final aplomb. I can't claim as much.

Here's how it works.

When someone jumps off the West Gate, they fall one hell of a long way. I've already told you how high the bridge is in metres, but all that matters when you're a human body plummeting from the bridge is that it's *one hell of a long way*. So, after falling for eternity within a brief moment, the body hits the water. It can get pretty messed up on impact, sure; but that doesn't concern us right now, because if they just end up in the water (or, if they miscalculate entirely, the riverbank), they don't need me to go get them. They float. Eventually. But I can tell you now, most of them don't *just* hit the water. Because—remember?—they fall such a long way. They're like fleshy torpedoes; they keep right on going. They part the water like a willing woman's legs, and they penetrate the fecund muddy cradle that lies beneath. And there they stay; implanted like sperm in an egg, only the merge is not one of life but of death.

And we can't just leave all those bodies planted in the mud down there, in the river our city plays in, gazes upon, drinks from (never mind the fact that it's already a polluted cesspit). No, somebody has to go and remove them. And that somebody is me.

I'm not the only one, of course. Victoria Police contract 10 divers from Any Dive, the HAZMAT diving company I am part of. But most of the other guys only do a West Gate suicide dive now and then; they also do the other stuff Vic Police need chumps like us to do for them—the raw sewage dives, the chemical infested pipelines, the simple body removals (usually murders, not suicides) from more placid lakes and waterways. Me? I'm a fulltime West Gate diver. I manage the Any Dive team. I'm on call. I'm *devoted*.

Not that it really matters, but my name is Ryan Deer. I'm 38, I'm single, and I live in a two bedroom apartment in West Brunswick. One bedroom for me. Another for the West Gate suicides who live with me always, their twisted limbs cavorting in my dreams, their agonised faces floating behind my eyes, breaking my heart over and over.

They are all my darlings; I have a memory slot in the computer of my brain allocated to saving each and every one of them. We tousle in the hungry soil of the riverbed together and we share an intimacy (them dead, me alive—in theory) that I never find above the roiling waterline of the Yarra. I have loved them all well.

But none as well as she.

• • •

It was a 4am dive, one summer Sunday.

We usually do them in the very late or early hours, when traffic on the West Gate is a sluggish crawl and we're not likely to be noticed. Berko—self-dubbed "King of the Yarra"—squatted on the boat as I dove, cigarette dangling from the corner of his wisened mouth, directing the big industrial spotlight on me and the sprawling riverbed. I've got my own kit, torches included, but that spotlight is vicious, and it slices deeply into the water without mercy. It's enough to see all I need to see. You'd be surprised just how much I *do* see under that glare.

The first thing I see is her hair. Well, some of it. It's lying on the riverbed about a metre from the rest of her. It's a lonely thing, swaying to and fro with the water's movement like flaxen seaweed.

It's anchored down by the hunk of scalp it's still implanted in; the bloody underside of the skin flap glued to the dark mud of the riverbed. I guess the impact of her body meeting the water—akin to smashing into a mass of concrete at great speed when you jump from such a height—caused half her scalp to shear right off her skull.

It's far from the worst thing I've seen down here on the scummy underside of the Yarra, but it might be the saddest. The portion of scalp and the endless riverbed, clinging to each other like star-crossed lovers while the owner of the scalp resides—alone, separate, discarded—elsewhere.

I hook the piece of scalp with my pick-up-stick, bagging it and sending it up the line to Berko. I'm not interested in that lost piece of her. It forsook her, and it must fend for itself now.

I move over towards her, approaching slowly; respectfully. Only her legs are visible, pointing up at the water's surface like accusations. They are naked, and streaked with deep furrows where her body has caved under the assault of the long jump. Blood and mud and pain are visible in her wounds. One of her feet is aimed backwards, bent double; her left leg is moving in a fluid way that boned limbs should not be able to achieve. At the point where her thighs should meld with her buttocks and pubic mound, there is only the riverbed; a muddy chastity belt, devouring her sex and the rest of her body; hiding her in the netherworld beneath the sod.

She's a head-first jumper. I don't see many of them. Most suicides literally step off their platform, or leap—but almost always feet-first. They hit the water in a messy heap, sideways or footways or any which ways—but rarely headways.

I have a sudden image of this woman, tall, blonde, and nude; arching her back as she reaches above herself with pale arms, looking at the sky before soaring away from the bridge in a perfect swan-dive.

Do-it-yourself fatality, head-first.

She must have been something. No doubts. No half-arsing. Just diving right into death, naked and determined. And how did she manage to climb to the middle of the West Gate with no clothes on? Did anyone try to stop her? Was she naked before she even got onto the bridge? Why?

Without thinking, without even pausing, I peel off one of my gloves and cup the curve of her right calf in my hand. She feels smooth and cool, and somehow *hard*. We stay like that for a while, she and I, clad in water and skin to skin. I have to fight the urge to wrench out my mouthpiece and press my lips to her legs; lick healing into them, taste her, know her. The compulsion to surrender my oxygen for her is overwhelming.

Then Berko jiggles the spotlight, impatient, and I know it's time to get to work.

I'm going to get you out, I mouth, chewing on my life-giving bit, the urge to spit it out still strong. *I'm going to free you from this river. I promise. Trust me.*

The alabaster tendrils of her legs move in my direction, and I know she is relying on me. I won't let her down. I've never let any of them down—I always get them out—but it's never mattered to me as much as it does right now.

Reluctantly, I flip the switch on the pack on my belt, activating voice communication with Berko as he bobs high above me. His voice barges down the umbilical line connecting me to the boat, ornery and indignant, violating my suit and flooding my head.

"Bin 'avin' fun down there, 'ave ya? What the fuck're ya doin', anyway? Courtin' the stiff?"

"Sorry, Berk. I've cleared the surrounding area now. Ready to excavate." My lips move with difficulty around my mouthpiece, and my voice is a clumsy wet murmur in my ears. I hate talking this way. The tinny electronic wail of it all is a profanity down here in the under-Yarra world.

"Cleared the area, yuh. If ya mean ya copped a feel of some dead legs, then you've cleared up *real* good. Think I can't see what yer up to from up here? I can see *everything*. Got it? Don't leave yer voice box off again. I'm not just gonna sit up here with me thumb up me arse while ya jerk off. Hear me?"

God, it's so wrong that he's even here; cranky old fart. I could steer the frigging boat myself, avoid his interference. They won't let me do a dive alone, though—safety reasons. I want to throw myself over her, wrap my body around her legs and shield her from his probing eyes and compassionless brain. *Fuck you!* I want to shout up to him. *Fuck off! Leave us alone! You don't belong here—you have no right!*

Instead, I wait without comment for him to feed the equipment down to me. After a moment, when he feels his point has been made, I see it break the surface above and begin to weave down. There are technical ways to explain how we get the bodies of the West Gate suicides out of the mud, but I'll keep it simple, because I don't care, and neither do you. Not about that stuff. We're here for them,

(*her*)

you and I.

Basically, we blast them out with a high-pressure hose. Berko's boat sucks in the river water—a hydraulic vampire, drinking the Yarra's blood—and spews it back out with enormous strength from the mouth of the hose that I've secured near the body. The riverbed is strong, but it's no match for the false strength of man-made power. My job is twofold. I have to try not to vapourise the corpse by putting the hose too close; it has to be near enough to get rid of the mud holding the body, but not so near that it hits the body itself. And, when the hose clears enough mud, I have to pull the body free. Then I take it up and after that, it's Berko's responsibility. He ferries his cargo to Vic Police, and who knows what they do with the bodies after that. Return them to their families for burial, I guess. If the suicide *has* any family.

The mouth of the hose nuzzles at my neck, a grotesque proboscis. I wrap both my hands around it and position it on the river floor. I used to need to spend time calculating precise measurements for positioning—in fact, I'm still meant to do that—but experience has given me a sixth sense for it now. I spend time with the jumpers, I dwell in their watery grave, and I just *know* where I have to put the hose in order to liberate them.

I follow this intuition now, and anchor the hose down. This does take a while, because if the hose comes free once the water is surging through it, I'll become the second corpse down here today. One blast of that water full in the chest and I'm the HAZMAT rather than the HAZMAT Diver.

"Hurry th'fuck up, Deer. I want that body onshore by sunrise."

"It takes the time it takes, Berk," I reply, the closest I get to snapping at him. It's unwise to bitch at the man who controls your air, your communications, your very body temperature with the warm water he sends into your suit. But more than that; if Berk complains about me enough, I could get taken off the West Gate team. And that would mean no more time spent under the water with the jumpers.

I need them. They need me. I'd be a fool to let anyone mess that up.

I test the last bolt on the hose's tether, and yank on the umbilical line six times, signaling Berk. The old bastard must have been waiting with his hand on the lever, because I feel the hose come alive in front of me immediately. Swearing, I propel myself backwards with all my strength (which is considerable, after years of this job).

As the first gout of water hits the mud around *her*—a near invisible stream of pure power, water in water—I stand on the riverbed and watch, my heart tight with anticipation.

In a matter of moments, she won't just be a pair of legs. I'll see the rest of her. I'll *hold* her. I'll save her.

God, I can't *breathe*.

When her legs thrash violently and begin to tilt like a felled tree, I jerk on the umbilical cord six times again. The torrent of force pouring from the hose ceases, and the hose wilts, its ardour spent.

I move forward, pushing against the stubborn water, wanting to get to her.

I catch her just as her legs crumple and fold in on her torso. I gently spin her, turning her right side up, pulling her head out of the hole she'd tunneled with her death-dive. She's bundled in my arms, a long baby, the hair left on her head trailing across my bare hand where I've forgotten to replace my glove.

"Send the stiff up, then git that hose dismantled and git your arse up here, Deer," Berko's voice grates in my ears, shattering the perfect moment. "Sun-up soon. Time t'go."

Her eyes are open. They're fixed on me; black rings in the white of her face. One of them is filled with blood, bulging against the thin skin of her eyeball, but still beautiful. Her lips are pale, torn a little in the corners where the water barreled in and stretched them, but they're curved in a smile, and that's beautiful, too. Her mottled cheekbones are high and wide, and her nose is straight and proud—even when it's pushed over to the right, broken. The white of her skull where half her scalp was torn off gleams at me like a bony hat, jauntily tilted to the side. Her remaining hair is long and golden, curling around me like tentacles. Her body is firm against my arms; I wish I could shrug off my suit and feel the coldness of her dead skin—that iciness that is so cold it's hot.

When she moves her hand to my face and speaks, I'm not even surprised. I've been waiting for this; for one of them to feel me, to respond to me. To reach them, and have them reach back.

We don't want to get out, she murmurs, her voice a liquid melody in my veins. *We want to get all the way* in.

"All the way in? You mean, under the riverbed?"

"Wha'the fuck're ya jawin' about, Deer?" Berko's voice is an obscenity, and I drop one hand to my belt, silencing my voice box before putting my hand back on her body.

Her hand reaches for my mouthpiece, and in a flick of her shattered wrist, it's gone. I'm breathless, and my first instinct is to panic; to gasp in lungful after lungful of dirty water. To choke. To drown. I see my mouthpiece, floating within arm's reach, and then her fingers brush my cheek. She draws my head down toward her, her lips waiting for me, her eyes closing.

Kiss me. Say goodbye to me. Take my secrets. Sing me home.

And I do. I take her in, mouthful after mouthful. We twirl in our sacred place beneath the water, beneath the city, beneath the world. She gifts me with her secrets, and I offer her mine, feeble though they are in comparison. The hum of the nothing that is everything fills my ears, and as we dance alone together, I sing her home.

• • •

I'm fired, of course. Berko really did see everything from his craven perch up there on the rolling boat. When he tells them he saw me remove my oxygen bit and smooch a corpse, I'm handed a tidy severance package and some complimentary counseling sessions. Trauma, they said. Understandable after spending as many years on the job as I had. Nobody held it against me. There would be no . . . repercussions.

When I laughed in their faces, they thought it was evidence I truly had lost it. But I couldn't help it. They were just so damned *funny*, sitting there quacking at me, utterly clueless. Poor bastards. But how could they know? They'd never been down there, beneath the world. There was always someone else to do their dirty work for them. And nobody else had spent as much time down there as I did; nobody even came close.

Nobody else had known the jumpers the way I had. Nobody had touched *her* the way I did. They didn't know anything, and it wasn't their fault. I pitied them. I told them so.

Berko was in the room. He didn't speak while they fired me. He just sat and stared at me, the corner of his left eye twitching now and then. From the little you know about Berko, you can probably already guess that was mighty strange behaviour for him. They left us alone in the room for a few minutes at one point. Berko leaned forward and put his hand on my leg. He was trembling.

"What was it like?" His voice was awed and he took great care to enunciate clearly. "Did she show you . . . y'know, what's there? I saw things twisting and shining . . . in the mud . . . God, they were *reaching* for you! Such beautiful things, they was."

That old bastard. He'd seen more than he deserved.

"I don't know what you're talking about," I said, smiling serenely into Berko's watery eyes. He snarled at me, all reverence gone.

"Why you fuckin' . . . who d'you think y'are? D'you know how long I've been workin' that river? Long before your daddy forgot to wear a condom, I was there. I've seen and heard things you wouldn't believe on and under that water. It ain't fair. Hear me? It ain't *fair*. Why should *you* be the one—"

They came back into the room then, and Berko jerked back into his seat, his mouth snapping shut and his eyes sinking back into his head. I offered to tell them what we'd been talking about, but they just exchanged odd looks and shook their heads.

I didn't offer to tell them the secrets she'd sang to me, though. I didn't go that far. They hadn't earnt it the way I had. They weren't ready.

But *I* was. Oh, God. I'd been ready for the longest time.

• • •

There are no walkways on the West Gate; it's not a walking bridge. As if it matters. As if the lack of designated areas for sad feet will somehow prevent people from scaling the bridge and leaping to their deaths.

There has been a call for "suicide fences" on the bridge for a long time, but they (the powers that be, the builders of fences, the rulers of bridges) have refused to erect any such thing. Think about that for a moment. Some simple fencing might save some desperate lives, but they won't oblige. Why? Don't they *want* the suicides to stop? Don't they care? Is it too much expense to save the sort of washed-up souls who shuffle off the West Gate every other week?

Or is it just that they know that it all goes much further

(deeper)

than it seems? Do they somehow understand that a fence wouldn't change a thing?

The mud is hungry, and deep, and we know that something better lies on the other side of it. If we could just . . . get . . . in.

She told me that, my darling in the river, whispering her secrets to my soul as I kissed the pulpy meat of her dead lips. I cradled her in my arms, she who didn't quite make it through the mud, and I sang her home. A song drawn in bubbles and silt and cold aquamarine. Not the song she dove in search of, but a song that put her searching essence at rest, all the same. My song was my love. She knew I cared, and in death she found the connection she

(we)

lacked in life. She was the culmination of my years under the Yarra; the end of my journey through the stories of the West Gate suicides. I always knew they had wonders to share with me. I knew I was there for a reason. I knew I was special, because they were special.

All of them.

I knew, and I was right. About that, and about other things, too.

Like what it would feel like to climb the West Gate and stand balancing on a ledge, the air expansive and shimmering around me, the water surging up greedily at me from far below.

It feels awful, and exhilarating, and terrifying, and wonderful, and primal, and all-encompassing. Just like I thought, and not at all like I thought. Perfect.

I'm naked; but not only that, I'm hairless. I've waxed everywhere—head, body, even my eyebrows. Pulling out my eyelashes (one by one with tweezers, slowing down to wait for the tears to clear each time) was the hardest part, but I wanted to be as aerodynamic as possible. No clothes. No hair. I'd remove my skin, if I could. I realised why she—my darling under the Yarra—was naked, you see. It was to make her travel further, faster. To get deeper under the mud.

But I've got an edge that she, poor angel, didn't have: my diving weights. I've lugged them all up here, to the top of the West Gate, in 20kg lots. I've got rather a lot of them, you see, over the years. Easily my own body weight. And I've gotten *strong*, diving under the Yarra and digging up its human treasures. I've put all the weights on the ledge I plan to leap from, and I'm confident that I can strap them all onto me and still be able to propel myself off the bridge with enough force to make my jump count. Even just falling with style will be enough, with all that weight on board.

The interesting thing is that it's taken me the better part of several hours to climb up and down the West Gate, naked, hairless, carrying weights and arranging them on a jutting platform. And do you think anyone has stopped their car, hung their head out their window, asked me if I'm ok? No. Of course they haven't. They haven't so much as slowed down, honked their horn, or flashed their lights; I'm not sure if they've even seen me. And it's midday; I'm noticeable. Don't get me wrong, I don't *want* anyone to stop me; I don't *need* their help.

But it just says a lot to me that they haven't offered.

Sooner or later, someone *will* call the Police, and I don't want that interference, so I know I need to act now. Enough musing about man's inhumanity to man—it's not as if it's news to me. I've seen the riverbed. I know how this gig—life—works. It stinks.

I've worked out the spot she would have jumped from, and that's where I am now. She came the closest out of all of them—all the jumpers I've seen—to getting right under that mud; getting all the way in, getting *through*. I'm heavier than she was. I'm streamlined. I've got my weights.

And the riverbed and I . . . we understand each other. I think it has wanted me for a long time. I know I've wanted it.

It feels like time is stretching, slowing, stopping; as I stand and look down at the river so far below me. My body feels pain from the burden of the weights and the chill wind on my naked skin, but it's a distant sensation to me; like a dream someone else is having in the next room. I can't hear the cars anymore; I can't feel the bridge platform under my bare feet. There's only me and the riverbed. The frothing water looks like a thin sheen of smoke over the mud that I know lies beneath, and I take a moment to calculate the exact angle I should fall at; the best way to shoot myself into the boggy target and hit it dead on. To penetrate and transcend.

Well, what do you know? Some people have stopped their cars after all, clogging up the flow of traffic on the bridge. I can see them in my peripherals, intruding only slightly on my holy communion with the Yarra. A woman is waving her arms above her head and screaming at me. Nice of her. She thinks she's trying to save me. You and I know better, don't we? I'm bound for shiny, beautiful things in that mud. Preventing me from reaching it would be a travesty.

Ah. See that man, to our far right? He's gotten out of his car, too, but he's not looking at you and I. He's peering over the edge of the bridge, down at the water, at the mud. He's wearing reflective sunglasses, and in the lenses . . . can you see that? Silvery tendrils of pure light, undulating and pulsing in a constant thready rhythm from their riverbed home. *He* sees it. He hears it, singing and cooing and whispering. He's already taking off his jacket and reaching down to untie his shoes. He shoots me a dark look. Knowing. Jealous. Sly.

I can't let him beat me. I was here first. And I've got weights.

I'm the happiest I've ever been as I shuffle forward and prepare to take my final steps this side of the mud. I can hear a murmur in my ear; my Yarra darling, singing *me* home this time.

And where is that home—where will I actually go, when I break through the mud, get all the way in at last?

Maybe it's the same marshy flesh that we all sprang from, as embryos implanted in our mother's wombs. Maybe the river is that same life-giving amniotic fluid we all swam in, once upon an unremembered time. Maybe it's an eventual rebirth I'm headed for, but not into this broken world; somewhere new, better, somewhere *good*.

Look, I'll be honest. I don't know. But I *will* know.

After the jump.

In the seconds when my feet leave the bridge and the air starts to tear at my skin like the razor-sharp tines of a thousand pitchforks, it occurs to me to wonder why that radiant something that I want so badly would also want *me*. Hell, it even wanted Berko, a man who freely admits to slipping his three year old granddaughter laxative-laced lollies for the joy of watching her face crumple and her legs pump as she runs for the toilet.

As I near the water—so quickly!—and those beckoning silver swirls solidify into something immense and hungry and suddenly not at all shiny, I ponder the fact that even now, the Yarra's next lover is parting the air only metres above my head, matching my own sacrifice with every pound of his falling flesh. How quickly he was hooked. How easily my own offering was bettered, before it was even complete.

In the very final second, my blonde riverbed angel reaches up from the water. She's going to grab me and pull me under, wrap me in her arms and share eternity on the other side of the mud with me. She'll answer all my questions, quell all my foolish doubts. But . . . no, she's trying to push me away! Her ethereal hands grasp my ankles, but they slide through my skin like smoke through mesh.

Her savaged mouth is open in a perfect O. It closes and opens, closes and opens again, and I can see what she's saying:

nononononononononononononono

Then a gargantuan column of writhing mud shoves her aside, and she's gone, leaving a seared after-image on the back of my eyes.

I'm hitting it it's hitting me we're together
I know now
I've made it
the mud is dirty silver
Oh, God! It's so col—

• • • • • • • • • • •

L'ESPRIT DE L'ESCALIER

PETER M BALL

Rat opens the double doors and the stairwell smells of baking, the air thick with dull warmth and the smell of yeasty dough. He wrinkles his long nose and wonders if it will be like this for the entire way down, or if the doughy stink will gradually transform itself into the aroma of fresh-baked. He hopes not. Rat worked in a bakery one summer, and he hasn't enjoyed the smell of bread since. It reminds him of the finger burns and the thick coats of lard painted into hot bread trays to keep the dough from sticking as it cooked.

He flexes his fingers. The big backpack is so heavy it's cutting off the circulation to his arms, so he has to remember to keep his fingers moving.

Someone has bolted a sign to the mahogany balustrade, warning people not to throw coins or pebbles down the centre of the stairwell. The guidebook says this is for the safety of fellow climbers. Every year someone is struck on the head when they're 130 flights below, and there's no chance of getting help in time when you're that far down.

There's another sign that warns people not to jump. Rat's guidebook says this isn't, in fact, the warning to the habitually stupid that it appears to be on the surface. Originally it was posted as a warning to the suicides that come to contemplate the twisting drop of the stairwell's core. It is easy to assume the stairwell has an end because that's what stairwells do, but the fact that no-one has ever reached the bottom leaves the question open. No-one ever thinks of stairwells as being bottomless, not even the people who stand on top of big buildings like the Empire State where the ground is a distant and hazy memory over 1,800 steps below. There's a hierarchy to such things determining what truly can go on forever. Wells? Yes. Pits? Yes. Trenches in the seabed where giant squid may live? Sure. But stairwells? No. Never. Hence there's a sign, a warning, to make the suicides rethink before leaping.

Rat isn't thinking about jumping over the railing. He turns around and looks at the first step. It's a foot high and four feet wide, a lump of grey marble that's cracked and covered with a random assortment of tags and graffiti. Rat looks at some of the things people have written and snorts. It's easy to write graffiti on the first step; it's the lower ones that require commitment. He wonders how far he'll need to descend before he reaches virgin territory.

The guidebook says that the lowest step anyone has reached is 120,828 steps down. People have probably gone lower, but they haven't come back. It's assumed that the suicides make it to the bottom.

If there is one.

If they were lucky.

The stairwell requires a lot of assumptions. The guidebook tells you to get used to that.

Rat figures the guy that hit the low-point 120,828 steps down probably had better things on his mind than leaving graffiti. He shrugs off the backpack and starts searching for his sharpie. It's a big backpack full of cunning pockets and hidey-holes for passports. The sharpie is in one of the cunning pockets Rat never uses, right next to the outer pocket that contains the plastic baggie filled with Marlo's ashes.

The smell of the uncapped sharpie is soothing. Its mentholated tang cuts through the yeasty heat. Rat chews on the cap for a few minutes, thinking, then leans over and writes *But I love you* on a blank patch of the first step. His handwriting is awkward, full of childish loops and a tendency to curve without the benefit of a ruled line.

Rat wishes he had something better to write; *But I love you* seems trite, and it probably didn't need to be said. He'd lost arguments with it before, with Marlo and others. He could have skipped the first step and used the first 500 to think of something better. He could have used the time to think of something poetic and elegant.

"No," he says, and his voice echoes down the stairwell. "No poetry."

Poetry would defeat the object. Just because something is trite, possibly even expected, doesn't make it any less true. He hasn't spent the last month preparing just so he could sacrifice truth for elegance. Marlo deserves better than that. So does he.

Rat puts the lid back on the sharpie and returns it to the backpack. He snaps everything shut and makes sure it's secure, twice. He's only packed three sharpies. It wouldn't do to lose them; he may need all of them before his descent is done.

He pulls the backpack onto his shoulders again, sagging with the weight. His hands are slippery. The air's not that hot; the guidebook says it'll get hotter, but Rat sweats easily. He spent a whole week planning ways he can stay hydrated. One hand rests against the railing, holding him steady. Rat places his left foot on the next step and lowers himself down.

"Two," he says, thumb hitting the click-counter at his belt. He keeps clicking away as the descent begins in earnest. "Three, four, five, six . . ."

• • •

The guidebook is small enough to fit in Rat's pocket, but he keeps it tucked into the backpack. Just in case.

They found the guidebook together, Rat and Marlo. It was hiding in the bottom of a used book bin, out the front of a Salvation Army store. Marlo found it; Rat has never been a big reader. The guidebook is the only book he's ever read all the way through. It's the only book he's ever attempted to read more than once.

"Check it out," Marlo said. "A book about the Endless Stairwell."

"What?" Rat said.

"The Stairwell. You know about the Stairwell, right?"

Rat shook his head. He'd never heard of the Stairwell before Marlo found the guidebook. That wasn't unusual. Rat rarely knew about the things Marlo knew about. Marlo was smart. Rat was smart, too, but he didn't think on his feet. Marlo said his talent lay in cunning, and Rat was okay with that.

"We should go one day," Marlo said. "Promise me we'll go."

Rat didn't promise. He thought an endless stairwell sounded stupid.

Rat meets six young couples coming up the stairs, all before he reaches step 500. The couples are young and giddy, with young men dressed with understated elegance. They are men dressed in casual clothes that are meant to look impressive. One of the couples has a camera.

Another couple, the second-last couple Rat passes, looks dour. They stand on separate sides of the steps, maximizing the space between them. Rat is forced to cut between, muttering an "excuse me" between clicks of his click-counter.

Rat's surprised by the number of couples he passes, but he shouldn't be. The guidebook says that step 657 is a popular place to propose, a landmark right up there with Niagara Falls and New Year's Eve fireworks.

When he reaches step 500, Rat uncaps a sharpie and thinks about the dour couple, unhappy in their long climb back to the surface. He leans over the step and writes *That would have been us, I think, if only things had gone differently.* He stands up and looks at his scrawl. Better, but still not great. Rat wonders if this really needs to be said.

"Five hundred and one," he says, "Five hundred and two."

He descends. There are no more couples. He has a smooth run between step 500 and step 657.

The romance step; the step where proposals happen. The guidebook gushes about its ambiance.

Rat schedules a rest stop on step 658. He drinks his water and looks up the stairwell, trying to work out what makes the step just above him so special. The step smells of old prophylactics. When Rat peers over the banister, he can see used condoms stuck to the side of the stairs. The stink mingles with the dough smell, turning Rat's stomach. There's nothing special here; grey marble with a worn patch on the centre; endless graffiti that links two sets of initials with a crude heart around the outside and the number "4" between the names.

Rat digs Marlo out of the backpack, cradles the plastic against his cheek.

"Will you marry me," he says. "You should say yes, you know. It's traditional to say yes when you love the person who asks you."

The baggie says nothing. It's cool against his cheek, but he feels cold talking to it.

It's hard to have a conversation with Marlo these days. Somehow, it just doesn't seem right.

Rat digs the ring out of a pocket in his jeans. There's only one diamond, small and flawed. It should have been better. Rat was going to propose to Marlo outside a cinema after a really good film, but the moment slipped away before he got the chance. He puts the ring on the romance step, the proposing step, right in the corner where step meets wall. Its yellow band is pale, hard to see against the darkness and the marble's whorls.

"Last chance, babe. You should have said something if you wanted the ring." Rat takes a long sip of water and shoulders the pack. "Six hundred and fifty-nine . . ."

At step 1,000 he writes out the lyrics to a Leonard Cohen song and underlines the refrain. He stops 500 steps later and writes out the number of times he thinks Marlo faked orgasm during their time together. He stares at the number, unsure of its accuracy, then adds a question mark. At 2,000 steps he admits in writing that Marlo was right, that he did sometimes fantasise about dating her sister.

There is a plaque on step 2,109. It tells Rat that he's climbed the length of the Sears tower. Rat doesn't look at the plaque; he knows what it says because he's read the guidebook.

He stops again at step 2,500. He writes: *I wish you were here. I'd like to kiss you right now.*

Rat stops when he reaches step 3,000. According the guidebook, most people turn before they reach step 3,000. A lot of people lie about reaching it. Rat takes out a sharpie and writes: *I wasn't sure if I would cry for you, but it appears that I can.*

It's a lie; Rat hasn't cried yet. Rat isn't a crier, not really.

He stops and camps on step 5,418. He drinks water and pecks at trail mix for dinner, saving the substantial fare in his pack for further down. Nights are cold on the Stair; the guidebook has warned him of this. He unpacks a green sleeping bag and nestles against his pack, using it as a pillow. He listens to the wind echo as it slides down the stairwell.

A Rastafarian is there when Rat wakes up, lounging against the balustrade while Rat struggles to open his eyes. Rat looks up, noting the long line of the Rastafarian's body, the black dreadlocks that brush against the marble step.

"Your hair must weigh a lot," Rat says. The Rastafarian grins, and his teeth are a flash of white amid his face. Marlo dated a Rastafarian once. She used to tell Rat stories about kissing him, letting her hands get lost in the tangled chords of his hair.

"It's light," she said. "So much lighter than you'd expect hair like that to be."

Rat wonders whether it was this Rastafarian. It seems unlikely, but so does an endless stairwell. Rat is prepared to embrace the unlikely at present.

"Good morning," the Rastafarian says. He has an English accent, upper crust. Rat keeps waiting for him to say "Mon", but he doesn't. The silence seems awkward.

"Hi," Rat says. He sits up, still wrapped in the sleeping bag. "Sorry, am I in your way?"

"Not at all," the Rastafarian says. "Maybe you were, once, but I've adapted, yes?"

The Rastafarian drops into a crouch, his face filling Rat's vision.

"Up or down?" the Rastafarian says.

"Down," Rat says.

"How far?" the Rastafarian says.

"As far as I can," Rat says. "Then a few steps further, just for good luck."

"Brave," the Rastafarian says.

"Maybe," Rat says. "Maybe I'm just stupid."

The Rastafarian grins again. His dreadlocks are pooled around, spreading over step 6,417. He looks at the backpack that Rat's been using as a pillow.

"Big pack," the Rastafarian says. "You're prepared, so you aren't stupid. Foolish, maybe, but not stupid."

The Rastafarian looks at Rat, his brown eyes so dark they look like giant pupils. Rat squirms.

"So," Rat says. "Up or down?"

"Both," the Rastafarian says. "Neither. Depends on my mood."

"You're a strange man," Rat says. The Rastafarian nods, dreadlocks sliding across the marble. He stands up and offers Rat a hand.

"Come on," the Rastafarian says. "Big day ahead."

Rat nods. He lets the Rastafarian lift him onto his feet. He folds the sleeping bag and stows it in the backpack while the Rastafarian watches. It's hot again, the air thick with yeast, but the Rastafarian smells like hair-oil and cinnamon.

The Rastafarian ascends. Rat descends. Both of them have their hands on the mahogany banister. Rat can hear the Rastafarian's hair swishing against the marble as the Rastafarian walks away.

• • •

Step 6,500: *I never wanted to hear about your exes.*

Marlo loved her Rasta boyfriend because he scored her free weed. She'd told Rat as much when she was explaining her ex-boyfriends. The revelation made Rat feel inadequate. He'd never scored Marlo weed, free or otherwise. The only greenery he'd given her was a potted plant, and that died on her windowsill after three weeks of neglect.

Step 7,000: *I loved you. I didn't love you. I can't really remember anymore.*

Rat stops for lunch. It isn't much; a cheese sandwich on rye bread, slightly squashed after two days in the pack. It tastes great. A day-and-a-half over, and Rat is already sick of trail mix. The cheese is waxy, a little flavourless, but it hits the spot. He wasn't supposed to eat it today, but the stairwell is hotter now, and the cheese wasn't travelling well.

He sips water from a flask. It's tepid. He digs through the pack and pulls out the guidebook, looking for the pink post-it tag that marks Rat's notes for the second day.

The guidebook says that this is the toughest part, the second day of descent. It's the part where most people start to think about turning around, heading back up to the surface in order to escape the heat. A day-and-a-half of climbing means you've lost sight of the top of the stairs.

Rat stands up and leans over the balustrade. He looks down. He looks up. The guidebook is right—both directions look the same. He knows the top is up there, somewhere, but he can't see it.

Rat checks the clicker. He has covered 8,369 steps. He could turn around now if he wanted. No-one would really know. It's not like he told anyone his plans. It's not like he should be ashamed. He's already eaten the sandwich he was saving for the third day.

Most people turn around on the second day of climbing. Rat has always been good at giving up.

He can't think of anything to write on step 8,500. He sits on the marble, chin in his hands, staring at Marlo's ashes. Eventually he uncaps the sharpie and writes *Happy Birthday*. It doesn't really work. Rat crosses it out. Then he writes *Happy Birthday Happy Birthday Happy Birthday*.

Marlo always said that repeating something thrice meant you didn't really mean it.

The world's second-longest stair is in Switzerland, dug into the side of a mountain. Rat knows this because the guidebook told him, and because someone has put a plaque on the appropriate step. The world's second-longest stair has 11,674 steps.

Rat stops to read the plaque this time, trying to feel like he's accomplished something.

He doesn't. He just feels sore. His legs are burning

He stops for the night on step 11,700. He writes *I'm sorry. I did love you* on the marble because he's too tired to think of anything better. He sets up his sleeping bag and uses it to cover the declaration. He tosses and turns all night, bothered by the heat. The yeasty smell gets worse at night. It makes Rat's nose twitch.

Marlo was going out with one of Rat's friends. He probably shouldn't have slept with her that first time, even after she said she'd broken up with the other guy. Rat wasn't always called Rat, but he'd earned himself the name and it suited him too well to go away.

On step 12,073 he sees his first suicide. The body whistles past, not even screaming anymore. Rat's surprised by the way the arms and legs twist, struggling against the fall.

On step 50,500 he writes *There were many expressions you used that drove me crazy. I still think of killing someone every time I hear the words "done and dusted" in conversation. Nothing is ever done. Nothing is ever dusted.*

He is on his second sharpie. He killed the first after forgetting to replace the cap while writing on step 15,000.

He runs out of sandwiches on the forth day of climbing, but there's plenty of trail mix and tins of beans. The plan was to descend until he ran out of things to say. Rat never bothered thinking about how he'd ascend once the task was done.

On step 120,000 he writes *Fuck cancer.* He crosses this out and writes *It wasn't my fault.* Deep down, he believes neither of these things, despite the fact that he should. The doctors were wrong; it wasn't the cancer that killed her.

The heat turns slick and humid 300 steps later. His rubber soles squeak against the moisture coating the ancient marble.

At step 120,828 he pauses and pulls the guidebook out of his backpack. He flicks through the worn pages, looking at the detailed notes he's scrawled into the margins. Pauses on the photograph of the step he's reached. The point of no return, the deepest step anyone's reached and still returned to the surface. He's followed the guidebook's advice when it comes to supplies. His pack is lighter now, easier to handle, but he could still return.

Rat tosses the book over the balustrade. He looks up the stairwell, then down. Sweat streams across his forehead, soaks through his T-shirt. Rat's been wearing the same outfit for days. He's pretty sure he smells.

"Hello?" he says, and his voice echoes across the stairwell. His throat is dry, so he drinks some water. More than he should, regardless of his decision. Rat figures he can extend his supply a little this far down, assuming he's willing to lick condensation off the stairs.

He pulls Marlo out of his pack and holds her in both hands. Better to do it now, regardless of the decision. This is where they were headed when they'd first planned to come here. Too many things could go wrong once he moved into uncharted territory.

"We made it, babe," Rat says. His thumbnail punctures the plastic and sets the ashes free. The cloud disperses across the empty space, descends on the breeze. Slow-moving, delicate, waiting for the next suicide to freefall through its mass. Even in death Marlo is beautiful. Rat misses her more than anything.

He sits down on step 120,829 and grieves, shedding tears for the first time.

Step 121,500: *We were never meant to be happy. I'm no longer sure that matters.*

On step 200,000 Rat commits an act of poetry. He chooses to keep descending. Poetry bothers him less this far down the stairwell.

Rat knows three things to be true. The first is this: he will run out of food and water before he runs out of things to say. Two: what goes down need not emerge at the surface. Three: there will be no ending. The ending lies above, at the first step, in the life he'd live if he walked away. Endings are destinations and the Stair has but one, found only by backtracking and returning to the beginning.

The heat gets worse as he hits the lower depths. The balustrade is hot enough to redden his palms. Rat sheds clothing, equipment, leaves his sleeping bag on a step. The sharpies leak in his pockets, bleeding ink across his thighs.

•••••••••••

THAT GIRL

KAARON WARREN

St Martin's was clean, you could say that at least. Apart from the fine mist of leg hair, that is. I watched as Sangeeta ("You know me. I am Sangeeta.") crawled through the women's legs, a long piece of thread hanging from between her teeth. She stroked a shin, a knee, looking for hairs to pluck.

"Come on, Sangeeta. All the ladies are bald, now. You'll have to find a dog." The head nurse was very kind when there were visitors, the inmates told me.

They sat along the wide verandah that wrapped around their dorm. Like many verandahs in Fiji, it acted as their social centre. It was the only place in the hospital with comfortable chairs. The dining hall, in a collapsing once-white building behind the dorm, had hard chairs designed to make you eat quickly; the art therapy room, across the loosely-pebbled driveway, had stools. This was one of the things I wanted to change; put comfy chairs in so the women could sit and stitch, or paint, or weave. At present they made small pandanus fans and carved turtles from soap to be sold at the annual bazaar. My funding covered a month, and came from a wealthy Australian woman who'd visited St Martins and been depressed at the state of the art therapy room, with paintings so old there was more dust than paint. They had no supplies at all. My benefactor hired me to sort out the physical therapy room, perhaps train the nurses in some art techniques. The nurses loved the sessions with me and used them to gossip, mostly.

Sangeeta dragged herself up using the band of my skirt. "You've got too many hairs in your eyebrows. And your lip is like a hairy worm."

I turned a stare on her and she shrank.

The head-nurse said, "You comment on our guest's appearance? Are you perfect? There are things you will need to learn, Sangeeta. If you want to return to your life in Suva."

Sangeeta primped her hair. "I am a beauty therapist. Of course I am beautiful." Her face was deeply scarred by acne. Open wounds went septic so easily in the tropics. There was a red slash across her throat, vivid shiny skin, and two of her fingers were bent sideways. The fingernails were painted and chipped, bitten to the quick. "I studied in Australia. I married an Australian man but he went mad every full moon."

"Of course he did," the head nurse said. "He was cursed on your honeymoon at Raki Raki."

"He upset the witches. He didn't believe they were witches and took a photo of me kissing one of their pigs. Then he said I smelled like bacon and could not make love to me."

"You are blessed," one of the other inmates said. "You will die untouched."

"My second husband turned out to be gay," Sangeeta said, all the time the thread hanging from her mouth. She held the thread taut. "Can I pluck your hairs? Make you smooth?"

The other women set up a clamor, all wanting to do something for me. To me.

Only the old lady at the end of the verandah sat quietly, her lips moving. I walked over to her and bent my head down. "What is it, dear?" I said.

"I am that girl," she said. "I am that girl."

She was very thin. Her skin was wrinkled, looking like the folds of brown velvet—a hand-made soft toy for an ungrateful child.

"I am that girl," the old woman said. Not much else. She would demand more porridge if it were on, and sometimes sing if the prayer was in Hindi. I would learn all this in the next few days.

She grabbed at me with sharp fingernails. They should have been clean; everything else was here, but I saw a dark red ridge I didn't like. If she was a painter I would have guessed at Russet

Red, but she was not a painter. A strong smell of bleach filled the air. I suspected it was their only cleaning fluid.

"What girl does she mean?"

The head nurse shook her head. "We don't know. Malvika has been saying that for a long time now. She's been here since she was a teenager. Appeared one night, they say. Filthy, torn up, you've never seen such a thing, the old nurse told me. Nobody wanted her. Her family said no thank you. She's not our worst, though." She put her hand on a mess of a girl curled in a chair. "This one here came out of the womb this way. Her family kept her in a small bure at the back of their house until she got pregnant. No one knows who the father was but they say it was a dog." The poor girl looked like she'd been grown in a jar. She was twisted and folded over herself and she chewed her lip as if it were food. My fingers itched to draw her, and the old woman, too. Not as part of my funding, but for pleasure. I paint the daily details of life, to make sense of the world and here the details were vast and many layered.

• • •

After the shift was over the head nurse took me to the suburb of Lami, where we looked at second-hand clothes which smelled so full of mould and mothballs you could never wash it out. We went into the dark, rotting shed which passed for a market. Piles of vegetable waste sat in their own sludge, but on the tables beautiful purple eggplant, hands of bananas, small, aromatic tomatoes. The nurse talked in Fijian to the stall holders and they smiled at me, nodding, welcoming.

"Artist!" one of them said. "Oh, mangosa!"

"Mangosa means smart," the head nurse said. "She says you are smart if you are an artist. There's the dog," she whispered. She pointed at an enormous yellow mongrel. He sat with his back against a post, his back legs stretched out, his front paws lolling. He sat like a man. I've never seen balls the size of those he displayed, bigger than cricket balls and a dark grayish pink.

"He's the one they say got poor Dog Girl pregnant. They say her children are running for local council." At last she laughed and it finally sank it she was joking. I felt thick, slow and patronising, that I would believe such a thing.

I paid for the vegetables and I paid for the taxi to drop her home and take me to my flat. Local wages are so low, my per diem from my Australian benefactor was higher than her weekly wage.

We passed St Martin's on the way. "They are mental in there," the taxi driver said, tapping his forehead. When I didn't respond he twisted to look at me, the steering wheel turning about so we veered across into traffic coming the other way. "Mental crazy," he said. "Don't go in there."

He seemed chatty, so I asked him who he thought 'that girl' might be. He looked at me in the mirror.

"It might mean anything to anyone."

"But what does it mean to you?"

"The same as it means to any taxi driver," he said. "In the story she never gets old. Fresh-faced, sparkle-eyed, she smells of mangoes in season. Not the skin part, the flesh, chopped up and sweet on the plate. She picks up a taxi near the handicraft market in town. It's always at 5:37. A lot of us won't pick up a girl from there, then. She climbs into the backseat and gives you such a smile you feel you heart melt, all thought of your family gone."

"Have you seen her?"

"No, but my brother has. She asks to go to the cemetery and if you pry and ask who is there, she will say, "My mother." You want to take her home and feed her. You keep driving and you can't help looking at her in the mirror because she is so beautiful. She wears no jewelry apart from a small pendant around her neck. It nestles just here." He touched his breastbone with a forefinger, then spread his fingers as if holding a breast.

"I think that's enough," I said.

"The pendant has a picture of Krisna, fat baby eating butter. You turn the corner to reach the graveyard and you wait for her to tell you where to pull in. You feel a great coldness but the door is closed. You turn around and she is gone. Nothing of her remains."

I shivered. It was an old story, true. But it frightened me.

Taxi drivers love to tell stories of the things they've seen, the people they've picked up. I dismissed it as an urban myth, but I heard it again, and again. Always a brother, or a best friend, and they always told it with a shiver, as if it hurt to talk.

• • •

On my next visit to St Martins' I walked up to the old lady, Malvika. "I am that girl," she said. Between her breasts I saw a pendant, Krisna eating butter.

"You had a taxi ride?" I asked. "Is that right?"

"I . . ." She nodded.

"Will you walk with me? Let's walk. I have sweets." I whispered this last to her, not wanting the others to follow. All the women here walked slowly, their feet dragging on the floor, as if their feet were lead and they were too tired, too weak, to lift them each step. The women looked up at visitors but their eagerness was frightening. They wanted to tell you, give you their stories, and they wanted treats. Sweets to suck is mostly what they craved, sugar being the easiest addiction. Sugar ran out here because the women spooned it into their pockets, poked a wet finger in there during prayer or while they swept, then sucked that sugar off.

We walked across the driveway and around behind the art therapy room. I didn't want to sit inside on the hard stools. It was dusty and it stank of bananas and sweat in the room. I wasn't sure how I'd fix it but fix it I would have to. We found an old bench in the shade behind the building and sat down. "I told this many times," Malvika said. "A hundred. Two hundred. They stopped writing it down."

"I can write it down," I said. I took out my sketchbook and I didn't write; I drew.

"My mother died and father was happy to find a girlfriend the next day. He didn't visit my mother's grave but at least he gave me money for a taxi. I finished my job at 5:30 and went to see Mother before going home. There were not many taxis because everybody had finished work but this one stopped. This one." She closed her eyes. I thought of the head nurse's description of Malvika's arrival and my heart started to beat. I didn't need to hear this story; I would do nothing about it. But I wanted to hear it. I did . I wanted to hear of suffering and pain. I wanted to draw it on my paper, capture the detail of it.

"Tell me," I said.

"He was a nice man and asked me questions about work and school. Then he asked about boys and my body, words I didn't like. I was not brave enough to tell him to stop but I didn't answer him.

"When we reached the cemetery he pulled right inside. It was raining and he said he didn't want me to get wet though of course I would, standing out there. He stopped the car and jumped out while I gathered my things. He opened the door for me and I thought that was kind. But he didn't let me out. No."

She squeezed her hands together. "He pushed into the back seat and he took what my husband should have had. He hit me many times. As he climbed out, I tried to get out the other door but he slammed my fingers. He dragged me out into the mud and forced my face down into it. Then he did more terrible things, tearing and hurting me."

She thrust her fingers into her pocket and brought them out covered with sugar. She sucked them.

"He picked me up and shoved me into the taxi. He could have left me there but he thought of a way to cover up his crime. He drove me up the hill to the hospital and dumped me here. I couldn't speak sense for two days and by then it was too late."

"And he invented the ghost story to explain where you had gone, in case people saw you getting in his taxi?"

The old lady looked at me and smiled. "I am that girl."

I thought, *You cling to your youth. You dream of being young again, before this happened to you.*

The head nurse came around the corner. "There you are! You shouldn't take her away. She is very unwell. Very fragile."

• • •

I went home to paint in the afternoon light. Rain obliterated Suva Bay and was headed our way, so I had to work fast. My painting of Malvika disturbed me, because I had the sense of her as a young girl more strongly than of her as an old woman.

The hair on her chin. I knew there was a long, dark hair, but did it curl? Which side of her face was it on?

I hailed a taxi and had him stop at a roadside market, where I bought bananas and pawpaw with the change in my purse. Nobody would question me if I came with fruit.

Out of habit I asked the driver about That Girl. This one said, "She disappears. I can show you the place."

• • •

I went to Malvika although it was close to dinnertime and the hospital didn't like a break in the routine. She sat outside the door of the dorm. The other inmates used the door at the end of the verandah.

She sat bolt upright, her eyes wide open. She didn't blink. Her mouth was open and saliva had dried around her lips.

"Omigod," I said. "She's dead."

The nurse stopped me. "No, she's in a state."

The old lady's eyes were reddened and dry. I stared into them, looking for a sign of life, but nothing. There was no pulse. No breath. I remembered nothing of my first aid training and didn't want to put my mouth on her anyway.

"We must lay her flat," I said. I could do that much. The others watched me.

"You should leave her comfortable," Sangeeta said, shaking her head. She smelled of burnt hair.

"We must call the doctor," I said, but even as I spoke I was thinking, "Prussian Blue. If I mix Prussian Blue with Titanium White, water it down, I'll get her dead eyes. I'll paint an image of herself as a young girl in there, then wipe it away and paint the blank."

"She's empty," the nurse whispered to me. "Her ghost is taking a holiday. She will be back. Just wait."

Five minutes passed and I knew I had to take charge. I called for the doctor on my cell phone. He said, "No hurry. The nurses will call for the morgue when they are ready."

I squatted beside Malvika. I wouldn't get this chance again. The hair on her chin; it didn't curl.

And it happened. After ten minutes, maybe fifteen, Malvika began to twitch, blink her eyes, then she curled over into a ball and rocked.

"She . . . has a doctor examined her?"

"They are not interested."

"How often does this happen?"

"Sometimes. It rests her. She is happier for days afterwards."

No one else seemed concerned and I wondered if it was my Western woman ways which made me so terrified of an old woman who could die and come back to life as if she was merely sleeping.

I sat quietly and sketched their night time routine. That calmed me. Malvika sat up, demanding sugar. Yellowish saliva trails covered her chin. Her lips were dry and cracked. Her eyes were still out of focus and almost purple, it seemed to me. Her left cheek was reddened, as if the blood had already started pooling there.

I sketched those marks of death.

• • •

I didn't go back to St Martin's for a while. I was offered a commission from a wealthy Frenchwoman and the lure of the money, plus the idea of having my work hang in France, convinced me to take it.

One afternoon, feeling frustrated with the pretty Frenchwoman's face, I pulled out my portrait of Malvika. It made me feel ill to look at it. I had not painted a dead woman before. In the background I had painted a clock, set at 5:37.

I thought of the taxi drivers and how easily they repeated the legend of the disappearing girl. How happily they unconsciously supported their rapist companion. I knew that I would not be able to finish my portrait of Malvika until I knew her as a young girl, traced her steps over and over again.

I began then a week, or was it two? Of catching taxis just after 5, outside the handicraft centre. I did it a dozen times, maybe more. Some of them told me proudly, "A lot of drivers won't pick up young girls from there. But I don't believe in ghosts."

One evening, the driver said, "You been shopping?" His eyes looked at me in the mirror but not at me. Beside me. I've always found cross-eyed people hard to talk to.

"Yes," I said, though I had no bags.

"You girls going dancing tonight?"

"Girls?"

"You and your friend." He nodded at me. Beside me.

I felt prickles down my right arm, as if someone had leaned close to me. I didn't believe there was anyone there, but I didn't want to look. I shifted nearer to the door, and turned my head.

Nothing. No one.

The driver said something in Hindi.

"I'm sorry, I don't speak Hindi," I said, but he spoke more, pausing now and then as you would in a conversation.

"Your friend is very shy," he said.

We turned up the road to the cemetery, heading for St Martin's. I had to continue, my heart beat with it. We passed the cemetery, pulled into St Martin's. The driver turned around.

"Where . . . is . . . your friend?" he shouted. He didn't look like a man who shouted. "Where is she? You pay me."

"Will you wait? I just want to see something."

He shook his head, already driving away as I shut the door. "Where is she? Where is that girl?"

• • •

Malvika sucked her fingers at me. "Sugar? Sugar?"

No one had cleaned her up and I could see the marks of death clearly, the yellowish saliva on her chin, the purple colour of her eyes. "Have you been away? Out?" I said.

She nodded. "I am that girl," and she smiled at me.

• • •

I finished my portrait of Malvika. The paint is very thick because I painted her over and over again; young, old, dead. Young, old dead. I could never decide which face captured her best.

WALKER

DIRK FLINTHART

Julie Kincaid's house seemed no different to many older houses in the suburb. White, peeling weatherboard with a picket fence and an overgrown garden, where two frangipani trees blossomed fragrantly, one in pink and the other in yellow. Jacarandas and poincianas shaded the back yard, sheltering myriad cicadas that chirred rhythmically in the building heat of the morning. Tufts of browning grass sprouted in the cracks of the cheerfully uneven concrete path from the gate to the verandah.

But seen from the corner of my eye, the whole house *shimmered*.

"There is power here," I said to Kan-yo, stepping back from the fence. "Why haven't we noticed so much power before? How did we miss it?"

From my pocket she pulsed back laughter. And yes, perhaps it was a foolish question. There are few Walkers, and we range widely. Easy to miss one simple house in an ocean of suburban lookalikes. Yet the power here was sufficient to disrupt hundreds of Anima inhabiting machinery all across the suburb. From the wall of display teevees in Retravision, locked mysteriously into Sesame Street, Kan-yo and I followed the trail through past vending machines that refused money, around an ATM quietly coughing twenties and fifties into the hot summer morning, down to CafeTronic where Max's Internet machines let me speak with Down Time and Sunlight Wires, the two Walkers nearest my region. Time and Wires knew of no other Walkers with business in the north of Brisbane, and we had tentatively decided it must be someone new when Max broke the news about the escalator failures in the mall.

A Walker new to the power, untrained in the laws of the Dreaming and the ways of the Anima—such a one posed a great danger. Kan-yo and I found the escalators too late. The power had already been shut off, consigning their Anima to the dark side of the Dreaming for a time. But nearby was a glass elevator, doors hissing open and closed at random. While I spoke to the security guard, Kan-yo soothed the Animus of the elevator, and in turn, she learned the scent of the Anima of all the phones which were in the elevator when this unknown Walker exerted her power—for Kan-yo insisted the Walker was 'she'. I should have known, for even I tasted the scraps and leavings of her power like milk and frangipani blossoms at the back of my throat, but Kan-yo, with her Animus senses and the clever tricks of her Nokia-built form, spoke with certainty of this Julie Kincaid.

And so we came to an ordinary-seeming house on a warm summer's day.

Kan-yo pulsed caution, and a query. "No," I said to her, watching the aluminium security door that led to the interior of the house. "I don't think we need the others yet. I don't want to frighten her. But—stay in contact with the Anima that Time and Wires carry, yes? A new Walker, no matter how strong she is, hasn't the knowledge to overcome me. Yet if she was strong enough, I might have to hurt her in defending myself. If it comes to that, we will retreat until the others come."

Halfway up the steps to the verandah, Kan-yo pulsed again, and I paused uneasily. "I feel it too," I said. "There's too much. There's a feeling . . ." A feeling of what? Something hidden, something behind and under the spilling, jittery energy of an untaught Walker. "I think we have little time, Kan-yo. Watch carefully!"

A slender young woman, comfortable in a big t-shirt and paint-spattered shorts, came within moments of my knock. From behind the security-mesh door, she frowned.

"Can I help you?"

I held up one of my business cards. "Canvassing for work, miss," I said. "You've got a 'sold' sign on your fence, so you've just moved in. An old place like this, likely you've found a few problems with the wiring. Maybe you've had trouble with the appliances?"

She withdrew a little into the shadowy interior, but her hand fell to the doorknob. "There have been a couple things, just lately. But—" she peered at my card, her blonde hair falling in wings about her face. "*Kadaitcha*? Does that mean something? I mean, it seems familiar."

"An old Aborigine term for a sort of magic-man," I offered. "It's kind of a joke. You're meant to think my repair work is magic, see? My grand-mum is aboriginal. Her people came from up Bundaberg way. She used to tell me about the Kadaitcha-man when I was little. But it's just a business name."

Still she hesitated. Through the haze of power that shimmered and sparked off the house, I couldn't get a real sense of her, or what she thought of me, so I stuck my card through the mail slot. "Look, I don't want to pressure you. If I've come at a bad time that's okay. You can use my card. Maybe call a few of the people around here. This is kind of my suburb. I do work for 'most everyone." I saw the toys scattered on the carpet behind her, in the hallway. "Call the school. I fixed their water coolers the other day. And I repaired the TV at the daycare centre in Winton street last week."

She picked up my card, looking at it carefully. "Actually—I really could use some help," she admitted, and I heard the deadlock snick back. "It's the ceiling fans. They keep coming on by themselves. It's a bit scary." The door swung back, and on her unspoken invitation, Kan-yo and I entered.

An old Queenslander, the house was cooler inside, and breezy. The ceilings were high, but I had to fight the urge to hunch my shoulders against the claustrophobic pressure of the power in the air, in the very walls and floor of the old place. Kan-yo shuddered on my chest, and I soothed her wordlessly.

"This way," said Julie Kincaid, showing us into a sunlit lounge room. Overhead, the ceiling fan chopped at the air, blasting it into the corners, rippling the curtains, flapping a newspaper on the worn brocade sofa. I didn't even have to glance at the switch on the wall. The distress of the Animus in the fan was clear, even through the distortion of the Dreaming in the house. The poor thing *hurt*.

Unthinking, I raised my hand and cleared the tangle of energies around it with a gesture. The fan slowed at once. To distract the young Walker, I asked a question. "How long has this been happening, Miss Kincaid?"

She stared at me, her eyes narrowing. "I don't remember telling you my name."

Kan-yo throbbed against my chest. I bit my lip. The ungrounded power in the place, that sense of something else—I wasn't thinking clearly. "Letters sticking out of the postbox on the fence," I said. "Name of Kincaid. I shouldn't have, but I looked."

Kan-yo buzzed again, and then again, while Julie Kincaid watched me. She reached into her pocket and brought out a mobile phone, keeping her eyes on me while she dialled. "I'm just going to check with the daycare centre, like you suggested," she said, in a quiet, even tone. "I don't know how you did that with the fan, by the way. I don't know whether to be grateful or not. Why don't you see what you can do for the one in the room opposite?"

A clear dismissal. I nodded, and stepped into the hall. Behind me, I heard her speaking calmly. Kan-yo confirmed she had called the daycare centre, so I opened the door of the room Julie Kincaid had indicated, and entered.

And stopped, staggered by a heavy, rolling wave of silence that almost pushed me back into the hall. There was no subtlety to it, but the sheer strength shook me, and Kan-yo shrilled wildly. I had no time to reassure her. The room commanded my whole attention. Stuffed plush toys. A small bed with gaily coloured sheets. Bright, crayon pictures decorated the walls; only crude stick figures, yes, but instantly recognisable to anyone who could walk the Dreaming. Here a car-Animus, obviously a Holden by its sturdy haunches and narrow forelimbs. There a cheerful kitchen-scene, complete with toaster-Animus, blender-Animus, and microwave-Animus. And there—

Kan-yo saw it too, and shrieked. I swept the picture from the wall, leaving the sticky-taped corners raggedly behind, and crossed to the lounge room in two strides. Julie Kincaid started as I entered, and I held the picture up between us, silencing her phone with a gesture. "Your daughter," I said. "Where is she?"

She blinked, summoning indignation, and I cut her off. "There is no time. Listen to me. This house has a cool room. One of those big, industrial fridges they use in pubs and restaurants. You've had electrical troubles since it arrived. It is dangerous. Your daughter is in danger." More than I could possibly explain to someone who couldn't walk in the Dreaming, and it was obvious that the daughter who slept in that bedroom, not Julie, was the new-fledged Walker.

"No," said Julie, confusion writ large on her face. "That's not—I mean . . . yes, my husband is a cook. We have a home catering business. The cool room was secondhand, and we had some trouble setting it up with the old electricals in this place. But there's no danger. Gracie can't even open it. And how—"

I grabbed her hand. "She won't need to open it. Come. She'll need us both."

I dragged her, protesting incoherently, into the hall. The cool room would be accessed from the kitchen, and in the old Queenslanders, that meant the back of the house. I could already feel it, if I concentrated. "Kan-yo, pass the word through Eve and Killayli to Sunlight Wires and Down Time. Whatever they're doing, stop and prepare. The creature here will know we've come. It will act quickly. If we have to go Darkside to reach it, I want help as near as I can get it."

"Who are you talking to?" Julie Kincaid shook off my hand and caught up with me as I burst into room at the end of the hallway.

"Mobile phone. Hands free," I said. It was the only explanation that would make sense to anyone but another Walker. "I'll need help for this." To my left, a dining room with an antique wooden table and matching, uncomfortable, curly-legged chairs. To my right, a modern kitchen dressed out in stainless steel, and at the back, a single, white door rimmed in steel. Waves of hatred poured off it, hitting me like soft hammers, and I stopped. "Secondhand," I said, glaring at Julie, who stared back at me, her eyes wide. "Where did you get it?"

Shrinking, she pulled away from me, reaching behind her for the telephone on the counter. I raised my voice. "*Where did you get it?*"

"A butcher," she whimpered. "In Zillmere. Going out of business. It was cheap because of the cleaning. Please, please, don't hurt us. If you just go, I won't say anything, please —"

I ignored her and studied the door. "A cool room," I muttered. "One with a history of blood and death. What kind of idiots?"

I checked myself, forcing calm. Two centuries ago, when the whites came to Australia, the people here lived with the Dreaming, and the Anima. Back then, the spirit-voices identified with the things that were important to the Aborigines: the animals, the plants, prominent features of the landscape. Some of the Aborigines could hear the Anima, perhaps, and in that way they learned. Or perhaps it was the other way around: perhaps the power of belief and story gave the Anima their path to the places and the things in the Dreaming that touched this world.

Either way: the whites changed all that. They broke the delicate web of lore and law, cut the strands that bound up the living, Dreaming whole. The Anima were driven out, or forgotten, or lost. Not until the whites built their own complicated, interdependent society with their own rules and beliefs did they return.

When they came back, they no longer identified with the animals, the plants, the features of the landscape. Those things weren't important in the white world. Nobody believed passionately in those things, not in the same way they supported Holden over Ford at Bathurst, or swore that Sony made better televisions than JVC, or lived and breathed Apple phones and computers and gadgets. When the Anima found their way back from the dark side of the Dreaming, they came to things of the new, white world that carried the potential for their secret life.

"Open the door," I said, gesturing at the white-and-steel maw set into the wall. Julie Kincaid blinked at me, tears running down her face. I tried to soften my voice. "Your daughter is inside," I told her. "Don't ask how I know. Just understand that it is true. If you act quickly, perhaps we can save her without . . ." I stopped. There really wasn't a way I could explain what would have to be done to save the girl if the Animus of the cool room had carried her to the dark side of the Dreaming. I could only hope that we were in time.

Hesitantly, her gaze fixed on me, Julie backed along the kitchen counter, and fumbled blindly with the handle to the door of the cool room. She paused, secured a better grip. Her eyes widened, and she turned away from me. I saw the muscles tighten in her shoulders. "I can't—it won't open," she said, and grabbed the emergency release, yanking with all the strength in her slight frame. "Oh my God! Grace! Gracie!"

Julie plastered her body against the whiteness of the cool room, slamming it with the flat of her hand, screaming her daughter's name. The sense of hatred from the thing changed subtly to a cruel and bitter *satisfaction*.

Some of the Anima still resented the changes forced on them by the new world. And some of them had been inimical to humankind even in the long gone days of old. This creature, the Animus of the cool room: it had a new-fledged Walker in its grasp. There would be no easy solution here. Time to Walk.

I put my hand on Julie's shoulder, above the t-shirt, skin to skin. Before she could jump away, I reached through, inside, and grasped at the Julie-within. By an act of will, I closed my eyes and the world around me bent, twisted. Tore. A soundless wind raked claws over my skin. I clenched my teeth against an impossible cold, muscles spasming against the blast. And then, with a sense of a vast door closing somewhere behind, we were through, and beyond, in the dark side of the Dreaming.

Cool, shadowed, fogged, like a dim, undeveloped photograph of the dayside, the dark side is part reflection, part blueprint, part reverse-image, part . . . indescribable. What senses we use to perceive it and interact with it, I do not know. Among ourselves, Walkers speak of sight, and sound and touch, even though there are none of these things. What other words are there? What other ways of knowing? This is the dark side of the Dreaming. Other laws hold sway.

I steadied Julie, pushing calm and strength down the connection between us until I felt her draw away from me, pull herself upright. "Where—" She paused. "Oh my God. What have you done?"

"This is the place your daughter has come," I told her. In this place, Julie Kincaid appeared as a slender, pale, big-eyed creature, like a cartoon ghost, staring at me in fear. I knew what she saw: the sigils and tattoos etched onto my skin glowing with power, turning me into a sort of animated scrawl in the were-light. At my chest, Kan-yo coiled sinously, graceful and strong in her true home. I set her on the ground, and she slithered away, questing into the dark. "This is not the time for questions, Julie Kincaid. This is a dangerous place. It is not for human beings. This is the home of dreams, and the things that live in them. I can come here when I must, and I am tolerated because I am . . . useful. There are things here that will help me, if I ask. But there are others that will harm. Stay close to me, and do as I say, and we will return safely, with your daughter."

Reassurances. They seemed to help her, or perhaps it was the strength I had already loaned her. Either way, she drew herself up, and looked around. "Where is she?"

I did not need to look. "There," I said, pointing at the shape I could literally feel, cold and vicious in the shadows. A thing of living darkness, it coiled, moving slowly upon itself. Squatting like a toad, it was at once vast and powerful, yet compact and dynamic. "That is the Animus of your cool room. That is its true shape in this place. It has taken your daughter within itself. It is our task to bring her back."

Julie made as if to move towards the Animus, then stopped. "How? How do you know? I—I can't see her. I don't know what that thing is. I don't know . . . all I've got is your word, and this place, this place . . ." She began to keen, a thin, wordless cry lost between fear and despair, and I lay my hand upon her, giving her of my strength again. A dangerous thing to do, yes, but I had no rightful claim on the daughter. I could come to the darkside, but once the girl had given herself into the Animus, the laws did not permit me to reclaim her. Even if I did overcome the Animus by strength and guile, my days as a Walker would be ended. A Walker who breaks the rules of the Dreaming is outcast, outlawed, rightfully to be harried and killed by the Anima in proper defense of their home. If there was any hope of recovering Grace Kincaid, it lay with her mother. I could not let her fail.

The keening faded, and Julie Kincaid drew a ragged breath. I released my grip.

Kan-yo whispered to me then. Killayli and Eve watched, she said. Down Times and Sunlight Wires prepared to enter the darkside at my need. Yet they could not come to my aid unless the Animus itself broke the accord. Until then, they could only observe, even if I failed. Even if it meant my death, and the death of Julie and Grace Kincaid. The laws of the Dreaming are uncompromising.

Such it is to be a Walker.

Bringing my power to my skin, I gripped the sigil on my left arm, pulled it free, and cast it on the ground where it burst into brilliant light. That sigil cost me many hours of meditation, preparation, and pain. In the dayside of the Dreaming, it would now be a whitely visible scar, puckered and shiny, until I could repeat the rituals, and restore its power. Sacrificing it bought just one advantage: as long as the light burned, the Animus could neither flee, nor change its shape. Now we could talk.

"Creature," I said. "I am Walker Clouds-In-Spring." My voice fell flat, without echoes in the newly lit space. Shadows crawled beyond the limits of my vision. "I am he that broke the Bridge Danyana with his song. It was I who drove the Dweller from the Mount Gravatt telephone exchange, and harried him back into the uttermost dark. I am the one who flew alongside Yuwattan of the steel eagle, from daylight to dusk without pause. I know the words of Kul-buru. I know the dances of One White Noise. I bear the sign of Iron, the sign of Glass, the sign of Copper, and the sign that burns. I bring this woman under my protection. She is the mother of the child you have taken, and claims her by the oldest right. Give up the girl as the Law demands, and we will go in peace. Deny this claim at your peril."

The shape before us moved and coiled. A bitter chill touched my skin, and Julie Kincaid shivered. For an instant, I thought the creature might risk defiance, hoping to overwhelm me here in its home. Those who dwell within the Dreaming have much more latitude than those of us who Walk there under sufferance. Their place; their laws. If the creature could destroy me swiftly, take my power for its own and harm no other Animus, no-one would take it to task except perhaps another Walker, and there are few of us.

Yet perhaps it had some suspicion of Sunlight Wires and Down Time, for the thing moved and coiled once more, and then it shifted, and somehow it opened. There, within the deeper darkness, lay three rounded, softly glowing shapes like the eggs of a titanic bird. My heart fell.

"What does it mean?" said Julie. "Where is Grace?"

"Grace is there," I said. "I came late. This is not the first time she has entered the darkness, through the Animus of your cool room. Twice before she has come, and willingly. Each of those," I pointed, "Is she, after a manner of speaking. One is the she-of-now. The others are she-before."

"Which one?" She stared into the darkness, her thin, pallid hands clenching and unclenching nervously.

"That's for you to determine. I have no right or claim to Grace. Only you, her mother, can bring her forth." I drew a deep breath, tasting old leaves and dry blood. "You have to choose."

"And . . . if I'm wrong?"

"Then we leave." I could not look at her. "And Grace does not. We will find her body cold, dead on the floor of the cool room. The rest of her will remain here."

"But that's not fair!"

I put my hand on her once more. "It isn't our world, Julie Kincaid. Grace came here of her own choice. You have a claim on her, by right, but if you can't make good that claim, Grace's choice stands."

Julie sobbed. "She's only a little girl! It was so hot. She hates the heat. We were going to get air conditioning as soon as we could afford it, but she was so hot, and she got a rash on her neck, and she cried. I took her into the cool room and we scraped some snow off the freezer. I put it on her neck, and she shivered, and then she laughed, and I loved her so much. I only wanted her to be happy!"

The bleak, vile satisfaction of the Animus rippled like rancid waves in a cesspit. I took Julie's shoulders in my hands, and forced her to look at me. "It is my strength which holds us here, Julie. Only the light of my sigil holds the Animus. Time is against us. You must choose, and choose now."

She looked past me, into the dark. "I can't choose. I can't do it."

"Then Grace dies."

"Don't say that!" Her voice rose to a shriek, and for a moment, her eyes flared with light. A little power of her own, then. Not enough, but perhaps a hint as to the strength of her daughter.

"Choose," I said. "Now."

She took a tentative step forward, then stopped, and looked back at me. "Aren't you coming?"

I shook my head. "Best I stay out here." If I entered the Animus—if it closed itself about us, took us entirely within its power . . . Could Sunlight Wires and Down Time act quickly enough to save us if the creature chose to kill, in defiance of the Law?

"Please," she said, her voice a thin whisper, her ghost-eyes wide and hollow. She glanced back at the living darkness, and the precious eggs within, and leaned close to me. "I'm afraid of the dark," she whispered in my ear.

I looked to the shadows where Kan-yo lay hidden, where presumably Eve and Killayli watched alongside her. Then I nodded, and took Julie Kincaid's hand in mine, and we stepped forward into the belly of the beast.

At once, the Animus closed itself about us, engulfing us in a tangible blackness. I felt Julie trembling violently against me, and I turned her face towards the egg-shapes. "There," I said. "Choose quickly. I will hold back the dark." With my free hand, I loosed the sigil from about my throat, and cast it down. The light it gave was wan and cold in that dark, bleak place, but it seemed to give Julie strength. While I stood, braced against the living dark that beat upon me like a thunderstorm, she knelt, and placed her free hand on one of the glowing shapes.

"Oh," she said. "She's so hot. So itchy. The cool room is scary. She knows she mustn't go there, but I'm there too, and it's all right, the snow is so cold on her neck." She looked up at me. "Not this one. This is the first time we went in." She pushed the egg away from her, and it faded.

There was a sound like the slaughter of a great beast, and the ground shuddered. The light of my sigil died, and the dark closed in. Julie gasped, and I gave up the sigil on my left thigh.

When she recovered herself, Julie touched another of the eggs. Hesitated. Touched the last. Pulled her hand back.

The sigil-light dimmed.

"Peppermint," said Julie, almost to herself, and pushed another egg away. "She had peppermints yesterday." She placed her hand on the final egg, and said clearly, "This is the one. This is my daughter. I've chosen."

The ground shook so violently that I fell, and the sigil-light blazed, then vanished. Desperately, I unwound the sigil from my left calf and hung it burning in the air. By its light, I saw a small girl, locked in her mother's embrace. The eggs were gone. There was no light except my fast-fading sigil. Julie Kincaid had chosen well.

"The claim is made by right," I said. "Release us." Nothing happened, save that the sigil-light faded, and the dark drew close around us. "Release us," I said again, "Or by right and by strength you will be destroyed."

The cold deepened to an ache that crushed bones and stole the breath from my throat. Fumbling, I unwound three more sigils in a blinding flare of light and welcome heat. As the living darkness recoiled from us, I spoke two more words, and flung the strength of my heart against the Animus. If I could break through, even for an instant, Kan-yo would know and the others could intervene. Power roared from me like a column of flame, beating against the dark, pushing it back, and farther back, even as the cold crept into my limbs. My breath burned in my throat. My body trembled, and ached, and still I pushed, and still the Animus held.

Held. Trembled. Pushed back, and I did not have the strength to stop it. Inch by inexorable inch, the Animus closed in upon us as all my power flared and raved against it. "Julie," I said, trying not to gasp. "Help me."

"How? I don't even know what you're doing." She held her daughter protectively to her chest. "What do I do?"

"I need the strength I gave you. I need your own strength." I stretched out my hand, and it trembled in the fading light. "Take my hand. Please." The weight of darkness came full upon me then, like a corpse across my shoulders, and I sank to one knee as Julie took my fingers in one hand. Gratefully, I drew from the fires within her, taking what strength she could spare, and she became even thinner and more ghostly, but the Animus recoiled. Hope flared, and I threw myself into the struggle anew. I could feel the dark life retreating, parting before the heat and light that raked at it—then Julie fell to her knees with a slow, sad, sigh, and I saw the terrible pallor of her skin, the fading light in her eyes.

She was done. We were lost.

The Animus bugled its triumph, and the terrible weight of its hatred redoubled, driving me down before it. I scrabbled for the last of my sigils, the spiral on my belly, preparing a final defiance. And then a small, sure hand clasped mine, and a great white light burst inside my head. Like a waterfall, strength and power rushed into me, filling me, stretching my skin taut and tingling. My hair stood on end, and a scream of rage and joy burst from my lips as Grace Kincaid, the newest and youngest Walker gave me her trust, and her power crawled like Tesla's tame lightnings over my body.

With a single word, I shaped a ball of dancing light at my fingertips and tossed it casually into the dark where it detonated with a soundless pulse. The Animus shuddered, and retreated, but I threw another, and another, and then I reached out, grabbed the slippery, rubbery, burningly cold stuff of the creature itself between my two hands, and ripped it apart.

The Animus screamed.

Light flooded in; real light, brilliant sunlight from the dayside of the Dreaming. I smelled frangipanis, and felt the warmth of summer. Under my hands, the were-flesh of the Animus flowed, and writhed, and changed until it was the door of the cool room that I clutched, forced wide with a strength greater than my own. The scream changed too, higher, flatter, more piercing, and I smelled smoke, and burning insulation. There was a flash, and a pop, and then near-silence as the compressor burned out completely. The Animus died then, on both sides of the Dreaming, and all that remained was the cool room itself, and the wreckage of the complex machine that had given the creature a home on the dayside.

I knelt, and collected Kan-yo's dayside form, tucking the phone away in my pocket. The white, puckery scar on my arm caught my eye briefly. There would be a long, wearisome price to pay for the power I had spent today, but for my pains, a new Walker stood beneath the sun. I smiled, and patted Kan-yo. Then I placed Julie Kincaid in the recovery position on the kitchen floor, and turned my attention to her daughter.

Grace Kincaid watched me steadily, with wide, grey eyes. She was perhaps five, maybe six years old, her hair bound in childish ponytails, but her eyes were older by far. I nodded acknowledgement, and gestured at the sink. "Is there a kettle? I think your mother will need a hot drink."

"I can do it," she said, and with a wave of her hand, she did. The little Animus of the electric kettle heard, and obeyed with a click and a hiss.

I frowned. "You must learn to listen to them as well," I said. "It isn't enough to command their obedience. A Walker stands between the Anima and humankind. We have to speak for both, if we are to share this world."

She nodded solemnly, and her eyes strayed to the still form of her mother.

"She isn't hurt," I said. "But she'll be tired, and what little she remembers will seem like a bad dream. You will have to be patient with her." I stood up.

"Are you going?" Grace's voice trembled a little. "What if it comes back?"

"It can't," I said. "We destroyed it. I will come back, in time. The cool room must be cleansed before it can be repaired, so that it is free of the taint of old death and violence. The next Animus it attracts will be different. You and I will see to it, little Walker."

Then her mother stirred, and groaned, and Grace ran to her side. I slipped away before Julie Kincaid could see me, and passed down the carpeted hallway to the brilliant Queensland sunshine beyond. Julie would forget, soon enough, but there would be my business card in the post-box when it came time to repair the cool room, and I would be called back. Grace would need guidance, and instruction, and for a time, protection. One day she would need a familiar Animus of her own, and on that day I would give her the name she would bear when she strode between the dark and the day, watching over all the creatures of the Dreaming.

Such it is to be a Walker.

· · · · · · · · · · ·

THE BONE MOTHER

ANGELA SLATTER

Baba Yaga sees the child from her window and knows that her daughter is dead. She bashes the pestle against the bottom of the mortar and swears she will not weep. The child is at the gate now, her hand nervously moving in the pocket of her apron. The old woman sits at the window to wait.

Vasilissa stares at the house. It is a tumble-down black dacha, somewhat forlorn in the late spring light. Chickens scratch at the dirt in a desultory fashion. A fence runs around the yard, and the gateposts are festooned with human skulls.

The blond girl shivers. Her stepmother sent her here and her mother, reduced to the tiny doll wiggling in her pocket, seconded the notion. She, however, is not so sure. Ludmilla, her father's second wife, means her harm but she is loath to think that her own mother has the same intent.

"Go to Baba Yaga and get us some coals for the fire," Ludmilla told her. Shura, her mother, said she should obey. "Ask Baba Yaga no questions she does not invite."

"Why, Mother, must I go?" Vasilissa had whispered to the twitching wooden doll. The thing had started speaking to her six months ago—five months after her mother's death, and one month after Ludmilla had married her father. She still doubted sometimes that the doll really did speak, but seeking out a priest and telling him the tale would be far worse than a little madness. Thus, she listened to the doll, who had never set her wrong.

"Because she is your grandmother, but she won't treat you any better for that. She has her own rules. Just do as I say and no harm will befall you."

Vasilissa had set out for Baba Yaga's compound. She walked a day and a night and on the evening of the second day she has come to the black dacha. A thundering of hooves splits the air and a torrent of air pushes past her, shoving her to the ground. She is familiar with the occurrence by now—in the mornings a woman in white charged past her, and at midday a fierce female rider in red did the same. Now, at dusk, a black rider takes her turn. She gallops past, through the gate, and disappears up the stairs of the dacha.

The little girl has spent the last hour sitting in the forest, watching the house, trying to ignore the tiny voice of the doll. At last the urging becomes too much and Vasilissa rises and drags her feet as she approaches the gate. The skulls glare down at her, eyes glowing red. She passes under their gaze, icy with fear.

Although she has been waiting for it, the child's knock startles Baba Yaga. She drops the pestle and it clunks heavily against the side of the mortar. From the air three sets of disembodied hands appear and she gestures for them to move the mortar back into a dark corner of the room, then she shuffles to the door.

The girl cowers under the Bone Mother's gaze. For the longest moment the old woman says nothing, just looks at the child, trying to see a trace of own daughter in the youthful features. Vasilissa peers with the same intent, thinking that the eyes set deep in the wrinkled face once looked out from her mother's face. A smile cracks the withered visage.

"What do you want, girl?" Her voice is the sound of the pestle grinding against the mortar. Vasilissa clears her throat.

"Please, Grandmother. My stepmother sent me to beg some coals from you. Our fire has gone out." Her feet are rooted to the spot as she stares up at her grandmother. Baba Yaga is tall and very thin, her face is a map of wrinkles, tattooed with age spots; she has a long nose and a surprisingly full mouth. Her hair is long and iron grey, pulled into an untidy plait hanging down her back.

"Stepmother? How long has she reigned?" Her heart trips at the idea of loss, of not knowing how long her daughter has been gone.

"Ludmilla and her daughters came to live with us five months ago," Vasilissa keeps her voice carefully neutral.

"How does she treat you?"

"As a stepmother does."

Baba Yaga grunts and steps aside so Vasilissa can pass into the parlour. The girl looks behind her surreptitiously.

"What, child?" The question is sharp. Vasilissa swallows hard.

"They say your house stands on the legs of giant chickens and moves around and around."

Her grandmother's bemusement is obvious. "Who would believe a stupid thing like that?" She leans down to the child. "When did you ever see a chicken big enough to support a dacha?"

Vasilissa giggles in spite of herself and steps across the threshold into a dim room filled with the smells of things that have lived for a long time. The doll in her pocket shakes.

• • •

After supper, Vasilissa watches her grandmother sleep in the big old bed across the room. Her face is less lined in repose but Vasilissa still thinks of each furrow as a journey taken, a map of her grandmother's past and perhaps one of Vasilissa's own future.

Will I look like her? Would my mother have looked like her had she lived? Is it so bad, to have lines to show where and who you have been?

Baba Yaga stirs, snores a little, settles. The little girl snuggles into the small bed she has been given and closes her eyes. Sleep comes quickly and she does not trouble the little doll for the first time in many nights.

• • •

They rise before dawn and eat a light breakfast, then Baba Yaga leads Vasilissa into the stable yard.

"Today, you must earn your keep. When I leave, you will clean the yard, clear out the stables, and sweep the floors. When you have finished that, take a quarter of a measure of wheat from my storehouse and pick out of it all the black grains and wild peas you find there. Then cook my supper." She leans down and whispers. "Or *you* will be my supper!"

The girl giggles, not in the least bit afraid.

"Yes, Grandmother. I bid you good day."

"My riders will come, my riders three. First is my glorious dawn, then my bright day, and last my tenebrous night. They cannot harm you, and will answer if you call." Baba Yaga climbs into the mortar, an ungainly scramble, grasps the pestle in her left hand and a long straw broom in her right.

The mortar, responding to her commands, rises in the air with a grinding sound and floats to the opening gate. Baba Yaga uses the pestle to steer and, with the broom, sweeps behind her to cover any trace of her passing. Vasilissa thinks it an extraordinary way to travel, when there are several fine horses peering at her from the stables. She shrugs.

When her grandmother has disappeared from view, Vasilissa pulls the little doll from her pocket. She puts a few crumbs of bread in front of the thing and a spoonful of milk.

"There, my little doll, take it. Eat a little, drink a little, and listen to my grief."

The doll shakes itself as if waking and eats up the morsels with alacrity. Vasilissa speaks once again.

"Today, little doll, I must clean the yard, clear out the stables, and sweep the floors, then separate a quarter measure of wheat from black grains and wild peas. Then I must cook supper. Tell me, little doll, what shall I do?"

"Cook the supper, of course. Leave the rest to me." The tiny thing jumps up and stands on the top step, raising her arms before she fixes the child with painted blue eyes. "Best you don't see this lest you become too old too soon."

Vasilissa bows her head and goes inside the dacha. She prepares her grandmother's supper, never tempted to look outside at the storm of activity the doll creates. Some things are best not known, some wisdoms should not come too soon.

• • •

The mortar makes it way through the trees doing surprisingly little damage. Baba Yaga knows her paths and, as she sweeps behind her, she ensures that no one can follow her trail, trace her back to the black dacha too easily. Not everyone appreciates her place in the scheme of things.

Baba Yaga is a woman who cannot be bound. She will bear no more children, she will bow to the wishes of no man; she is independent, adrift from the world and its demands. The world, in ceasing to recognise her value, has granted her a freedom unknown to maids and mothers. Only the crone may stand alone. She heals when she can and, when she cannot, she ushers others along their path, easing suffering, tempering fear.

The people of the forest know enough to leave signs when she is needed: a red rag tied to a fence or gate post. An offering is left, too, so as not to actually hand anything over to the old woman and risk the catching of old age, which some of them seem to think of as a contagion. She's a last hope to most, too feared to be willingly approached except in desperation. Oftentimes they wait too long. Mourners put such deaths down not to their own inaction, but to malice, to the crone being hungry to take a life, to feed herself on the juices of the living. She is deathless, strange thing that she is, and they assume she must feed off them to maintain this ever-life.

When she does manage to save someone, there is still fear—gratitude becomes a strange, haunted animal, constrained by a niggling unease, an idea, however unreasonable, that the price of her aid is too high. She should, she tells herself over and again, be used to it; inured to the ache it causes her. But she isn't; she suspects she never will be, and she fears for herself if she ever does become numb. Pain tells her she is still just a little human; something less than mortal, but more than a stone. This comforts, sometimes.

Today she saves a child and helps an old woman along the path, all in the same cottage. The child has a fever, easily quelled by a tea of herbs. She hands the child's mother enough of the mixture for two days more. The woman's mother-in-law lies quietly in a shadowed corner, waiting for the last darkness to fall. There is no request for her help with this one, it's as if the old woman is not worth the trouble, not worth an offering to the dark woman who roams the woods.

Baba Yaga sits by the narrow pallet, hands waving the hovering younger woman away. Her nose twitches at the stale smell of the old woman's body. She has not been bathed and she has soiled herself some time today or the day before. Baba Yaga looks at the younger woman.

"I hope your daughter treats you thus when your time comes. I hope she pays you the same respect, gives you the same dignity at your dying time," she spits and the woman shrinks away to sink against a wall on the far side of the cottage, hoping the curse will somehow slip from her skin, not embed itself in her pores.

Baba Yaga takes the hand of the old woman. The last vestiges of life have collected in her eyes, which shine in the dim room, and she smiles at the dark woman, grateful, for once, without fear. "Bless you, Baba. I beg you to help me pass on."

The deathless one nods and pulls a flask from the folds of her faded dress. She holds it to the lips of the woman, who drinks greedily. The old woman falls back and sighs her last breath.

Who would do this for me? wonders Baba Yaga. *Who would perform these things for me?*

The fact that she is deathless does not make the absence of an answer any less painful. She closes the old woman's eyes and rises, giving a final glance to the woman's daughter-in-law. "Bury her well. I will know if you do not."

The grinding noise of the mortar barely troubles her; she is so deep in thought that she forgets to sweep away the traces of her passing.

• • •

The old woman's son returns late that evening. He has been deep in the forest for almost a month and when he left his mother was hale and hearty. Her illness was sudden, occasioned by a summer cold and compounded by her daughter-in-law's neglect. His shock at her loss is acute.

His wife, afraid of Baba Yaga's curse and in full knowledge of her own culpability, seeks a scapegoat. She is desperate to stay her husband's hand, to keep his grief away from her, to keep him from ever thinking that she had a hand in his mother's demise.

"It was Baba Yaga. The Bone Mother came and took her." She does not mention that their daughter was ill, nor that Baba Yaga saved the child's life. She lets her husband believe that the dark woman took his mother out of spite, to extend her own life. He stays hollow-eyed beside his mother's corpse, sitting the death watch through the deep hours.

In the morning he buries she who gave him life, and when he finishes shovelling earth on top of the still form, he notices the path of broken branches and crushed grass left by Baba Yaga's mortar. Without a word to his wife, he pulls the axe from the block beside the woodpile and sets out.

• • •

Vasilissa, exhausted by her labours in the kitchen and anesthetised by the honey wine her grandmother had let her try, sleeps so soundly that she does not feel Baba Yaga's long-fingered hand slip under her pillow and grasp the little wooden doll. She does not hear the old woman shuffle from the room and shut the door quietly behind her. The child sleeps on, blissfully ignorant.

Baba Yaga, having eased herself into a chair by the fire, props the doll on a small table beside her and watches to see what the thing will do. At first there is nothing, no sign of life, but there is something about the doll that reminds her of a forest creature pretending to be a rock or a log in the face of a predator. She drops crumbs of bread into the small creature's lap and places a thimble of wine beside it. Her eyes gleam over the golden hair, the large blue eyes so like her own, and the full lips that, if her eyes do not deceive her, begin to pout at the extended scrutiny.

"There, my little doll, take it. Eat a little, drink a little, and listen to my grief." She leans forward, certain of herself now. "My daughter ran away with a worthless man and I did not see her again."

"Oh, Mother!" The doll jumps up and stamps its tiny feet, almost upsetting the thimble of wine.

"Ah! I knew it. You're a cunning little bitch, Shura," Baba Yaga sits back, shaking her head. "Not even properly dead."

"Dead enough it would seem."

"How did you come to this, daughter?"

"My penance for leaving you alone is to watch over my daughter as long as she needs me. In this ridiculous shape. Imagine my surprise when I died and woke up like this. Hoping for heaven or purgatory—at least—and this is what I get." Shura sits heavily and takes a deep draught of wine. "If I didn't know better I'd say you had something to do with it."

"Who's to say I didn't?" Baba Yaga runs a finger down one of the golden curls, seeing for a moment the little girl Shura had been.

Wilful, selfish, demanding. Leaving her mother when she was ill unto death to go off with a man.

"Was *he* her father? The one you left with?"

"Of course not, Mother. Did you really think *him* the type to stick around?" Shura sighed. "Vasilissa's father would have had your approval. He was a rich merchant, kind and gentle. *Is* a rich merchant if Ludmilla's kept him safe."

Baba Yaga sits back and releases a pent-up breath.

"What's *she* like?"

"Like me, I suppose. She's looking out for her own daughters, but it's at the expense of mine and I don't like that." She looks down at her tiny fingers. "Truth be told, if I could kick her out of my bed and out of my house I would."

"But you can't."

"But I can't, Mother, no. You could, though. Or take Vasilissa into your own." The painted eyes shine as if alive. "You could do that, Mother, look after my beautiful girl."

The old woman's face collapses in on itself, as if her age has suddenly arrived with no warning, like a fat guest walking across a weak threshold. Shura watches as something liquid and silver makes its way down one of the furrows of her mother's face. This is the first time she has faced the devastation she caused. Her wooden heart, kinder than her human one was, twists painfully in her otherwise hollow chest.

"Don't cry, Mama. Please don't cry. Look after my child. Set me free." She regrets this the moment it leaves her lips. Baba Yaga's eyes snap open, turned to angry obsidian.

"Thinking of yourself to the last." She lifts the doll and holds it in her strong hand. If the doll could breathe, she would struggle for breath. "You want me to take your child so you can rest in peace. Then she can leave me when I need her, just like you did."

She holds the toy high, contemplating throwing it into the fire, stirring up the coals once more and watching the doll be consumed. Shura, sensing the direction of her mother's thoughts, is smart enough to shut up, to lie limp in the claw-like grip, and to hope as hard as she can that her mother's anger is not as strong as her love.

In the end the old woman simply shakes the doll in frustration, rather like a dog worrying a bone. Shura remains silent: she has retreated to her state of wood and varnish to ignore the horror of what her end could have been, of what her life may continue to be.

• • •

Baba Yaga does not leave the dacha that day. Vasilissa finds her in the morning, still sitting by the dead fire, motionless as a stone; although she breathes, her hands and face are very cold. She cannot move her grandmother from the chair, nor will the old woman answer her; the Bone Mother merely shifts her stare from the dead fire to the window that overlooks the yard.

Vasilissa brings cold compresses and drips sips of water between Baba Yaga's dry lips, but the old woman does not stir; her eyes have all the animation of glass. Vasilissa, fearful beyond measure, picks Shura up from the floor by the fireplace. The side of the doll lying nearest the fire is slightly burnt. Shura guzzles down the wine Vasilissa gives her first of all, finishing her meal with cake crumbs.

"There my little doll, take it. Eat a little, drink a little, and listen to my grief." Vasilissa takes a deep breath. "I fear my grandmother is dying."

Shura sags, a marionette whose strings have been cut. "She cannot die, but she can become a stone. She did for almost a year after my father left."

"What must I do, little doll? What must I do, my little mother?" To her distress, Vasilissa sees her mother shrug and shake her head. The child flares up. "We must do something! We cannot leave her like this."

"It's her heart that troubles her, not any physical ailment, Vasilissa." Shura's voice fractures. "How do you cure loneliness? How do you ease the pain of singularity? She stands alone. She stands outside."

Vasilissa gives her mother a frustrated shake and sets her on the mantle. She settles herself on Baba Yaga's lap, curling her child's form around her grandmother, wrapping her arms around the thin shoulders, burying her smooth face in the corrugated skin of Baba Yaga's neck. Her voice is soft as she makes her promises.

"Don't leave me, Grandmother. I will not leave you. You will not stand alone any longer. Do not become stone." Her voice strengthens. "I love you, Grandmother. I will not leave you."

She falls asleep, her promise still on her lips, sticky and sweet like honey. Her dreams, though, are fraught: she sees a man hunting through the woods, following her grandmother's trail, his axe sharp and his temper frayed by grief.

Vasilissa is woken by a noise in the yard. She looks out the window and sees the skulls on the gateposts, their teeth clattering a warning. Beyond them, in among the tree trunks, she can see someone moving, a man, with the late afternoon sun glittering on the edge of his blade. She grabs Shura and rushes to the kitchen, unsure how much time she may have while he stalks around the dacha, trying to learn its defences.

The little girl makes her offering to the doll and cries: "There my little doll, take it. Eat a little, drink a little, and listen to my grief. A man comes, his axe sharp and bright. I fear for us all." She takes Shura to the window where they can see him clearly, standing just outside the fence, angry and uncertain.

"The black rider is coming, I can feel the earth shaking beneath her tread. Tell her to cast her darkest night over us and I will deal with this man. Be brave!" Shura exhorts her daughter.

Vasilissa runs through the dacha and throws open the front door. The man is inside the gate. When he sees her, he moves faster: it seems his anger will be spread over anyone he can find. Vasilissa can hear the beat of hooves and she shouts.

"Black rider, black rider, come to my aid! Throw your darkest night upon us!"

Her last glimpse is of the man tossed about by three sets of disembodied hands, then all goes black, as black as the inside of the deepest cave. She hears Shura's voice rising, chanting, calling upon spells of forgetfulness, of disorientation, to send the man far away, with no memory of the path to this dacha. For a long while all is silent.

Vasilissa waits and waits. She stretches forth and finds the doll lying not far from her hand, and she gathers Shura up, holding her in her lap. After a time (she does not know how long), the darkness does not seem so heavy and she hears a scratching sound and a torch flares. Baba Yaga stands at the door of the dacha and lights Vasilissa's way inside.

Baba Yaga takes Shura from her granddaughter and rubs a drop of water on the doll's lips, holds cake crumbs out for her.

"There my little doll, take it. Eat a little, drink a little, and listen to my joy." She says quietly. "I will look after your daughter, Shura."

The doll's eyes shine, her painted mouth moving in a smile. "Thank you, mother. My Vasilissa is faithful above all things."

"And when the time comes, Shura, I will let her go," Baba Yaga promises. "As I release you now, daughter. Rest."

• • • • • • • • • • •

CHILDREN'S STORY

BOB FRANKLIN

My name is Liam and this is the story of Boots the dog and the holiday I had with Mum and Dad and Boots. I am leaving spaces for the pictures like in my favourite books.

(The first picture goes here. It is a picture of me and Mum and Dad and Boots. Everyone is smiling even Boots)

We got up early because Dad said its a long drive. We are going to a place called Aireys Inlet. I said Hairys Inlet and Mum laughed. Its by the sea. We are going to live in a house there for a week. Some of Mum and Dads friends are coming there as well. It will be fun dad said we will play games of football and cricket and frisbee and swimming. We packed the car full. Boots tried to help but was just trouble.

(Here is a picture of Dad tripping over Boots and stuff going flying)

When everything was packed in the car Dad said there was no room for Boots and he would have to stay behind. No way I said but dad was just joking. Boots sat in the back with me on his rug. We played games of I-spy on the long drive and Boots slept on his rug. It was a lovely day with the sun shining and mum and Dad were happy because of the holiday.

(Here is a picture of our car packed with stuff with Boots with his head out of the window)

We got takeaway food on the drive. I had a hamburger and chips and Boots tried to eat dads hamburger and dad smacked him and mum said don't hit him and there was quiet for a bit. But then we got to the sea and all the hills and the bendy road and dad smiled and then mum smiled. They smiled more when we got to the house because it was really great with a big lawn for cricket and everything. Boots jumped out of the car and tried to do his toilet on the lawn and dad said get off the pitch.

(Here is a picture of Dad chasing Boots with a cricket bat)

Mum said let's explore the house and we did and saw lots of rooms and my room had bunk beds and a big box with toys in. Then we went to the beach and we all went in the sea and Boots barked because no one was with him. Dad said be quiet because dogs can't be on the beach. I said there might be a shark and Boots was telling us but dad took Boots to the car.

(Here is a picture of Boots chasing away a shark. His tail is like legs like cartoons)

We played some more but I was sad with Boots in the car and dad got angry and said bloody dog we're going home. So we went home and mum and dads friends called Dave and Kath were there and they said this is our friend Tim and Boots started going all funny he went down low and his teeth were showing. Dad said stop it sorry Tim but Boots didn't stop it and dad said that's enough and tied Boots up.

(Here is a picture of Boots looking sad)

Dad said time for a beer and everyone had one except me I had fizzy orange. I played frisbee with Tim he had a long coat and shoes on which was stupid in the sun. Dave put the barbecue on and Tim tried to be friends with Boots with dad standing there but Boots growled and dad smacked him. We played cricket and Tim went for a walk so Boots was let off but he ran away with the ball and dad got angry again.

(Here is a picture of Boots with the ball and everyone chasing him)

Then we had sausages and chops and Boots wanted some even with his own dinner. Then Tim came home and Boots ran at him and Tim got scared and dad got so angry and said that's it he's tied up outside for the whole night.

(Here is a picture of Boots looking sad and the moon is in the sky)

We played word games and everyone had beer except me I had more orange drink. Tim got angry about a word with Kath and then Dave got angry. Mum said time for my bedtime. I said can I say goodnight to Boots and dad said no he's bad.

(Here is a picture of me looking at Boots outside the glass door he has the rope in his mouth)

I went to sleep and woke up and dad and Tim were angry I could hear them. Then Dave and Kath were angry with Tim then mum said time for bed. Tim went away to his room I could hear his shoes. I went to sleep and had a bad dream.

(Here is a picture of the dream it is Boots he is barking at Tim because Tim has got no eyes just blackness)

I woke up scared and Boots was barking like mad and jumping. I ran to mum and dads room and saw Tim he was going to Dave and Kaths room. Mum and dad were messy like the kangaroos on the road. I pulled their arms but they just looked. Tim started coming I could hear his shoes.

(Here is a picture of Tim coming his eyes are black his mouth is like a sharks mouth)

I got under mum and dads bed. Tim came in I could see his shoes. Please go away I said but not loud. Tim got on his knees and I peed in my pyjamas. Then there was a smash it was Boots in the glass door. Tim stopped getting on his knees fast and went outside. Please don't hurt Boots I said but Boots was hurt because of the glass.

(Here is a picture of Boots with glass in him)

Then there was banging at the front door and shouting. Tim went away I heard the door open. I ran outside Boots was on the floor he was making a sound like a train whistle. I went on my knees and stroked his head and he went quiet. Uncle Kev said hes with mum and dad now I wish I was with Boots and mum and dad. I am writing all this because Tim is somewhere and he looks like anyone but dogs know so watch out.

(Here is a picture of Mum and dad and Boots and Boots is barking and dad is listening)

··········

NIGHT SHIFT

DALE ELVY

I hate the night shift.

There's a change comes over the city when the last rays of the sun finally shrink into nothing, and the shadows grow fat. A slyness that takes hold, as the city lights wink on, bathing the streets in a weak orange glow. Everything has a dreamy feel, as though nothing is really as it seems. Sometimes you even feel a presence in the streets that seems to whisper that things normally taken for granted in daylight; consequences and rules, no longer apply. People aren't themselves at night.

I tried to give up working nights after I got stabbed the second time; twenty-six stitches, but the captain gave me a long speech about how we all need to do our part, then I was right back on the night shift again.

By the time I arrive, the crowd has grown to an impressive size. People push and jostle, their other business forgotten at the chance to glimpse a stranger's misfortune. Gangs of women in their night finery elbow peddlers and sweepers they'd normally cross the street to avoid. Hawkers and urchins crane their necks and whisper to one another, all natural animosity forgotten in the excitement. Funny how someone else's tragedy can bring people together for a time.

I make my way through the press of the crowd almost unnoticed, I don't cut much of a figure in my crumpled suit. That's just fine by me.

The plaza is ringed by tumble-down apartments. Plaster has sloughed away to reveal brick and now the weather is eating at the dry mortar dust that glues the bricks together, spreading a spider web of cracks up the walls and giving the apartments a drunken lean. Lines of washing are strung between windows up there, flapping like strings of dark flags against the night. There're a hundred nameless places like this in the city.

"Carera, get in here."

Sergeant Dalo has spotted me in the crowd, and gestures impatiently. People look briefly interested as I make my way past the ring of watchmen keeping the crowd at bay. Murmuring follows my passage. I probably resemble a suspect more than a watchman.

"What took you so long?"

"Had trouble finding it."

Dalo doesn't believe me. We've worked together for long enough that he has my measure. But he has a job to do, and so do I. He leads me into the middle of the plaza where a dirty blanket covers a corpse; my work for the night.

"She was found about an hour ago. " Dalo pulls back the blanket.

The woman beneath looks like she might almost be asleep, eyes closed and face relaxed. It's rare for death to leave so little trace. Her skin is pale, but there's no sign of violence. Her hair is spread like a halo around her head, damp now from the seeping, cracked cobblestones that line the plaza. She is, without a doubt, strikingly beautiful.

Her clothes are plain, nondescript. A simple dark dress and jacket and sensible shoes. She was either trying to blend in, or she's that rare breed of woman who doesn't play on her looks. Either way is interesting, although I judge her the former, given the deft traces of makeup now visible against bloodless cheeks.

I look up to see Krimpa, the corpse-taker, across the plaza standing patiently with his hand-cart.

"Evening Carera." He tips his hat with a happy smile. Soon enough she'll be his to tend.

I nod to him as Dalo drones on. "Not much on her, no papers, just an amulet and a small amount of change," he hands me a small paper bag that clinks as I take it. "As you can see, no obvious signs of foul play, she just dropped dead by the look of it."

"Any witnesses?"

Dalo gives me a look. I should have known better than to ask. "I'll leave a couple of men to keep the crowd back until you're finished. She's all yours." He signals and the patrol departs with a clatter.

I look at the crowd, and they look right back, expectantly. The show is just beginning.

With a sigh, I bend down and mutter the words of a spell. It takes a little while to catch, but then I feel the magic take me, and focus on the corpse of the young woman. Abruptly she sits up, jerked like a marionette on invisible strings. She turns her head toward me. There are screams from the crowd and they edge back from the nervous watchmen.

Her corpse opens its eyes and light pours out. I will myself to meet its gaze. I can see her last moments of life.

She's been running. Her legs are aching, lungs burning. She's in a hurry to see someone. Time is running out. Across busy streets, up winding stairs, then she's in the plaza. Still a long way to go. If only she could risk the trolley. Washing flaps above her, making her jump and in that instant, the wind tugs the scrap of paper from her hand, carrying it to the far corner of the plaza. She curses and goes to fetch it before the wind can steal it, and in that moment, something strikes. She doesn't see it. She doesn't hear it, but she can sense it at the last moment, a small thing that darts, lightning quick, from the shadows. A brief sting of pain in her calf and she's falling. She's confused, doesn't know what has happened or how such a small sting could unbalance her. Then the cobbles come to meet her and she knows nothing else.

The corpse slumps back, as though the strings are suddenly cut. The light is gone, and there is a faint smell of sulphur in the air. The crowd hush expectantly. This is the part where an investigator usually makes an arrest; they press forward again willing me to make a grand announcement, or name one of their number. But I've seen no face, got no clue as to who is responsible. I disappoint them, as I turn back to the corpse and examine the leg. It takes me a moment or two to find it, but there are a series of small punctures on her left calf. They hardly look more than pin pricks.

I sigh. The crowd's breaking up. A dissatisfied murmur fills the plaza. There'll be no instant justice tonight.

I examine the bag of her effects. A collection of small change, of no interest, and a small amulet. *That*, I recognise immediately. The etched outline of a griffon against an elaborate arch, and for those who knew where to look, something more. A fine incantation to enhance the bearer's authority, worked into the flat lines, masquerading as artistic shading.

I know where to look because I used to wear one.

An apprentice then. I look at her again, but can't place her face. It was years ago they threw me out, so she probably hadn't even taken her vows when I started working the night shift.

I'm a little shaken now. An apprentice killed like this, out in the open. To pull it off you'd need a good measure of skill, and nerve to match. I reach for the flask I keep in my pocket, and realise it's empty. Damn.

Krimpa has appeared beside me, looking down at her.

"Got some leads then chief?"

"Perhaps."

Everyone meets Krimpa eventually, although most will never know it. Street sweeper or Alderman, watchmen or merchant, if you die in the city, and they manage to find your remains, Krimpa will tend to you.

"Mind if I take her then? It'd be a shame to leave her in the wet for too long."

I nod, slipping the amulet into my pocket. As I step away, I remember the small piece of paper. It' a windy night, but this plaza is ringed with buildings, trapping leaves and other debris. It's a chance.

It takes me almost an hour to search the dark corners of the plaza, and I ruin my best pair of trousers before I finally find the clogged sewer grate. Amidst the sludge and leaves I find a small, folded piece of parchment. The last thing the dead apprentice was thinking of.

I open it slowly, savouring a momentary victory for my weary brain. There is a single line of script, written in a spidery hand:

Special Investigator Carera, 3rd Precinct.

My name. I drop the paper, and it disappears straight down into the dark open sewer I've just cleared. Why was she looking for me? Now things are worse. Now I'm involved in this somehow, and I don't even know what this is.

I leave the plaza. I need a drink.

The kind of bar that will still let me run a tab isn't the kind of place you want to go. Bleary, bloodshot eyes and faces rich with broken blood vessels crowd me. There're loud, drunken arguments, same as every night, and someone gets a jagged bottle-end jammed in their gut. They haul him out cursing and bleeding after they settle his bill. I don't care.

She finds me there before I'm completely insensible. Lara was a watch sergeant before an addict smashed her arm in a dozen places; that's the night shift for you. Now she runs the investigators in the precinct. Not in charge exactly, but she makes sure we do what we're supposed to, go where we're supposed to, and most importantly, that we turn mysteries into cases, and cases into convictions.

She gives me a long look. I don't like it and squirm under her gaze. There was a time when Lara used to look at me differently. Like she could change me, maybe even make me a better man. But what you see is what you get. Now she's burning off the pleasant buzz that I've been carefully building.

"What happened?"

"Nothing. Don't want to talk about it."

Her mouth firms. "Then you'd better get on with it. You get a reading on the killer?"

"Nope."

"The captain wants this one wrapped up quickly. There's pressure from downtown."

Worse and worse.

"Got a lead?"

"Sort of." I can't lie to her, which is probably why the captain sent her.

"Good." She looks across at the barman. "Modokian Fish-Hook please."

I eye the drink unhappily. This is going to be messy.

"Drink it."

Two minutes later I'm emptying my guts against an alley wall. Lara leans nearby, unperturbed by the violent, putrid stream.

"I got a look at the body. A pretty girl, killed out in the open like that. Perhaps she was seeing someone she shouldn't have been? Perhaps she threatened to let someone's wife know what was going on?"

"Perhaps." Another wave hits me and I choke and splutter as it pours out.

"Poison then. A professional job?"

I spit and wipe my mouth. "Definitely professional." I don't want to tell her my suspicions yet. It's bad enough that I'm somehow involved in this mess. The smart thing to do would be to turn it over to another investigator, but then I'd be looked into, and I don't want that.

"Feel better?"

"No." I take the mints she offers and stuff them in my mouth. My stomach is still churning but my head feels clearer. I'm not convinced it's an improvement. Lara walks me to the trolley stop and hands me a ticket.

"Just do your job Carera; figure out if it's murder, and if so, who did it, and why. What happens after that isn't your problem. Let the captain figure it out."

"Sure." Somehow I don't think the captain will thank me for dumping this on his door. The trolley arrives, grinding up the narrow street and hissing steam. I wearily clamber on. Lara meets my eye from the pavement.

"Don't make me drag you out of another bar tonight Carera. I mean it."

I'm grateful as the noise of the trolley pulling out drowns anything I might say. The other passengers don't seem eager to share their trolley with me, there's a general move away as I slouch into a seat; can't say as I blame them. I pull my hat down over my eyes and run over things again in my mind.

I must've dozed off, because I don't remember much of the trip across town. When I open my eyes the jagged outline of the Opal Fortress is looming over the city. A cluster of its squat towers and halls, some ancient, others merely old, crowding the skyline with their drab majesty. The other trolley passengers are mesmerised, some stare openly, others sneak glances out of the corner of their eyes. But none can ignore the powerful presence. Like a python coiled, dangerous and fascinating.

I've managed to avoid the Opal Fortress for the last decade, blocked it out of my mind. A hole in my past I'd rather ignore. But I suppose it was inevitable I'd be back one day.

The gates are just as I remember, large and intimidating, hinting at the arcane mysteries within. The security is new though. Two large men look me over suspiciously. They won't entertain the notion that I'm an investigator, until I fish out my badge, and even then they're skeptical; like someone might be playing a prank. They frisk me, and seem disappointed when they don't find the enchanted short-sword watchmen are issued by the city. I pawned it months ago; instead they find the small replacement hatchet I keep inside my jacket, and confiscate that instead.

Suitably screened I'm escorted through the great hall. Long dead Deacon's look down on me with frozen disdain from grand life-sized portraits. Each represents a different era of power and growth for the Opal Fortress. There was a time I knew all their names, but for the life of me I can't remember even one now.

It's much quieter than I remember, although I was a creature of the daylight back then, and rarely had cause to wander the Fortress at night. Rather than treat me to the grand Generation Stair, I'm hustled in the back way, into the bowels of the Fortress, where opulent elegance melts into dirty function, and a stair has no more pretence than a grimy, well worn series of treads. Up we climb, until we reach the heights of the old keep, where the corridors are small and narrow. Cleaners are working in the hallways. They look at me suspiciously as we pass, as though I might be conspiring to contribute to their workload.

The Deacon's office is pretty much as I remember it, which is a surprise, because I was only ever admitted here once, for an hour, on the day they threw me out. Lined with yellowed scrolls and tattered tomes, it's exactly the sort of place you imagine a master of magic should reside. The desk is cluttered with papers and other curiosities pickled in jars and preserved for later study. The Deacon is scribbling away, but looks up as we enter. A flash of surprise crosses his face when he sees me, then is gone again. So he does remember me. I file that away for later thought.

"Yes?"

"Good evening Deacon. I'm Investigator Carera from the city watch. I'd like to ask you a few questions."

I can see he's considering denying the request. But he knows that the watch has authority here, despite all the arcane pretensions.

"Certainly." He motions to a high-backed chair

I sit and my large escort takes up a position behind me. Clearly they don't trust me at all.

"A young woman died tonight Deacon, she was an apprentice." I dump the amulet onto his desk. His eyes flicker. He knows something.

"Oh dear." His hands tap out an irregular beat on the desk. He's nervous.

"Well, if you'd care to liaise with the registrar, we can provide you with her next of kin of course."

He hasn't even asked who she is. The old bastard knows. In spite of myself, I'm surprised. I knew there were dark things happening in the Fortress, but I wouldn't have suspected the Deacon himself of involvement. How times have changed. Time to push a little.

"I believe she was murdered Deacon, most likely by magical means."

"Murdered? " The Deacon licks his lips. His fingers are still fidgeting on the desk. "Preposterous. You shouldn't believe the talk in the street investigator. It is almost impossible to kill by magic."

I know it. Of course I know it. The first thing they teach new apprentices is how difficult it is to affect other people directly with magic. Even the notorious Eagin twist, where the caster attempts to rupture a blood vessel in the target's brain requires formidable talent and focus, and even then only works on one person in four. But I'm not your average investigator. I have an inkling of the Fortress' secrets.

"There are other kinds of magic. Summonings for instance." I see it again in my mind's eye, the years melting away. The worn circle in the vaulted chamber beneath the Fortress. That terrible thing, a mass of writhing grey flesh that had emerged, when I had finished the incantation. Consuming and devouring as we fled.

"Summonings are strictly forbidden by the Fortress. They have been so for more than a decade, as you would know Inspector Carera."

Tap, tap, tap. Fingers drumming on the desk.

"So you say Deacon." Ten years ago. The last time I was in this office. The Deacon's face is tight with anger as I stammer my explanation. It sounds weak; summoning is the final frontier of the magical arts. A chance to further our knowledge exponentially. I never meant for anyone to die.

I don't like the memory. I stand abruptly, aware of the guard tensing behind me.

"Arrange for the apprentice's details to be sent to the Precinct House directly, Deacon. I'm sure I'll have other questions in due course." There's something going on here, but I'm not going to find anything using the direct approach, the Fortress is too good at covering up its dirty laundry. I should know.

"Her name was Ella."

I look over my shoulder. The Deacon is holding the amulet, watching it spin. He looks old and sad. I have no pity for him, the bastard is neck deep in whatever is going on. I'd haul him downtown right now, but no-one's going to believe me over the city's foremost practitioner of magic. I need more.

By the time I get back outside, night has given way to the weak grey of first light. My city is going to bed, as their city is waking up. My shift is over, so I catch the trolley back to my flat. I ignore the wrappers and half eaten food that litter the floor, and fall into bed.

At some point during the day I'm woken by furtive scurrying sounds; something small moving around in the other room. Rats. Not surprising given the state of the place. I feel drained, so don't even bother stirring, instead, I trigger one of the small fire wards that I had carefully inscribed for practice during my studious days as an apprentice. I'm rewarded by a frantic scrabbling and the faint smell of scorched meat. Satisfied that now there's a rat that feels even worse than I do, I close my eyes again.

It's a real challenge finding a suit that is anything even resembling clean. There's a dark scorch mark near the door, and a smear of goo running to the broken window the overlooks the street. A big rat then. I really should clean up a bit, and fix the windows, but I'm more preoccupied with searching the empty bottles for dregs. First thing in the evening the world feels fuzzy and hostile.

On the trolley to the Precinct house I run over things in my mind. The Deacon, the dead apprentice and secrets of the Fortress.

Tap, tap, tap.

My name on a note. Pressure from downtown.

Tap, tap, tap.

The city seems unusually quiet. An old woman in the seat opposite is staring at me intently. I ignore her and get off at my regular spot, a block from the precinct house, near the large tavern normally frequented by the watch. I'm trying to think of someone on the day shift who might be convinced to buy me a drink, when strong hands grab me and propel me into an alley.

A big man punches me square in the stomach, and I double over. Probably would've broken my ribs if not for the vest I wear under my shirt.

"Investigator Carera, it's time to talk."

I don't want to talk. While I'm sucking in breath I slip my hatchet from its holster. Any fool who thinks I'm going to follow a script is going to regret it.

He grabs me by the neck, and opens his mouth to continue the speech. My hand lashes out with the hatchet. The razor sharp blade bites into his thigh. A big man, he takes a moment to go down. Long enough to make me wonder if I hit my target. But the blood hosing from the severed femoral artery in his leg can't be argued with. In less than a minute the alley is soaked in his blood and he crumples, pale and surprised, still trying to form words. I watch dispassionately, then clean my hatchet on his shirt as the light goes out of his eyes.

He looks a bit like the guard from the Fortress.

Tap, tap, tap.

I check his pockets but don't find anything interesting, although I pocket the few dollars in his wallet.

After the dead man has bought me a drink, I file a report at the precinct house. No questions are asked. The night shift has an open mandate to bring order to the night, and an attack on one is an attack on all.

Lara is waiting at my desk.

"You're late."

"Had some trouble. Case took an unexpected turn."

"Yeah?" She eyes my blood stained suit.

"I think this might be something big, perhaps even involving the Deacon."

"Damn Carera. That's just what we need. Are you sure you're not dragging in some unfinished business from your past?"

I sketch it out for her. Not my suspicions, just the evidence that seems to point to something going on at the Opal Fortress. She looks less happy with every word.

"You really want to see where this goes Carera? It might not be pretty."

"You'd prefer I blame the murder on the heavy from the Fortress who tried to jump me? He's not in a position to deny it. Then we could just punch out and get a drink . . ."

She rubs the stump of her arm ruefully. "And watch you sink deeper into a bottle? No thanks, just focus on doing one of the few things in this world that you're actually good at. C'mon I want to show you something. There've been developments."

Lara takes me up town to the farm. At least that's what Krimpa calls it. The final pasture for the departed. A sleek grey lowrise bordered by reflecting pools that shimmer in the night. We walk across the wide stone ramp and down into the bowels of the farm. Our footsteps are unnaturally loud, as we pass row after row of sleek columns. Krimpa is waiting, his grey gown stained dark with gore.

"Investigator Carera, I see you've already been busy tonight. Here to see your latest addition to the farm?"

"Just show us last night's additions Krimpa." Lara doesn't care for Krimpa. There's something unsettling about anyone who takes that level of pleasure in their work.

"Of course Sergeant, this way."

There are less bodies than I was expecting. No more than a dozen, each carefully laid out in a small alcove for the rites of passing. I spot Ella, the apprentice at the far end, pale and pristine.

"Quiet night then Krimpa?"

"Indeed. And so far, tonight has been slow as well, with the exception of your own work, of course Investigator. A very neat job, that."

I grunt.

"Thanks Krimpa, I can take it from here." Lara waits until he is gone, shuffling off into the darkness to tend his farm. She moves to a corpse, a middle aged man, and unfolds a piece of paper from her pocket. "According to the reports filed last night this is, or was, Gulino Tranda."

I tilt my head to regard the body, and find it disappointingly unremarkable. "The Iron Falcon?"

"None other. The Lord-Mayor's Chief of Staff was found at dawn. No obvious cause of death listed, but Krimpa's report notes there are some small punctures on his back."

The Falcon ran the city. Everyone who had any reason to work with downtown knew that. The Lord-Mayor cut ribbons and kissed babies, behind the scenes the Falcon cut million dollar building and servicing contracts and kissed whoever he damn well pleased. He had spies in every department, and always made sure the Lord-Mayor came up smelling of roses. No matter what.

"Laticia Huron, better known as the Viper." The next corpse is a woman whose blond hair was streaked with grey. Her body is a spiderweb of old scars. "Same thing, only the puncture marks were in her foot." The Viper was a powerful underworld figure. She took a cut of every bar and brothel in the city, and was ruthless with anyone who tried to stand against her.

"And Emil Asuln, the union boss." A bloated corpse, bluish and mottled. "They fished him out of the river, but I don't think he drowned. Krimpa has yet to confirm it, but I'd suspect he died the same way as the others."

Three of the most powerful people in the city, killed in a single night. Each of them had carved out a significant personal empire through force of will. Every one was formidable and well protected. Killing one alone would create a significant power vacuum, but killing all three at once? That spoke of a grand strategy. Who could possibly have the resources to capitalise on the ensuing chaos?

"Readings?"

"Asuln was too far gone, but neither of the other two saw their killers. They died quickly. It's likely the perpetrators went out of their way to avoid detection in a post-mortem reading."

There's one person missing. If you were to name the most powerful, influential, people in the city these three would top the list, but another name would make that list as well. The Deacon of the Opal Fortress. The sort of person who'd know how the readings work, and could contrive to thwart them. But what was his game? What possible advantage could he secure through this kind of assassination? He was already undisputed master of his field, with power and resources to match.

Tap, tap, tap.

As I focus on the Deacon, I remember his fingers tapping away on his desk. I'd thought it a tell. A manifestation of his nervousness, but the sound means something more . . .

A memory from years ago; one class among many in my second year as an apprentice. The art of communication through non-vocal methods. Castings can work through purely auditory medium, but you need to know what the sounds mean. A language of clicks, bangs and taps.

Tap, tap, tap. Help us.

Suddenly I know. I know why the apprentice had my name. I know why the guard remained in the room during my interview with the Deacon. I know why the Opal Fortress seemed so quiet. I know why these three are lying here and the Deacon isn't.

"We've got to go. I need to see the Captain right now!" I'm practically flying out of the farm. Not smart. I make it as far as the ramp out to the street before I'm panting and wheezing. Lara catches me easily. She helps me on and we struggle together to a trolley. A badge is waved and the trolley delivers us directly to the precinct house as fast as it will go, much to the annoyance of the other passengers.

Despite the sweat soaking my shirt, I storm up the cracked worn steps, past the duty sergeant and on into the Captain's office. There's no time to waste.

He's sitting at his desk reading from a large file. He looks up calmly as I enter and try to gasp an explanation.

"Sit down Carera. Get your breath."

I try to insist that I don't need to sit, but then I feel my legs trembling and slump down, panting. Outside I can see Lara through the glass, waiting near the investigators' section. She looks only mildly out of breath.

I switch my attention to the Captain's office as I try and sort out the words I want. It's filled with miscellany from thirty years of service on the watch. Badges and shields gleam from plaques. Pictures of the Captain with important people, smiling and shaking hands. I recognise one with the Iron Falcon. Weapons of all sorts, given ceremonially, or confiscated from criminals. Watchmen love to collect things. The pride of the Captain's collection is a scaled down model of the city sprawling on a low table near his desk. Tiny towers and spires loom over miniature streets and plazas. Every detail has been faithfully depicted, from the metallic gleam of the trolley tracks to the blue twist of the river. A world in miniature, with the precincts jurisdiction carefully marked.

"Captain, something's gone wrong at the Opal Fortress. I think they've summoned something. It's taken over there, and is trying to take the rest of the city."

"Well Carera, I suppose you'd know about that sort of thing." The Captain looks up from the page, and I recognise my name written in large text on the page. He's reading my file.

"It says here that you were expelled from the Fortress for trying to make contact with an unauthorised summoning as part of your thesis." He turns the page. "And you didn't much like what you found. Six dead and three who needed to be institutionalised. It took them three hours to finally subdue what you summoned. The title of your thesis was to be 'contacting the void, the future of magic'." He says it slowly, as though tasting the words.

I'm numb. I suppose I knew the full record would be in my file, although I had always told myself that the Fortress would have left no trace of the scandal.

The Captain leans back in his chair. "If it hadn't been for that first, rather clumsy effort, I doubt the Fortress would ever have decided to explore the idea of summoning further. Trying to contact something more refined and powerful. Not that you were to know, they turned you out after all. Left you to a life of drinking and violence on the night shift. Ironic then, that they should turn to you when everything gets out of hand, and those that they summoned, decided they'd rather stay."

I have a sick feeling in my stomach.

The Captain rises and moves absently to the miniature city, peering into the tiny streets. "Of course, the Fortress had to fall first. The practice of magic makes you so much more difficult to control, and almost impossible to possess. But the Deacon thought he'd outfoxed us by sending his daughter Ella to warn you—the black sheep that they tossed aside years ago. As an investigator in the watch you'd have been able to mount a response, perhaps even take back the Fortress if you'd acted swiftly. But we were watching. The message was never delivered."

I get to my feet. This isn't happening.

"We hadn't expected you to draw the case, but fortunately you were too busy drinking yourself to an early grave to put it together in time. Even after the visit to the Fortress, you didn't move against us."

I move slowly back to the wall, behind my back my fingers fumble with a polished sword mounted on a plaque.

"What do you want?"

"We want what you want Carera. I've read report after report in your file detailing the violence and depravity of the city after dark. We can't understand why you'd build such a fine place, and spend all your time trying to escape it. Trying to seek temporary oblivion in drink and drugs. But we're happy to enjoy it on your behalf. Once there are more of us, we'll become everything you wanted to, but were too weak and selfish to embrace. We've already moved against the leaders of the city, those too strong willed to succumb to a new order. Now we're moving into positions of authority, starting with the night shift."

I lunge forward, driving the sword into the captain's chest and sending him tumbling back into the wall. Something dark and terrible writhes in the skin beneath his neck. Something that's been riding inside him, controlling him like a puppet. The Captain looks at me blearily and gets back up to his feet, movements uncertain, as blood turns his shirt a dark crimson.

Outside I see Lara struggling with two watchmen. They're holding something that looks like an eel which is squirming eagerly toward her face. She meets my eye.

"Carera help!"

The Captain has drawn his own sword now and advances on me. I'm no hero. I charge the window of the Captain's office and smash right through, landing hard on the street below in a shower of glass. Pain lances through my foot, and I'm bleeding in a dozen places.

The Captain appears in the window, looking down at me still impaled on the polished blade. "You can run, Carera, but this city is ours now. We are your future. The future you predicted."

I get to my feet and limp into the night.

· · · · · · · · · · ·

MANIFEST DESTINY

JANEEN WEBB

The mob had been foraging when he first caught sight of them, but they had scattered in all directions before the explorer could ride them down. He crested a rocky outcrop that gave him an unexpected view of the tangled forest, unbroken as far as the eye could see. But there was no time to contemplate the landscape, to get his bearings. He quickly crossed himself as he gave chase, trying in vain to catch one of the younger ones.

Low branches tore at him. He forced his tired horse to a last spurt of speed over steep ground dangerously full of wombat holes and slippery with leaf litter. The gap was narrowing now. Both man and horse were sweating heavily in the relentless January heat. A broad damp patch spread down the back of the explorer's shirt, almost joining with the sweat-soaked rings under his arms. He felt the perspiration trickling down, his wet collar chafing against his sunburnt neck. His trousers soaked up sweat from the horse's lathered flanks.

We both stink, he thought wryly. *This had better be worth it.* He was almost there, the rope now coiled ready in his hand.

The mob was still too quick for him, zigzagging away into the densely wooded ravine, using the treacherously uneven terrain to advantage. He managed, at the last, to separate one of the older ones from the tail-end stragglers. This one was struggling to keep up with the others, but still running for its life.

"Gotcha!"

The rope snaked out, tightened.

The quarry staggered, fell to its knees.

The explorer wheeled in close, leaned down to slide the noose up the body until it was a halter about the neck.

"Up you come," he grunted, breathing hard. He pulled sharply. "Let's go."

It jerked to its feet, no longer resisting as the man tied the rope to his saddle bow. He forced the creature to move along beside, dragging it when it faltered.

It was not a long ride back to camp. The man took it slowly, resting the horse, following the trail of broken vegetation that marked his passage through the undergrowth.

In a small, trampled clearing in the midst of the dense shade of native forest the other men were going quietly about the necessary chores—mending harness, splicing rope, repairing their gear. One, a tall, fair-haired man with pale blue eyes, was bent carefully over a plant press. The makeshift camp seemed irritatingly peaceful when the explorer rode in. Shafts of slanting sunlight lit up the massive tree trunks that surrounded the glade like the pillars of some primitive cathedral. There was distant birdsong, and the ceaseless sounds of insects grated on his senses. The whole thing annoyed the man. He swung out of the saddle, tugging the rope free. The captive sank to the ground, spent. He haltered it by its neck to the nearest tree, grimacing in distaste.

"I got one," he said.

"So I see, Richard," the naturalist replied, straightening up. "And what do you intend to do with it?"

The explorer walked across to join the other men, picked up his canteen, drank deeply. "You know what, Karl," he replied testily. He took another long swig, wiped his hand on his sleeve. "You know we're short of food, after that landslip. We lost one of our packhorses, supplies and all, all gone to the bottom of that cliff."

"That still leaves us with what the other horse is carrying. The men have repaired most of the gear, and we have our guns, and the ammunition."

"But we can't get a clear shot in this god-forsaken forest. We haven't brought down anything edible in days."

"You winged a parrot, boss," one of the others said, smiling broadly. "Karl says it was a crimson parrot—very pretty."

Richard glared at him. "As I said, Thomas: nothing edible. And so far Karl hasn't managed to hit a single thing on this whole trip. I thought Norwegians were supposed to be good hunters."

Karl shrugged. "Not all of us, alas," he said.

"Well, Thomas?" the explorer continued. "You didn't do any better than me, did you?"

"I'll take another crack at it, come dusk, boss. I've set up a hide, down there." He gestured vaguely towards a spot where the earth seemed to fold itself into a narrow slot that angled down the hill. "I found tracks."

The explorer turned away, exasperated. "I'll try my own methods," he said.

"Seriously," Karl went on, ignoring the warning signs, "do you really think you can make this one show you how to find native food?"

"It worked before."

"The last one got away, gnawed through the rope. It was quite a thick hair-rope, as I recall."

"Alright, I admit that one was a failure." Richard's voice was harder, more aggressive now. "But the buck before that gave us some useful information."

"You tortured him."

"I didn't do anything we don't do to our own convicts."

"He died, Richard."

"So? You said yourself, they are scarcely human."

The naturalist shook his head. "You English," he said. "You are a cruel people."

"No more than most, Karl," Richard replied. "We do what's necessary." He stared hard at the naturalist, grey eyes at blue, daring the scientist to contradict him. "And why have you suddenly become such a great defender of savages?"

"Because I am here," Karl said mildly. "And I do not like what I see."

"Let me remind you that I am leading this expedition. I provide for all of us the best way I can. I notice you consume your share."

Karl shrugged. "You were happy enough to take my money to finance this trip."

"And you'll be taking your share of the gold when we find it."

"*If* we find it. But you always knew that my reasons for travelling with you are more scientific than mercenary."

"Well, that's as may be," the explorer went on. "I did offer you the buck's skull for your collection."

"I've told you, Richard. I no longer collect such things."

"But you did."

"Once, yes, before I realised the landholders were shooting specimens to bring to me. On this trip my specimens are strictly botanical, and entomological."

"There's no shortage of bugs, at least," said Thomas, slapping futilely at the ubiquitous bush flies.

But Richard wouldn't let the argument go. "So what exactly *did* you do, Karl? With the shot specimens, that is?" The question had a nasty edge to it.

Karl noticed that the other five men were finding reasons to be elsewhere. One got up, muttering something about taking the horse for a drink. Another, he noted with satisfaction, was sneaking water to the exhausted captive, behind the explorer's back.

"I conducted some scientific experiments, Richard," the naturalist said. "I contributed measurements to some European colleagues who were producing comparative tables of human development."

"And they found?"

"A number of indicators that Australian natives have a low plane of intellectual advancement: small development of the cranium, low receding forehead that restricts the frontal lobes, and so on."

"So they *are* no better than animals."

Karl was exasperated. "I have studied them further. They have their own languages, customs. They don't understand us, nor we them, but they are a species of human for all that."

"They can understand when they want to," Richard replied stubbornly. "No doubt about that. Uncooperative savages, that's what they are."

"That doesn't mean you can just kill them."

"Doesn't it?" he said. "Who's going to stop me?"

"It's not right, Richard. It's sad that they will inevitably die out now that a more evolved species has arrived," Karl said patiently. "It's a natural process. We should observe their ways before the end."

"In that case, they're dying anyway. I'm just helping things along a bit, and helping myself into the bargain." The explorer's thin-lipped smile was mean. "You should stick to your observations, Karl, while you can."

Karl turned to Thomas. "What do you think?" he asked.

Thomas spat. "I'm just here for the gold," he said. "I'll leave the philosophy to you."

"Very wise," said the explorer, unsheathing his hunting knife. "And leave the interrogation to me.' He turned back towards the captive, knife in hand. "You don't have to watch," he said. "I can always make myself understood."

As the man took his first step towards her, the old woman started keening, a rising, high-pitched wail that cut through the summer air, a sound to set the teeth on edge. The birdsong stilled, the forest itself seemed to be leaning into the glade, listening.

Karl tried again. "Leave off, Richard. At least think of her sex. Decent people don't torture women."

"She's not a proper woman. A decent woman would at least cover her nakedness."

"It's not their way, Richard, and you know it."

"Listen to me, science man. She's a witch. Look at her. Open your eyes and look. Anyone can see she's a witch." Richard poked his knife at his captive. The old woman howled louder. She scrabbled backwards, pressing her bent back against the tree. The scent of bruised eucalyptus rose around her on the hot air.

"She's black, she's filthy, she smells bad. She's evil." The leader of the expedition was ticking off points on his fingers now. "Look again, man: bloodshot eyes, matted hair, toothless mouth, gibbering in tongues—she's a witch. And she's cursing us."

"Probably," Karl said. He sighed wearily. "She's a frightened old woman, Richard. You only caught her because she was too old to get away. The others were too quick for you, that's all. There's nothing sinister about her."

"Then what's all this then?" Richard pointed at the woven belt and dilly bag that hung awry about his captive's skinny hips. "I'll warrant those dried things are poisonous—charms and talismans. She'll put a hex on us."

"Superstitious nonsense! I had thought you a more enlightened man than that. Spells and ghost stories are entertainments for romantic women. Sensible men of the world no longer believe them."

"Where I come from," Richard said, "we don't have time for luxuries and your middle class entertainments." He fingered his crucifix on its chain in his pocket as he spoke. "Where I come from, we know what we know. And I know a witch when I see one."

Karl raised a hand, palm out, in defeat. "Then I'l leave you to your beliefs. But I will still ask you to do the honourable thing. Let her go."

"No." Richard's freckled face flamed as red as his hair. "We can't let her go," he shouted. "Don't you understand? If we let her go she'll bring back the others in the dead of night. They'll murder us in our sleep."

"They've more sense than that. They know we're armed. In my experience, they'll get as far away from us as they can," Karl said.

Richard did not reply, just stood there, radiating stubborn defiance.

Karl tried another tack. "You could at least wait until after Thomas takes a shot at the local game from his hide. If he bags any meat, you won't have to resort to torture."

"I suppose so," Richard replied, nodding to Thomas. "Do your best, Tom. We can find out what the witch knows in the morning if you have no luck with your gun." He turned back to Karl. "Will that satisfy you? The old hag gets a reprieve until tomorrow. But I'll do what I must if I have to." He shrugged. "I take no pleasure in the pain of others."

"No?"

"No!" The explorer turned on his heel. "I have better things to do than argue with you," he said as he stormed out of the clearing.

• • •

Exhausted, the explorer slept fitfully as the stifling afternoon dragged finally into dusk. The men who had remained in the camp dozed too.

Even the old woman rested against her tree, eyes closed. It was too hot to do otherwise.

They woke suddenly to the sharp crack of rifle fire. There were shouts from the valley, and then the sound of snapping undergrowth as Thomas and two of his friends dragged the kill back to the campsite.

"Not a bad effort, even if I say so myself." Thomas grinned broadly, posing theatrically with one foot on the large kangaroo he had shot.

"We'll dine well tonight."

"It's an eastern grey buck," said the naturalist, coming to look more closely. "It's a very fine specimen."

"It's dinner," Tom said testily. "What's the point of knowing what things are properly called if you can't make use of them? Plain kangaroo is good eating." He turned to the others. "John, Harry, come and help me butcher it. We'll sear steaks now, and cook the rest. No sense in wasting any of it."

"Right," said Richard, reasserting his authority. "Well done, Tom. The rest of you, build up the fire. Karl, you make a rack for cooking the strips."

Karl spread his hands, miming helplessness. "I'm not sure . . ." he began.

The explorer lost patience. "Never mind," he said. "Harry will do it for you. He usually does. Harry?"

"Right away, boss."

Richard turned back to the naturalist. "You wouldn't survive a day out here on your own, would you?"

Karl shrugged. "Probably not," he agreed. "I know I don't have any bushman skills. That's why I paid such a lot of money to come with you."

"Right," said Richard. "We know where we stand." He gestured at Karl's growing pile of plant specimens. "Tom's in the right of it, you know. It would make more sense to the rest of us if you could tell us which plants we could eat, instead of just collecting and naming them."

"All in due course," Karl replied equably. "It takes a lot of basic research to construct a valid taxonomy. I'm identifying small pieces of the bigger puzzle."

"Even so," Richard replied, "isn't there a way you could make your work more immediately useful?"

"I do have one helpful suggestion to make right now," Karl said.

"And what would that be?"

"I do think we should hobble the horses and make sure our gear is tied down tonight."

"Why?" said Richard. "It's totally still here. Not a breath of air anywhere."

"That's what I mean," said Karl. "It's thunderstorm weather. I've seen it before."

"Now who's jumping at shadows?" Richard said. "If there's a storm here, it will be because the witch has summoned it. And you've already told me that can't happen." He shrugged. "I don't see any need to make extra work for ourselves. We'll be leaving at first light."

"You're the leader." Karl turned away. He was quietly packing his scientific equipment into its cases and covering it in a sheltered spot beside his own carefully tethered horse when he chanced to glance across the glade at the captive.

She was alert now, and sniffing the air suspiciously.

• • •

Before long a greasy blue-grey smoke haze hung low in the still air, filling the glade with the smell of cooking meat. The men wolfed down singed steaks while the rest of the kangaroo sizzled on its rack over the fire. The light was fading fast, and the fat-splashed firelight cast flickering red shadows that glowed like stained glass between the pillars of the tall trees.

Karl made a point of sharing his meal with the captive. "There you are, grandmother," he said, holding a strip of charred meat to her mouth.

The woman nodded warily, then greedily gobbled her portion.

Karl resumed his seat by the fire. "She's as hungry as we are," he said.

"Waste of good food," Richard muttered.

"She might help us in return," Karl replied. "She certainly won't show us native supplies if she realises she won't get anything herself."

"Maybe," the explorer said. "Maybe not: who knows what a witch thinks?"

"Do you have witches in Norway, Karl?" Harry asked.

"I thought it was trolls," said Thomas. "Where did you say you came from?"

"I grew up in Bergen," Karl replied, "and of course we have such stories to frighten the children. But as I told Richard, I outgrew such fancies."

"Then I'll tell you a true story that should scare you," Thomas replied. "I was up country last year, and the squatters were all talking about it." He settled himself more comfortably. "You know that human flesh is a great delicacy for the blacks." The other men nodded sagely. "They call it *talgoro*. They eat the torso and the limbs, but never the head or the entrails. The most prized morsel is the fat about the kidneys—they think that by eating it they acquire the strength of the victim. It's because they believe that the kidneys are the centre of life."

"How interesting," said Karl. "For the ancient Greeks, it was the liver."

Thomas ignored the interruption. "What happened," he said, "was that a white policeman was attacked by the blacks. They beat him with clubs until he was knocked senseless, and they thought he was dead. Then they slit his skin and took out his kidneys, and ran away." He paused for effect. "But the poor fellow wasn't dead," he went on, his voice low. "His men found him, and he woke up long enough to tell them what had happened. He died properly a few hours later."

"What happened next?" Harry asked.

"Nothing," Thomas replied darkly. "They never caught the murdering blacks."

"I heard that they like the taste of Chinese best," John said. "They say that up on the Palmer gold fields they've been killed and eaten in big numbers."

Karl was skeptical. "Has anyone actually seen the natives committing these acts of cannibalism?" he asked.

"I for one never want to," Thomas replied. "Do you think your witch is a cannibal, boss?"

"She could be," the explorer replied, considering. "I wouldn't be surprised." He shrugged. "But there's nothing to worry about now. She's securely tied. She won't be eating anyone tonight."

The men laughed uneasily.

"Whites can be cannibals too," Karl said. "We've all heard about those Port Arthur escapees eating their friends."

"That's different," Richard put in. "That was a matter of survival. We'd all do it if we had to."

Karl shuddered. "I know I couldn't," he said.

"No," Richard agreed. "You'd starve defending your principles." He grinned suddenly. "We'd probably eat you."

Thomas grinned back. "Too stringy, boss," he said. "We'd choose someone with more meat on the bones."

"You're right," said Harry. "John here is much heavier."

"It's all muscle," John replied, laughing along with the others. "I'd be too tough."

"All right, all right," said the explorer. "That's enough. You're shocking our scientist." He yawned. "I'm too tired to think about anything right now. Tomorrow's another day. We'll worry about what to do with the cannibal witch then." He began settling himself by the fire. "Goodnight, lads. Goodnight, Karl. Get some rest."

"Goodnight." Karl hesitated, wanting to say more. But he resisted the impulse and moved quietly to where his gear was stowed. He laid his blanket carefully in the little hollow, making a shallow nest for himself. He stretched out, watching as the others found comfortable places. Before long, the camp was all quiet, all still. Clouds were building, and Karl lay a long time wakeful in the starless darkness before he too finally drifted into sleep.

• • •

The storm, when it came, came without warning. Lightning arced across the sullen sky and the smell of scorched ozone barely preceded the huge crack of thunder that startled the men awake. Then the sky was alive with lightning flashes and the thunder rumbled like an earthquake.

The explorer and his men woke to chaos. The horses were screaming, bucking to break their light tethers. Two had already bolted. The captive was screeching too, struggling to free herself from the strangling halter that held her in harm's way. The men ran in all directions, desperate to secure the remaining mounts, snatching up their rifles where they could, scrambling to grab their scattered gear.

"One, two . . ." Under his breath Karl began counting seconds between the flashes of forked lightning and the thunder peals. He didn't get to three. The storm front was upon them. And the wind was rising fast. The noise began as a low moaning in the tree tops.

The moaning became a howling, and the howling a shriek. Tall trees whipped and bent, straining in the windstorm. Branches came crashing down. A wattle split, tore, whirled away into the darkness. The men were pelted with stinging leaves and bark and heavier gum nuts that bruised where they struck. Karl grabbed for his horse, but was driven back by the gale. He crouched in the lee of a boulder, sheltering as best he could.

Then the rain came. A few fat drops at first, then a wind-driven downpour that tore apart the forest canopy. The rain became hail, chunks of ice that bombarded the landscape, round ice balls that collected in drifts around trees and filled the cracks and crevices of the campsite. Karl watched, hunched behind his rock against the punishing onslaught. The pulsing lightning lit a madly shifting scene of flying debris and bouncing white hailstones, with a lurid red fire-glow at its heart. He could no longer tell if the screams that echoed in his ears were human, animal or elemental.

I don't belong here, he thought.

And suddenly he was aware that there were flitting black shadows amongst the shifting shapes of the trees, shadows that moved with purpose despite the wild storm. The tribe had come.

The naturalist stayed as still as he could, peering at the confusion of the campsite. But then the fire was smothered, the glow went out, and he had only flashes of vision when the lightning flared. He glimpsed spears, and the tall warriors who carried them. Weaponless and terrified, he shut his eyes and turned his face away.

The storm raged on, but no blow fell upon him. He lost track of the hours, wretchedly holding on for his life against the elements, until finally the rain eased a little. The thick darkness began to shade to predawn grey, and just as Karl risked movement to ease the stiffness from his limbs, the manic laughter of kookaburras pealed across the soggy sky. The dawn chorus had begun. The carolling of native magpies joining their raucous cousins to greet the day served only to remind the naturalist that he was a stranger in a frighteningly strange land.

The light grew, and Karl looked about him, badly shaken. He called, and called again, but no-one answered. He was alone. To calm his rising panic, he forced himself to take stock of his position. He was soaked to the skin, bruised and tired, but whole. His equipment was intact—though he noticed wryly that his blanket had been anchored in its hollow only by the weight of melting hail stones it contained.

The rest of the camp had not fared so well. The explorer's gear was strewn about, badly damaged, the tools scattered and ruined.

Everything edible was gone, even the kangaroo meat they had left over the cooking fire. The tribe had been thorough. As Karl had expected, the captive was gone. Her rescuers had left a neatly cut halter rope dropped at the base of her tree. The naturalist stooped to retrieve a length of leather rein, realising as he did so that this too had been deftly severed. His tethered horse was missing. All of the horses had been driven off, under cover of the thunderstorm. He had to assume that they were gone for good.

The enormity of his situation was becoming horribly clear. He would, of course, wait for his companions. He hoped they lived yet, and would somehow make their way back to the campsite. He knew there was no sense in his getting himself lost searching the dense forest for them: better he should re-build the fire so that the smoke might guide them. He would not, could not think of them lying dead with their throats cut, or worse. Last night's lurid tales of native cannibalism rose unbidden in his mind. This must not be. He had refused to believe such things at the time, he would not countenance them now. No more than he would countenance the old beliefs in witchcraft—these were tales from his European childhood, not fit for a grown man of science, a logical man. Grimly, he pushed the clamouring thoughts aside and began to sift through the wreckage of the camp, setting aside anything that might be useful, salvaging anything that might be mended.

The sun was rising now, but the dark fears only grew stronger with the daylight. Hope faded to despair. The explorer would not be coming back. There would be no help, no search party, no reprieve. Without food or tools or the bush skills of his companions, the naturalist was all too aware that the chances of his retracing their path on foot, of making it back alive to the tiny Port Albert settlement were vanishingly small.

Overwhelmed, he sat by the dead ashes of the cooking fire, staring at the useless bits of cut leather that lay about him. Sunlight touched his face, and somewhere above him a native thrush trilled its liquid song into the cool morning air. The forest stirred around him, indifferent to his plight.

The scientific man put his head in his hands, and wept.

• • • • • • • • • • •

HIVE

STEPHEN M IRWIN

The sky was blue as a vein the day I killed my father. It wouldn't stay that way; that strange, ice-fire blue eventually gave way to eerie grey, then to the red of sick blood. Everything tilted that day; the world shifted and lurched on its invisible spine, revealing things in new dimensions, ugly as those cubist paintings you see in art books. Ugly, but beautiful. Secret. I've looked for that secret beauty every day since. I found glimpses of it in the craquelure on the ceiling of my room at *Joondalup*, the boys' home, in the wrinkles of worried faces in hospital waiting rooms, in the marbled beef from cattle I boned. Even yesterday, as I strained in the rain hitching my boat to the car, I caught hints of it in the twisting swirls of grey water flooding down the driveway. But I've never really found it. Not the complete beauty—whole, tiny and perfect enough to turn on your palm—that I saw that day.

I'd woken late that morning. I was ten years old, and rarely slept past dawn. But by the sunlight blaring in under the torn pull-down blind, it was after eight o'clock when I opened my eyes. There was no school on, so no watching Mum rush about looking for her keys; she'd gone to Cumby to see Aunt Trish, her sister. It was just me and Dad at Canterbury.

Canterbury was a saucer of hard, red land lipped by black rock hills. A river ambled through it, barely wide enough to be called a creek and never more than sluggish with the heat of summer or the dry dread cold of winter. As often as not, the riverbed was dry, just a seemingly endless path of brown skullcaps running north-south. I never saw fish in the water at Canterbury; maybe they were wise enough to stay away. At weekends, when I wasn't needed for rounding, drenching or shooting sheep, I would fossick among the stones on the riverbank for diamonds. I'd read at school about diamonds, and how ordinary they appear uncut, and found a stone I was convinced was a gem that would change our lives forever. Dad took a hammer to it, to show me it was worthless quartz. Our lot was not to find diamonds.

Three or four years ago I learned that half of Canterbury had been acquired by the government and flooded to make a reservoir. The river had been dammed and that saucer of land filled with water. In all likelihood, our white house with the rust-red roof was demolished. But in my dreams, the house is still there, deep under brown water. And I am inside, swimming through the rooms of my childhood, down the hall through the shimmering gloom, accompanied by schools of grey catfish as I strain, lungs burning, into the kitchen, past the old fridge, to the back door. Which is always locked.

But that morning—when I was ten and the drowning dreams had not yet started—I found the back door wide open when I scuffed into the kitchen. I was sore, and confused. Either something good had happened, but bad things were due today, or vice versa. All I was certain of was that I had overslept, there was no school, and Dad had left the back door swung wide. I looked outside, squinting against the glare. Across a hundred yards of red dirt was the shed. Movement. Dad was fixing something on one of the tractors. A glint, like a blue diamond, and a puff of orange flame— he was brazing.

"Dad!"

The flame swung low. Like insect eyes, the green-black goggles turned toward me.

"You want tea?"

The round goggles fixed on me for a long moment. Dark and inscrutable. Then, a hint of a white smile below, and Dad shook his head.

I nodded, and turned to make my breakfast. In the fridge, the raft of yellow cream floating on the milk was almost gone—Dad liked to eat it with a spoon when Mum wasn't watching. I carefully poured a glass, unable to dislodge the dark stone in my belly that said something was wrong. But what? I opened the pantry and reached to get out the honey flakes—then stiffened as if electrified. On the front of the box, benevolent cartoon bees buzzed around the bowl. I'd remembered.

For weeks—months, really—I'd pestered my parents to let me build a beehive. My fixation on bees had begun in the school library. Researching for a class project on the conquests of Alexander, I found a photograph of an ancient Persian amulet; this shiny, glinting insect of gold and mother of pearl and polished anthracite lodged in my mind, as firmly stuck as a real bee's barb. Starting my own hive, I could have dozens—thousands!—of living, delicate, golden bees, rich (in my own mind) as any Achaemenid prince. I saw myself donning the keeper's hat, cool as Steve McQueen in his silver suit about to battle *The Towering Inferno*, smoker in hand, ready to plunge into the dark, moist, sweetly dangerous vault of my own hive.

Mum and Dad were set against it. Mum because she felt there was insufficient pollen for bees to survive on in Canterbury, and Dad because he didn't need to waste his time driving me three hours to hospital covered in bee stings. My protests, my research, my charts showing bee range and numbers of flowering trees, my tables highlighting limited likelihood of allergy were in vain. My hive was vetoed.

But I'd ordered a Queen, anyway.

Lunchtimes in the school library gave me the time to investigate beekeeping suppliers in the classifieds of city newspapers. I couldn't afford a smoker or frames for a hive, but I knew I could make them, and I did. I had started making my hive from a warped and peeling dog kennel that I'd found hidden in long whip grass near the station's original mud-brick house, about a mile from ours. I'd begun constructing frames for the hive from the scraps of windows and doorjambs that hung awry in that cadaverous place. My experimental smoker was hidden skilfully in the work shed, along with a paper bag full of wattle twigs, the closest thing I could find to pine needles. What I couldn't fabricate was the essence of a hive—the Queen. She, some workers, drones and foundation wax would cost me $18, delivered. I timed things well, saving pocket money for weeks with a view to having her arrive in her dark, perforated box during the school holidays. Which started today.

In order to keep my purchase secret, I needed to be the first to our letterbox, two miles from the house, when the postie drove up in his dusty van some time after lunch. The original station house was halfway to the post box, hunched in the lee of a rocky rise; so, to while away the morning, I'd go there to finish the comb frames for the hive. Congratulating myself on my cleverness, I packed a lunch, made a mix of cordial, and packed them in an old cardboard school port that had almost outworn its usefulness. I left the back stoop to go to the shed. Stepping on to the red dirt and into the sun seemed to drop fifty pounds onto my shoulders; the light was blinding, and the heat was heavy and solid enough to chew. I hurried to the shade of the shed.

My father was at back of a tractor, one hand leaning on the frame that held the greasy PTO shaft he was repairing. His other held the oxy wand, and the flame hissed idly into space, a titian snake with nothing to bite. He was forty-one, then, and I could see the grey at his temples. He wasn't moving, and the goggles stopped me seeing where he was looking.

"Dad."

He didn't stir.

"Dad?"

Slowly, he turned. Again, the black discs of the goggles regarded me, a giant beetle with a fiery stinger. Then, his hand holding the oxy torch swung up, the arc of a flaming arrow, right to his head, and pulled the goggles off his eyes. They fixed on me, and a slight frown folded the skin above his nose, as if he was concentrating, trying to put a name to my face.

"Hey."

He was staring at me, hard, like I was some Rosetta Stone that could unlock some puzzle that had stumped him. For the first and last time in my life, I felt uncomfortable under my father's gaze. I shifted the port on my shoulder.

"You okay?" I asked.

He nodded slowly. His lips were dry, and he hadn't shaved. "Are you okay?"

Now I was really flipping out. Dad sometimes became a bit vague when Mum went away—but I thought that was just because he missed her. This was unsettling. And I had things to do.

"I'm going to the old house for a look. I've got lunch."

Dad nodded, and his eyes ratcheted down to the flame in his hands. He shut it off.

I turned and stepped into the sun.

"Michael," he said.

I stopped and looked back. With me in the sun and him in the dark, he was just a shadow. I couldn't see his face, but I knew he was looking at me. Framing words. Important words. I waited, baking.

"Nothing."

I nodded, and turned and ran.

• • •

The old house was just a shell perched halfway up a dusted, rocky slope that rose to a sharp outcrop above. This stony hill was the highest part of Canterbury; over the rise was a steep gully that flooded suddenly when it rained, and was treacherously spiked with broken branches any other time. But the old house was in a good spot, overlooking the plains of ruddy dirt and brown grass. Just a mile away, near a solitary grove of gums, was our red-roofed home. In the far distance, I could see a puff of red dust anchored by a shifting spot of grey-white—our sheep.

I laboured in the sun for two hours, pulling down window frames with the hammer and chisel I'd spirited from the shed, then cut them as best I could, one foot pinning the timber to the dry-rotted verandah, one hand inexpertly hacking with a rusty saw. Twice I'd hit my thumb with the hammer. The sharp pain took my mind away from my aches.

The old kennel, my new hive, sat beside the old house like a forgotten sedan chair surrounded by bowed, worshipful grass. I'd cut the roof away, nailed in rails, and slotted my makeshift frames into the top box. I'd pulled one slat of chamferboard from a side of the kennel, and for the hole fashioned a bottom box for the brood; somewhere dark and safe where my queen could pulse and squirt out more and more servants. And an heir.

Lunchtime. I clawed up the rocky hillside to the skeletal remains of a tree that afforded a bit of shade. I checked for ants and sat, but the hot earth scalded my buttocks, making me wince. I removed my drink and sandwiches from the old school port and sat on it. The sides crushed with a tired sigh—the bag's usefulness had finally passed.

The day was at its high hinge. The sun glared down from overhead, and the horizon had cooked to a colourless plasma. I unfolded the greaseproof paper and chewed, looking over the abandoned station house. It was big, with wooden floors that must have looked quite fine before the roof thatching dislodged, and sun and rain twisted the boards. The walls were largely solid, but dark cracks grew at angry angles from the corners of doorways and windows. The view here was . . . well, breathtaking. But even when my parents had bought Canterbury fifteen years ago, the station house was already long empty. I wondered why. Why had the original owners abandoned a perfectly good house with a beautiful view?

"Because she wasn't s'posed to be here."

I yelped and jumped away from the voice at my right elbow. I lost my footing on the sharp shale and fell on one knee, bending my already wounded thumb under my hand. But that pain came later; right then, I was staring wide-eyed at a woman who'd appeared silently from nowhere.

"Snuck up on ya?"

She was sitting on her haunches next to my crumpled school bag. She wore a plain floral shift, and her skin was black as coal. Pureblood. Her hair had grey in it, but it was thick and, once, it would have been as black as her skin and her eyes. She seemed rooted to the ground, solid as rock. Smiling at me. Maybe laughing.

"Come on. Not gonna bite ya." She grinned. "Not yet."

I blinked, not moving. She rolled her eyes, showing pearl white, and gestured me with mock annoyance to come back. I stole a look around. My father was a mile away. Beyond him, the nearest neighbour was five or more. I was alone with her.

"Young Michael, innit?" she asked, patting the crumpled port. I nodded and cautiously sat. She was staring out across the plain, just the thinnest sliver of eye visible under her thick lashes. My heart was pumping, and sweat was leaking out of me everywhere. But her skin was dry. Black and dry and smooth. Beautiful. Still.

"Who are you?" I asked.

I wasn't sure if she'd heard me. She didn't move, just kept watching plains below. I was about to ask again, when she spoke.

"You'd know it if you heard it." She turned and looked at me, and smiled. Her teeth were perfect white. "But you can call me Joan, eh? Like St Joan. St Joan d'Arc, eh?"

I nodded. I'd read last term how the Maiden of Orléans had burned for heresy.

"Old d'Arcy, eh? That's me, eh? Dark? d'Arc? Geddit?"

I watched her to see if there was meanness in her words. But her smile seemed sincere. I nodded again.

"No, they wouldn't burn me. I just hide somewhere black, they never find me." She chuckled. But her eyes didn't laugh—they were watching me carefully, the slivers of curved dark iris glinting, reminding me of something. This was the first time I'd sat with a black woman. The Aboriginal settlement was twelve miles south, and the only black kids at school were the Douglas brothers, and no one in their right mind sat with them. There were blacks in town, usually sitting in groups of three or four under the fig tree near the Great War memorial; Mum always hurried me past them. Dad had hired a black stockman when I was little. Bill. Bill had his own horse. But he'd stopped working for us by the time was five, and I'd never asked why he'd left.

Joan hummed contentedly to herself, idly cleaning under her nails with a thorn. Then I remembered what I was thinking when she'd arrived—I'd been thinking . . .

"About the ol' house," she said, and looked at me. Her eyes were black pearls. "You were oglin' the house. She still all right lookin', even though she's getting' old. Bit like me, eh?"

Joan grinned, and I opened my mouth to answer, but couldn't think what to say. She shook her head—don't worry.

"Thought I'd tell you why the white fellas give 'er up." She raised her eyebrows—do you want to know?

I nodded.

"Didn't like the colour," she said. She paused, then burst into deep laughter. It bounced off the rocks and carried away in the breeze. For a guilty moment, I was afraid Dad would hear it, look out, and somehow see me all this way away talking to an abo.

"Only kidding," said Joan."'No, this ain't ground for building. This is special ground. Precious ground. You can feel it, can't you, Michael?"

I thought about that. "It's got a good view," I said.

She laughed again, deep and good, refreshing as a waterhole. "Good view, yeah." She sniffed. The sound echoed slightly off the rocks above and the red mud walls below. "No, this a *wunona* place. A place to come and sleep, dream the understanding of things. But you sleep here every night like them folk," she nodded down at the empty house, "you see too much."

She pursed her lips and looked at me. I could feel her eyes testing mine, poking to see if I understood.

"Bad dreams?" I said.

She nodded. Good.

"This place gave them nightmares?"

She shifted. For the first time, I noticed the pattern on her dress wasn't of flowers at all, but intertwined insects, and what I'd thought were petals were their wings.

"No, not nightmares. Just things. Things how they are." Joan shrugged. "Seein' things how they are, it's not everyone's cup of tea."

I looked at the abandoned house. When it was first built, it would have been the only structure in a hundred square miles. If every night in it were plagued by fitful dreams, how would you feel? No one to hear you cry out. Nowhere to run. Alone and haunted.

"Where's that postman of yours?" asked Joan.

"I don't know," I answered. And my heart did a funny little drop. She knew I was waiting for the mail. How did she know? I looked at her. But, again, she was still as stone, a black sphinx watching the whipsnake dust road a mile away.

"Oh, I know bits and pieces, Michael." She winked at me. "I know you don't have bad dreams."

My mouth was dry. The cordial had soaked into the bread in my gut, making a soggy ball that sat queasily. She was right. I never dreamed. I woke each morning in a muzzy headed malaise that lifted like fog by breakfast. I never remembered what went through my head in the night.

"Are you . . . are you a *kadaitcha* woman, Joan?"

I'd heard that the Douglas boys had an uncle who was a kadaitcha, a medicine man. He pointed the bone at some bloke who'd sold the family a dud washing machine, and the salesman had wasted away and died just two months later. Or so I'd heard.

Joan looked at me, and raised her eyebrows. Maybe impressed that I knew the word. Maybe offended.

"Not me. Just a silly old black bitch, me, eh? Talkin' shit with a silly young white fella."

She nudged me and smiled. It was a brilliant smile—pure black and pure white. I would remember it many years later, walking across the checkerboard tile floor of a hotel foyer in Marseilles. I'd broken down there, curled on the marble staircase, bawling like a toddler, unable to stop. All the other tourists shrank away.

But then, that kiln-dry midday sitting above the old station house, everything was in equilibrium. The future hadn't started, and the past hadn't unveiled. Joan held the scales. Smiling.

I smiled back.

The air was still. No breeze wishpered sand at the dead tree trunk we sat under. No crows called their kin to meat. There was no hint, just then, of the dust storm that was brewing at the edge of the world, ready to smother this awful day. Just an ignorant white boy and a mysterious black woman, talking shit.

"Talking shit," I said. I think that was the first time I'd sworn in front of an adult. I turned to see if I was in trouble. Joan just smiled at me. But not at what I'd said, I now know, but at what was coming.

"You a gamblin' man, Mister Michael?" asked Joan.

I blinked and frowned. Was I? I'd gambled that my parents wouldn't learn that I'd bought stuff through the mail against their wishes. I'd gambled that they wouldn't find my secret hive here in this special, ghostly place. I'd gambled that I could come up with a year's worth of excuses to regularly visit my hive once it took hold.

"I reckon," I replied.

Joan nodded. "Righto, then," she said.

Still on her haunches, she dusted her hands, like a sideshow huckster readying to display some sleight of hand. And as I watched her fingers twitch, I noticed that the pattern on her dress wasn't made of generic insects. They were bees. Blue and green and yellow, with honeycomb wings. My jaw slid open.

"You watchin' my arse or my hands, boy?" asked Joan.

She was smiling again.

I dragged my eyes back to her hands. She held them both in front of her as lightly clenched fists. I could see the sweet gradation of her skin colour from the black back of her hand to the coffee colour on the side of her palm; I could see the stark crescents of white nails on black whorls. And, still, not a drop of sweat.

"Two choices, Mister Michael: left or right."

She turned her closed fists toward me, grinning.

If the sun heating the earth makes a sound, I heard it then. Because there wasn't another noise. The world was deathly still.

"What's the deal?" I asked.

"Well. You pick one. You pick the right one, you get another choice. You pick the wrong one, you go away from here and never come back up. Never have no bad dreams. Never have no good ones, neither."

Her lips pulled back further. Her eyes closed tighter—just thin slices of shining white and glistening black. And I remembered, then, what her eyes reminded me of: the Persian bee brooch, the one in the book, with its stripes of mother of pearl and polished jet. Untouched by time. Ancient, unsettling beauty. And suddenly, this all seemed very serious. My heart began to thud a little harder.

"What if I don't choose?"

Joan cocked her head and laughed.

"Oh, I reckon you'll choose, Michael. You're a gamblin' man."

She was right. I would choose. And I did. Before I could stop myself, I tapped her right fist.

She smiled, and uncurled her fingers. On her umber palm sat a bee. A bee unlike any I'd ever seen. At least, not with waking eyes.

It was large, half as big as the cardboard rolls of ten-cent pieces checkout girls crack open into their tills. Its body was gold-furred, and its eyes were sapphire. The bands of its abdomen weren't brown and yellow, but silver and blood red, shining like a crystal. Its legs were jet black and long. And it moved. It crooked one slender leg to draw its divinely fine antenna down for preening. It was the Queen. The Queen I dreamed of, and the Queen I'd forgotten. Memories flooded back in a torrent. Memories of the weeks after I'd first seen the Persian brooch when nights were thick with dreams of starting my own hive. In those dreams, I'd wake to a golden morning and rush to the ice-white hive. Cocooned in a safe aura of sweet blue smoke, I'd crack open the brood box and find her. Not plain and bloated and wormish, as I later found real Queen bees later to appear, but gemlike and scintillating and perfect—exactly like the bee on the black woman's palm.

"Remember?" Joan whispered.

I nodded, transfixed. The Queen flexed her wings: flawless mica teardrops. Her compound eyes glittered under the white sun—each a hundred eyes, watching me.

"She's not real," I whispered.

Joan shrugged. "Take her. See."

I stretched out my hand. She opened her other fist—empty—and with that free hand grabbed my wrist. Her skin was dry and cool, and her grip strong as iron. She dropped the bee into my palm. I could feel her weight, the touch of her fine feet on my pale, damp skin.

"See?" asked Joan. "You do dream."

The Queen stung.

Pain flared in my hand and swept up my arm—like flames, it burned, dwarfing the throbbing in my thumb, the stab in my knee, the bruises on my neck and . . .

"And?" asked Joan.

And the other pain.

The pain that came at night. When I couldn't breathe. When my head was pushed against the mattress. When Mum was away. The pain I dreamed, and forgot I dreamed.

"No dream, Mister Michael."

The acid burning of the poison spread into my shoulder, up my neck, into my face—a bonfire.

I screamed.

But my cries were muffled by my pillow, enough so I could hear the sobbing behind me.

The poison tightened my throat and filled my eyes. Everything burned. Fire roared in my ears. Everything was red and swollen, ready to burst. The sky, the land, everything—except Joan. Black as ash. Still as rock. She smiled.

"Remember, now?"

The world flooded. My eyes swam wet. My throat gagged tight. I was drowning, unable to breathe. Underwater . . . with the back door locked.

I nodded.

The pain stopped.

I sucked hot air into my lungs. My heart sprinted to catch it.

The world was silent again, the quiet broken only by my snotty breaths shuddering in and out, echoing off the rocks.

Joan, carved from black granite, watched the sky. Sniffing back mucus, I followed her gaze.

A quadrant of the sky was closing over in a red-black eyelid. Dust storm coming.

Then I remembered: the bee.

Joan still held my left wrist, but my right palm was empty. I looked around. The jewelled bee was seated, again, on Joan's hand. As I reached for it, her fingers closed over it—a strong obsidian cage.

"Gamblin' man?"

I looked up to her face. All trace of smile was gone. Her eyes watched me, cool as the insect's.

"You want your daddy dead?"

I blinked. And felt the first touch of a breeze. Air drawn from the north, down toward the hungry dust storm.

"No." My voice was a weak croak.

Joan cocked her head.

"No wonder you white folks lie so good. Start 'em early. But man . . . "

She looked at the bee turning itself in her hand, sparkling in the sun, red on red, white on silver. "Your dreams, they are beauties." She looked up at me.

"Tell you what, gamblin' man. "Nuther shot. Left or right. Left, I let you go, you run and save your daddy. Right, you keep your dream."

The haze preceding the storm crept over the sun, casting a pewter pall over the plain. In the far distance, the sheep were running. The pernicious eyelid of the dust crept closer to our home. I figured ten minutes was about how long it would take to get there.

My whisper was cracked and broken. "You are a *kadaitcha* woman."

"Whatever you want, gamblin' man. Just choose."

I looked down at our farm house. So white and small under such a huge, red wave. How can so much poison come from such a little thing?

I tapped Joan's right hand, the hand which held the Queen bee.

For a long moment, nothing happened. Then, she let out a sigh, and rocked back on her haunches. The flowers of her dress were nondescript. Not bees, just flowers. Plain daisies. She chuckled, and casually dropped the bee into my palm. I quickly cupped my other hand over it.

"Know why the real Joan Darky got all burned up?" asked Joan. My eyes were locked on the dust rolling toward our house.

"For wearin' pants. They just didn't like seein' a girl in pants. Still, she hadn'a worn pants, none of us would know her, would we? Funny how people got to die to get a point across."

We sat for a while, me cradling my jewelled bee, and her rocking gently on her heels, Joan humming to herself as the storm came closer. Wind began to whip our hair, and devil-devils swirled in the dirt around us. As the sky grew dark, Joan stood.

"Reckon you oughta get into that house, gamblin' man."

Her eyes were dark tar drops.

"No need for you to come back up here."

With that, she turned and stepped lightly away up the escarpment and over the rocks. Gone.

I hurried down the hill, sliding on the loose rocks, and reached the old mud brick house as the dust storm hit with a violence that shook me. Wind as red and thick as cow's blood howled around me. It grew so thick, I couldn't see. I curled into a corner of a room, tucked my face against my knees, and put my hands over my ears as the dust storm pounded with a roar as loud as the end of the world. I lost time. A minute became an hour. An hour became ten. I forgot where I was, forgot I was awake and not dreaming, and got to my feet. I pushed through red mist, trying to get to the kitchen, before remembering I wasn't in our house. I gagged on the dust, so I pulled off my shirt and tied it around my face. Finally, I went back to my corner, curled again into a tiny tadpole, and waited.

• • •

When I woke, I was covered in a second skin of dust. Sunlight flickered weakly through the open window hole; a tiny red orb near the horizon. The day was nearly done. I sat up. Both my hands were open, and empty. The Queen, if there had ever been a Queen, was gone.

I found my father hanging by his belt in the shed. The police later told my Aunt Trish he died just before the storm hit, because there was no red dirt in his lungs. I grew quite close to Aunt Trish after Mum went funny. Mum killed herself, too, some eighteen months later, after drinking a tea made from mouse poison.

I survived a series of boys' homes, where the abuse my father dealt was commonplace for some others, but never again for me. I fought. I left at seventeen, and after that money and jobs came and went. Dreams returned vividly; not just the one where I was caught in the drowning house, but other dreams. Dreams where I chose Joan's other fist. Where I run across the red dirt, lungs afire, racing to beat the storm. Finding Dad standing on the tractor with a belt around his neck, not yet stepped off. In time to talk him down . . . but never doing so. Being there to watch him step away . . .

I saved, and travelled to Iran, searching. I found a brooch not unlike the one I wondered over as a child—but never the exact golden bee that had caught in my eye and mind. Finally, I tried my hand at beekeeping. I laughed as I stuck my hand in my first hive, knowing it would come out unscathed, and it did. I'd had enough stings. Now I run a honey farm. But every time I open a brood box, my breath stops for a moment, and some small part inside me flutters in hope. But the queens are always drab; never beauties made of the blood and silver.

Tomorrow, I am driving home to Canterbury. They've had no good rain in a year, and the reservoir, I hear, is low. I've hired a boat. If the water is low enough, I'm rowing over to the rocky escarpment there. It's a special place. I'm a gambling man, you see, and I'm hoping to lose some dreams.

• • • • • • • • • • •

ACCEPTION

TESSA KUM

I.

Forty-four seconds ago, I heard a knock at the door.
Forty-two seconds ago, I considered ignoring it.
Twenty-seven seconds ago, I answered it.

"Tessa Kum?"
Here we go.
Again.

NOTICE OF RELOCATION

Dear Ms T Kum (CID# 19800806-F787-A/C2/M3-2009),

Re: the Revised and Updated *Collective Unconscious Research and Privacy Act (2009)*, *Equal Opportunity Act (1995)*, *Racial and Religious Tolerance Act (2001)*, *Thought Artefact Identification and Spatial Differentiation Act (2009)*, and the Department of Human Services (Housing) and Deep Research and Ethical Oversight Committee Co-operative 2009.

Thanks to your assistance, the first stage of the Cultural Identification Program has been a resounding success. The joint efforts of DHS and DREOC in recognising and classifying each of Victoria's rich and diverse cultural zones has yielded excellent results. We are now able to begin extrapolating artifacts in the psyche of the collective waking conscious, specifically those stemming from cultural structures. As such, our understanding of the collective unconscious and the human condition is deeper than ever before, and continues to grow.

Your support has been greatly appreciated, and with the insight gained from the initial CID Program, it is now possible for the community to take the next exciting step.

You have been identified as being of Asian Stock (second-tier Chinese/third-tier Malaysian). Our records indicate you have already taken up residence within one of the designated Asian Cultural Zones (Box Hill, SE CHINA, Third Precinct), a neighbourhood reflecting your lush and vibrant heritage.

Psychic Waypoint Tower #ACC217 has returned anomalous readings in the nocturnal waveband in your area. The nocturnal wave band—a state of the art new initiative—monitors the unconscious while asleep, gaining us valuable research data into the true unconscious with no disruption or inconvenience to you. Further investigation has pinpointed you as the aberrant mind within PWT #ACC217's field of surveillance.

Your true unconscious is not compatible with the specifications laid out for an Asian Cultural Zone (Box Hill, SE CHINA, Third Precinct), as stated in the *Collective Unconscious Research and Privacy Act (2009)*.

New accommodation in a more suitable zone has been found for you.

It is our responsibility to lead the world forward in this new and exciting era, and it is with pride, humility and determination that we accept this responsibility. There has never been a time of greater unity within our nation than now.

Thank you for your cooperation in this matter.

Together, we are building a better future.

• • •

DREOC officers are of the same breed as ticket inspectors. Even in plain clothes they're easy to pick. It's written in their posture, the heavy armour in their voices. They know they're unpopular and they're bracing for pent-up and projectile vitriol. It's building in the four of them now, as my gaze is dragged along the sentences. The further down the page I get, the wider they hold their shoulders. They're blocking the light.

Half the breath I have been holding comes out, not a sigh, and I look up at the wall of muscle around me.

"Do you understand?"

The officer asking curls down toward me, a nametag on his coat announcing him as Colin Brown. He looks like a Colin Brown. Clean-cut, neat, and with an odd mix of apprehension and confidence—they outnumber me, but he doesn't want to be here. Ancient acne scars and out-going ears make him look younger than he is. He taps over his PDA without doing anything.

"Certainly. We're building a better future." I fold the letter and run the seams between my fingers, and that action releases me from their attention. They disperse around the room.

Colin's sarcasm detector isn't switched on. "A better future. Exactly. Let's see here." He scans his PDA again. "Our records indicate you are of Asian stock."

"So you keep telling me. I assume that's why you moved me here, to an Asian Cultural Zone, right?"

He won't look at me. "You sound like you disagree."

"It doesn't matter what I think."

In the kitchen his companions coalesce, murmuring and shifting impatiently.

"You know you can contest a cultural classification—"

"I know. I have. Several times."

Colin winces, or smiles, or attempts to do both and ends up with a face of dishonest wrinkles. He changes the subject. "You seem prepared for this. Were you contacted by DREOC, by any chance?" He gestures at the boxes crowding the room.

"No." I clasp my hands before me and dig my nails and my anger into my palms. "Your agents forcibly removed me from Northcote and placed me here three weeks ago, and I have not unpacked. Doing so would mean accepting a classification you have no right to force on me, accepting the creation of the zones and my non-consensual relocation, accepting that it is now illegal for me to see my family and friends, accepting that I have let the bad guys destroy my life, and I accept none of these things."

"Oh." Colin taps his PDA once, twice. "Well."

I think Colin would be more comfortable if I were yelling at him.

• • •

They have a truck waiting downstairs.

Fifty-eight minutes after I open the door, every trace of me is removed from the apartment I refused to call home.

• • •

I have no idea what road we're on. They've taken me through Asian, Mediterranean, British, Sub-Continent, Pacific and East African Cultural Zones, and now we're out west. I don't know the west. It's almost a foreign country. They do things differently here, with big houses on small blocks and not a tree to be seen. The night sky sags over the rooftops, pushing everything down against the dead lawns.

"What was it that singled me out for this special treatment?"

The checkpoint falls away behind us, the glimmer of razor wire in the spotlights slipping back from the road and stretching into the darkness, the border between some African and Middle Eastern Cultural Zone. There are no Indigenous Cultural Zones this close to the city.

Colin winds up the window, the car weaving in the lane. "Ah. I don't know if I should tell you that."

"It's in my head. I already know."

He taps his thumbs thoughtfully on the steering wheel, and finally digs his PDA out of his pocket. "It states here you dream of the end of the world—" he quirks an eyebrow, it's oh so amusing—"which is not within the acceptable parameters laid out for Asian stock, Chinese and Malaysian inclusive, according to the *Collective Unconscious Research and Privacy Act (2009)*, with particular reference to the Herman-Biscuit Paper, and made legislation last week. Specifically, the inclusion of zombies—" He pauses and reads over that again, his mouth moving silently. It's a good thing it's a straight road. "Zombies? Really?"

Every morning I wake up full of terror and adrenaline after spending my sleep running for my life. Some mornings, I wake before the zombies corner me. Some mornings, I don't.

Mum told me, sitting at the kitchen table with two cups of tea and DREOC bold and unstoppable on the front page of *The Age*, that it was an unsubtle metaphor my unconscious or subconscious or whatever-conscious was employing to act out my waking fears: an unstoppable and uncaring force would invade and destroy my world, and stand on my lounge room carpet in dirty shoes and acne scars, and smile weakly at me while doing so. At the time, I thought she was projecting.

Who knew zombies were against the law?

Some disquiet stirs in the back of my mind, doubt cast on my doubt. They really can read minds. There are no walls left in the world.

"That's an odd thing to dream about."

"Apparently." I stare at him with my dark Asian eyes.

He flicks me a nervous glance without turning his head, and licks his lips. He isn't someone who can sit in silence. Unfortunately, he's no good at making conversation.

"Well, I mean, it's odd for a Malaysian to dream about. You know, it's not all that exotic, and Malaysians don't have zombies. Um. Do they?"

"I'm not Malaysian."

"But our records- wait, we've been over this already. You're Chinese. Sorry."

"I'm not Chinese either."

I have this conversation with everyone I meet, eventually.

He looks at me, the road, me, the road, the dash, the road, me, the rear view mirror, me. My face doesn't tell him much.

"Is this how you dispute their findings? Flat out deny everything?"

I turn away and look in the side view mirror. The truck carrying my boxes is driven by a compulsive tailgater, the headlights bright in my eyes.

It's all in the record he just read, if he paid attention. If any of them paid any attention.

• • •

Colin's use of it lodges the word in my head. It's a pretty word, with a meaning that is not so pretty.

"A guy at work said my lunch was 'exotic'."

Dad pulled a face at me, one of his many faces to indicate he had heard but probably wasn't paying attention. He lifted the lid from the wok, dragging up a roil of steam and releasing the smell of pork, char sieu sauce and cloud mushrooms. The hiss and spit conquered the kitchen and I waited till he clanged the lid back down.

"It was only two-minute noodles. Not even any meat or veggies. Just the noodles. In the microwave."

Dad pulled another face, disdaining my choice of lunch.

"There are other people in the office who eat the exact same noodles, and they aren't told it's 'exotic'."

He pointed at the rice cooker, and I obeyed.

"Maybe it's because I was using chopsticks," I said, pushing the steamed bok choi and wom bok aside.

Dad was nodding, but not listening. Pork and cloud mushrooms out of the wok, into a dish. Oil and garlic into the wok. Soy sauce on the silken tofu. The snapping and cracking garlic and oil on the silken tofu.

This was not exotic either.

• • •

Not even those who lived in the western suburbs had much to do with this place. It was intended to be an industrial estate, until DREOC claimed it, and overnight it was made over with portable rooms and portable toilets and portable showers, all shuffled in and planted amid scaffolding and abandoned foundations and pipes and silos.

We pull up at the final checkpoint, and as our convoy is confirmed against the registered database, Colin turns to me. "Your new home. What do you think?"

Ropes have been strung between the portables, some laden with laundry. I doubt anything dries quickly in the cold. The area isn't paved, the portables are set on cinderblocks and all else is potholed gravel. Skips sit at the end of a row, lids raised with the bulge of sodden plastic bags, two listing at an angle with the stumps left by missing wheels sunk in the mud. A high fence marks the perimeter. Barbed wire, clean and new and yet unrusted. Puddles glisten sick little rainbows of oil on leaked grey water, that careless reek wafting in through the car vents.

A couple of women smoking by the toilets watch us, a mixture of apathy and raw seething hatred in the creases around their eyes, the twist of their mouths and the pinch of their noses as smoke leaves and rises around them.

This is so far removed from the eucalypt-lined streets of my home and the tragically-hip and curious alleys of the city. There will be no possums on the roof here, no chai lattes and no urban exploration. No joyous discoveries of great restaurants, surprise street art, secret hot chocolate.

Colin can't keep his hands still on the wheel. Weirdly eager and afraid, as though he'll take any rejection of the place as a personal failure. There was a time I would have been sensitive to his sensitivity. There was a time I'd have even tried to dress the situation in a positive light, for my own wellbeing.

I stare at him until he has to look away, and then I stare at him some more. Passive aggressive is all I have in me, and it isn't all that aggressive.

I'm given one half of a portable. A cracked chipboard partition provides a thin veneer of privacy between me and my neighbour, but does nothing to drown out the sound of the TV, 60 *Minutes* covering something on shopping-trolley rage. No curtains, anyone walking by can see my everything. It's not insulated. The air feels heavy, settled, a faint thread of mildew souring the edges. No one has moved through it for some time.

Colin offers to help me put my bed together, but I don't want him to be nice, I won't let him be nice, I'm going to hate him and everything he is.

"I'm just trying to help," he says, too much the kicked puppy.

"You're the bad guy," I say. "You don't get to help."

He ducks his head and leaves me in another place I will not call home.

• • •

I pull up Mum's number on my mobile. I pull up close friends, distant friends, co-workers. I cycle through them all, over and over, and don't call any of them.

There is nothing to say.

• • •

Kim lives in the portable across from me, sharing with an elderly Brazilian-Rhodesian man who yells abuse at everyone equally.

She's not a mongrel like me. She grew up in four different countries, her parents doing some sort of diplomatic work, which is enough reason to lock her up in here ("the kennel," she says, without a smile but not without amusement).

"My mind is a spaghetti jambalaya goulash stirfry." There is some pride in this statement, but I've yet to hear her say something unexpected.

She passes me a cigarette. I don't smoke, but I've now confirmed that I cannot leave the camp without 'special permission', and even if I could there are no trains or buses this far out and thus I cannot get to work and so no longer have a job, not to mention I can't get to any of my stowed books in order to read, so I smoke. Or rather, I suck on the filter, hold the smoke in my mouth, nettled acridity muting fast on my tongue, and dare myself to inhale without choking.

This is how dogs in the kennel pass the time.

"I'm just a banana."

"Like most of the people here. Bananas, coconuts, eggplants—"

"Kiwi fruit."

She laughs.

"I don't get the point of that. Not here." I point at the Psychic Waypoint Tower mounted over an unused silo at the southern end of the camp. "Waste of time. All right for reading all the nicely sorted zones, I mean, there probably are patterns there to recognise, but here?" I watch one of the camp guards jog to the toilet. "They've never explained how the towers work."

She exhales gustily, silent, and smoke spills from her nose.

"It isn't for data, you know. It's so we know we're always being watched. We're the aberrant cultural cells in the larger body of Australia. Everything else is neat and orderly, and we're the cancer, and they've got their eye on us, to make sure we don't get out of hand."

"You sound like Agent Smith."

I return the cigarette. "It isn't neat and orderly. It's never been neat and orderly. This is Australia." The smoke has coated my teeth and they're tacky against my tongue.

I hate this place; the cold and the mud, the stagnant air infected with stewing sewerage and old steam from the mess hall, the emptiness of trees, the absence of all I've taken for granted—loose leaf tea, magpies stalking me on the nature strip, fog over the railway tracks, hot soft-boiled eggs, overheard laughter, running water, light switches that work, colour, colour, colour—I hate this temporary third-world country. I might be in shock.

"Why aren't there any Australian Cultural Zones, anyway?"

I never did fit in the Asian Cultural Zone. To everyone else, I was Asian enough to be labelled 'Asian', but to all Asians, I was white. The looks I'd get as I left the railway station at Box Hill varied from surprise to hostility. I didn't belong, and if they must be segregated, then they didn't want me there.

There was never a question of whether I would be placed in a British Cultural Zone.

No one belongs in here either, and there is an equality in that misfitism like a balm on a burn.

Kim squints at me. "You haven't even been here a day."

"Don't tell me I have to earn my bitterness."

She laughs again, and some of the tension slides from my neck.

• • •

Colin is in the mess hall. Why is Colin in the mess hall? Too late, I've made eye contact. He parks himself at our table, the plastic chair stammering across the lino, a forced casualness in his white knuckles and clasped hands, that ticket inspector paranoia waiting to be challenged.

"Soooooo." He can't help but fill the silence he's created. "Tess—I can call you Tess, right? You're not Malaysian, and you're not Chinese. What are you then?"

"Fuck off," Kim suggests.

"I'm Australian."

To his credit, he does not say *yeah, but what are you really?* "Your family, then."

"It's all in my file."

"I'd rather hear it from you."

The sound Kim makes could be at Colin, or at her carbonara.

The look he directs at me, this government-sanctioned bully, this clueless boy, this ordinary guy, unhinges my jaw. He's all expectation, eager and open-minded, and trying so hard.

Okay then.

"Mum is white Australian. Her Mum came over from England, and her Dad is seventh generation white settler."

"Then your Dad is Malaysian."

"Yes. No." I poke my carbonara with equal distaste. "He's Chinese-Malaysian, which means the family is Chinese, but they live in Malaysia. Not Malaysian, though. Different cultural group. Sorta."

"Doesn't that mean he's just Chinese?"

Dad, tucking into rendang and sneering at the group at the table opposite. "From northern China," he said. "You can tell from the sallow skin and the pudgy faces."

Mum met my eyes and we shared a shrug.

"Really?"

"Yeah." *A disapproving sniff.* "You can tell."

"Yes. No. He's never been to China, and the family has been in Malaysia for generations. There's geographical cross-pollination of the culture."

Colin's mouth puckers in thought.

"Like all the Greeks here, who've never been to Greece," I add.

"But there aren't many of them." He dismisses them with an easy wave that floors my appetite faster than the cafeteria food. Kim glances at me, resignation in the slope of her mouth.

"There are enough to make several Mediterranean Cultural Zones."

"Yeah, but not that many—"

"Do you think Australia is white?"

Finding himself suddenly pinned between us, he stalls. He knows the answer he wants to give will be shot down, and we know it too. He knows we'll sniff out any dishonest reply, and we know he knows that too.

"The majority is," he offers lamely.

Kim curls her lip. "I'm white. What the fuck am I doing in here?"

He raises his hands helplessly. "It's not my call, you know, I'm just trying to get a fix on Tess here, you see. Your Dad, I mean." He can't change the subject fast enough. "If he were deported—"

"Not 'were'. He has been." *Thirty-nine missed calls. Seventeen messages. Mum standing alone in the kitchen with the dogs sitting in the hallway, waiting for Dad to come home.* "You didn't even give me enough notice to get to the airport and say goodbye."

Colin raises his hands again, against the accusation in my voice. "That wasn't me personally, come on now, I'm trying to understand."

Which is more than most DREOC officers do, I'll give him that. I bite down the tired tirade stirring on my tongue.

"So, since he was deported from here for not being Australian, will he be deported from Malaysia for not being Malaysian?"

I tell myself I could answer, if I chose to.

"Would they send him to China? Would China take your family?"

"It's a detention centre," Dad said, weeks ago, a weak connection forcing his voice under water. "For everyone who gave up their Malaysian citizenship to live overseas. There's not enough space. There isn't any running water. There aren't any beds. They won't let any of your uncles contact me. They don't want us—" He cut himself off, but not before I heard the catch in his voice. When he continued, he was steady, collected, even had a weak laugh. "And the squat toilets are just holes in the courtyard. They're not screened off. You should have seen the queue after they served curry for dinner. What a mess. Oh dear. Oh dear, oh dear."

He was pretending to be okay.

The battery in his phone died, and that was the last I heard of him.

"Sorry. I know you don't know, I shouldn't be asking. Um." Colin's eyes dart to my plate. "Are you going to eat that? No? Thanks." He grabs the plastic fork from my hand and shovels tortellini in his mouth. "It must be hard," he says, cream sauce thickening the saliva strings between his teeth.

"Jesus—" A touch on Kim's arm and she quiets.

I could stop here. I could. I could get up and walk away.

"How do you justify it?" I ask, keeping my voice level.

"Pardon?"

I swallow, control cold and hard in my throat. "You kick people out of the country and divide up families and make people live where you say they can live. DREOC is destroying lives. Destroying *us*. How do you justify it?"

Chewing slower, he shrugs uncomfortably. *"I'm* not destroying anything, I mean, it's only temporary stuff. I don't have any say in it, you know. It's just a job. All the higher ups make the decisions. We just get told what to do."

I swallow again, control getting harder to hold. "You have to pay the bills?"

"Exactly!"

"Pretty sure that's what a lot of the guards in the World War II Nazi concentration camps said."

"What, hey! That's not fair!" Flecks of pasta spray from between his teeth and he clasps a hand over his mouth, chewing and swallowing hastily. "We're not going around killing anyone, Jesus! This isn't ethnic cleansing, or, or, genocide, or anything like that, it's not permanent, it's just, just—"

"Bringing some order?" Kim suggests.

"Tidying up?"

"Yeah. Yeah. Tidying up. That's all." He looks down at the plate, oil congealed around the bacon.

I lean forward. "Tidying and cleansing mean the same thing."

"It's not like that and you know it!"

His shout echoes across the mess hall, a sudden quiet focus unfurling in its wake.

"Do I know it?" I hiss. "Do I fucking know it? Do you? Do you know how it *really* is then? If you do, then please, by all means, educate us!" I can't keep it down. "Have you had men in uniform drag you out your door and throw you in the back of a truck and haul you away without telling you where to? How about being told you are no longer allowed to associate with your friends and family because they're white and you're not? Has your father been kicked out of the country? No? Are you coming to terms with the fact you may never see him again? No? I bet you still live at home and none of this has ever occurred to you, you take it all for granted, you pathetic whitebread fuck!" He looks away, wavering protests silenced. Horrified I said it, horrified I meant it, but not enough to stop, I don't stop, I can't stop, I won't stop. "How about this place, then? This prison camp, don't pretend this shit hole isn't a fucking prison. Have you just been thrown into a scungy-arse portable with no water and no power and no privacy and nothing, *nothing*, and told you can't leave because you might contaminate the rest of the fucking state?!"

It's a roar an eruption a nova whiting out the mess hall and snarling in my ears. It shakes me and shakes me, my fists on the table, Colin wide-eyed and flinching. There isn't enough air in me, but still it comes out, this final razor opening everyone within earshot.

"Despite being born here, and having lived only here, have you been told you are not Australian?"

I can hear nothing. There is nothing to hear. No one says a word. No one can speak over the answering roar in their own hearts. It has shaken me, and I am shaken, frightened by the violence in my blood and bones, but I swallow, taste bile, and swallow it down.

After a long pause spent probing a grey crescent of mushroom with the tip of his fork, Colin shakes his head.

"It's just a job," he repeats, barely a whisper.

"Just a job," I repeat.

"Do you know what you're doing?" Kim murmurs.

"Yes," I lie.

Colin draws in a shuddering breath and looks up, the muscles in his neck taut against his spine, raising his head in rusty wincing judders. There is nothing he rests his gaze on, no safe place to look here, among us, until he meets my eyes. I don't know what he sees, but in him I see a hunger.

"I'm just . . ." His breath is heavy with cream and garlic, which doesn't hide the rank cold sweat. "I want to help."

I loosen my fingers. "We don't want help," I say, and my voice carries, clear and calm in the aftermath, addressing not just him and Kim, but everyone, all the misfits and oddballs and mongrels and mixtures.

"We want change."

This isn't fury. This is an offer.

The realisation widens his eyes and parts his lips. Is the breath he draws laden with hope? With anticipation? I can see right through him and watch that first spark catch and light up. All he needs is one last push.

His eyes are so clear, so bright.

I will change that.

"Tell me how the Psychic Waypoint Towers work."

This enemy, this ordinary person, he doesn't want to be the bad guy.

I won't let him.

II.

There's no escaping the smell.

It saturates the air, lends it a fullness that sits heavy in the lungs and coats the back of the throat. We cover our faces with rags and masks already carrying the stench. It wends its way into all closed spaces. It seeps into the skin and hair. No one is carefree with the air they breathe. No one gets used to it.

Melbourne's birds, the magpies and seagulls and crows, have grown fat and torpid. They need never hunt, they need never compete. There is more food than they can eat, and they waddle about the streets, complacent and lazy, not even pausing to peck at a thumb rolled into a gutter, the fingernail hanging loose and ready to fall.

Occasionally, when there is a lull in hostilities, new fires are lit. Whether once revolutionaries or DREOC militia, nearby bodies are collected and heaped. In burnt-out ambulances. In florist kiosks. In derailed trams. Ruins given a new purpose. The dead drape careless arms across each other. They all look the same. Precious fuel and they burn and the smell changes. We don't linger.

We need food, and we do what we must to have it.

And no matter what it is—spam, tinned asparagus, vegemite, a jar of anchovies, a can of mock turkey—when opened, when cooked, when that first bite hits the tongue-

It tastes like the dead.

It's come down to this.

"It's not worth it," I say, sitting on the roof of the municipal hall on Ruckers Hill, binoculars pointed towards the city, the sunset in my eyes. Last night, DREOC made an enormous push and took back the Atherton Gardens housing blocks in Fitzroy, despite our best efforts.

Colin rubs his thumb on my hairline, behind my ear, making a clean patch in the grime. "You keep saying that."

"Because it's true."

This was, in another life, my favourite view of Melbourne. It was a grand surprise opening up beyond the petrol station and houses without warning. I'd take long looping walks, always culminating on this hill, with the sun gone, and the city rising graceful and clean into the night sky. Full of glass, full of light, full of determinedly individual architecture, each building making a unique statement, each building clashing with its neighbours.

Now the glass is broken and crumbed on the streets, the buildings blasted, and everything is smoke and dust and smoke and dust.

The DREOC militia have wasted no time. A fresh Psychic Waypoint Tower, gleaming clean and orange in the sinking light, is growing on the commission block roof, amid the air-conditioning vents and mobile phone towers. If they complete it, they'll have a live feed into Melbourne once again. They'll be able to see us. They'll be able to find us.

They'll know our plan.

"We're not finished. There's still a lot of work to be done. Later, you'll see you're wrong." There is a conviction in his voice that wasn't always there. I haven't seen uncertainty in him for a long time, not since that first day, back in the camp, standing in the ruins of the first Psychic Waypoint Tower destroyed, rag-tag army of misfits and mongrels around us and the camp's director kneeling at my feet. I pulled the trigger, and watched the spark within him become an inferno.

The wind changes, and smoke obscures my view. Burning tyres, burning houses, burning petrol stations; every sunset is spectacular.

"We were a minority." I lower the binoculars. They're dropping smoke flares around the roof to mask the tower's construction, and on the ground mounds of trash are set alight to screen their movements.

I doubt we'll miraculously stumble across any rocket launchers before they bring the tower online. We have to make our move now, even if we're not ready.

"Maybe," I say, thinking back to a camp of cheap temporary housing on an industrial site in the far western suburbs, one camp out of an entire state, and I wonder where Mum is, if she got out with the rest of the refugees, or- no, don't think about that. "Maybe we should have been left to suffer so the majority could live in peace."

He leans in close, close enough I can hear him swallow, throat tight and tense and dry. "It's too late," he says through clenched teeth. "To change your mind."

It's never too late to change, I think, but do not say.

A scuffle on the ladder, and Kim pops up through the trapdoor. "Slop's up. Pickled dace and marmalade, picked it special just for you, Col."

"We should eat before we meet the others." I stand and head back to the trapdoor. He'll follow. He always does.

• • •

What signs there are read *Bonds Warehouse* and WARNING CONDEMNED BUILDING DO NOT ENTER and ASBESTOS HAZARD *All Personnel Must Wear Protective Clothing.* A derelict storage warehouse in Thomastown, all grime-coated gutters and stone-broken windows, dribbles of rust and pigeon shit caked down the walls. That wet taste of old metal and cold stone in the vast empty spaces surrounding it. A chain-link fence with a crusted gate and padlock sealing off a bare concrete courtyard spackled with weed.

This is not DREOC's primary research facility. That one is signposted, advertised, and even ran guided tours on the weekends.

This is DREOC's real research facility.

Before, all transmissions from every Psychic Waypoint Tower in the state came to this site. Everything read in the unconscious, nocturnal and waking conscious wavebands came silent through the sky to an antenna array concealed within the structure. The neighbourhood died from the psychic pollution, although no one knew it at the time. The thoughtfog broke everyone, eventually.

The complex extends beneath the surface, surprisingly far down, safe from the poisonous space it created. We have only the original planning blue prints. We could be wrong about a lot of things.

And we certainly are.

When we reach the twelfth sub-level, when we turn the corner and see the featureless corridor terminate at a cell door bearing no name or number, when we finally reach our objective, my hands are still clean, but I am not. I am uninjured, my breathing even, but something inside me cannot stop howling.

With such operations, I like to guess how many years of therapy it would take to undo the evening's actions. The answer is always: none. I don't like counsellors. If I can't absolve myself of this, then no one can.

"Stay here." Kim nods, and Colin leaves the team guarding the stairwell and joins me at the door.

"Just a swipe card?" he asks. The reader flicks to green and the passageway echoes with the thunk of the bolt flung back. I don't let my relief show. The swipe card cost too much for doubt.

I push the door open.

Small, square, unornamented. Empty walls, no carpet. One hospital bed, devoid of extraneous medical equipment. In it, one girl, beneath a doona. A floral doona. With bees. Heavy leather restrains all her limbs with only minimal slack for movement. The smell of piss and shit.

She starts awake—was she asleep?—and I was wrong, she's not a girl, she's a woman. She can't be much older than me. No, that's not true. Maybe her body has only lived for so many years, but her mind is like nothing else on Earth.

A surprised frown dips beneath her matted bed hair, quickly melting away as she rolls her eyes and sighs, this amused exasperation her only greeting. Her head drops back on the pillow, eyes closed. She's seen all she needs to see.

"One at a time." I push Colin back out the door. He resists for a moment, staring at her. She's not unattractive and a feather of envy brushes up my throat. "Get the helmet." I shut the door behind him.

"I know you probably need some time to figure me out," I say, approaching the bed. My voice rasps too loud in the silent room, tongue and lips dry and coarse from yelling. "I can't give you that time, sorry. We need to be out that door and up that corridor and out of this place, and we needed to have done it ten minutes ago. We've got your helmet, you won't leave this room without it on."

I tug angrily at her straps. She lies here for all hours of all days, and can't take herself to the toilet. She reeks. Rage at this small indignity is easier to hold than rage at the greater crime against her.

"You knew." The words form in her mouth slowly, as if spooling from a single thread drawn across a great distance. "Right away. Why the straps."

I glance at her face. Proud Greek nose, smooth olive skin gone sallow without the sun, fierce eyebrows. She looks at me looking at her, some tired recognition in the faint tilt to her chin. Already, she *sees* me. Maybe she doesn't need that much time. Maybe I'm not that hard to figure out. I try not to feel insulted by this.

The first strap comes loose. "It's what I'd do, in your situation." My knuckles brush against the inside of her wrist, and the pearled scars there.

Her hand twists, and her grip is not weak. "How do you know I won't do it again once you've freed me?"

"I don't."

"Will you stop me?"

I don't answer. She can read my mind and see the truth for herself.

• • •

She was the first psychic ever created. The lab rat DREOC used to trial and error their research and streamline the process for the mindreaders to come. She woke with all her walls demolished, able to read everyone, unable to hold herself apart from the collective conscious. After weeks alternating between screaming and sedation, they built a shielded room, providing the walls they'd taken from her, and she never left.

Later, she'll try to tell me what it was like. "Like drowning, never dying," she says, or, "Noise torture, like the CIA use," or, "Chemical burn in your brain." Her mind was levered open and the world swept through and swept her out. She can't explain, and I can't understand.

The records refer to her as Yvonne, but she hasn't been Yvonne for some time. She is everyone, and no one.

From her, they were able to design the first Psychic Waypoint Towers and extract some meaning from the data they collected. From her, DREOC built everything.

She is the end of the world, sitting here in green pyjamas.

• • •

Kim holds the door open for Colin, huffing beneath the helmet's weight. There's no time, but he launches into his speech before he's crossed the threshold.

"We've been fighting DREOC from the beginning. Anyone could see that tapping into the collective unconscious was the highest breach of privacy, an abuse of power justified as being for 'the good of all mankind'. Exploring the human condition, establishing Australia's psychic signature, enhancing anti-discrimination laws; it never ends, and people were surprised when segregation became legislation."

Kim ignores my gesture to leave and darts after Colin, catching the other side of the helmet. He nods briefly, not breaking his monologue. "That's not what Australia is. See Tessa?" He can never quite meet my eye when using me as an example. "Unclassifiable, indefinable, she is her own person. As we all should be. DREOC has forgone the individual. We won't let it happen, not without a fight. Aussie battlers, that's what we are. The underdog. Fighting for a fair go." They heave the helmet onto the bed with a grunt.

I've heard him practicing this in the bathroom. I wonder if he believes it.

"Six minutes," Kim mouths. This is taking too long.

A bemused smile touches Yvonne's face, distant, as everything she says and does comes through so many layers of everyone else she appears to forget her body, and he trails off like a stunned school boy.

"But, you know that, of course."

I suck in my cheek and give him a look before turning to the helmet. "Is there a trick to this, or do you just put it on?" It isn't glass, but looks it. It's reminiscent of an old diving helmet, and the shoulders are heavily padded to soften its ridiculous weight. Our greasy handprints are all over it. "Kim, get out there and get the others ready to move."

"Wait." Kim hesitates, but Colin isn't talking to her. He nods at Yvonne. "Prove it."

"We don't have time for this." The militia is coming, if not here already. We have to *go*.

"We do," Kim backs him up.

"We can't do this again," Colin says. "If she's the wrong person—"

Yvonne slips from the bed and crosses the floor with small steps, and beckons him down to whisper in his ear.

All the blood rushes from his face, etching out his acne scars, the graze on his forehead and the grime on his chin. His looks down at Kim, and I see something there I don't want to see, before he looks at me, then away, resolutely away. The question on Kim's lips stalls with a quiet shake of his head, and some invisible and undeniable chasm opens between us.

What did she tell him? I think I know. I wish I didn't know. I add another year to my hypothetical therapy.

"Satisfied?" I can't keep the edge out of my voice.

He nods, once.

"Kim," I snap, ignoring the half-formed guilt on her face. The lights flicker and die momentarily. There is no time. "I said go tell the others, we're leaving." She can't leave the room fast enough. "Help me with this."

Colin casts quick furtive looks at my face as we lift the helmet. He never did master forced casualness. The helmet settles and Yvonne straightens awkwardly beneath it.

"I haven't had any contact with anyone outside for . . . I don't know. Time is a different language with too many parallel memories. Not since they made the other mindreaders, at any rate." The helmet fogs with her breath. With halting steps she heads to the door. Too slow, too slow.

She looks at me. "I've read you. I know everything about you." I pause. "Everything."

Old disquiet stirs in the back of my mind. There are no walls left in the world.

"Even the zombies." There's no amusement in that statement.

"I haven't dreamed for a long time."

"Liar." Her smile fades fast. "I know the way they work. I can see why they put you in the reject bin, with all the other pieces that didn't fit in their jigsaw. I know what you've done." I expect judgement, but there is none. "I know why you've done it. For Australia."

"No, not for Australia."

I can hear Colin not saying anything. I can read his silences as easily as Yvonne read me.

"You would say this country does not know what it is."

Kids threw rocks at me after school, calling me a dirty chink and telling me to go home. Which is exactly where I was going. At least the irony amused my parents.

"It will know, in the end." And it will not like what it sees.

She shakes her head, shuffling ever onward. "You can't lie to me," she says. There is almost a question in her voice, a question she knows there is no point in asking.

I reach out to steady her, swaying beneath the helmet's weight, but don't touch her. "No. I can't. Everything you saw in my head is true."

The corners of her mouth sag.

"I'm sorry," I add, as the pitch in the room alters. The air-conditioning has stopped.

"I can never go home."

I unholster my gun, signalling for Colin to get the door. "None of us can."

He cracks it, peers through, and confirming the corridor clear, ducks out.

"I'm sorry too," she murmurs. I can barely hear her. It's not a diving helmet, it's a fish tank.

I stare down the corridor at Colin's back, at the fingertips Kim lays on his wrist. He recoils from her. He knows I'm watching. I keep my finger off the trigger.

"I know you know."

"And you know I chose to say nothing."

Colin flips off signals in a flurry. Fuck. We're not alone.

Yvonne slips a hand into mine. The creases of my palm are black with cordite and sweat, my knuckles bruised, and her skin is paper dry and cold. Back pressed to the wall, I step out, but she doesn't follow and stops me short.

"Choices." The word sounds hollow, drooping from her tongue. "You have given me no choice here. You're no different from DREOC."

There is no time. Kim catches my eye and beckons urgently. Their impatience claws beneath my shoulder blades. Echoing down the stairwell, the sound of boots, the rasp of flak jackets. Deep in the building something rumbles, and the lights go out for good.

There are too many things I can't grant her, but I ask. I have to know. "What do you want?"

She sighs, soft and airless as a failing moth.

"I want to die."

And the shooting starts again.

. . .

We speed down the Western Ring Road in an old jeep. My ribs shriek with every bounce, and on the cracked road there is a lot of bouncing. The freeway is clotted with the husks of burnt out trucks jack-knifed across the lanes, the remaining wreckage of conquered barricades and cars half-crushed by the passage of tanks. Flitting between the warehouses is the occasional glimpse of what was the city, baleful and weary beyond orange-bellied smoke.

We left at least six behind at the research facility, and beside me Kim writhes and kicks at the seat in front. She can't breathe, she's choking on her own blood.

Four nooses hang from the sign for Pascoe Vale Road. One of them has snapped. I can't tell if the dead are theirs or ours. Yvonne looks at me, and her look is terrible.

"What have you done?"

She doesn't need to ask. She knew. Now, she understands.

. . .

Colin is speaking, but no one hears him. They're looking at Yvonne, tired and wilting and ridiculous in her begrimed pyjamas and helmet. They're looking at the unhappy turn of her lips and downcast eyes. They're looking at her hand, clinging fast to mine. They're looking at the bullet-proof vest I'm still wearing, and the small but significant hole in the outer lining. They're looking at my straight back, set shoulders and lifted chin. They can't see my pain. Here in the main bunker in our underground base, all they see is the revolution, and our victory.

Colin finishes listing the lost and dead, his voice breaking on Kim's name. Her last packet of cigarettes in his hand, already tapping one out. I never did pick up the habit. "The price was high," he says, meeting my eyes briefly. This time he does not tell me it was worth it.

"There is still a lot of work to be done," I say.

Unlike him, I am very good at pretending nothing is wrong.

. . .

Yvonne finally releases my hand, after taking it in the corridor all those hours ago. Her flesh is crimped with the impression of my fingers where I'd gripped too hard in pain, the bruising already showing. She shucks off the helmet with a groan of relief.

"It's noisy," she says of the room we prepared, "but keeps enough out."

I sit gingerly on the edge of the bed, too aware of her. As the Psychic Waypoint Tower invaded my sleep, so she is once again invading my thoughts, and I don't like it and don't hide it. Although there's little of interest to see right now. Intense hurt. Colin. Betrayal. Fatigue. Grief. Kim. A sudden savage craving for chicken parmigiana.

She holds up her bruised hand. "If I can touch you, I can read you."

Oh.

There's no small amount of malicious enjoyment in her pronouncement.

I don't deserve to feel betrayed. I assumed her to be passive, just a tool. She's right. I am no different from DREOC.

She shakes her head in agreement. "No, the Face of the Revolution is not."

I could convince her. I could put forth all the reasons she has to work with us. I could.

"But you want to let me choose," she says, simply. "You see me as a person first. You would let me choose even though none of your comrades has considered doing so, and will oppose you if they find out."

I haven't said a word. There's no need.

Yvonne crouches before me. Her face, protected by the helmet, is starkly clean compared to the rest of her. There's a faint memory of air-conditioning in her hair.

"Who am I talking to; the revolutionary leader, the heart-broken daughter, the jilted lover, who?" She touches my face, a touch that is only a touch.

Chicken parmigiana, followed by a lamb souvlaki.

And then, hot apple pie and cream.

"Me," I croak. "You're talking to me."

III.

I pull the trigger. Again.

The crack of gunfire joins the echoes already bouncing around Federation Square. None of them truly fade away. I wanted to use a silencer, but Colin said it would ruin the effect.

It's amazing how much blood comes out of a head wound. The body, greasy blonde hair and heavy jowls, is dragged from the stage before it has finished collapsing, but there is still so much blood, spilling on top of all the blood spilt before, thick and black.

Colin actually used the phrase 'thoughtcrime' that time, and I don't believe he was being ironic. I don't believe he's read *1984* either.

"Bring the next," he says. *Next. Next.* Like the echoing gunshot, the word never fades away.

Pieces of the outside world reach us; a pirate broadcast on shortwave, a briefly stolen satellite hookup, an unreliable spliced phone line. The picture pieced together is contradictory, both hopeful and hopeless. DREOC is proceeding as planned and has started a program for reading the minds of high school students to determine their future occupations. DREOC is tangled in international red tape and is being charged with human rights abuse. Martial law has been declared in all states. More underground rebellions have formed. The cultural zones have become entirely sealed off and no one can leave them. The rebellions are quite literally underground and go where they please.

Australia is frightened. Australia is joyous. Australia doesn't know what it is or what it is becoming.

The original plan—and it was a fine plan—was to have Yvonne act as our own Psychic Waypoint Tower and gather information regarding DREOC's capabilities and movements, the location of their stations, and their future plans. We had no moles, no inside intelligence to speak of. She was to be the turning point in our campaign.

And she was.

Oh, she was.

Colin pronounces the sentence, and I pull the trigger. Again.

"Bring the next," he says.

We're on the stage backing the Transport Bar. When Prime Minister Rudd made a formal apology to the indigenous people of Australia, I was here, watching this stage. Colin liked this resonance with the past, thought it fitting. The square is packed, the incline towards the twisted remains of the Atrium rises in the receding distance, until all I can see is a wall of faces.

There was cheering when we began, when the first DREOC militia member was executed, and what I saw in those faces sickened me. All these executions later, and there is no cheering, and what I see in those faces now is worse.

We don't have enough ammunition to waste on a firing squad. There are no bullet holes in the wall. We have left no mark to tell those who will come later what has happened here.

There is just me, hand and gun so splattered with blood it drips like an open wound, waiting for the word.

I pull the trigger. Again.

"Bring the next."

This used to be such a *cultured* space; cultural exhibitions, curious art installations, activists and petition-signers, street-performers and sponsored jazz bands, free tai chi and salsa classes, book fairs and green energy expos; all these things aimed at making the world a better place.

Not all blood smells the same. Not all blood flows the same. It creeps across the stage and oozes around my boot.

I have to be the one to pull the trigger, Colin said. It is symbolic. It is what history wants. I fired the first shot, the shot that started this, and so I must fire the shot that will end it for these criminals.

He said these things, and I knew, blinded by the blaze of his conviction, he couldn't see *me* anymore.

Colin is reading, again, the charges against one of the seventy-nine DREOC militia members remaining in our captivity. Try-hard tribal tattoos, a weak chin and mutton chops. He's just some guy. Some guy who needed a job to get his parents off his back. Some guy who got caught up in the hysteria. Some guy paying rent. Some guy trying to make himself big. Some guy with nothing better to do. Some guy, pulling Samoans and Somalis and Indonesians and Vietnamese and Greeks and Turks and Lebanese and Koreans out of their homes and telling them where to go. I have to keep reminding myself of this. It gets harder each time I pull the trigger.

There is no end to these ordinary people. There never will be.

This guy, this enemy, this guy, he cringes away from Yvonne's hand. Yvonne can't take the helmet off outside, or lose her mind in the roar of the world's collective conscious. Her hand has become the hand of judgement, resting on the back of his neck. With a touch she can see, and with a touch she sees him. There are no walls left in the world.

The final charge is read, and Colin pauses to lick his lips, the break in speech tripping my attention. All the charges are the same, for all our prisoners. A mass sentencing and execution would be more efficient, I'd joked.

But, no. It is the rights of the individual that DREOC has not respected. Thus it is the individual we must honour, and condemn.

No one talks about Australia anymore. I stopped counting the number of times I've had to reload after the sixth clip.

"We are prepared to waive these charges," Colin says. "If you can put aside your prejudices and judgements and let go of the collective mentality you've so blindly followed, if you can do this, you may join us. You can help us change Australia. You have a choice: to change.

"Together," Colin says. "We are building a better future."

He can't say the DREOC motto without emphasising it. He still thinks it's clever.

Blood seeps over the lip of the stage to the patterned paving below. The slope has funnelled it down through the cracks towards St Kilda Road, and the crowd has given way before its advance. On the edge, by that creeping tide, an Indian woman and red-bearded man stand behind a girl, hands on her shoulders. Her face is dirty, thin, and the features ambiguous in origin. She covers her nose and mouth and hasn't looked up from the blood in a long time.

This enemy, this guy, this frightened man, he is kneeling in the blood of those tried before him. It's soaked his pants and the stain is climbing the fabric. It isn't much of a choice. He nods. He has no loyalty to DREOC. It was just a job.

Colin looks at Yvonne, and with a small shake of her head, she removes her hand.

She is so quick to judge.

Colin doesn't skip a beat. "You do not possess the qualities necessary to make the world and our future what it must be. You have no place here." I can't tell if Colin enjoys this or not. I don't know if I can even hear him over the memory of all the previous judgements and the growing howl in my heart.

"This is Tessa. You can't classify her just by looking at her face, and her background confuses you because she cannot be so easily defined as 'Asian' or 'Caucasian'. For that, you treated her as less than human."

And you won't let me be only human, merely human, *just* human.

"You locked her up because she was inconvenient."

And you're the one who carried that out.

"She is the face of the future, the Face of the Revolution, and the revolution has won!"

There are no cheers. This is no triumph.

In this breath, in this moment no different from all the others preceding it, I touch my finger to the trigger. The hush in the square is outlined by the complacent murmur of seagulls, gathering by the trucks to the side of the stage, the tray beds heaped high with all the people I have executed, no, murdered today. To the other side, the beer garden converted to a cattle pen, are all the prisoners yet to be tried, heads down, some crying.

No please no please no please no his lips move. This frightened man, this enemy, his voice has fled. Yvonne took it from him, negated any choice he might have made with a shake of her head.

My wrist aches, hand gloved in gore, cordite and blood on my tongue, ears ringing, the gun too hot in my hand but I can't put it down. There are more to come, we have to read them, we have to decide what they are, we have to-

Colin steps back, clear of any spatter, and I say, "No."

The word cuts through all the other words hanging in the air, soft and undeniable and waking the crowd from their acceptance.

"These blokes, they thought I was some old Chinese fuddy-duddy, they started telling me what I should be saying, and I thought, uh oh, here we go, I'll show them. Nobody tells me what to be."

"You know I'm just going to throw those words back at you when you tell me what I should be, right, Dad?"

I tilt my chin, just enough of a negative to assure the guards below.

"You were this man. Just doing your job. Not malicious. You worked for DREOC and did all that he did. You changed."

"And he won't change," Colin counters. "Yvonne has seen him. She knows. None of us can lie to her."

"No," I repeat. "Seeing is not understanding." A ripple runs through the crowd. These people have lost as much as I have, if not more. They fought beside me. They died doing what I commanded. They did terrible things because I ordered it. They believed.

"His death won't solve anything. None of these deaths will. This isn't what we wanted."

"This is what we *need*." Colin turns to the audience, prisoners and comrades, and points at the enemy, the guy, the victim. "He will not change! He will look at you and see a chink, a wog, a skinny, a boong, a curry, a towelhead. It is ingrained. It cannot be undone."

The audience shivers like wind passing over water. Here and there I see a nod, or a frown of doubt. Even the guards, friends who've been with us since that first camp, lean towards each other and whisper uncertainly, eyes darting between us. They all believed, because we never gave them a reason not to.

Colin has become a fluent orator in his time, but I am the Face of the Revolution, and there is blood, bone and brain spattered on my trousers, shirt, face and hair.

The girl in the crowd isn't listening to Colin. She doesn't need to be told of all the wrongs DREOC perpetuated in the name of a better future. She doesn't need fine speeches to mollify her conscience.

". . . It will only happen again unless we erase it. We must remove the minds that pollute the collective with narrow and out-dated thoughts . . ."

All she can see is the blood at her feet.

". . . We can only take what we have learned, and start anew. A society that recognises the individual as equally as the group."

Out of my line of sight, Yvonne is silent, still, almost nonexistent. Knowingly or not, she has become the tool DREOC created her to be. I am fortunate for the helmet, and that—here, now—she cannot see what I am thinking.

Colin turns to me, and it's just him, me, and the disappointment in his voice.

"It was you who taught me this simple truth."

"Then why don't you understand?" I whisper.

The crowd stills. I have never grown used to being the focus of so much attention.

This time, I can't give them what they want.

"Don't you see what we're doing? You put me in that camp because someone read my mind and I dreamed of zombies, and that was incompatible with your checklist. Now we're standing here, passing out judgement on these people because we've read their minds and what we find is incompatible with our checklist. This new world order we're building, now we have our own psychic; we're telling people what they are, and what they are allowed to be—" I swallow. I can't look at Yvonne. "We've become them."

"This is different, Tessa." He couldn't fake this frightening calm. "You're losing sight of the bigger picture."

"This is not different."

The frown in Colin's brow deepens. He doesn't want to hear this, doesn't want me to be this, doesn't have time for this. "Everything has changed. We're giving this man a chance, which is more than you were given. You know this. You've known this your whole life. This is the change *you* brought about."

The rift is complete. This is what we have become. In the empty space between us is the memory of Kim. This is why he ended up in Kim's bed; he had not put her on a pedestal. She was like him, just some person.

I bow my head, and nod.

He says, "Then you know what must be done."

He says, lower, "It is too late to change your mind."

I don't trust myself to speak.

For a moment, I think he's going to reach out a hand to me, or I to him, but the moment passes, and with a final nod, he turns away from me.

"Doubt is in all of us!" He addresses the crowd again as I step up. "Even she, the spark and inspiration that brought us so far, even she doubts! We have endured so much to reach this point, we have suffered and we have lost so much, and there's still a lot of work to be done." The stillness in the audience remains, but the flavour of the air has changed, the welling expectation heavy like a distant storm. "The path forward is still one we must fight for, every step of the way. We all doubt. We will continue to doubt, but we shall never, *never* let doubt win!"

They cheer. They no longer doubt.

Yvonne puts her hand on the back of my neck. I feel a tremble run through her fingers, but she does not pull away.

This enemy, this victim, this guy at my feet, he won't look at me. I don't doubt Yvonne. She sees people clearly, all they have ever been. I judge him, and harshly.

She cannot see what people will become.

In another time, in another place, to another person, my mother said she would be proud of me, no matter who I was, and even though he hassled me for not becoming an astronaut, my father agreed.

Finally, I meet Yvonne's eyes.

She's smiling, a broad, relieved smile, and with that smile the world changes, no, the world never changed, and my doubts leave me.

And I put a bullet through her heart.

· · · · · · · · · · ·

BRAVE FACE

PETE KEMPSHALL

They made me watch.

It took about a minute. Doesn't sound long, does it? But a minute . . .

Count it. Go on, count it out. One one-thousand. Two one-thousand. Three one-thousand. And while you're getting up to sixty, think about watching. Not on the net like everyone else, but right there in the room, close enough to look into his eyes. Unable to turn it off, unable to look away.

Then tell me a minute's not long.

Afterwards, they tied on the blindfold again, trapping me inside my head with the sight, and with the knowledge that sooner or later they'd come for me. That's how this will end. Not with negotiations, not with exchanges or concessions, or release, but on my knees, under lights.

I concentrate on other things.

I'm with Beth, squeezing her tight in Departures. She tells me to be careful, I tell her not to worry. I'm a civilian. I'm going there to help, not to fight. It'll be fine. Promise.

I kiss her and she touches my face. Her hands smell of baby wipes.

The memory aches, but the ache gives me strength. If I hold on to it like I held onto her, they can't touch me, not where it matters most.

Jerry begged. God, how he begged. They had to shout their demands into the camera just to be heard. And then the screaming, as they set to work with the knife, slicing first, then sawing, holding him up by the hair as the rest of him fell away.

That's why they made me watch. That's why they took away the cloth, held my head still and my eyelids open. They wanted me to know what's coming. Because when you know what's coming, when you've seen it happen . . . you're going to beg. That's what they want, for me to beg, to bargain, to plead.

But I won't. Behind my eyes I see them doing to me what they did to Jerry and I want to scream. I want to howl and thrash and kick and bite and cling to my life with every last particle of my strength. But I won't.

I picture her watching when they drag me in front of the lens, picture how she'll see me every time she closes her eyes. Every time she thinks of me—for every day after, despite everything we've shared—her first thought will be of this. And I imagine how one day, when he's old enough, she'll have to explain it to our boy.

I can't stop this. Not by begging. Not by pleading. All I can do is make it easier for the people I love. So I pray, for a brave face and a sharper knife.

It'll be fine.

Promise.

•••••••••••

HOME

MARTIN LIVINGS

Jack sits, dead, in the passenger seat of a white sedan driven by a familiar stranger. It's hot in the car, hot like an open oven, hot like a burning lake of oil; rivulets of sweat trickle down his brow and back, along his arms. His wrist itches and aches where his watch strap digs into it, but he doesn't dare look at it, doesn't want to know the time. Half past death, a quarter to hell.

"How are you holding up, soldier?" the man asks him, without taking his eyes from the road ahead, straight and featureless as the barrel of a rifle. On either side of the road, misty buildings stream past them, their walls transparent. Nebulous tree spirits line the street, barely there at all. And, beyond and beneath and behind them all, the desert, always the desert, dry, flat, dead. Dead like Jack.

Jack looks down from the road ahead, at his once-pristine army dress uniform, rumpled by heat and sweat. There, in the middle of his chest, the shirt is torn and burnt, hanging away in ragged flaps. Beneath that, the gaping hole in his chest. His fingers flutter unconsciously to the wound, feeling the jagged edges of his shattered ribs.

"Jack?"

Jack looks up at the driver, a well-dressed man in his middle years with dark, thin hair greying and flat against his scalp. Small, delicate glasses sit on the bridge of his thin nose. He wears a stylish dark blue suit and seems blissfully untouched by the heat that torments Jack, who feels like he should know him. The man keeps watching the road.

"Jack, I asked you how you were holding up." There is a searching quality in the man's voice, a piercing lighthouse beam of concern that makes Jack shrivel in his seat.

Jack doesn't say anything, can't find the air in his ruined chest. He wants to ask where he is, who the driver is, where they're going, but there's dust in his throat, sand in his lungs. He shrugs instead.

"Not too far to go now," the man says. "Nearly there." He glances across at Jack.

Jack flinches away from the driver. The man's eyes are carnival mirrors, each one holding a twisted, misshapen reflection of Jack, throwing it back at him like a foul curse. He turns, looks out his window instead, anything to escape those mirrored eyes. Outside, the ghost houses pass them by, their fences swirling with pale luminescent smoke. They stand above the arid sands on foundations long dead, faded memories of brick and wood and concrete. Only the desert is real now. The desert, and the road, and the heat.

The car slows, pulls over. Jack feels the bump as it stops, and the buildings around them emerge from the smoke, become more real, more solid. It looks like a service station, a low-slung building with huge glass windows and doors plastered with garish advertisements for a thousand things a dead man no longer needs. The driver turns to Jack, he sees it in his peripheral vision, but he doesn't return the look, doesn't dare meet those eyes again. "I'm sorry," the man says, "but we need to get some petrol. Can I get you anything? Some water?"

Water. Jack's dry mouth and throat cry out for it, but he controls them. He can't trust anything, not from this man, this *thing* that looks like a man. He shakes his head.

"Suit yourself," says the man, and climbs out of the car. He walks around and pumps some petrol into the tank, stands casually in the mist, the buildings languidly fading in and out of existence around them. The harsh clunk-clunk-clunk of the bowser makes his head hurt. Then it stops, and the driver puts the nozzle back and walks into the smoke, towards the hazy shop. In a second or two, he's gone. Jack holds his breath, waits for the man to reappear, but he doesn't. Then Jack reaches for the door handle, expecting it to be locked. It clicks and opens beneath his hand.

Outside, the air is even hotter than within, drier, dustier. He coughs as he steps out of the car, wobbles on his feet as if he's never walked a step in his life. He leans against the vehicle for a moment, then pushes himself off. He walks away, away from the car, away from the phantom petrol station. Away from it and towards the only thing that's real. The road and the desert beyond.

He stands at the edge of the road, swaying a little. His head spins. The sweat is under his watch band again, making his wrist hurt. Even outside the car, he can smell the stink of his corpse, the flesh rotten, blood congealed and tacky. He looks down at his chest, sees flies buzzing around the open wound. He feels sick at the sight of them.

He looks up, up at the road, and glances to his left. There's a car approaching, a dirty black car, dented and rusted, travelling fast down the straight, barren highway. Then a noise to his right distracts him, a sharp rhythmic drum roll. He recognises the sound immediately, looks in its direction. There is a jeep approaching, an army jeep painted pale yellow and brown, desert camouflage colours. The muzzle-flash of its rear-mounted heavy machine gun flickers like a faulty light bulb. He hears the triple-bangs of the bullets, the gunfire, the sonic booms, the impact explosions. He looks down and sees the road at his feet splinter, shattered pieces of rough bitumen dancing like startled crickets. He turns back to his left as the bullets finally find their target. The dark car shudders and shivers beneath the assault, metal torn, glass shattered. It veers off to the side of the road.

His side of the road.

It's coming right at him, collision course, but he feels no fear, just a curious detachment. It slides sideways in the soft sand at the road's shoulder, engulfed in a plume of dust. The cloud reaches Jack, slaps him in the face, and he closes his eyes, flinches away from the stinging sands. When he opens his eyes again, the car has come to a halt.

Jack hears footsteps to his right. He turns and sees that the jeep has stopped, maybe ten metres away, and a man in army fatigues is jogging towards him, sidearm drawn and at the ready. His pale helmet is low on his face, shading his eyes. The soldier runs straight past Jack, close enough to reach out and touch if he wanted, and approaches the ruined black car. He looks through the shattered windscreen, at the dead man slumped behind the wheel. The driver doesn't look much older than Jack, maybe in his thirties, with olive skin and dark hair. He's dressed in civilian clothes, his white button-down shirt soaked with blood. Sunglasses cover his eyes, a small mercy. The soldier carefully walks around to the side of the car, to the rear door. He reaches out and opens it.

No . . .

There's a man with a shotgun crouched in the back seat, swathed in black robes. Only his eyes are visible, dark eyes, almost feminine. Jack hears the man's battle cry, high-pitched and filled with terrible rage. Then the shotgun goes off with a muffled bang and the soldier stumbles backwards, away from the car. He lands hard on his back in the dirt, his ruined chest already soaked with blood. The chinstrap of the soldier's helmet snaps, and it comes loose and rolls aside. Jack sees the man's face, lying there in the reddening sand, the horrified expression, the pain. The moment of death.

It's Jack's face. As he knew it would be.

He watches himself die in the blood-stained dirt, transfixed, but at the far edges of his awareness something else is bothering him. A deep drone, barely audible at first, but getting louder. It fills his head, makes his vision blur. He closes his eyes and covers his ears with his hands, hunched over on the side of the road. It gets louder, more insistent.

Strong hands grasp his shoulders and yank him over backwards. He yelps and tumbles, flails blind and useless at his assailant. A hot gust of air rushes over him, dragon's breath, filled with the stink of smoke and oil. Then the deep drone becomes deeper still, and slowly fades to nothing. Jack is on his back, and that man, that familiar stranger is standing over him, looking down at him with those damned mirror eyes. In them, Jack looks tiny, pathetic, like a frightened child.

"Jesus, Jack," the man gasps, "that was bloody close! Are you okay?"

Jack doesn't respond, just climbs to his feet. His legs are shaky. He turns away from the man, back to the road. The black car and jeep are gone. *He* is gone. His body, dead in the sand.

"Come on," the driver says, "let's go." He puts his hand on Jack's shoulder. The man's touch scorches like a hot iron, straight through Jack's uniform to the tender flesh beneath, and he twists away. He looks once more to the road, to the desert, but he knows now that there's no escape there, no escape anywhere.

Defeated, he returns to the car.

They pull out of the station and continue to drive in silence. Jack doesn't know how long they've been driving now. It feels like days, weeks maybe, though the sun's never gone down, the temperature's never dropped. It's always been hot and bright. Jack would give anything to see the sunset, to be wrapped in the cool night air. Instead he's here, in this car, with this man-shaped thing behind the wheel. It's his fate, like that story of the man who spends eternity pushing the rock up a hill. No, more than his fate. His *punishment*.

He sees something on the road in front of them. There, in the distance, almost lost in the ripples of heat haze, is another car. It shimmers and becomes the army jeep, on the same side of the road as them, coming fast.

He looks over at the driver to see if he's noticed the oncoming jeep, but the man has changed. He's now the dark complexioned younger man, the driver of the black car, his large sunglasses covering his eyes. Sweat trickles down his face. He looks frightened. The car has changed as well, become older, the seats upholstered in cracked brown leather, a musty, *used* smell filling the air. The heat, though, the heat is the same. The heat is always the same.

Jack looks back to the road ahead, across a bonnet now black and dirty and dented, and sees the flashes from the back of the approaching jeep. Chunks of the road ahead leap into the air. Then bullets pierce the bonnet of the car, holes appear like magic tricks, pop pop pop. The windscreen explodes inwards, shatters into a million geometric pieces. The driver jerks back and forth in his chair, and splashes of blood burst from his white shirt, shockingly red. He doesn't make a sound, not so much as a grunt. The car swerves, a little at first, then more, as the man's dead hands pull it this way and that. Jack knows it's going to crash.

No . . .

Then another bullet, far behind all the others, finally finds him. It enters him, pierces him. Violates him. It doesn't even touch the edges of the hole in his chest, but he still feels his heart explode, his dead ghost of a heart, like the houses on the street outside, gone yet still there. The seat against his back rips open, and a sound he can't quite identify comes from behind him, a horrible animal-like shriek that makes his guts twist inside him. He gasps.

"Jack?" a voice asks him, a familiar voice, still filled with that quiet concern.

Jack looks over at the driver, the dead man with the bloodied white shirt, and he's gone, replaced again by the man in the dark suit with mirrors for eyes. He's not sure which is worse. The windscreen is whole once more, the bonnet intact. But the sounds still ring in his ears, echo and hum. He shakes his head, looks away from the eyes, those looking-glass eyes.

"It's all right, soldier," the man says, his attention mercifully back on the road again. "We're almost there. Almost home."

Jack's chest hurts. If he had a heart, it would be breaking. This was too cruel. All he'd ever wanted was to go home, all through his time overseas. And now he's dead, and home is nothing but a distant memory, a heat mirage on a long desert highway. A brutal illusion.

The car slows again, pulls into a driveway. A house appears out of the mists, red-bricked and tin-roofed. Three windows and a door, painted in nostalgic watercolours in Jack's eyes. He watches as they pull up in front of it, mesmerised and appalled.

It's his house. He's home.

The lie is almost perfect. The gardens aren't as lush as he remembers them, the roses wilted and faded by the ceaseless sun above. The windows are dirty, the path dotted with scattered brown leaves. But it's so close, so damn close, that it makes him feel dizzy. He wants to cry, but there are no tears in him, he's as dry as the desert, dry as old bones, dry as dust.

The driver gets out of the car, then walks around and opens Jack's door. Jack steps out, gravel crunching beneath his booted feet. He looks around, at this house surrounded by thick blue vapours, the house he grew up in. No, *not* the house he grew up in, just a good likeness, it has to be. The man leads him away from the car, towards the front door.

He's only taken a few steps when the door opens, and he sees his parents.

For a moment, one wondrous moment, he *believes* it, believes it all. The mists disappear and he's in the front yard of his childhood home, surrounded by the streets and houses of familiar memories. There are the musical sounds of birds coming from the many native trees and bushes planted all around. Cars drive past at a sensible speed on the road behind him, making soft comforting roars. He can smell the lemon tree in the front garden, the sharp citrus tang in the cool autumn air. And there, on the front door step, are his mum and dad; older, yes, but still his mum and dad, still real. They look at him and . . .

The make-believe world fractures and fades when he sees his parents' eyes. They're the same as the driver's, terrible silver-plated mirrors embedded deep in their sockets. He is trapped in them, once, twice, three times, four. Each reflection smaller and more misbegotten than the one before. Most of all, he sees the hole in his chest, dark and deep and decayed. These . . . these *things* masquerading as his parents, these monsters in human costumes, walk towards him, their arms open, ready to gather him up like a helpless baby, carry him away into his own private hell. The mists roll in again, the suburban paradise engulfed once more by the desert and the heat and the smell of old blood and rotting meat.

Jack turns away from them, from the house and the people and the lies, turns back to the car. All he wants now is to be driven away from here, anywhere, anywhere but here. But the car is wrecked, peppered with bullet holes, tyres half-buried in the sands. The windscreen is a ruined glass jigsaw puzzle, jagged pieces scattered across the front seats, across the bloodied corpse of the olive-skinned man behind the wheel. Jack's hands are hot and sore from firing the heavy machine gun in the nearby jeep, battered by the recoil. He holds his pistol out in front of him with both hands, arms straight like he was trained. He approaches the back door, releases his gun with one hand to open it up. Pulls on the handle, and inside . . .

No . . .

The dead woman looks like she's in her twenties. She's dressed in a traditional Islamic hijab, all black, but the veil has fallen away from her face, revealing high cheekbones, those beautiful dark eyes. Her mouth is slightly open. A bullet has struck her in the temple, torn away the flesh and bone there, leaving a ruined jagged crater the size of a man's fist. Jack can see fragments of her skull, and beneath them, the sponge-like pink tissues of her brain. The side of her face is painted bright red. One arm is flung back on the seat, a blood-splattered finger raised to the sky.

The other cradles her baby.

The child is wrapped in a blanket, once white, but now stained with blood, its mother's and its own. Its head lolls to one side, small chubby hands held out, palms up, imploring, begging, pleading. It's been struck in its tiny chest, the impact of the bullet all but quartering the baby. A jumbled bloody mess lies in its lap, and it takes Jack an awful moment to realise that it's the baby's internal organs, guts and lungs and heart, all shredded up and spat out by the force of the gunshot.

Jack hears a noise, a sickening high keening like an animal caught in a trap, and for a second or two he thinks that the child is somehow still alive, wailing for its dead mother. But the sound isn't coming from the baby. It's coming from Jack. He feels something crumble and fall deep inside himself, in his chest, like he's collapsing into himself.

"Doctor?" a voice so much like his mother's says softly from somewhere behind him, thousands of miles away. "What's wrong with him?"

His wrist still itches and hurts, where his watch strap digs into it. He scratches at it, but there's no watch there. His fingernails dig at the bandages, and blood blooms beneath them again. From far away, he can hear their voices, the creatures with his parents' faces and mirrorballs for eyes, concerned, worried. Gentle hands on his shoulders, on his back, soothing. He doesn't feel them, can't feel them. Can't face them, can't see himself reflected in them. Can't.

His heart is gone. His heart is gone, and he can never go home.

• • • • • • • • • • • •

SOIL FROM MY FINGERS

LISA L HANNETT

I could convince falconers to trade six hawks for two of my hens. I could navigate borderlands without steering the caravan into Meito ghost fields. I could ford winter rivers, violent with fast-moving ice, without losing any of my stock. If duty called I could lead the Pasha's warriors into battle, and guide most of them back out again. My clan was ten wagons strong; my brothers' sons would add three more to that count before we set out on our next travelling days. Some believed I could make dead vines bear fruit or teach lame goats to walk, if only I wielded the right tools. Had the right ingredients. Spoke the right words. These things I could do and more. But it all meant nothing if no one remembered me, if I couldn't give my wife a child.

It wasn't for lack of trying. When we were first married, mystery and excitement drove me to Astrith's wagon every night. I'd walk past the campfires above which spitted hares roasted, ignoring the rumble in my belly in favour of a lower hunger, earning smiles from my cousins and brothers. It was bad luck for husbands to live with their brides until after a first child was born; skittish young ghosts shy away from wombs when men are forever booming into them. I was determined to get Astrith with child, so we could start our life together. Properly. Without risking barrenness, or worse, being cursed with the unnatural offspring breaking this taboo would bring.

Astrith's laugh gave me shivers, her touch was assured, her embrace was open and warm. I couldn't wait to join her in bed each night, to renew our efforts at giving our House an heir. The clanwives would serenade me with a chorus of luck-giving whistles as I stepped out of the flickering light into evening's deepening shadows; more often than not, my mother would give me a skin of fermented mare's milk to bring as a gift. Thus armed, my hands and face and cock scrubbed clean, I would knock on the fresh green paint of my wife's door, and wait for her to invite me in.

Deep yellow candle glow spilled down the wooden steps leading up to her caravan when she opened the door that first night. Astrith had been beautiful then. Her fair skin was made tawny in the ambient light, her black hair unplaited, her blouse unlaced and revealing. I nearly dropped the skin of milk when I saw her. Nearly tumbled back down the stairs and into the familiar sounds of falling night: cook pots clinking on heated stones, knives being honed by the fireside, axes splitting enough logs to keep darkness at bay, stories being told in murmurs. Closing the door, I'd turned to Astrith and blamed my clumsiness on the green-eyed cat winding itself around my ankles. I'd had a reputation among traders and warriors to uphold. Never let it be said that Tomaken is a stumbler.

Astrith had laughed at my excuses; a resonant, healthy sound. She'd bent down and shooed Sorokin, her favourite cat, away from my feet. While she was down there, she'd made quick work of my pants' drawstring. Within moments, I was praying to the Meitoshi, thanking them for blessing me with such joy.

• • •

My knuckles were stained green from three years of nightly knockings. One thousand nights joining my wife, observed by her broods of kittens; one thousand days of tears marking Astrith's wan features, and mine, as the cradle I'd built remained empty. She continued to welcome me, with arms and legs and heart; but after she'd twice expelled the bloody husk of a baby long before it was due in this world, Astrith's enthusiasm for my affections grew thin.

"Keep trying," my mother said, her breath visible in the late winter air. She took my hands, gave me a milk-skin kept warm by the fire. I placed it beneath my thick woollen vest; its heat did little to thaw the block of ice in my chest. "The moon is waxing, the

stars are spinning. The time for growth and change is at hand."
When she patted my cheek, her hand was shaky. The whistle she
sounded as I shuffled to Astrith's wagon was more than a little
forced.

My wife was sitting at the small fold-out table in the caravan's
far end, next to a potbellied stove that exuded more heat than
was needed for such a small space. Her doeskin mantle was
bundled in her lap, wrapped around something I couldn't quite
see. *Not the baby*, I prayed, when I noticed Astrith's eyes were red
from crying. Six months she had kept this one; I dreaded seeing
the infant's lifeless form, shrivelled in her lap. But there was no
blood-stained nightdress, the woven floor-coverings hadn't been
rolled back to expose scrub-able boards, the tin chamber pot was
still empty and tucked away in a corner. I held the door open,
thinking Sorokin would want to escape the stifling heat—she had
grown to be an outside cat, one who preferred being cold. When
she didn't appear, I closed the door and took a few halting steps
toward my wife.

"I've looked everywhere," she said, staring down at the mewling,
writhing mass in her arms. "Beneath the mattress, in all the
cupboards, behind curtains. In the footlocker, the undercarriage,
in the crawlspace above the bed. I even pried slats away from the
walls"—I saw two wooden boards, leaning next to Astrith's horse-
head fiddle—"but I couldn't find it anywhere."

"Couldn't find what, Breath of My Heart?"

Dark circles ringed her eyes, and her voice broke when she said,
"The curse against mothers that plagues this house. There must be
a hidden fetish, a poisoned charm in these walls. How will I carry
this child to term when even poor Sorokin has been taken from
me?"

My heartbeat quickened. I loosened Astrith's grip on the cloak,
pulled its covering folds away, revealed Sorokin's still form. Six
naked kittens squirmed at their mother's cold teats, blinking blindly
and struggling for supremacy. The two smallest ones looked like
they wouldn't endure the next five minutes; the four others weren't
faring much better.

"Only one need survive," I said, plucking the strongest kitten
from the litter, shifting the rest to the floor. I whispered life-giving
words, pierced a small hole in the milk-skin with my teeth, then

pressed the charmed liquid to the creature's mouth. She snuffled and gulped greedily.

"We'll defy this curse as a family. You and me, and Katla here." Astrith smiled at the name. "The moon has changed for us three, My Breath. You'll see."

• • •

The baby seemed reluctant to join us. Our clan had journeyed throughout the travelling days: we'd crossed the heart of the grasslands; we'd scaled the steppes (avoiding the bandits that roamed those lands); and our path had reached the wooded foothills surrounding Zhureem Ordon, the Pasha's mountain-top fortress, when my daughter declared she was ready to be born.

She was more than two weeks late; Astrith's confinement was long and painful. The midwives earned their keep all day—their cheeks grew ruddy, their summer tunics stained with sweat, as they ran to and from the river carrying canteens of water for boiling or for rinsing blood-soaked rags. They wouldn't cut the child from her mother's womb, no matter how badly it pained them to see Astrith struggle: to remove a creature thus would deem it unborn. The ancestors would keep its spirit, leaving only the shell of an infant behind. It would be better for mother and child to die than to bring such an abomination into the world. Our clan prided itself on its band of heirs; we had yet to lose any of our offspring to the ghost fields. With the Meitoshi behind me, we wouldn't start with my child.

I remained at our camp while my men went hunting in the forest. They nodded their approval when I volunteered to tend the horses, beasts renowned for their wiliness, before they disappeared into the trees. For hours I dug post-holes for the animals' temporary pens in the clearing opposite our wagons and tents. I could hear Astrith's cries even there. They'd started off strong, but had grown weaker and weaker until my spade, ringing against rocky soil, drowned them out.

The sun had passed her torch to night's guardian before Chinta, the eldest midwife, came to collect me. She placed her wizened hand on my shoulder, not flinching at the filth and sweat she found there, and whispered, "It's time for you to come."

Her expression was unreadable. I dropped the spade, grabbed my sheepskin jerkin, and followed Chinta to Astrith's caravan. The camp was quiet. The men were only now starting to return from their hunt; the women hovered in hushed circles near my wife's dwelling, waiting for news of the birth. The crunch of my boots on brittle grass echoed in my ears, the beads dangling from my long black braid clicked together with each step I took. Chinta left me at the stairs, her head bowed. I'm sure I heard voices rise in speculation as soon as the door snicked shut behind me.

Astrith sat up in bed, nestled beneath a mound of quilts and furs. Wet tendrils of hair clung to her cheeks, which were the greyish white of old teeth and dewy from her labour. Her head was propped up against stained pillows; her eyes were open but moved sleepily as I approached. Two large bowls filled with crimson water had been abandoned at the foot of her bed. In her arms a bundle, not unlike the one she'd held three months earlier.

"We've a beautiful girl," my wife said. A smile wavered at the edges of her lips.

"A girl," I breathed. I perched on the edge of the mattress, tried to disturb my girls as little as possible. "A daughter." Astrith's nod was barely perceptible. "May I?" I asked, then scooped the bundle into my arms before my wife had a chance to respond.

The baby was much smaller than I'd expected. Her skin was also bluer than seemed normal. She was so tightly swaddled all that was visible was her head, which was topped with a shock of black fuzz. Full lips, tiny nose, two delicate ears, two puffy eyes. Each feature appeared in its proper place. Her eyes were closed for the most part, but she'd peeked at me long enough to show off the deep brown of her irises. Flecked with gold, just like my mother's. "She's stunning," I whispered.

Katla wound through my legs, just like Sorokin used to, and meowed to get my attention. "Look, Katla," I said, crouching down to the cat. "A perfect little sister for you." But I felt uneasy as I said it. The cat recoiled at the sight of my daughter; she swatted at the baby with claws extended. The girl didn't react in the slightest. Her breathing shallowed.

"Something's wrong," I said to Astrith. "This infant is too cold."

Tears spilled over my wife's pale cheeks, but she remained silent.

"We must get the midwives, get them back here to fix her—"

Astrith shook her head. "They know she's not right, Tomaken. Why else would they have summoned you? You know a husband doesn't see his child until it's been named."

I'd forgotten, in my excitement.

"You are here to say goodbye, nothing more," she said.

"No," I replied. "No," as the baby grew still. "Nothing's wrong with her, Breath of My Heart. All she needs is to get some fresh air.' I chuckled, tried to keep my voice even as I scoured the room for ingredients. "I've told you not to keep your stove so warm,"— *there's blood*, grabbing a handful of soaked rags from the bowls— "and in the middle of summer no less,"—*there's hair*, snatching a few inky strands from my wife's bone-handled brush—"but I'm sure you'll learn these things,"—*there's dirt aplenty outside*— "when you've had more time as a mother."

All I need now, I thought, *is an appropriate vessel . . .*

The cat yowled as I stepped on her tail. I smiled, shook my head at her. "Come here, my Katla. We're going for a little walk."

All eyes were averted as I exited the caravan. Yet even a blind man would have seen the burden I carried, would have noticed the speed with which I left the enclosure of our camp. Not many would have paid attention to the cat-shaped flicker of darkness at my heels, or would have thought it unusual if they had. No one stopped me as I blended in with the shadows; it was only fitting I bury the child before its spirit grew too accustomed to the warmth of our homes, the taste of our breath.

And I had every intention of putting my girl in the earth, but none of leaving her there.

First, I took her to the river where the waters thrummed like ancestral voices. I immersed my daughter, ridding all traces of her human birth. Then I gathered my supplies in one arm, the baby and Katla in the other. The cat fought against me until I pinned her to my side, trapped her small head in my large hand; she wailed like a newborn, which I took as a good sign. I hoped the fight would stay in her until it was needed most.

I returned to the site of my afternoon's toils. Without hesitation, I dropped the baby and accompanying magics into the freshly turned earth, which was rich brown and smelled of horse dung. I lifted the cat up, looked her straight in the eyes: they were as vibrant an emerald as her dam's had been. "Thank you, my Katla," I said—and with a silent prayer for the Meito to send a strong spirit, I snapped the cat's neck and buried her in the same pit as my daughter.

I could have left it there, and almost did. One final element was needed, to quicken the spell, but I didn't think I had the will to provide it. *If it took this long to work the proper way*, I thought, *there's no chance it's going to work now*. My mind made up, I turned toward the river, ready to cleanse myself of the night's events. To wash everything away.

I'd gone no more than three steps when a picture of Astrith, exhausted and probably barren, flitted across my mind. It was for her I was doing this. For her, and my heir. I walked back to the mound of tamped dirt, used the spade handle to drill a deep hole in its centre. Bile rose in the back of my throat. I took a deep breath, let the chill breeze soothe me. Exhaling, I reminded myself that Tomaken is no stumbler. I knelt, not to bury my girl but to bring her back.

Almost a fortnight had passed since I'd had a night visit with my wife; it wasn't long before my stroking hand coaxed warm spurts of semen onto the earth. There was no pleasure in this act, only need. When my racing pulse slowed, I pulled up my trousers, watched my seed seep into the ground, then cried until my head pounded.

• • •

Astrith didn't question where I'd found our green-eyed daughter. She didn't mention the filth I'd carried into the room on my boots, merely brushed crumbs of dirt off our wriggling infant as I placed her on the bed. We'd been married long enough now for her to know my secrets. To know what I was capable of doing. I slipped into bed beside her in the grey twilight that masquerades as daybreak, and tucked the girl snugly between us.

"We'll have to give her a name," Astrith said. It was clear from my wife's expression that she was already besotted. "Before we can introduce her to the rest of the clan."

"Her name is Katla," I said. "You'll find she won't answer to anything else."

Astrith looked at me for a moment too long, but didn't say anything. My strong wife, always proving I was lucky to love her.

I kissed her full on the lips then, as I hadn't done in weeks. She responded in kind, though we were both so exhausted our mouths soon parted. I ran my finger along her smooth brow, traced the line of her high cheekbones, then cradled her square jaw in my palm. "Get some rest," I said. Her contented smile was a welcome pressure against my hand. "We'll give our Katla the introduction she deserves when the rooster has properly greeted morning."

I looked down at Katla as Astrith slept. The baby was restless, her eyes wide open. She gave off an incredible heat. In my fatigue, I thought I saw her frown as if concentrating. Darkness pooled around her head, making her hair appear longer than it had been when we were outside. The air seemed to shimmer around her; in my mind I chastised my wife for insisting on stoking the fire so fervently. But the coals had been banked hours ago.

Katla's struggles subsided and with them my worries. My head was leaden with weariness, so I laid it on the edge of Astrith's pillow, telling myself I'd hear the cock's crow soon enough. I just needed to rest my eyes.

The sun was well above the horizon, her rusty light streaming through the caravan's west-facing windows, when I was woken by Astrith's insistent shaking. I blinked to clear away the sleep, rolled over to discover that Katla was no longer on the bed beside me.

"What's wrong?" I asked, instantly awake. "What's wrong with the baby?"

Astrith clucked her tongue at me, like a practised mother already. Her voice wasn't nearly so assured. "Nothing's wrong, Tomaken. Not really. It's just . . . Do you think it's possible for a child to be *too* healthy?"

As she stepped aside I got a clear view of the cradle. I didn't have to ask what she meant.

Katla was sitting up.

My daughter blinked at me as I met her gaze—her knowing, flashing green gaze. She stretched her mouth wide in a yawn. Her gums, glistening with dribble, were studded with the tips of white teeth.

My stomach clenched as I looked at the child I'd created. Less than a day on this earth, and already more robust than my brother's two-year-old son. I knew the colour was draining from my tanned face: I could tell this by the look of fear on my wife's.

"Perhaps it's always this way," I said, sitting up, my mind racing. "Growth-spurts aren't uncommon—"

A knock at the door interrupted my flawed explanations.

"I've brought some dried curds for you, Tomaken." My mother's scratchy voice barely penetrated the wagon's thick panelling. Words must be whispered around a house of the dead, for fear of calling the spirit's attention before it reaches the ghost fields. "And some *bantan* for Astrith, to help her regain her strength.' I tapped three times on the wall, a sign of thanks that wouldn't invite further conversation.

I waited until the sound of my mother's shuffling bootsteps had moved beyond earshot before I dared speak again. "Do you think she heard us?"

Astrith ignored the question, silenced me with a sharp gesture. "We mustn't introduce Katla like this."

I got out of bed, paced over to the cradle, took Katla up in my arms. She was heavy, and smelled of sour milk. Her skin was pale to the point of translucence. And she was enchanting, no matter her size.

"But what if she cries?" I asked. "What will we do with the clothes she soils? They'll know she's here eventually, and I'd rather not enrage the ancestors. Not when we've become a real family at last."

My wife, always sensible, shook her head. "The clan won't see her now, not without suspecting—as we do, My Breath—that the Meito are playing tricks with us."

Once again I looked at my daughter, knowing full well it wasn't the guardians who were responsible. Not this time.

"Give me a day to think," I said. I pressed a kiss on my wife's forehead and the child into her arms. "Just keep her quiet until I return."

• • •

I avoided my kin as I left Astrith's caravan. Head down, I skirted the clearing and broke a new path through the forest. Walking would do me good; it clears the mind, gives a man the distance he needs to think. The air was still, pungent with the scent of damp leaves. Fresh, with an undertone of rot. I felt my blood pumping as I blazed the trail, filling me with good energy, releasing the bad.

My face, chest, armpits, crotch all grew moist with sweat—still I walked. Over the river, whispering now that it was day; through the copse of silver birch, where I gathered strips of bark for luck; past the sentinel pines whose needles seemed tipped with flames, silhouetted against the setting sun; until the moon had risen high overhead, burnishing leaves and branches and animal eyes with silver.

My pulse throbbed in my ears as I emerged on the other side of the woods. The plains stretched out before me, a vast sea of grey and black. Long blades of sweet-grass undulated in an unfelt wind; the ancestors busily moved from place to place, shifting grasses the only sign of their passing. Hours of walking had taken me far away from my problem, but no closer to a solution. I crouched down, caught my breath, and dug my fingers into the earth.

The grasses waved in a hypnotic rhythm. Night predators rustled in the undergrowth behind me. Clouds streamed past the moon, strobing its soft light. Treetops swayed, shushed. My heartbeat slowed, evened out. Loose soil streamed through my fingers. The night was filled with echoes of the ancestors' busy feet.

I must have dozed, then. A waking sleep in which time passed but I remained frozen, eyes open. A kestrel swooped down before me; the yellow ring around her eyes, the bright cere of her beak, and her dangerous feet were luminous in the waning moonlight. In a flash, she snatched a vole, who had innocently poked his head out of the ground not two feet in front of me. Her shrill cry of triumph shook me out of my stupor, set my heart pounding once more.

As I stood, my joints stiff and aching, my boots covered in dew, I noticed a russet feather sticking up out of the earth where the kestrel had made her kill. Smiling, I plucked it like a flower. The Meito had given me a sign—and signs, unlike the swift growth of cat-infants, could easily be deciphered.

I would consult with Temudzhin, the Meito's interpreter. My smile broadened. Clutching the feather tightly in my fist, I turned back to the woods, my heart and footsteps light.

• • •

They did not remain so for long.

I arrived back at our encampment by mid-afternoon, only to notice a flattened patch of grass where Temudzhin's wagon and supply tent should have been. My cousin, Chuluun, walked past as I stood gaping at the deep ruts Temudzhin's caravan had left in the ground. Chuluun bowed his head, touched fingers to brow by way of greeting.

"How long has he been gone?" I asked, pointing at the white scattering of Temudzhin's fire, noticing new shoots of grass already sprouting where the tent had been staked. His departure was clearly not recent.

"Four sunrises ago," Chuluun replied. "The Pasha wanted an audience with him before the autumn markets get too hectic." Chuluun looked up at the sky, gauging the sun's path. "If his journey has gone smoothly, he shouldn't be too long in reaching Zhureem Ordon."

I thanked my cousin, then headed for Astrith's wagon. If anything, my heart was heavier now than it had been yesterday. Even if I left right away, I'd never catch Temudzhin before he ascended the Pasha's mountain, before he passed the palace's bronze gates. And if I tried, there was no doubt the clan would discover Katla before my return. They would see what I'd done, and they would banish me for it. It's one thing to heal a wounded yak, to encourage horses to stud or to provide supplies from next to nothing—it was another thing altogether to invite ghosts into our community and to make one my heir.

Astrith opened the caravan's door before my foot had made contact with the bottom step. She looked as frantic as I felt.

"Hurry, Tomaken," she whispered. "Get inside."

Her hands were shaking, but still she closed the door gently to avoid waking the child curled up on our bed. And she was a child now, no longer an infant. One who didn't know better would think she was a girl of four or five years. Her hair was glossy, long and black, just like her namesake's. Astrith had tied it back with red ribbons, as was custom for girls of that age. The tips of the ribbons were frayed and wet; Katla was chewing one in her sleep. She was wrapped in one of my wife's old shifts, which was too big by far. Her pale shoulders and long, sinewy legs were exposed but Katla didn't seem to mind the cold. A soft rumble, like purring, escaped her throat as she exhaled.

"Get rid of it," Astrith snapped. "We can't care for it, Tomaken. I can't."

I looked at my wife, my mouth pressed firmly shut.

"Get rid of it," she repeated.

I breathed out slowly. Closed my eyes. A plan started to form in my mind.

Four days to reach the Pasha's markets. Four days to send a bird ahead, to organise an audience with my lord. Four days for the girl to grow.

I opened my eyes again, and nodded.

• • •

No bride would ever be as pure as my Katla. She had never been stained with moon blood; she had hardly yet learned to speak. *This last trait alone will increase her value*, I thought.

My sturdy horse seemed delighted to be free of the wagon's halter. He sped us across hills, his footing sure and steadfast as wooded knolls grew into stony mountains. I gave him free rein, adjusting his course only when his exuberance threatened to lead us away from the Pasha's territory. The horse's unshod hooves were swift; we reached Yangjugol, the valley curving around the cliff-top palace, by the time Katla had stretched into a beautiful girl of twelve. I had hoped she would've reached sixteen after four days' time; that her hips and breasts would have become more pronounced. Softer and more enticingly full.

But my horse was too fleet—we'd arrived along with the third sunrise, carried on gusts of wintry mountain air—and Katla's growth spurts were erratic and slowing. Still, I had no doubt she would appeal to my lord. The transaction would be brief; she would be purchased instantly. I would be back on my horse before the ache of three days' riding had had a chance to leave my legs.

As we rode through the valley, I realised a few dozen merchants must've had the same idea as me: reach Yangjugol early enough to prise the fattest coins from our Pasha's tight grasp, make a profit before the chill settled in too securely, leave before the autumn markets began in earnest. All the men, regardless of clan or age, stopped their work as we passed. Openly stared at Katla, sitting in the saddle before me. In their place, I too would have stared.

Several stalls had already been erected in the shadow of Zhureem Ordon. The palace's blood-red rooftops and peaked gables were barely visible from the mountain's base, hidden as they were behind a high impenetrable wall. A road switch-backed up the mountain face, ending in a closed bronze gate; it would take us more than a few hours' hard walking to reach it.

I tethered my horse by the snow leopards' enclosure, which stood taller than the height of two men and, as far as I could see, ran the length of the mountain. These great felines were the Pasha's pride, his favourite possessions; and like all treasures, kept under lock and key. I had no fondness for leopards. Their crystal blue eyes were too knowing, like they'd seen my misdeeds and were only keeping silent to torment me. I slapped Katla's hand when she looked ready to reach through the cage's evenly spaced bars. She blinked, but did not cry out as a normal child would. Her hand fell limply to her side.

"She's a frigid little thing isn't she, Tomaken?"

"Bitter words spoil beauty," I replied, watching Setseh and the Pasha's two other wives approach. "You should bite your tongue before it curdles."

Setseh's hair was streaked with grey, pulled back from her lined face in a loose horse-tail. As first wife, she had earned the silk scarves draped over her burgundy woollens, and poking out of the basket she carried. She had also earned her sharp tongue. Yarmaa and Dzhol walked two paces behind her; the twins had tinted their hair since I saw them last, it was now the hue of dried henna. The colour didn't become them. The wives' skirts flapped in the valley's katabatic winds, unhindered by buckles or pride. Their soft cotton shirts gaped unrestrained, the effect too familiar to be tempting. They knew men lusted not for women they had already enjoyed, but for those who were yet unexplored. Even so, they regularly came down to Yangjugol, and strutted around the merchants as if they were still girls of eighteen.

"And how will you be using your tongue today, Tomaken?" Setseh asked. She bent down and placed the basket near the snow leopards' enclosure. "As warrior? Pauper? Supplicant?" She took strips of dried ox-meat out of the basket, slipped them through the bars as she spoke.

I stepped away from the cage as the leopards wrestled over these morsels, their saliva flying in gobbets, their breath rank.

"I approach our lord as a father," I said. "And as a merchant."

Setseh hissed as Katla snatched a strip of meat out of the basket and began nibbling on it. She slapped the girl's face and hands until they were red. Katla dropped the titbit, but continued to lick the salt from her fingers.

"Are you an imbecile, girl? Stealing from the Pasha's pride?" Yarmaa and Dzhol snorted as Katla's brow furrowed in confusion. "Get this creature out of my sight!"

I gathered Katla into my arms, more to steady myself than to comfort her. She didn't seem disturbed in the least by Setseh's anger. But the first wife's disdain reassured me. The wives always turned vicious when the Pasha was ready to add to their number: Setseh had been unbearable when Yarmaa arrived; and the pair of them were fit to be tied when Dzhol followed her sister to Zhureem Ordon. Looking now at the flush in their weathered faces, I couldn't help but think it was my Katla's icy skin that infuriated them. So translucent, so bruisable, so different from their own brash colouring. Their hides had been worn tough with use, like well-ridden stallions. My Katla wasn't yet broken in. She would be the Pasha's youngest wife yet. The most tender. The most disconcerting.

. . .

"One condition," I said, "and my little daughter will be yours."

The Pasha stood proudly in the fortress's reception hall. A silk vest stretched over his thick robes, a mink hat topped his grey head. He stroked the wealthy expanse of his belly with jewel-encrusted fingers and stared out the window, surveying the lands his father had conquered. I was forced to speak to his back.

"You may buy her now," I informed him, "but you may not enjoy her until she has had her first bloods." It was perhaps an arbitrary rule, but necessary. Prohibition makes all purchases more enticing, and I wanted to be sure the Pasha would bite. It would do none of us any good, seeing her ravished and left unbought. I could not take her home again.

I bowed my head as I spoke, wrapped Katla in my finest embroidered cloak, fastened its toggles tight beneath her chin. My hand lingered there, enjoying her warmth after our cold trek up the mountain, until her unflinching green gaze made me shiver. The Pasha turned at that moment and caught the gesture. He stood with one eyebrow raised.

Let him think I yearn for her, I thought. *That this restriction springs from lust instead of fear. He can think what he likes. Just so long as he believes my act, and takes her. This creature will not be Tomaken's heir.*

"Let me inspect the girl more closely," he said.

Never had a prospective bride approached the Pasha with such a sinuous gait. She hadn't done it intentionally, of that I am sure; but if he hadn't been interested before, my lord certainly was now. He appraised my Katla—by all accounts a chieftain's daughter, a warrior's daughter—as he would the treasures we men had won for him in the wars. Like porcelain or rice, leather saddlebags, or snow leopard tails like the three dangling limply on his banner above the hall's great fireplace. But my Katla was more precious to him than cinnamon, than jade, than ivory.

Good girl, I thought. I was forced to look out the window, beyond the Pasha's bulk. The price I got would be lower if my lord saw me smile.

The forest was a dark smudge at the edge of my vision, sketched beyond the vast valley aproning out before us. Its dense foliage and closely-packed trees harboured my clan, kept them hidden in the empire's margins. I yearned to be back with them, for this deal to be done. The clan could use the profit Katla's body would gain for us. And Astrith and I could use some peace.

My lord wanted to keep Katla out of any other man's reach, to balance her firmly on the tip of his tower. I knew this the moment his eyes widened at the sight of her. His coffers were full; his bed empty. He had no use for haggard wives.

So he agreed to my condition.

• • •

Flurries of snow fell, carried dusk in their wake, as I placed the heavy purse in my saddlebag. The horse was restless, eager to be on the road and away from the mountain's chill climate. I planned to ride through the night, taking rest only when I couldn't avoid it. The summer snows wouldn't last, but their arrival was a harbinger of worse times to come. I was anxious to be on my way; to be back in Astrith's stifling caravan, with her arms and legs wrapped around me. Perhaps there was time yet, to earn a child. To replace Katla. To forget her.

"Aren't you forgetting something?"

Setseh's voice was shrill. Her hand was gripped tightly around the neck of Katla's cloak. She dragged the girl behind her, toward me.

"You do us no favours, Tomaken. Leaving such trash behind." She pushed the girl in the back, knocked her to the ground at my feet. "Take her. Or else let the Meito take you."

I bent to help Katla stand; took a pinch of earth between my fingertips and scattered it to the winds to counteract the first wife's curse. "I wouldn't let your husband hear such profanity," I said, brushing Katla off. "You of all people should know what the Meito do to those who curse the Pasha's wife."

Yarmaa and Dzhol looked at each other, then at Setseh. As one, the three women approached my Katla, began fussing with her hair, straightening her cloak, smoothing the thin shift she wore beneath it.

"It is done then, is it?"

I nodded and mounted my horse. The sky was growing increasingly dark. I prayed the storm would hold until I was well beyond the Pasha's territory.

Setseh pulled Katla close, placed a gloved hand on her shoulder. She kept her gaze locked on mine and said, "Well, well, little wife. Be sure you lie still when our husband comes to you, else you will feel the pain of his knife."

"A knife in your heart," Yarmaa said, undoing and taking the girl's cloak, poking her slight chest. "To accompany the plunge of his shaft down below." Dzhol smiled, and giggled. Third wives are of little use for much else.

In this way the women tried to taunt me, as if I were a true father. As if I cared what happened to Katla, as if I cared that they threatened her. I was glad to be rid of her, glad to avoid seeing her grow any older. Katla, too, seemed undisturbed. A hint of pink tipped her nose, the ends of her fingers. She held her head high while the women hissed and cooed in her ears. She was rose-coloured, but not afraid.

The wives were oblivious to the sound of the Pasha's stately footsteps crunching down the road to Yangjugol. His pace was not hurried but not slow. He descended from Zhureem Ordon with controlled anticipation. Katla watched silently as her new husband slapped his first wife, then tossed her aside like gnawed bones. She did not flinch when Setseh's head clashed against metal bars, nor when Yarmaa and Dzhol began whimpering. She blinked when his voice boomed across the valley, announcing his claim. Declaring her his property, his wife.

A puff of relief escaped my lips, dispersed into the twilight.

She was his. No longer my Katla, no longer my concern. His.

The bitter rattle of iron on metal told me I was mistaken to relax so soon. I steered my mount around, just in time to see Setseh throwing open the door to the snow leopards' cage. There was no time for her to scurry out of the way before they sprang; the gleam in her eye revealed that safety came second to her revenge. One leopard wrapped its teeth around the first wife's throat, silencing her venomous words. Years of captivity hadn't slowed the Pasha's pets in the least. Their movements were lithe and swift.

The scant crowd of merchants scattered with fear, several running without being chased. These men were not warriors: they fled like selfish children, saving themselves with no thought for their lord's plight. The Pasha was left to confront a muscular leopard with no army to support him. My lord wielded nothing more than a belt, which he lashed about like a whip. He fought bravely, even when a second cat slinked up behind him and took a great swipe at his hamstrings. A trio of leopards sped toward me; my horse reared but did not unseat me. His nimble hooves danced around slashing paws, striking teeth. He edged us closer to Katla, away from the road. The Pasha now lay wounded at her side, his leg a mess of blood and ligaments. She paid him no attention. Great cats appeared and disappeared in the thinning crowd—she followed them with her eyes.

Her gaze caught mine just as the leopard pounced. The sky twisted. The earth rushed up to meet me. My teeth crashed together, blood poured from my nose. I inhaled in sharp gasps. I looked at my horse, splayed on the ground, his back snapped. Saw my leg twisted in the stirrup, bent at an unnatural angle. I smelled the leopard's stale breath before I felt its paws on my back. Without meaning to, I moaned. Death in battle is honourable; it should not be feared. But only shame can come from a death such as this.

My head snapped up as I heard the soft tread of footsteps. Katla crouched down before me, placed her hand on my head, met the leopard's gaze evenly. I felt the weight of his forelegs leave my back. He snorted, drew closer to the girl I had made. His pale eyes were a shade darker than Katla's; his composure rivalled a king's. A low growl rumbled from his soft, white throat. There was no threat of a roar from one such as him. It was merely a purr.

She stroked my hair as the leopard coiled its long tail around her. Threaded it around her legs, beneath the thin cloth of her shift. His purrs intensified as he flicked his tail, in and out. Katla's fingers spasmed, dug into my scalp—then went still for a moment. She draped her other arm around the thick fur of the great feline's neck, then resumed gently patting my head. She licked the leopard's cheek, the dark rosettes of his pelt round shadows beneath her wet tongue. Her gaze was fierce, unflinching, as she threw her leg over his back, pulled herself up, away from me. The chaos surrounding us seemed muted and unimportant. She looked down at her steed, then at me. It was the only time I'd see her smile.

The tip of the leopard's tail trailed behind them as they left the clearing together, streaking the snow with moist dirt instead of blood. I watched them blend into the forest, stealthy as only cats can be, blinking as tears filled my eyes.

I could keep clouds at bay with a glance and a well-spoken word. I could outwit a Pasha and survive his snow leopards' attacks. I would see love in my wife's face until the end of my days and, Meitoshi willing, she would see the same. My clan would be strong with men; warriors and traders who would outlive and thrive without me. But only their names would be recorded in our people's annals; their names and their children's. Not mine. The bravest, the strongest, the wiliest clan-child would steal my title, gain control of our family. It was settled the moment Katla and her mate disappeared into the shadows. I knew then, as I had known from the moment I made her: no matter how mighty my deeds or how valiant, I would only ever be remembered as the master of dust and dirt.

• • • • • • • • • • •

FEAST OR FAMINE

GARY KEMBLE

Don never realised how good a cinder-block wall could taste.

Another little tidbit for his front-page exclusive, or his book, if they ever got out of this. Rick, the photographer, was over by the bunker's steel door, licking the puddle oozing underneath it. They'd tossed a coin to decide who got first go at the puddle. Rick won.

The bastard.

Don pressed his swollen tongue against the cool brick. All around them, they could hear the maddening gurgle of trickling water. He should have been thankful. Sikaram mountain, west of Kabul, was normally frozen solid in February, which would have meant no water trickling in under the doorway or down the walls. Without this unseasonable warmth, he would have been dead rather than just bitching about having to lick a wall.

It was a fortnight since they left Azram in Abdul's ancient Ford truck, on their way to an exclusive interview with one of Afghanistan's most feared warlords. Abdul phoned them ten minutes before pulling up outside the fleapit hotel they were staying in. No-one knew where they were.

A fortnight since that terrifying ride up the winding road that snaked around Sikaram, in the foothills of the Himalayas. Countless buses had plunged off that very goat track while Allah was looking the other way.

A fortnight since they followed Abdul down the two steps into the bunker, buried in the side of the mountain. Abdul promised to return with Marco, leader of the Afghan chapter of the Al-Aqsa

Terror Brigades. The press pass hanging around Don's neck hadn't seemed like such a powerful amulet waiting in that bloodstained death room, with the green and white banner hanging on one wall, a video camera poised to capture some new atrocity. And the Butcher of Kabul was on his way, with his trademark cigar cutter and Desert Eagle pistol, both souvenired from a US General who strayed too close to the badlands. Suddenly, it had seemed insane trying to interview a man whose regard for human life stretched only as far as his warped interpretation of the Koran. This man had killed journalists—Don had seen the video.

Now weak with hunger, Don would welcome him with open arms.

Hold his hands out, laugh at the meaty snickety-snick of steel slicing through flesh, bone, and sinew. Gobble his own fingers with relish and praise Allah as he dropped to his knees and waited for the .44-calibre hollow-point. Death by bullet would be a blessing right now.

After Abdul left, Don had tried the door—just out of interest—and it was definitely locked, secured with a heavy duty deadbolt.

It was thirteen days since the avalanche hit and the power went out. They hid under the table, clutching each other, praying the snow would smash the bunker open but somehow leave them alive.

For his part, Don knew what he'd do. Run back to Azrow, catch the next donkey back to Kabul, a white-knuckle DC-9 to Lahore, then home via London to Brisbane, where he'd appear on radio talk shows and start writing his memoirs: Afghanistan—A Coward's Tale. If Rick still wanted the story, he could wait for Marco alone and do a photo spread. But Don didn't think that would be the case. He figured, after all they'd gone through, he would be booking a donkey for two.

The bunker held. The lights flickered out and the roof groaned under the weight of the snow—but it held. It was clearly a Grade-A insurgent hideout, endorsed by Osama bin Laden himself. The rumbling subsided, and in the darkness, in that moment of silence, Don thought he'd go insane. Then Rick screamed a string of expletives and Don knew they were still alive. He wasn't sure how he felt about that.

They stumbled around in the dark, looking for things they'd seen while the lights were still on. There were candles and matches, a big bag of road salt by the door, and a cheap transistor radio that broadcast nothing but static and the occasional burst of traditional Pakistani music. They lit a candle and stared at each other over the table, trying to make a joke of it all.

It was twelve days since the last of their food—a half-melted Mars bar Rick had in his jacket pocket—disappeared. They tossed a coin to decide who got the first bite. And then when it was gone, Rick had to go and mention that Stephen King story—"Survivor Type"—the one where a doctor is trapped on a desert island and decides to eat himself. Good thing we're not doctors, Don had joked. But it stayed with him. Plump, juicy flesh.

They took turns kicking the steel door with their hiking boots.

Each blow produced a low, solid thump. Maybe they would've had better luck before the avalanche when they were still strong.

And then ten days of licking a wall, resting, and praying for someone to find them. Don's stomach was a shrivelled sack. It didn't even grumble any more. Don missed the grumbling. It was a sign he was still alive. He tried to focus on his wall, but his mind rebelled, sending him visions of thick, bloody steaks, French fries coated in chicken salt, and fat fingers, falling from Marco's cigar cutter. He pushed the thought away but his mouth kept watering.

He turned, slumped back against the wall, and watched Rick lapping up water. The table was covered in wax, the last candle burning down to the stub. The thought of being trapped in here in the dark would've terrified him a week ago. Now he was too frail for terror. Mild apprehension was the best he could muster.

"Do you reckon he's coming back?" Don said.

Rick turned, face wet and shiny. He sat beside the door, all eyes and teeth. Concentration camp chic.

"Why bother?"

"Maybe he really wants to be in The Daily?" Don said, then laughed. A low chuckle, conserving energy.

Rick went back to his puddle.

Some time later, the candle guttered and the last of the wax dripped off the table edge. Don had been hoping for some scrap of light, a grey beam telling them they weren't buried that deep, that maybe they had some hope. So he waited, but the darkness was an impenetrable shroud. He was taunted by visions of Marco in that video, hostage with duct tape over his mouth, the cigar cutter, fingers dropping to the floor. Plump, juicy fingers. Drool slipped over his bottom lip, down his chin. He let it go. Who was he keeping up appearances for now?

Time passed. Maybe minutes, maybe hours or days. Outside, the infuriating cascade of melting snow continued. The pool of water under the door got big enough to share. Thank God for global warming.

Don pushed himself up from the puddle. "I can't stop thinking about it."

"What?"

"That story. The Stephen King story."

" 'Survivor Type'?"

"Yeah."

Don waited, expecting Rick to make some pre-emptive strike, pooh-poohing the idea before he'd even voiced it. But he didn't.

"We're not surgeons. But we could tear up the banner for tourniquets, use the road salt to stem the blood flow," Don said.

"Oh, Jesus."

"I'd eat myself, but we don't have a knife. I can't bear the thought of biting into my own flesh."

"Oh, Jesus."

"Think of it this way. If we survive, you'll live off this story for the rest of your life. They'll probably make a movie about it."

There was a long pause. Don thought Rick had fallen asleep. But eventually, he spoke.

"How . . . how to we decide who goes first?"

"The usual way."

More silence, then the noise of Rick fishing the coin out of his top pocket. Don got a match ready.

"Call," Rick said. The coin whistled briefly through the darkness, before the slap of flesh on flesh.

"Heads."

Don lit the match as Rick pulled his hand away. Tails.

"Shit."

By match light, they tore the Islamist banner into strips, and moved everything they would need beside the door.

"Arm or leg?" Rick said.

"Leg. We can hobble out of here on one leg, but we need our arms."

Don pulled his pants off, then sat on them on the cold floor.

Together, they tied a tourniquet around the top of his leg, and readied some salt and a makeshift bandage. And then they were quiet again.

Don's breath rasped in time with the throbbing in his leg.

"Are you ready?" Rick said.

"No. But do it anyway."

Don squeezed his eyes shut—a childhood habit useless in the pitch black. There was a rumbling noise—so low that, at first, he thought he was imagining it. He felt Rick's hands against his leg, then lips and teeth.

"Wait!"

Rick pulled away. They could both hear it now. The bunker vibrated.

"Holy shit!" Don said. "It's the truck!"

But it wasn't. The noise grew louder and louder, until the bunker rattled with the force of it. Another avalanche. The two men embraced, swearing and calling on a God neither really believed in. The flood of snow passed overhead and the darkness and silence seemed even more impenetrable. They peered around, hoping for some ray of light, a glimmer of hope, but the darkness was unbroken.

"Go on, then," Don said. "Make it quick."

The hands grabbed his leg again, this time more forcefully. Lips pressed against his flesh and then there was an explosion of pain, bright red on black. Don let fly with a torrent of curses, each one bouncing back off the bunker walls. He pressed a hand to his leg and felt the wound, blood pulsing slowly. He could hear Rick gagging.

"Don't you spew, you bastard. The damage is done," he said.

Don heard hands slide against dusty concrete, then felt a new bloom of agony as Rick thrust salt into his wound. He greyed out, and when he came to his leg was throbbing again, red pulsing through his eyeballs. Rick panted in the darkness.

"I guess it's your turn now," he said.

"Uh-huh."

Don waited until Rick was ready and then lowered his face to the plump thigh. He smelt sweat and piss; Rick's leg hairs tickled his lips. He opened his mouth as wide as he could and visualised a rump steak at the Brekkie Creek Hotel, rare and bloody, just the way he liked it. He bit down and tasted flesh. Warm blood pumped over his face, as Rick's abuse battered his eardrums. He resisted the urge to jerk away, instead sucking the blood into his mouth and swallowing.

No point letting good food go to waste, he thought, and hysteria bubbled at the back of his mind.

Don rolled to one side, panting, enjoying the surge of energy the fresh blood was already providing. After a moment, he slid his hands around on the floor, looking for the bag of salt. He grabbed a handful, shoved it into Rick's wound. Rick screamed. Don was glad.

Now you know what it feels like, you prick.

They spent what felt like hours telling each other they'd done the right thing, that it was their only hope of survival, but the lie was bitter on Don's tongue. There was always a choice. Brave men chose to die. He knew that if he survived, he would never purge himself of that strangely exotic flavour. He was stained.

Guilt subsided, hunger filled the void. They feasted, with no way of knowing how much closer to rescue—if any—they were edging.

They told each other how vile it was to eat another living being's flesh. But in truth, Don enjoyed it this time. Like sheep's brains or bird nest soup, it was only disgusting because we told ourselves it should be. Any qualms he earlier had were quieted by the coppery tang of blood.

Rick cried a lot. He prayed a lot. Rick knew more prayers than Don would have given him credit for. Catholic education? It dawned on Don that he didn't really know this man at all, although they'd worked together many times. Over the years, they'd swapped war stories, chatted about the here and now, but never once got personal.

Rick was a stranger, getting stranger by the minute. A blank slab of meat. Don's meal ticket.

"What if God's punishing us?" Rick said. "What if this is a test? What if each bite we take dooms us to another week in here?"

Don sighed. "What if we're already dead?" he said. Darkness cloaked his smile. "What if this is purgatory."

Rick fell silent. Don could smell the waves of fear coming off the photojournalist. He waited a heartbeat.

"Dinner time," he said.

"Don't call it that!"

"Calm down. You know stress causes meat to toughen up?"

"Don!" He was crying again now.

"Keep you pants on. Or off, as it were."

Don waited for Rick to remove his bandage, then crawled across the floor. His own wound pulsed in sympathy. What they were doing was wrong; Rick was right about that. But not because of the snapper's new-found morality. It was wrong because they couldn't sustain each other indefinitely. No such thing as perpetual motion.

All they were doing was lining their bellies with tainted meat.

Despite the salt, Rick's wound smelled bad. Don chose a new cut, further down the thigh. He latched on then snapped his head to one side, guzzling blood, relishing the screams. When he was done, he flopped back, savouring the meat, then wiped his mouth and licked the blood off his hand. He waited until Rick's sobs had died down.

"Your wound doesn't smell too good, Ricky-boy," he said.

"No shit."

"I think we should take a look at it."

"And how do you propose we do that?"

"Your camera. We can take a look on the screen. I'm amazed you didn't think of it earlier."

"You're sick."

"No, but you might be if we don't take a look at that wound. Where's the camera?"

"You can't have it."

Don threw himself onto the photographer, hands sliding around on the dusty cement, looking for the camera. Rick got to it first, but Don easily snatched it away from him.

"Please, Don. Don't."

"Don't be such a baby."

Don fumbled for the on switch. A metallic chime sounded.

"Say 'flesh'," Don said, and pressed the shutter release.

Both men cried out at the sudden shock of light. Don blinked away the after-image then peered at the small LCD screen on the back of the camera. It shocked him. Rick's gaunt face, mouth caked in dried blood. Clothes tattered and grimy. He aimed the camera down at the leg this time, shielded his eyes and hit the button again.

The wound was a stomach-churning mix of bloodied salt, white flesh, and yellow pus. It was turning dark around the edges. Don sucked in breath between his teeth.

"Doesn't look too good," he said.

Rick turned away. "I don't want to see."

Don shoved the camera at him, but he covered his face. He was crying again.

"Baby. C'mon—it's your turn to eat."

"I don't want to."

"It's your turn."

"I can't."

Don couldn't force Rick to eat. Therefore, Rick would die. There was no point waiting for him to wither away.

Don switched the camera off, then hefted it in his hand. He climbed onto Rick's lap.

"Don?"

Don slammed the camera into Rick's upturned face. Blood splashed onto Don's grinning teeth. Rick cried out, and the journalist hit him again, the lens snapping off with the force of the impact. Rick's hands came up and Don batted them away. On the third strike, the camera body split in two. He cast it to one side and grabbed Rick around the throat.

"Here's a prayer for you. For what I am about to receive . . ."

He smashed Rick's head against the bunker wall.

". . . I am truly, truly grateful . . ."

Don smacked Rick's head against the wall again, and felt blood and something meatier sliding over his hands.

". . . Amen."

Don fell on Rick, licking the blood from his ruined face. None of this one bite at a time crap, he thought, and feasted properly. When his belly was full he rolled up next to his partner and slept.

Don woke in the eternal darkness, belly full, face sticky with gore.

For a moment, he thought he heard Rick praying, then remembered

Rick was dead. But still . . .

Our father in heaven . . .

"Rick?"

His fingers crawled along the floor, searching for Rick's body. At first, he couldn't find it and panic gripped him. He imagined Rick sitting on the table, feet swinging, leering down at him. Then he touched something cold and sticky and realised he'd just rolled away from the body in his sleep. He explored the corpse, trying to figure out which bit was which. It took a while, but eventually he found the empty eye sockets and then the mouth. He held his hand against the smashed ruins of teeth until he was satisfied there was no talking or breathing going on. He drifted back to sleep with his head on Rick's chest.

Rick spoke to him often as Don stripped the body clean. Prayers for his soul, mostly. But sometimes, he'd be angry and lay some of that vengeful God shit on Don.

"If God hates me, why am I still alive?" Don spat back.

He paused, realising he hadn't asked, "If there is a God, why am I still alive?" But he let it go. Rick was silent, and that was the main thing.

Rick sulked for what could have been days, but then again, may have been hours or minutes or seconds. Don gnawed on a bone, then paused. Had imagined it? No, there it was. A low rumbling sound, way off in the distance. Not another avalanche. This was sporadic.

It made Don think of thunder or drumbeats. Rick laughed.

"He's coming for you, Don," he said. "I told you he would."

"No!"

Don scrambled around the bunker until he found the table. He scurried underneath, which only prompted fresh gales of laughter from Rick.

"He's going to tear you apart. Just like you did me."

"Shut the fuck up!"

"Except you're going to be alive the whole time, screaming in agony. And God won't give a shit."

"You don't even have a tongue, or lips, or vocal cords. You're nothing!"

Rick's laughter stretched into a long, piercing scream. But even the scream was drowned out by the sound of God's thunderous footsteps, so close now Don's fillings vibrated and small bits of cement clattered on the tabletop. Warm piss trickled down Don's trouser leg.

Don waited for death. But gradually, the footsteps retreated. Don opened his eyes. A thin line of light sliced through the darkness, so narrow that Don thought he was imagining it.

He crept out from under the table and edged across the floor, squinting. A gust of wind rattled the door. The line of light disappeared for an eternity, then reappeared.

Don pushed at the door, barely daring to believe. The frame was warped, the brickwork cracked, the lock bent out of shape. He staggered up the steps into the bright sunshine, crying as the light speared his eyes. He fell to the ground, smelling dirt, trees, a hint of floral perfume, and something else. A metallic, burning smell he vaguely remembered from his past life. He clutched at the dirt, crying, howling as he rubbed the fine powder on his face.

He opened his eyes and realised he was looking at one of God's footprints. The crater was black, all life extinguished.

"It's a miracle," he whispered, then grinned as the hunger came upon him once more.

• • •

Marco rode tall in the passenger seat, puffing on one of the Cuban cigars gifted to him at his daughter's wedding. He had it on good authority they had once been owned by Saddam Hussein himself—a token from the CIA back in the 80s. The truck laboured over the pockmarked dirt road, winding its way up Sikaram. Abdul was a good driver, and he'd traversed this road many times.

Snow still dusted the higher peaks, but down here, it was all brown rocks, with the odd flower pushing up to taste the spring sunshine.

From the back of the truck came the occasional grunt or cry of pain when they passed over a particularly bumpy patch. There were fifty or so government soldiers back there, hooded and roped together.

They would soon have more to worry about than a few bumps and bruises. Marco pulled the cigar cutter out of his pocket and clicked it open and shut a couple of times.

The sun had dipped down behind the mountains by the time the truck's headlights swung across the bunker's grey face. Someone in the back of the truck screamed for help and Marco chuckled. The laugh caught in his throat when he saw the crater.

He climbed out of the truck, so transfixed he missed the muddy footprints leading to and from the bunker's only entrance, shreds of cloth hanging from the tree branches, a lone peasant's sandal, almost black with dried blood.

The crater was about a bus-length across. New shoots of grass had just started sprouting in the depths of the charred pit. Marco stared out across the valley. He could see the path of destruction down there. He had heard of at least one family turned to ash by this latest atrocity, still more who had lost property or animals. Bile and excitement churned in his guts. This batch of collaborators was going to suffer even more than usual. If that were possible. Abdul lurked in his peripheral vision.

"Get them out," Marco said, patting the Desert Eagle strapped to his thigh. He watched the light drain out of the valley below before turning for the bunker. At least, that was still intact, he thought.

Abdul trudged around the back of the truck and unlocked the rear gates. He caught a whiff of shit and piss before an icy mountain breeze carried it away, rippling the canvas cover over the truck bed.

He looked in at the cargo—soldiers with flour sacks over their heads.

Then the pleading began. Promises of money, women, livestock. He fed them the lie they wanted to hear.

"Do as you are told, and tonight, you will be eating with your families," he said. "Get out."

He grabbed the nearest soldier under the arms and hauled him out of the truck, dumping him onto the road. The rope tugged at the ankles of the next man, who got the idea. They clambered off the truck then hunched in the road, backs against the wind.

Marco called out from the steps leading down to the bunker.

"Abdul, whatever happened to those journalists?"

Abdul looked blank for a moment. "I forgot! The avalanche, then the air raid. They're still in there."

Abdul and Marco shared a glance.

"That's a shame," Marco said. "I was really looking forward to killing those Australian dogs."

Marco leant beside the battered steel door as Abdul hauled the prisoners off the truck. He watched the prisoners so intently he didn't notice the door wasn't quite shut. The pungent aroma of his cigar masked the stench of carrion wafting from the death room. A gust of wind whistled through the tree, covering the sound of laboured breathing, barely a metre from his face.

Abdul slung his AK-47 over his shoulder and unclipped a ring of keys from his belt. He turned towards the bunker door. Marco was gone. The bunker door squealed shut.

"Marco?"

A scream gouged the air. Abdul sprinted towards the bunker. The howl gained a liquid, gurgling property. The prisoners joined in and begged Allah to save them. Abdul shouldered the door open, levelling his assault rifle at the darkness. Marco's Desert Eagle discharged, drowning out the scream, lighting up the room.

Blood. On the walls. Floor. Everywhere.

Marco's finger jittered against the trigger as the life drained from his body, offering Abdul staccato glimpses of the horror unfolding.

Abdul's jaw dropped, terror sapping his strength. The AK fell impotent to his side.

Bodies, stripped of flesh.

Bloodied clothes. Backpacks. Shoes.

Dismembered arms, legs, heads.

The monster, tearing open Marco's throat with its teeth.

Blood gushing over its face.

A stained press pass, hanging around its neck.

A filthy bandage around one bare thigh.

Abdul turned to run but it was too late. The monster was on him.

Outside, the prisoners huddled together in the darkness, moaning, waiting for the cannibal of Sikaram to get hungry once more.

....

JOHNNY & BABUSHKA

R J ASTRUC

I *love* Christmas.

I think it's mainly the tinsel.

But also the wrapping paper and the crackers and the presents and the carolling and Harrods and the Queen's Message and the goodwill-to-all-mankind and the way my home-town Wickley looks in winter, all tucked up in a white fleece of snow.

My flat-neighbour Johnny Flannery says it's weird for me to celebrate Christmas, on account of who I am and, more specifically, *what* I am. He has a point, I suppose. I'm a fairy. Genus: *Perisan peri,* or *Perfume-eater.* Era: *7th millenium BCE.* Mythos: *Zoroastrian.* Traditionally, Zorastrians do Nouruz, we do Sadeh, we do Pateti, we do six gahambars and eleven Jashans; we do Khordad Sal (the anniversary of Zarathushtra's birth) and, to even things up, we also do Zartosht No-Diso (the anniversary of Zarathushtra's death).

We technically *don't* do Christmas—but look, it's all secular and commercial now, right? Sure, back in my day, it wasn't all this jolly mince-pies-and-Tannenbaum stuff. Far from it. In 7000 BCE the Christ-child himself was a mere twinkle in his father's eye—and a very faint twinkle at that. We didn't get any decent December festivities until the Romans invented *Dies Natalis Solis Invicti* in the early two hundreds and invited every solar god and his dog to join the fun.

Christmas in the middle ages was a good laugh, what with the gambling and the carolling and the pageants and the rest. But to my mind, nothing can beat Christmas in twenty-first century London. Maybe it's the vibe. Maybe it's the festivities. Maybe it's the way families come together, exchange gifts, and share the year's joys and hardships over eggnog and turkey . . .

Okay, thinking about it, it's probably the tinsel.

Anyway. This—the story that follows—isn't a story about a Christmas miracle but I feel like it *ought* to be.

You're welcome to suspend your disbelief.

• • •

Christmas Eve. The night before Christmas, and as it happens there *is* something stirring in my shitty ten-by-fifteen metre tenement flat: me.

I'm in the middle of making myself a Christmas crown out of foil, glue, beads and sticky-tape (I saw it on Playschool) when there's a knock on my door. I unstick myself from the table, the wall, and my own sleeve and go to find out who it is.

Outside, bouncing from foot to foot in the corridor of our tenements, is my flat-neighbour Johnny Flannery. You know Johnny: six-foot eleven, brown, handsome, leather-clad, nominally Irish, with a grin that makes grannies feel faint and a police record almost as long as his *very* long arms. Last seen climbing out your bedroom window with a stereo in one hand and some Tupperware for the girlfriend in the other—yes, *that* Johnny Flannery.

Johnny is also sort-of-kind-of my best friend. I'd make a joke about that, but this is West London and I'm five-foot-flat *and* ethnic *and* a fucking fairy and I've come to be rather grateful for Johnny's company. And, of course, his loyal silence regarding my supernatural origins. There's not terribly much you can hide from your neighbour, particularly when he keeps breaking into your house to watch late-night cable.

"Zeeeem," goes Johnny.

"Johnny," I riposte. Then burp. I've spent much of the afternoon eating glitter, which I understand is bad for people and also quite bad for fairies too, but not in the same way. "I suppose you'd like to come in . . ."

But he already is in, his feet up on my coffee table, his arse on my couch, and the remote control in the palm of his hand. "Didn't know if ancient Zoroastrian fairies celebrated Christmas," he says, digging a hastily-wrapped present out of the pocket of his jacket. "So, like, if you do, here's something. If you don't, though, I'll 'ave it back . . ."

"I do, ta, Johnny."

"It's a personal organiser," he explains, as I tear away the paper. Of course it is. I'm always asking him to get me something *practical*, and the personal organiser is the very epitome of practical. I switch it on and check the specs. It has an electronic diary, an alarm, a calendar, GPS, email and even an inbuilt web browser, which I guess would be useful if I ever felt masochistic enough to try surfing the net on a three-inch screen. Admittedly from certain angles it looks a little like the case Johnny's girlfriend keeps her mascara in (which I'm certain he did on purpose, one of his less than subtle digs at my masculinity) . . .

"I figured it'd be useful, like," says Johnny. "On account of you havin' so many associates to keep up with. Banshees and demons and vampires and the rest of them types you fairy folk hang out with."

"I'm a veritable supernatural socialite," I agree, scrolling through Google street view with my thumbs. I might've been born nine millennia ago, but when it comes to technology I'm totally *cutting-edge*. I've even got my own Facebook page. "So where did you steal it from?"

Johnny pulls a face, a face that's now full of the Christmas pudding I'd left out on the coffee table in case any hungry young carollers came knocking. "Ah now, Zeem, don't look yer gift horse in his mouth. Where's yer Christmas spirit?"

I give him a look. My flat is positively *redolent* with Christmas spirit, and has been since early November. I'm a fairy, after all; we get excitable around shiny things. There's not a cupboard or table or chair I haven't swathed in brightly coloured bunting; every doorknob is wearing its very own tiny Santa's hat. My Christmas tree—an eight foot monstrosity I had to wheel home from Tescos in a shopping trolley—is bent double underneath the weight of the hundred-thousand odd decorations I've accumulated over the years and enough tinsel to moor a warship. (Personally, I think it compares quite favourably to the charity Giving Tree in Wickley's shopping centre . . .) Sprigs of mistletoe sprout somewhat optimistically from the light-fittings.

"Don't you roll yer eyes at me, fairy-boy," Johnny says, one figure jabbing the bulls-eye of my Rudolf-the-Red-Nosed-Reindeer jumper. "Cynical folks like you always ferget the true meanin' of Christmas. Ain't about bleeding tinsel and presents and the like. It's all about givin' somethin' back to those who need it."

"No, that's the true meaning of your court-ordered community service. I've *done* my charity work, thanks. I advised the Giving Tree people on their tinsel choices—"

Johnny's about to clip me one over the ear when we hear someone yelling outside–and then, close, *too* close, the squeal of brakes.

And then a thump.

Johnny and I look at each other.

We're out the door in record time.

• • •

The victim of the crash is an old woman. A trio of young hoods stand dumbly around her body, which is spread-eagled on the pavement like a clumsy snow-angel. The pooling light of the streetlamps gives this sad little tableaux a strangely ethereal quality. Ethereal and still. There's no sign of the car that hit her. Or a sign that help is on its way. Or a sign that anyone except the hoods have even *noticed* the woman on the ground. And at this time of the evening there's few cars on the road (which is iced up and slippery), and all the shops across the way have already closed their doors for the holidays.

"Ambulance," I say, puffing up—Johnny a half-step behind me. "Did you call an—"

"Course we done," says a hood. "We ain't stupid, mate. They says they'll be here in a half hour, like, on account of how the traffic's bogged in round the top end of town. Christmas shopping n all."

"Said we had to watch her, like, until they came. So's we is. It's the charitable thing, innit.' This little slice of Dickensian Christmas spirit comes from the lips of a fat white kid in a yellow hoodie. She stares down at the crumpled woman and sighs. "God bless the old cunt."

I look down, too. There's no blood. The woman's left arm's sitting at a funny angle and her chest looks dented, curving inward where it shouldn't. She's breathing, sort of, little whistles and whispers like a sleeping child. Her head's wrapped up in one of those patterned scarfs that Russian ladies sometimes wear, and her clothes are quaintly old-fashioned, layers of gypsy skirts and a belt of chain and flat silver discs.

In one hand she's clutching a sack that's almost as big as she is. Gently I bend down and pry away her fingers.

And—because I'm curious—I look inside.

It's filled with presents.

Each one is wrapped up in shiny Christmas paper, with the name and address of a lucky child pasted to the front.

"Oh, yer kiddin'," says Johnny, who's looking over my shoulder. "Oh. Oh geez. Oh geez, Zeem. Do you know who that is? I mean, is that bleedin'—"

"Yes. Poor woman. I wonder what she's doing out at this time."

"Oh, *we know*," says Johnny, tapping the side of his nose to intimate a secret shared. "We *know* why."

"We do?"

"Sure we do. Old lady with a bag full of presents . . ." If he intimates any harder he might take a nostril off. "Not that hard to guess who it is, is it?"

"Guess who—oh." I don't know the specifics of the British school syllabus, but I *do* know that there's a big focus on cultural diversity. I expect that Johnny has heard the stories of Babushka; that he's familiar with the old Russian woman in a headscarf, a sack of presents over her shoulder, chasing the Christ-child from house to house with the tenacity of an insurance salesman. "That's nice, Johnny," I say uneasily. "But actually—"

Johnny bounces, energised. "You know what we got to do now, don't you? We got to deliver 'em."

"*What?*" I look at the hoods, hoping for a sensibly derisive teenage response, but the hoods are already looking at Johnny—tattooed, six foot eleven, serial offender Johnny Flannery—and have appeared to come to the consensus that this man is a Role Model. "Christmas spirit," they chime. "'Tis the reason for the season."

"Please, Johnny. If it was any other day of the year you'd be going through her wallet for her credit cards. It'll take us ages to find these people, anyway. Do I look like I know where . . ." I check a present. " . . . Holsbury Street in Upper Wickley is off the top of my head?"

Johnny nudges my arm, and I realise I'm still holding my personal organiser.

"Don't you got a GPS on that thing, mate?" he asks, grinning.

• • •

So, on the night before Christmas, when I *should* be at home eating glitter and watching the BBC's *Carols from Kings*, I am instead tramping up the streets of Wickley behind a convicted felon and three probable-felons-to-be. I'm not really sure why I'm doing it, only that Johnny is very persuasive and also very tall. And maybe I feel a tiny bit guilty, too. I'm a creature of goodness and light and happiness, but tonight my conscience has been upstaged by the humanitarian instincts of a bunch of local thugs.

We've left the Russian lady in the hands of the paramedics. (They say she'll pull through, which I can tell Johnny's having a hard time not declaring a *Christmas miracle*). The first address on our Christmas list—for a present Johnny's carefully selected by the age-old method of lucky dipping—is on Mercy Street. According to the GPS, this is a casual five minute stroll away for someone who's six foot eleven and fit, and a horrible five minute *sobbingpantingstumble* away for someone who's five foot flat and has a belly full of glitter.

But it's too much to hope the others will slow down for me. Johnny, striding along with a sack of presents slung over his shoulder, is unmistakeably a man on a mission; the hoods follow in his footsteps like loyal pages after their Good King Wenceslas.

I catch up with the group as Johnny's knocking on the front door, the present—a medium-sized rectangular box in pink sparkly paper—tucked under his chin. I'm about to voice my misgivings about blindly handing out mysterious boxes to small children, when a middle-aged woman wearing a Santa's hat and a tinsel boa appears at the ingress. Her face fairly sours when she sees who's on her doorstep.

"Hello," says Johnny, whose Christmas spirit appears indefatigable. "I'm 'ere to deliver—"

"Wait." The woman squints. "Aren't you the Irish bastard who stole my Playstation last month?"

Johnny is politely disarming. "I 'ave brought a present for yer daughter. A very merry Christmas to you, ma'am."

The woman is pushing up her sleeves, a very un-merry scowl on her face, when a grubby little girl appears at her hip. Johnny's gaze shifts from mother to daughter; he bends from his great height until he and the girl are at eye level.

"Are you Fei Ling?" he asks.

The child wrinkles her face. "Yes," she says.

"Then this is for you," says Johnny graciously, and places the present into Fei's small hands.

"Don't you open that," says her mother automatically, but her plea falls on deaf ears. Fei is already ripping off the paper. Amongst the immutable truths I've learnt in my long existence is the fact it is not physically possible to separate a small child from an unwrapped Christmas present. Rankled, the mother turns her attention back to Johnny. "Flannery, isn't it?" she says. "Aren't you meant to be in jail?"

"Doin' community service this time," says Johnny. "On account o' me good behavior."

"Good behavior? Community service?" The mother snorts. "Well I tell you now, Johnny Flannery, you ain't done this community any favours. You theivin' shit, that Playstation cost us good money."

"Mummy, look, it's a Barbie," says Fei.

"Can't we let bygones be bygones?" Johnny tries, smiling the winning smile I've personally witnessed turn a one year sentence into six months.

"'Tis the reason for the season," chime the hoods, a little more uncertainly this time.

"I should call the cops on you right now."

"Mummy-mummy-mummy-*mummy*, it's a Barbie, *mummy*."

Fei's mother looks down finally at her child, who is fairly *windmilling* the plastic doll to get some parental attention. "Oh," she says, softening a little. "It's the one you wanted, isn't it? What are you going to call her?"

"Barbie," says Fei, in that tone that says: Don't you know anything, Mum? "Her name is Barbie."

Johnny, a man with well honed get-away skills, chooses this moment to start inching away from the door. The hoods follow his lead; and soon we're all half-way down the street, back-patting and grinning and congratulating each other for a job more-or-lessly well done . . . and for the life of me, I can't help but get swept up in their good cheer. What's more Christmasy, after all, than bringing toys to small children?

"Okay, fairy-boy, where are we off to next?" says Johnny, flicking his fingers at my belly and Rudolf-the-Red-Nosed-Reindeer's nose. "We got a big night ahead of us."

"Wait, there's at least thirty presents in there," I say, my good cheer faltering at the thought of the *very* long roads ahead of us, and the *very* short legs I have to traverse with them. "We really can't—"

But Johnny's already lucky-dipped another present from his sack. "Number 8 Hemmingway Close!" he declares, as the hoods cheer. "Ain't that just past the pub?"

• • •

I am, as I've mentioned, nine millenia old and I'm used to seeing history repeat itself, practically *ad infinitum* (and certainly *ad nauseum*). There's a saying that goes: there are no new stories ever written—and I feel now, more than ever, like we're walking along a path already well-trodden. But Christmas has always been about traditions and signs and the curious little things mortals do to make sense of a world too bloody complicated for them to ever understand.

Babushka's story is, of course, a story about apologies. When the three kings of the Nativity invite Babushka to join them as they follow their star-of-wonder, Babushka has other things to do. Her house needs cleaning; the floors must be scrubbed; food must be cooked and, most importantly, she needs to find the right gift for the Christ-child. (And what *do* you buy for the son of a god, really?) And while Babushka procrastinates, the Christ-child slips away from her; he is gone by the time she finally reaches Bethlehem, her ungiveable gift clutched to her chest.

Babushka is still looking for him. She sublimates her guilt for failing him by leaving presents for other children—it is a sort of penance. A community service, in fact, that's very much like the one Johnny does every Monday, Tuesday, and Friday.

And, of course, the community service he's performing now.

There's a light snow falling as we walk the streets of Wickley— the kind of light snow you often see peppering the outermost branches of Christmas card Christmas trees, or sprinkled across the roofs of barn-yards and farm houses in pastoral idylls. (Not the usual sort of snow we get in Wickley, which predominantly comes in *slush*.) Johnny's taught the hoods the dirty versions to some classic holiday favourites; they carol away merrily, the yellow hoodie taking the high notes that the two boys can't reach.

Like Babushka before us, we do our rounds. This little boy gets a fire engine. This little girl, hiding behind her father, gets a book about origami. This family gets a hamper of small gifts: bits and pieces for the Christmas tree, a couple of CDs, and that special Tescos Christmas pudding that no one but visiting uncles eat. This little girl gets an astronaut's helmet. This little girl gets a DVD of early *Star Trek* episodes, and gives us a traditional Vulcan salute as we leave.

After a dozen or so successful present deliveries, Johnny starts to regale the hoods with his unique take on the Christmas mythology.

"Parents invented Santa so's little kids wouldn't know where presents came from," he explains, in the most paternal of tones. "He's sort of like god, right, only fer little baby Christians."

"Actually," I say, still lagging behind the pack, "Santa is generally associated with Woden, who's pure heathen."

Johnny frowns, but rallies on. "Anyway, y'know how god 'as angels, right? Well, Santa 'as little elves instead fer helpin' him—"

"Not in the Netherlands," I say. "In the Netherlands he's got a helper called Zwarte Piet who cheerfully beats the shit out of kids on the naughty list. And in parts of Eastern Europe he used to have the Krampus, who wear black masks and drag chains which they throw at passing children—"

"And it's called Xmas on account o' how Jesus were nailed to a great big X," Johnny snaps.

"No, Johnny," I say automatically, "it's called Xmas because in Greek and Roman, X is the first letter of the word Christ."

The hoods look suspiciously between us. Trying to work out who's telling the truth—which, frankly, as both a mythological creature *and* someone without a police record, I find rather offensive.

Surprisingly it's Johnny who breaks the tension. "I ain't no expert," he says mildly, tossing a sparkly-pink present in his hand.

"You should listen a Zeem 'ere. He's always got 'is facts straight on this sort o' stuff. I reckon I'll stick wit' gift-givin', eh?"

He double-checks the address on the back of the present, then trots off to knock on a door. The hoods, still playing page, aren't far behind him.

I watch them do their Babushka business from the pavement. Johnny is a thief and the hoods are a bunch of little bastards who've a reputation for ringing doorbells in the middle of the night, writing misspelled graffiti on people's fences and pissing in public places. This is *their* pilgrimage, not mine; their chance to give back. And yet what they're doing here, as we walk from house to house, seems less like a penance than an impulse.

Sure they're doing good in the Christmas tradition—in, specifically, *Babushka's* tradition—but it doesn't fit in my head in the neat way I'd prefer it to.

• • •

We deliver the last presents to a pair of snotty-nosed twins just outside the town centre; they squeak happily and hug the yellow hoodie. Their father invites us in to sample his home-made eggnog, but it's getting close to midnight now and the hoods have parental curfews. We say our goodbyes before the hoods think to serenade the twins with a farewell carol.

Our route back to the tenements takes us down main street, where the lamp posts are swathed in red tinsel like barber's poles and every shop window is printed with a *Merry Christmas* decal. (Naturally the French bakery's reads: *Joyeux Noel.*) The pavements are crowded with people returning from late church services and the annual carols by candlelight held in Wickley's community centre. Johnny, who's always got an eye for an opportunity, nicks someone's wallet and uses the cash in it to buy the hoods a kebab each.

Then the yellow hoodie finds some mistletoe hanging from a street sign and gets in a snog with the better looking of the two other hoods. And the less attractive male hood carves his name into a bus time table with a penknife.

Johnny and I leave them to it and walk home through the snow, which is looking slushier by the minute. At my place, Johnny flips through repeats of *Carols from Kings* while I potter off to the kitchen to pour him a glass of brandy and myself a glass of *Chanel No. 5.*

"You know all that present-giving doesn't count as community service, right?" I say, returning with drinks.

Johnny shrugs. "I know."

"Then why do it?"

"Dunno. Why wouldn't I?"

I look at Johnny for a long time.

"Merry Christmas, Johnny," I say eventually. "Thank you for being my friend."

"Merry Christmas, Zeem," says Johnny. "Thank you fer bein' mine."

We clink glasses. We drink. And I don't wince, even though I want to. I'll admit it freely: I'm nine millennia old and I still haven't gotten used to the indignity of being taught *life lessons* by humans. Especially not on bloody Christmas day.

• • •

This story has an ending, but it's not magical or miraculous.

Three days after Christmas, Johnny and I go to the hospital. We've got a patient to see, and a Christmas miracle to verify. Patient visiting hours are almost up, but tall, dark, handsome Johnny manages to flirt his way past two duty nurses and a janitor without too much trouble.

We find our Babushka in the private wing. As we enter her room, she starts awake, and the monitor at her side peep-peep-peeps like a hungry chick. Her heartbeats zigzag irregularly on the screen. An elaborate pulley system is keeping her bandaged left leg raised; her right arm has a plaster cast. Without her patterned scarf she doesn't look particularly Russian. She's just a small, broken woman. She looks like no one special at all.

"Are—are—" the broken woman begins, rubbing her eyes, but Johnny puts a finger to his lips to quiet her.

"Hullo, Missus B," he says. "Don't you bother gettin' up on my account. I jus' came by to say that you ain't got nothin' to worry about. With the presents. Me 'n' my friends, we delivered 'em. All them kids got their presents. So don't worry 'bout a thing, you hear? You concentrate on restin' yourself and getting better."

The broken lady's face crinkles in confusion. I put a hand on Johnny's arm before he can go in for an over-friendly, over-Christmasy hug of *togetherliness*.

"You should probably head off now, Johnny," I whisper. "I'll take it from here. The lady Babushka and I have things to talk about. One mythological being to another."

"Oh, aye," says Johnny, intimating with his finger again. "I'll meet you outside then, fairy-boy. G'bye, Missus B."

He strides out, a hero's exit, ducking ever so slightly to clear the door frame. The broken woman and I watch him go.

"It's Kazeem, isn't it?" asks the broken woman finally. "I 'member you helped us some with setting up the Giving Tree. You had opinions about our tinsel."

"That's right," I say. "And that was my friend Johnny Flannery. It's okay, he's nothing to worry about. He got out of Wandsworth for good behaviour."

"Did he really deliver those presents? I should thank him. I think *everyone* needs to thank him."

"Ah, no. I think it might be better if you didn't."

"What do you mean?"

An unfortunate side effect of my fairy biology means I've an awful time trying to lie, but that doesn't mean I can't prevaricate with the best of them. "Johnny's an unassuming kind of man, Mrs Edgeworth," I say. "Wouldn't want anyone to make a fuss of him."

"I was worried someone might have stolen all the gifts," says Mrs Edgeworth, leaning back on her pillows. The pulley system creaks in relief. "What a disaster that would be! Especially considering how much support the Giving Tree got this year. Dozens of presents donated. Those poor unfortunate children would have been so disappointed—"

"Quite," I say. "Lucky we had Johnny Flannery, eh."

On the way out I stop at the hospital gift shop to browse their assortment of fluffy bears and balloons and plastic flowers and other Get Well Soon paraphernalia. I'm not going to tell Johnny about Mrs Edgeworth and the Giving Tree, of course. I want Johnny to have the dream of saving Christmas, but I also I owe him a real gift, something a little more solid than bloody Christmas spirit. Call it an impulse, or maybe just plain old *peer pressure* . . .

Tis the reason for the season, and all that.

•••••••••••

SCHUBERT BY CANDLELIGHT

MATTHEW CHRULEW

I smile as Samuel hesitates in the doorway, three-quarters full of self-pity and one-quarter of cognac. His gaze sweeps the room, pausing on curious articles: me standing in the centre of his Savonnerie rug; the decanter of Premier Grand Cru set out on the cabinet; Narcissus Absolute candles arranged on the mantlepiece. The familiar melancholy of Schubert's *Rosamunde* drifts from the corner. Already, from the quickening of his lips, I can begin to penetrate his mind: a flicker of repressed desire within the gloom.

"Adam," he says. "You're here."

I had begun to worry that he would work it out and wouldn't come home at all. At least, not on his own. I even found myself biting my nails again. Habits die hard, both old and new. But here he is, shutting the door gently behind him.

It turns out, after all, that I had weighed his infatuation perfectly.

"Of course I'm here," I say, and beneath the despondency on his round, soft face, the half-drunk waver in his eyes, I can sense his surprise and anticipation. That fearful longing, thinking tonight might be his big night.

Well, if you look at it the right way, it *will*.

Then the misery regains its grip, and he puts his head in his hands.

"Samuel, sit down." I guide him into his pride and joy, the Victorian mahogany elbowchair by the wall. "You look like something got the better of you."

"You wouldn't believe the day I've had," he says. I cross his precious wool rug, light the sweetly fragrant candles, and pour him a cognac. Three cubes, two shots, one swirl: the only thing not neat about him.

"Really?" I hand him the drink, allowing our fingers almost to touch, and then adjust the volume on the record to play softly in the background. "This should cheer you up," I say, knowing better.

He contrives a half-enthusiastic smile, sinks into his chair and breathes in the cognac vapours.

"Not likely. I'm finished," he exhales quickly. "I've been set up."

I shake my head and hold out his pills. "I have no idea what you're talking about."

He looks up, as if only now registering my presence. He takes the pills and swallows them with the Grand Cru.

"Overnight, there was an intruder."

"What? Was anybody harmed?"

He gazes at me over the crystal snifter. I maintain my concerned expression.

"No, no, there was no-one there. It was just . . . corporate espionage. The system was compromised and vital information was exposed." He shakes his head. "The thing is, they breached security using *my* passwords!"

"What? How did they get them?"

"I have *no* idea, but half the board believed it was me, the traitors. I finally convinced them that I couldn't possibly gain anything—I'm not going anywhere!—but of course they still hold me responsible."

I feign a groan of shock and sympathy as he squanders the liquor with a masochistic gulp.

"So now we just have to wait. If it's a whistle-blower, they'll still throw me to the wolves, but it won't matter. The media will tear the company apart just the same." He concedes a wincing smile. "But if it's blackmail, it's a matter of waiting for the message. We'll pay big, too. Either way, that's the end of me."

He leans back with an air of practised misfortune, indulging this newfound justification. "Oh, I'm too miserable. Let's talk about something else."

"Yes, let's. You need to relax." I pour him another drink, the decanter flickering ostentatiously under the candlelight. He glances at the piano, notices my suitcases, and looks up at me. I lower my eyes.

It's tempting: I want to suggest that he sit at the grand and purge himself through his fingers. He always plays most beautifully when depressed, losing himself in the sorrow of the music.

That's how it was the first time I met him, quietly gatecrashing that intolerable work party. I watched as he sat there in that hand-carved seat, politely brushing aside the under-dressed and over-rouged tarts and making boring intelligent conversation with the dissolute execs, the PR men, the other neurochemists-for-hire. His fingers fidgeted at his knees, enticed by the Unfinished Symphony which played in the background. He was obviously desperate for company—younger, male, and unrelated to work—but too governed by his Catholic superego to admit it, let alone act on it. And it was noticeably frowned upon by his peers, just like with Schubert—as if, two centuries later, we were still in the grips of that stifling taboo. So he pined, wielding his melancholy like a lure. I saw my moment and took it, stood by the piano and offered him a glance.

"You play," I said.

When everyone else had left, he sat before the parlor grand and slowly, softly, released himself into the *Rosamunde* Impromptu in B-flat major. That's how it's been ever since: Schubert and longing. Never altering his mood, but mirroring it perfectly—and that reflection, too, entranced him.

Like the composer, he felt himself to be the most unhappy and wretched creature in the world.

I was beguiled. It was then that this undertaking became about so much more than Bryce Pharmaceuticals' dirty secrets.

We had dinner the following night; within a week, I was staying in his spare room.

It wasn't a problem, playing this game with another man; he was too repressed to even approach me for a fortnight and accepted my gentle rejection as if it were fate. But his desire remained, undiminished. I found myself wondering, with an ironic smirk, whether it might somehow rub off.

But that would be all right; I wouldn't mind. I could be anything for a while. Even that which he found unspeakable.

It was his habits that got under my skin: his minute and rigid patterns and affectations, his tedious Oedipal conflicts and hypocritical boys'-school morality. God. He was so predictable that

I found myself pre-empting his incessant, conflicted grudge-stories about his mother, unknowingly conceding to his preciousness over his furniture, and counting the clock by his insufferable fixations. At least he's not a smoker; the amount of times I've had to withstand *that* godforsaken addiction.

The trick is to survive such annoyances while remaining open to what is worthwhile. His one superlative talent.

But to expect him to play now would be wishful thinking; instead, I turn up the record as the ominous strains of the second Entr'acte die away.

"Tell me, though, Samuel, I'm intrigued. What is so worrying about the data that was breached?" I'm curious about how much he actually knows.

He makes a show of sniffing the vapours wafting from the crystal and studies me with delicate consideration. "You know my research is confidential." But his motives are so easily deciphered: he is judging, not if he can trust me, but how he might play this confidence to his advantage.

I smile. "Well, it *was*."

He grunts in acknowledgement. "Let me put it this way. Bryce Pharmaceuticals' interests extend into some . . . ethically sensitive areas." He can't help but pause and glance around as a Ducati hums past, its headlight driving inkblot shadows across the walls.

"How do you mean?"

"The last few years, Bryce has concentrated its R&D on a certain area of neuropharmacology—controversial, but potentially extremely profitable. Nootropics, it's called: cognitive enhancers that act directly on the brain, boosting neurotransmitter levels, for example, to improve memory, concentration, alertness, things like that. The military's been dabbling in it for decades, but industry has avoided this sort of cosmetic enhancement. Since Viagra, though . . ." He blushes ever so slightly. "Well, the idea has become more acceptable to consumers. Now there's heavy competition among biotech start-ups, not to mention big pharma, to develop effective drugs and corner the market. I mean, with regulations being what they are, officially they're intended for diseases like Alzheimer's. Though this whole diagnostics business has proven quite elastic—there's always some new disorder or condition we can target. But the real profit is in the massive off-label demand;

we're talking students, aging baby boomers . . . Heck, my whole team is on modafinil—narcolepsy meds. They pretty much have to be, given the hours I make them work."

He laughs with disdain at the image of his medicated lab rats, and I smile along.

"Our competitors have been experimenting with ampakines, CREB enhancers, BDNF . . . not that those will mean anything to you."

I open my hands in ignorance.

"While we've been synthesising a new compound—MN1704, we call it."

"Smart drugs?"

"Well, yes, some use that term."

"Giving yourself the chance at something that fate never saw fit to equip you with. I understand the appeal of that."

He inclines his head forward. "I can see that about you. Critics complain that we're messing with nature, but what is 'normal', anyway? People have always modified themselves with the best means available. Will we deny them that choice today, just when we're finally getting good at it?"

I throw in my old favourite. "I remember reading somewhere about this dream of inventing memory pills. There were these experiments, in the sixties I think, where this scientist taught worms to behave a particular way, and then ground them up and fed them to some other worms. Apparently the untrained worms acquired the learned behaviour of the ones they had eaten. Suddenly everybody was hoping they could take a tablet and— *voila! On parle Français!*"

He laughs. "Ah, *oui*, the planaria controversy. So . . . *bête*. No, no, those results were refuted long ago. Nothing so extravagant is claimed for next gen nootropics. Though I personally find the prospect of enhanced recall to be sufficiently exciting in itself."

"But I don't understand. I see how some might object, but it hardly seems illegal."

"Not as such, no. You must understand that Bryce's number one concern is to protect their investment—securing intellectual property. With this incident, the threat to that alone has them panicking. But there's also the issue of . . . well, let's just say that I'm not sure how much scrutiny our testing procedures could handle."

"You mean on animals?"

He laughs again and waves his hand. "Absolutely routine and unquestioned. As is that on humans, mind you. No, it's all about fast-tracking FDA approval, you see. Which makes it very profitable for clinical investigators and contract research organisations to quickly produce supportive research—and very . . . unprofitable for them to bother too much about negative results and side-effects."

"I see."

He hesitates, chinking ice in consideration before resuming. "And if that requires such research to be exported to poorer areas, or third world countries, where regulation is not so stringent, and less than desirable effects on the local population are not so noticeable . . . then so be it."

I nod, ever his confidant. "Well, those sound like the sorts of things Bryce would have good reason to keep under wraps."

"A fact they impress upon their staff in the strongest possible manner."

I raise my eyebrows. "You've been threatened? What are you going to do?"

"Others have tried to leave, but they never . . ." He trails off, then takes a controlled sip of his cognac.

I push him no further, returning instead to the record player to tweak the volume; the Geisterchor is drawing near.

Some of my contacts had worked for Bryce. My main collaborator, J, barely escaped with his life, let alone the fruits of his research.

"So what do you think?" I ask. "Do they want to ruin the company by going public? Or are they after money?"

"Perhaps even the research itself," he says. "We have competitors who know that we're close to market—when their takeover bid failed, they offered me double what I earn at Bryce, but I've never even considered it. Everything's locked up in proprietary agreements anyway. I've always been careful with security; I just have no idea how they got their hands on *my* codes."

He gulps back the remains of his drink now, still working everything through. The insight is taking its time coming. I could never actually tell him, of course; what a waste that would be. I want to see his face as he realises it himself. But that doesn't mean I can't help him along.

"You really shouldn't blame yourself," I lie. "I mean, you only did what was in your nature." As predictable as that was.

His eyes narrow as he considers my statement. I stand by the piano, fingering the key in the ornamental lock on the lid.

"I don't know what you mean," he says tentatively.

"You couldn't help but take me in."

His body visibly jerks—and now enlightenment.

"It was you!" The words rush from his mouth with a burst of spit and air, as though his brain wants nothing to do with them. The balloon at his right hand gleams under the candles. Then a lip flutter and a small jolt forward as the understanding is absorbed.

"It was you, wasn't it, you bastard?"

What a wonderful indulgence, to stand and savour his moment of recognition. What a gift! Sunk deep in that ornate chair, he seems to shrink. Only his brown-flecked eyes acknowledge the clamour behind them. The waxing strains of the third act fall around our strange duel. All the scene needs is for him to drop his glass, have it scatter ice in a slow descent, and then smash on the tiles to spray flickering chunks of crystal at his feet.

"'Bastard'?" I smile, mock-offended. His hands shake, but he controls them, gripping the carved arms of the chair. "Samuel, that's not like you. Here, let me fix you another, help you calm your nerves."

"You did it? This whole time . . . This is the sort of thing I expose myself to." Such a wounded soul, unable to appreciate his sublime mental state. "I trusted you." He searches me with those irritating dejected eyes. "You little upstart, you . . . *parvenu*."

"You were born a victim, weren't you, Samuel?"

"Fuck you. I treated you well. But this whole time you've been deceiving me."

"You've been deceiving yourself. I let you think what you wanted, what you *needed*. I gave you something to live for."

"And you want me to thank you?"

"Of course you won't understand, but I do have your best interests in mind."

He screws up his face as if he might actually scream, or try to get up, or throw his glass and grant me that shattering of sharpness and light. But passive as always, he reins in the animus and the questions come.

"Is it money that you want? You could have just asked." Though he would have preferred the transaction to involve more than that. "And if you're trying to blackmail Bryce, I'm no use to you now."

He's right. If I wanted money, I could have just fucked him, or killed him, or gone straight to the source. "Of course, but I have all the expensive furniture I need, Samuel. That is, none." The only motivations he can ascribe to me are his own ephemera. He thinks his trimmings separate him from the rat race he accelerates, but he's just a different class of worm. Enslaved by their prepackaged appetites for buying, watching, eating, fucking. Fixed in the same tiresome patterns.

For Samuel, the secure repetition of professional success and private disappointment, unable to recognise the singular quality that sets him apart. Unable to take those habits and impulses as a target and work on them for his own improvement.

There's even a tempting carnality to my business, to which many end up chained. To survive in this game, you must elevate yourself above those short-term opiates and focus on the only goal that matters: the becoming of one's art.

"Unless you only want to take us down. Who are you working for? NooGen? Temporal Globe? Or are you some crusader for goddamn truth and morality?"

I can't stand this pathetic groping. "What you're missing here, Samuel, what hasn't even crossed your mind, is that maybe I couldn't care less about your disease mongering, or how you got the job done. How many Africans you experimented on, how many vagrants you harvested. You should consider this: there might be some for whom merely ingesting nootropics to enhance cognitive function is fucking *passé*." I mouth the last word priggishly in my best imitation of his faux-French.

It takes a second for that to sink in, yet still he won't accept it. "What do you mean?"

"Imagine being able to learn a skill or language, to implant a memory or knowledge, simply through ingestion."

His hand twitches on the glass as he considers my comment. Eventually he settles on scorn. "Memory transfer? You actually think that works? I told you, that rubbish was discredited! It never even really worked with simple worms, let alone organisms of greater complexity. It's ridiculed these days as an object lesson in bad science!"

I laugh. "What, you've done the experiments, have you? No, of course not. You think you've stepped over the line with your little slum trials, but you couldn't even begin to take the necessary steps. You still deprive yourself of the means to determine the precise effects of your own timid drugs."

He scoffs. "Today's scanning technology is amazingly sophisticated. Short of dissecting the brain, there's . . ." He stops in response to my impassive gaze, then continues with emphasis: "As in, killing one's subjects."

"Well, as J would say, that archaic prohibition is precisely what's preventing neuroscience from truly entering the twenty-first century."

He runs his hand through his thick grey hair.

"I know, Samuel, it sounds unbelieveable. But we've got data, *objective results* that would blow you away. Christ! We've got the *product*." I lean down to open the pocket of one suitcase and remove a pill bottle to shake in his face. He stares at the case as if I'd only now shattered his hopeful illusion, until the rattling breaks his reverie.

"Are you trying to tell me . . ." he says, but I interrupt him.

"Actually, no. I'm messing with you, Samuel." I roll the bottle around in my hand. "Of course, these don't really provide the content themselves. They're much like yours—Bryce's. They help it on its way. Which is why we wanted your research, see. We're still a long way from isolating the appropriate engram and facilitating its delivery. No, I still have to consent to become like those lowly worms, reduce myself to the task of ingestion—unpleasant, old-fashioned, but effective."

After a pause, he says, "*Not* the pills."

"Straight to the source."

He twitches at the jowls, blinks twice. It's gratifying to watch the acquisition of enlightenment, however slow and sporadic. "You mean through eating brain matter? That is simply not possible."

I open my hands. "*À la mémoire de mon vieil ami Bruno, je dois objecter. Je parle Français avec son hémispherè gauche.*"

He baulks. The orchestra pauses before the strings once more unfold, awaiting the hunter's chorus. I watch the tremors of his facial nerves until he ultimately shakes his head and pushes further.

"Are you even aware of the dangers? Have you heard of kuru? A mental disease savages *acquired* from eating each others' brains! It's just like BSE." He reverts to his patronising scientist's tone. "You know, mad cow disease?"

"Oh, I know," I say. "I'd certainly be worried if I was working with cannibals." I offer my best ironic smile. "But as you well know, among us civilised folk the risk of sporadic prion disease is the proverbial one in a million. I mean, you're a special boy, Samuel, but . . ."

He tries to scoff at my dismissal, but ends up coughing and spitting into a handkerchief. He sips at the cognac to recover.

"Nobody knows the risks of what you're taking, Adam. The documented harmful side-effects that I've had to conceal are bad enough."

I can't help but smile at his admission. "Spare me your hypocrisy. And spare Hippocrates, too. You are kind to worry after me, though. Thankyou. But no-one is more aware of the dangers. I've found that with care and proper procedure, the risks can be minimised. And the gains maximised. Speaking of which . . ." I open the pill bottle and count three into my palm. "The human brain—so complex! So much potential! And so adaptable. Well, sometimes. When we try. Plasticity—that's the term you guys use, isn't it? J certainly does, all the time." I roll my eyes. "Of course, as you say, it's impossible to precisely separate the relevant areas, at least at this stage of our knowledge. As convenient as a map of localised function would be, so much turns out to also be distributed. Especially with procedural memory. That's both the beauty and bane of the whole project. You wouldn't want to leave out parts that might hold important information—like, say, Heschl's gyrus. There's nothing worse than gaining a skill piecemeal."

"You're serious, aren't you?"

"But on the other hand, you have to be careful of acquiring too many unwanted elements. I should know. God, you make one mistake as a rookie and you pay for it over and over." Though I'd been doing very well. Before tonight, I hadn't bitten my nails in months. I know, now, it's a matter of planning, and of hard ascetic work after the fact. It's the unforeseen ones that get you. "You don't have any secret habits I should know about, do you?" I ask, peering into his face.

The *Rosamunde* crescendos as he stares at me, the melody leaping beyond the harmonic groundwork.

"You—you're a psycho! You're like some . . . Hannibal Lecter tryhard!" Again with the projection. "Actually, no, Dahmer's more like it." Wish-fulfilment now. I hold up a hand to placate him.

"Please," I say. "Give me some credit." Samuel almost looks relieved. "It's nothing like that."

It takes a second before he asks. "How so?"

"Well, no offense, but excuse me if I don't crack open a big Amarone. As valuable as your brain is to me, it's far from a delicacy. Or a fetish. Sorry."

The colour drains from his face.

"As a matter of fact, the whole process is quite the ordeal." If only he could appreciate how severely I struggle with the chore. "But Samuel: I don't do it to degrade you—or restrain you. I wish to exalt you, my virtuoso worm!"

He flinches again. Another slip in perspective. It's finally forced its way through. Back straightens, hands twitch, and his brain competes in a fiery battle until it overwhelms him and he's basking in his new awareness.

He knows he's going to die.

I walk the length of the lounge, and turning back, I'm transfixed by the panic sharpening his few deep-set wrinkles.

"You're going to eat me. You actually intend to . . . you . . ." His finger taps the rim of his near-empty glass; his other hand is stretched over the carved chair-arm. "What will you do, just *eat* my brain?"

There is nothing to do but laugh at such simplicity. "Of course."

"Why?" He looks down at his hands in a moment of melodrama. "What is it about *me* that you want?"

It can't be pleasant to think you've left nothing behind. That this is it. But I couldn't expect him to comprehend his true value, to accept his sacrifice for the higher beauty. Few do. But really— after having resigned himself to this timorous life, death couldn't be much worse.

"Everything I know, all my research was in the computer system," he pleads, "and you obviously already have my password! Whatever you want, there are easier ways. Just ask!"

"If only I could, Samuel, but I'm afraid that anything of real value demands risk, effort, anguish—of us both. This is how it must be."

Feeling the sweat of my palm, I realise the pills are still in my hand. "J tells me these will be especially helpful for this project. 'Accentuate the appropriate faculty,' he said." I swallow them and turn away, fingertips once more on the still-closed grand, waiting for what might come out of his mouth now.

Then I hear him lunge from the chair and feel him thud into my back, slamming me into the piano and cracking the wood of the lid. I swing my arm around and knock the glass from his hand as he brings it down towards me. It smashes on the rug, glinting as he pummels me, his chest heaving with the effort of his panic. I shove him off and he collapses on the floor.

I bend down, hovering at his throat, my face millimetres from his.

"You fuck," his voice strains. I drag his chair over to the damaged grand and lift him up to sit back in his proper position. I retrieve some tape from a case and bind his wrists to the scrollwork arms. Not the conventional pose for a fenestration, but it's important to keep things familiar.

"You have to learn to relax. Just accept this."

He kicks out pathetically, then sinks back, sobbing, into the hardwood. I take out my plastic mats and lay them down.

"As I was saying, Samuel, I have accumulated a number of effective techniques. Like stimulating the relevant neural pathways."

I draw the curtains and gather the candles behind him one by one, trailing the rich, floral scent of narcissus. "The light would only be a distraction." I turn the volume of the Schubert to full.

Instantly, it sparks through my body and echoes, throbbing, through the room. I feel I can clutch the mournful notes from the air, breathe in their patterns and allow myself to be smothered.

I open the cases, put on my scrub suit and gloves, and lay out my equipment: drill, scalpel, receptacles. There is something reassuringly pleasant about the arrangement of steel.

"Fourteen-hundred and twenty grams, Samuel. That's how much Schubert's brain is said to have weighed. Quite unexceptional, but we know full well now, it's not just size that counts. And my, the things he did with it!" I flourish my scalpel like a baton, tracing a surge in the refrain. "What a consumption that would have been. But alas, the substrate always decays. Which is why I am so grateful for the enduring gift of his genius. And for *you*, Samuel, its present vessel!"

He spits and wrenches his neck, a last show of life. Such an unbalanced composition. But his true talent will survive him, just as the *Rosamunde* did the worthless play it was written for.

Just as all Schubert's music did the 1420 grams of grey matter that spawned it. And here it is now, incorporated in the spongy folds cradled by this stout but penetrable skull. So precious.

The rich treasure and its glorious hope, no longer buried. True immortality, beyond the decline of legacy, the betrayals of children, the faltering of memory. We will perish together and be reborn beyond, emerging, purged, on the other side.

I blink. Filigree waves encircle me, filling the room. They vibrate in perfect harmonies. The sonorous figures move, build, enter my head, intense and pure. I can see Samuel's fingers dancing on the arms of the chair in his suspense before the event.

As I circle him one last time, I can even see the resignation in his eyes as he atones to the music.

"That's it, my friend. Relax. Listen to the harmony, the footsteps, the breathing. No more wretched isolation. This is your greatest moment. You always wanted to be inside me."

I grew up to the sounds of cars and planes. Pop music. Radio talkback. Debased noise everywhere—but still it suggested a world beyond. I took a few guitar lessons when I was eight, but they didn't last long. I had the feel, I knew the music, I'd make up songs in my head. God, the music in my head.

But I never had the discipline to learn an instrument, nor the straight-backed mother with stifled musical ambition and a cane. Such a missed opportunity.

The spread of shattered crystal on his multi-hued rug refracts the muted candlelight as he plays. He hardly needs my encouragement; he can't help but revert to his true being. Schubert's genius, worked into him through years of practice. I can see it at his fingertips, struggling to be free.

The bliss is on him now, like a spark against the void. He is one of the lucky ones, to avoid the scrap heap. To have his essence survive.

He is worth learning.

I approach his exhausted frame from behind, and steadily trace the scalpel from behind his right ear over the crown of his head. But he twitches, ever so slightly, and I withdraw my hand. Practicality must prevail over symbolism. I lean him back from the piano and lay him onto the floor like a mated king. I pull away his antique chair, an arced spatter of deep red now staining its hand-embroidered upholstery.

He is still now, his head resting snugly on the cutting block, ready for his ascent. I finish the incision and return the scalpel to its place beside the drill. The *Rosamunde* is actualised in the cloying air, strands of still lightning waiting to enter me.

We will make such beautiful music together.

· · · · · · · · · · ·

SLOW COOKIN'

ANGELA REGA

So Nonna Elba gets the shits big time and cracks a silent but deadly one at the kitchen table. She says that's it—if my sister Lilli and I are going to insist on eating all this rubbish and nothing else—then she's going to rip out the old slow cooking combustion stove in our kitchen and buy a new electric cooker.

"What do I need a stove that you need to still bloody chop wood for when you can just turn a switch on?" She says blowing minty smoke into our faces. "I spend hours preparing something good to eat and you come home and tell me you've eaten pizza that looks like it has been deep fried in fat that's three days old."

I eye the table and notice that she's been reading the White Goods junk mail. It's so thick; there's ten new cigarette stubs in the ashtray. She's on the page that says that all installations come with a free scratch lottery ticket. I suppose this is what happens when your Grandma trades in reading grimoires for junk mail catalogues. She's become quite hooked on the stuff. Nonna Elba reckons that reading junk mail makes her feel less guilty about smoking. She's reading so much junk mail, she's chaining a pack and a half of Alpines each day.

"Eden," she says to me. "What do we need this old slow cooking stove when you don't eat my home made pizza dough anymore? Eh? I might as well buy an electric cooker. No chopping wood, just turn on a switch and hey, presto!"

I suppose Nonna Elba has a point. I look over at the old combustion stove. It has sat in the right hand corner of Nonna's kitchen from the first day she arrived here from Sicily in 1966. She carted the thing all the way over on one of the last ships to sail through the Suez Canal: *they wanted to buy it off me,* she always says to us when she's had too much to drink. *Could have swapped it for a camel and two sheep and some apple tobacco. But I said no. I love this thing.*

The slow cooker sits in that corner of the kitchen, a heap of dirty beige enamel with all the green knobs worn from use. It has a temperamental water boiler, crumbling fire bricks and a plate warming section that Nonna swears works better than any microwave the neighbours have.

How could she be ready to part with it?

"And another thing, you two," she says taking a slurp of her cold espresso. "I'm getting old, you know, how are you going to live when I'm gone? You've got the gifts and you're not developing them. This is your heritage! Don't cry to me if you don't pass your Clairvoyant test in two weeks time. Donna Lola is coming all the way from my Solichiatta near Etna to conduct your exams and she'll be jet lagged and very cranky if it is obvious you haven't prepared properly!"

I roll my eyes and pour a packet of pop rocks into my mouth.

Nonna Elba slams her coffee cup down on the table, spilling espresso on the glossy white goods brochure. "You eat that shit all the time; it's going to make you sick. Don't tell me if you get sick, okay? I can predict the future, remember? You keep eating that shit and not practicing your magic you're both going to end up married to guys like those two fat slobs down the street and working at McDonalds for the rest of your life."

There's a knock at the door.

"Who is it, Nonna?" I ask her. I hate it when she tells me my future.

"How the hell should I know?" She says exhaling a smoke ring.

Nonna points to the door and I point at Lilli. My sister goes to answer the door and returns with a parcel wrapped in an Ezy Buy Catalogue.

"Ah hah! Just what I've been waiting for!" Nonna Elba puts out the cigarette stub in the ashtray, pulls a cigarette out of the nearly empty packet and lights up. Cigarette in mouth, she rips open the parcel. "A toilet paper holder and magazine stand in one! Perfect for bathroom reading! And a toilet brush holder in the shape of a toilet!"

Lilli and I laugh, and I regurgitate some of the Pop Rocks onto the plastic tablecloth. Nonna Elba eyeballs her and Lilli grabs me a napkin to clean it up.

"We'll buy the stove this afternoon." Nonna Elba coughs up a half her breakfast and swallows it down again. "I really have to give up smoking. And you, Eden, you're growing a donut ring around your waist!"

• • •

The White Goods Warehouse is a sparse factory outlet with exposed pink bats hanging from the ceiling. Nonna's managed to get a $150 discount on the electric stove we've chosen because she made a scratch with a paper clip on one of the hotplates when no one was looking.

She grabs an acne ridden teenage guy with a name badge that states, 'Customer Service is my Specialty' and says, "So, with this free installation and scratchie, what time will you come?"

The guy clears his throat. "Well . . . we can't give you an exact time, Madam. It will be anytime on Friday between 7 am and 5 pm. Would you like your *free* scratchie you get with your *free* installation now?"

Nonna turns her back to him, bends over and lets out a huge fart. Lilli and I try to stifle our giggles. Nonna always tells us that sometimes the best magic is the magic you blow out of your arse.

"I'll take the booklet of ten you've got there, young man," Nonna says pulling the tickets out of his pocket. "Give me something to do while I'm waiting around at home instead of scratching my arse."

The stove arrives wrapped in really cool bubble wrap. Lilli and I spend an entire afternoon popping the bubbles. Nonna screams twice that we are supposed to be practising our summoning and banishing spells as that's 55 percent of the exam and twice we tell that we'll do it later. Popping plastic bubble wrap has to be the most satisfying way to procrastinate.

"Eden! Lilli! If I hear another plastic bubble pop—I'll pop your heads! Now try and move the slow cooker to make way for the new electric." Nonna means business.

It's really weird but when I look over at our old stove, it's like the poor thing knows its days are numbered and it seems sad. Maxi, our cat, has been sleeping wrapped around one of the legs all afternoon.

We squat on either side of the old cooker and give it a heave but it does not budge. Maxi hisses at us and skulks away, pissed off that we have disturbed him.

"It's too heavy! You'll have to wait for the installation guys to come!" We both scream out to Nonna.

"I won't hold my bloody breath!" She yells back at us. The toilet flushes and her footsteps get closer to the kitchen; we run away from the bubble wrap.

"And, what did I say to you?" She says biting the side of her hand at us.

"Summoning Practice?" I say.

"Don't forget to do it or else you are going to lose your skills! I've ruined you two!" She shoots the Medusa look at us and we both cross our hearts. She stays staring at us until I walk over to the drawer where the Summoning and Banishing Spells book is, pull it out it and drop it onto the kitchen table. We open it to Nonna's notes on page one and I read aloud to Lilli.

The first rule is: Practice Every Day.

Avoiding Practice in the developing years can be detrimental to the teenage witch's progress. From the ages of thirteen to sixteen, girls are prone to summon demons instead of elementals and elementals instead of the dead. This can prove disastrous for those working in the area of séance and channelling. Add the fact that due to migration, dissociated from their lands and beliefs, the arts of clairvoyancy are a part of our Sicilian culture that is rapidly disappearing. Practice must be maintained as must be the ability to banish the unwanted summoned—

"I'm hungry," Lilli interrupts.

I smile. Sometimes being a twin means you don't have to explain to the other what you are thinking. We hear *Days of Our Lives* on the television, Nonna's favourite soap and sneak out the back door, creeping down the drive until we reach the footpath and walk down to Pizza Hut on the Princess Highway. The vouchers we use are for a free soft serve ice cream with every Cabanossi Lovers Pizza.

When we get back home, Nonna hasn't bothered to cook anything for dinner and sits with a hunk of cheese, some green olives and a glass of wine for her dinner. She doesn't say anything about our little escapade either. We put the left over pizza in the fridge.

Reprieve.

• • •

The noise starts at 2.23 a.m. Lilli and I both almost jump out of our bunk beds at the clanging in the kitchen. Someone was banging a fry pan in the kitchen with a wooden spoon to a 4/4 rhythm.

"What the hell is that?" Lilli whispers to me.

"How the hell should I know? Ask Nonna, she's the psychic!"

"Maybe Maxi is chasing a mouse in the kitchen."

"Yeah to a marching beat! I left him outside tonight."

We link arms and I grab the hairspray from the dresser—it would make a good weapon if it is a burglar in the house. We tiptoe in the dark, down the corridor, until we reach the kitchen and switch on the light. Fry pans, saucepans, baking dishes, all of them lie strewn on the floor. On the kitchen table, written in salt are the words: *SLOW COOKIN.*

"Lilli!" I whisper and pinch my sister hard on the arm. "Have you been practising summoning without using the book? You know that is really, really stupid."

"I haven't been doing any summoning practice!"

"Me neither. I've been so slack that Nonna told me she's going to give up on me soon and I can go and work at McDonald's instead of the clairvoyant arts when I leave school!" She pinches my arm right back and I let go of hers.

"Well, there is definitely something that's been summoned here—something that doesn't like the idea of our new stove!"

I turn my head to look at the electric cooker, wrapped in half popped bubble wrap, it now lay on the floor, horizontal and smeared in the left over Cabanossi Lovers pizzas we had left in the fridge. "Well, let's clean this mess up and try not to wake Nonna. She's going to go off at us about our summoning practice again. She's going to say we've brought this on."

Nonna Elba's snoring could be heard from the kitchen.

"I can't believe she has managed to sleep through that racket," Lilli says.

"I can," I say, waving an empty bottle of Jameson's whiskey in her face.

We both jump at the sound of scratching at the back door. Lilli and I creep over towards the sound. Me, with the empty whiskey bottle in hand and Lilli with the can of hairspray, maybe whatever it was, was out near the laundry. We both exhale in relief. It's Maxi, wanting to be let in. The poor cat meows in surprise at all the loving attention, flicks his tail at us and runs down the corridor straight to Nonna Elba's room.

"Well, I think we both better get back to our books and work out what the hell was in our kitchen tonight before Nonna finds out!" I say to Lilli, licking the rim of the whiskey bottle.

"Tomorrow morning," Lilli answers.

"Okay, let's just have a bit more of that leftover KFC in the fridge, all we had was that Pizza Hut for dinner."

"That KFC is three days old," Lilli grimaces but she's already opening the fridge. "Whatever or whoever it is has covered our KFC with chook feathers and chicken feet."

I snatch the plate from Lilli's hands and throw the chicken bits, feathers, feet and plate into the bin. "Eehhew! That's gross! We should clean this up now, Nonna Elba's going to lose it if she sees all this mess in the kitchen tomorrow morning."

Lilli nods her head and walks towards the sink to grab the sponge. Nonna was going to have something to say about the fact that we had been avoiding Summoning and Banishing for the last three days. We would have a better chance to escape her wrath if we at least cleared the evidence of kitchen poltergeist activity before the morning.

It was too late. We could hear her already shuffling down the corridor in her fluffy slippers.

"Right! What's going on?" She says, hands on hips. She walks over the table, looks at the words SLOW COOKIN written in salt, dips her finger in it, tastes it and smacks her lips.

"You've bloody summoned a Mumacca! What did I say to you girls about summoning the elementals without consulting the right books—eh? I told you, you need to practice every day, you need to say the exact words in the book or else the wrong creatures can come. Ones you don't want around!"

"We were in bed! We didn't do any summoning—" I said.

"Exactly my point!" Nonna Elba banged on the table for maximum effect. "You haven't been doing any summoning or banishing spells lately. All the certified documents from the Etna Inherited Magic Board I had to organise in order for your school to approve your study leave and you have both done nothing!"

"But we've still got a week and half," I answered.

"I don't want to hear it! You and your sister—no summoning and banishing, no practice and no proper home cooking. You're going to lose our old magic and I'm not getting any younger and you both are making me lose it! What will you do when I'm gone? I think I've over-compensated for you two losing your mother. I've ruined you!"

"Well, Nonna. What about you reading all the junk mail? You're the one that got us hooked on the junk mail with the fast food in it."

"I'm an old lady and can do what I bloody well like! Why should I read the grimoires when I know them by heart?"

Something clanged inside the wall behind the cupboards.

"Well girls, he or she or it is not gone." Nonna Elba walked over to the drawer and pulled out the Summoning and Banishing Spells book; it was as thick as a telephone directory. She threw it at us. Lilli ducked just in time and it landed with a thud on the table.

"It's just like the yellow pages," Nonna says lighting up a cigarette. "I could have bashed you with it and have left no bruises. Now clean this kitchen up and get studying on how to get rid of whatever it is! You'll find Mumacca under "M'."

We clean up the kitchen and take the book with us to bed. We last five minutes before Lilli starts to drool a little and it drips onto the page. I turn out the light and decide to get some sleep. Banishing and how the heck this thing was summoned in the first place can wait until the morning.

· · ·

So procrastinating has finally kicked us back in the butt. And we don't have anymore plastic bubbles to pop, either. Lilli's gone to do a tarot reading to earn money to support her Pizza Hut habit and I've just found the entry under "B' for "Brownies' in a book on folklore I borrowed from our local Library. After reading the first paragraph, I realise we don't have the friendly British variety.

Those brownies like to clean things up. No. We've really got the Sicilian version—just like our Grandma.

It seems that Nonna Elba knew I would seek information from anything but the book she carted on the boat back in 1966 with the old slow cooker because at the end of the entry she's written in Sicilian, in very small print: *now that you've read through the fairy tale version please go back to THE BOOK and see "M" for Mumacca*.

Mumaccas are supposed to be Southern Italian brownies that wear cute red hats and like to hang out around wine cellars all day. This doesn't fit because we don't have a wine cellar but Nonna has plenty of grog around the house to drink. We know that he doesn't like KFC chicken and prefers slow cooking to fast food. But none of this makes sense.

Lilli walks in with a box of donuts. She's made enough to start her own franchise in a donut shop by reading Mrs Simoncetta's tarot cards every second day. The woman is as addicted to readings as we are to junk food. Lilli knows exactly what to say to women like her wanting answers about love and prospects. *There's an ending and a new beginning coming your way. And you're at a crossroads in your life, and you may not know it but you're very loved,* and Mrs Simoncetta thinks my sister is Madame Blavatsky or something. Me, I can't be bothered but then again, I'm not as hooked on Pizza Hut and Pop Rocks are much cheaper than pizza. But I am just a bit jealous. Nonna has never threatened Lilli with working at McDonald's until the end of her days as much as she does with me. I have found how to placate the little bastard but I'm not telling her. I just might win my own brownie points with Nonna if I keep this titbit of information to myself.

"Eden, have you found out how to send the Mumacca back?"

I shake my head.

"Holy Shit! Eden!" She screams as she opens the box and a putrid smell of rotten eggs fills the kitchen. "He's left a little turd in the hole of each donut!" Lilli throws the box onto the floor. "Did you find the banishing chapter? How do we banish him?" Lilli is frantic.

I shrug my shoulders. "Mumaccas are from Southern Italy, they're not from Australia. I thought we're supposed to have the friendly British variety here." I can't help but like him a bit for ruining Lilli's donuts.

"You mean he's probably like, from Sicily like Nonna?"

"Yep! And sorry to change the subject but we really have to get this old slow cooker out of the way. Council clean up is Saturday morning and the new electric stove is installed on Friday. It's Thursday today so we'd better get a move on. And the exam is next Friday!"

"Great!" Lilli yells. "Right! We so have to start studying. Let's start with this Banishing and then move onto the channelling of the dead. I heard there's no multiple choice in the exams—it's all *viva voce*. Let's have a chocolate reward two hours from now."

I pull out two Mars Bars from my pocket. "Let's have a motivating chocolate now!"

We sit at the kitchen table and open up the exercise books that Nonna has left out for us to take notes.

"It says here that Mumaccas are notoriously bad at arithmetic and can't count past twelve!" Lilli says.

I nod my head and keep the other bit of information to myself. Maybe Nonna has made the book that way so she can see who's done the study. If Lilli shines at the tarot readings at least I can earn some brownie points with banishing him.

We fall into a rare silence as we start taking notes when I feel a pulling on my left plait.

"Lilli, stop it!" I slap my sister on the arm.

"Stop what?"

"You just pulled my hair."

"No I didn't."

And then my sister's face goes white and she grabs at her own hair. "Run!"

Lilli jumps out of her chair and onto the table, I stumble out of my chair and see a little ruddy dirty face, a bulbous nose and nostril hairs protruding to his upper lip. It is the Mumacca and he's not happy. In his hand, he has the chicken scissors.

I scream and start running around the kitchen table. Lucky his stubby legs are a lot shorter than mine. I grab the kitchen stool to use as a mount to get to the top of the fridge. He catches my plait and pulls it really hard. There is the sound of a snip and a light feeling on the left side of my head as my plait falls to the floor. He's cut my plait off! I make it up to the top of the fridge but he has forgotten me and moves towards Lilli. He hoists himself up on the table and tries to reach her long hair but she has rolled it tight into a bun on top of her head. She grabs the book, jumps down and runs around the table.

I know I can't withhold my knowledge anymore. "Give him a gift, Lilli! One of the junk mail things. Anything!"

Lilli's hair starts to unravel out of the bun as she runs towards the boxes of Nonna Elba's unopened junk mail orders. She rips the nearest box open, while the little Mumacca is pulling at one of her long curls and snipping madly at the air. He opens the scissors to cut the long strands in his hand but Lilli has already handed him the bright orange colander still in plastic and says, "A gift just for you!"

The Mumacca drops the scissors and grabs at the colander. You can see from the delight in his eyes, the gurgle of snot coming out of his nose and the big toothy grin that he loves the gift, just like the manual says. He plops himself down with his back against the stove and sits cross-legged with the colander in his lap and starts to count the holes in it. He puts a stubby finger onto each hole and counts, "Water go, Spaghetti Stop. Water go, Spaghetti Stop. Water go, Spaghetti Stop."

"It's a colander," Lilli says as she twists her hair back into a bun and backs away from him. I want to laugh but don't want to distract the little man in case he decides to cut my other plait!

Lilli reads the bits that I had kept to myself about giving Mumaccas a gift to placate them. I've managed to leave my chocolate fingerprint there.

"Hey! So you already read the bit about the gift and decided to tell me only when he's about to stab me with the chicken scissors!"

"Well, I didn't know he was going to appear so soon! Anyway, we seem to have distracted him now. Look at him! Each time he gets to twelve the poor little thing has to start all over again."

"We can't get rid of the stove," Lilli says to me while watching him totally engrossed in counting the holes in the colander.

"Why not?" I ask. I'm pretty pissed that I have lost half a head of hair.

"If we do, he's going to be homeless. An elemental refugee so to speak. I can't let him be homeless!" Lilli sighs. I know that sigh. It's the same sigh she makes every time she walks past the pet shop when there are dachshund puppies for sale.

"He's probably been living behind the stove since 1966, helping Nonna with all cooking since then."

"I suppose that's why everyone loves her food. She's got a little helper. Every woman I've done a tarot reading for this week has said how lucky we are to have Nonna's slow cooking."

"Don't make me feel guilty now about eating junk!" I'm feeling a bit feral now and jump down off the top of the fridge and make my way to the bread tin and pull out a packet of salt and vinegar chips. The bag makes a popping sound and stops the Mumacca at number eleven. He lets out a screech, drops the colander and lunges towards me to seize the bag of chips.

"Hey! They're mine!" I yell at him but he isn't scared. He yanks the packet out of my hand, throws them on the floor and stamps on the packet until it is nothing but foil and sawdust. Picking up the colander, he runs inside the pantry cupboard next to the stove. We hear the sound of rummaging and he comes out looking pleased as punch with a colander full of potatoes, pulls out a small knife from his faded blue overalls and starts peeling the spuds cross legged on the floor.

"I think he's making us real chips," Lilli says. "I don't think we should try and banish him now. I'm hungry."

We creep backwards out of the kitchen and watch him from the doorway peel the potatoes, slicing them into thick wedges. He drags the old fry pan out of the cupboard, places it on the old slow cooker and lights up the kindling with a click of his fingers. He puts lashings of olive oil into the pan and when it is sizzling he tosses in the wedges, sprinkling big flakes of sea salt on top.

The aroma makes our stomachs rumble. He must have heard mine because he claps and jumps up and down with that toothy grin again and hands us the wedges on a plate.

As we sit around the old slow cooker crunching into home cooked chips, the Mumacca opens the empty Nescafe jar with our collected junk food vouchers and throws them in with the kindling. And we don't protest.

He doesn't do the same with Nonna's Ezy Life Home Shopping Catalogue.

We hear the front door open and Nonna's Cuban heeled sandals walk up the hallway.

"Aahh, so you've studied the manual, I see," she says as the Mumacca has gone back to sitting back against the stove counting colander holes.

"Do we have to banish him, Nonna?" Lilli asks.

"We do if we get rid of the old slow cooker," she says matter of factly. "I can't chop the wood for the fire on my own anymore; you girls have to chip in too." She opens her handbag and puts our exam registration forms on the table. "And if you keep eating all the junk, then there's no point keeping the stove or the Mumacca."

There's a knock at the door.

"Well, one of you go and get it!" Nonna rolls her eyes. "Such lazy granddaughters!"

I jump up and run down the corridor towards the door. I'm still pretty pissed at the Mumacca for chopping my hair but hey, it is the eighties and I just might get away with having half a head of long hair and a bob on the other. And he is pretty cute—in a dachshund puppy kind of a way.

I open the door. A courier has left a parcel behind our screen door. It's a vertical chicken roaster Nonna Elba must have ordered and a new roll of bubble wrap.

I run back down the corridor with the vertical chicken roaster and hand it to the Mumacca. "A gift for you," I say.

He blows me a kiss and starts to play with the metal contraption.

I suppose Nonna's junk mail addiction might come in handy after all.

That afternoon, Lilli and I re-wrap the electric stove in the fresh bubble wrap for the installation guys to take back on Friday. And Lilli swears she sees Nonna wink at the Mumacca and him wink back at her.

Now just to study for those exams . . . .

• • • • • • • • • • •

THE SCHOOL BUS

JASON FISCHER

Nan said that Dad was at the wall tonight, keeping lookout for kangaroos. The sun was nearly at the treeline, so I rode there on my bike as quick as I could. Dad says only bloody idiots stay outside after dusk.

The wall wasn't a proper wall made out of bricks or stones. It was a junk wall— piled up truck tires and car bodies and sheets of rusty tin. Two and a half metres high, which is about how high the roos can jump. Nan says they used to jump much higher in the old days, so at least we got one thing to be thankful of.

Dad was at the lookout spot facing the main highway, and he was testing the spotlights. They had a bunch of car batteries up there, connected with bent-out coat hangers and jumper leads.

"Light," he yelled out to Mr Wenham, who was the next lookout along. I leaned my bike against a broken TV set and climbed up the ladder.

"Tom!" Dad said. "What the hell you doing here? Go home and get indoors before I tan your bloody backside."

"I got a note from school," I said, and dug the paper slip out of my pocket. "If you don't sign this, Mrs Hamilton says I'll be in even more trouble."

"Gimme that.' Dad squinted at the note. "Says you didn't finish your homework."

"It's stupid and boring. And Mrs Hamilton has only got one leg."

"You've got a bloody cheek on you. Respect your elders." Dad had a nib of a pencil in his pocket and scribbled his mark on the slip.

"We work hard to give you kids a school. If you keep mucking about in class, I'll turf you over the wall and let the roos sort you out."

The sun was starting to sink through the scrub, and all I could see out there was the cracked black ribbon—the old highway. Beats me how they spotted the roos anyway, I reckon if the lights didn't scare them off, the rifles would.

One night, Billy Wenham and I snuck out to watch a roo attack. There were dozens of them, bright eyes shining as they ran from the searchlights. We saw a roo scrabbling to the top of the wall right near our hiding spot, its face all rotten and bits of bone showing in its tail. It nearly got over but Mr Richards shot it in the face. We didn't dare sneak out again after that.

It only takes one roo getting over the wall and we're all dead meat.

"Tell your Nan that I said you get no supper," Dad said. "And you can attend to Miss Stewart on your way home."

"Aw Dad! She's really gross."

"Just feed her boy, don't go doing any of the other stuff. Understand?"

"What other stuff?" I really didn't know what he was talking about. Everyone was really weird whenever I asked about Miss Stewart.

"No backtalk. You can feed the pigs in the morning too."

I slid down the ladder and rode towards Miss Stewart's house. No supper and two extra chores. Stupid Mrs Hamilton.

By the time I got to Miss Stewart's house, it was well into dusk, and I felt a bit nervous. I should have gone to see Dad in the morning, like Nan said. But I figured he would be cranky after pulling an all-nighter.

The door was open. I'm always getting told to mind my manners, and even though Miss Stewart isn't one of the grown-ups who can get me in trouble, I knocked.

There are men coming and going all the time to see her. I guess they take pity on her on account of her situation. Sometimes they even queue out the front door, waiting to pay their respects.

"Come in," she said. Her voice was all weird and quiet. She never sounded happy or sad or anything. Dad says there's no point being miserable. He says there's no room in this town for anyone who wants to whinge and whine.

She slept in the front room of the house. There was nothing in there but an old saggy mattress and some newspapers laid out across the floor. We used to have to change the newspaper every week or so but we stopped doing that a while ago. It smelled really bad in there.

"Hello, Tom," she said, and I nodded hello. I know she can't help it, but it's really disgusting. She doesn't have arms or legs, and she's missing all of her teeth too. She's just a torso and a head.

"I'm glad you came, I'm really busting.' I find the rusty saucepan that they've given her to use as a potty. The next bit's a little tricky, but I found that the best way was to sit on the edge of the mattress, resting her across my lap like a big baby. She's not allowed to wear clothes anymore, and it's weird to be able to see her boobs and everything. Some of the other boys laugh about it.

So the trick is to point her bottom end at the pan, and then she goes. The Council said all of our toilet pans are needed for the town garden, especially this year because it's heaps dry. Dad caught me peeing on the back fence once and he gave me a right belting.

When Miss Stewart is finished I help her wipe up with a bit of paper from the floor. She gets a bath twice a week, which was Nan's idea. I don't see why she's so special, I only get one bath each Sunday *and* I have to share the water with Dad and Nan.

"You're a good boy, Tom," she said, and I put her back on the mattress. It's going to be a cold night tonight, so I fetch her two blankets from a pile by the door. They don't allow Miss Stewart a fire.

There's a couple of crates of baby food in the kitchen, and a plastic tub full of rainwater. I pull out a few jars and scoop an enamel mug into the tub for her to drink out of.

"Here's your dinner, Miss Stewart," I said and sit her up on some pillows. I spoon her the apple one first, I know it's her favourite.

"How was school today?" she asked, and so I told her all about the stupid book report and how I got in trouble for not doing my homework.

"I remember reading Picnic at Hanging Rock when I went to school," she said, her gummy jaws working on the baby mush. "I thought it was a very boring book, but that's only because they made me read it. I tried it again, when I was all grown up, and you know what Tom?"

"What's that, Miss Stewart?"

"I still didn't like it."

Miss Stewart isn't from around here. She came in a few years ago, with a bunch of out-of-towners. Before everything went bad, she was actually a famous lady and an actress on the television. They showed us a video of her show once, but they don't play the videos anymore because all the batteries are needed for the town lights.

The grown-ups put posters of her all over the wall. It's weird to see pictures of her with arms and legs, and her hair all pretty. She's smiling in the pictures, but I can't remember ever seeing her smile. "Alison Stewart—star of Outback Glamour!" one of the posters says.

You can see wet gummy marks from where she's tried to pull down the posters on the lowest bit of the wall. I'm not sure why they put the posters there. If it's meant to cheer her up it does the opposite. I know I wouldn't want to look at my old pictures every day if I had lost my arms and legs.

Dad won't let me take the posters down, and told me not to mention it ever again.

It was getting really late, and I was so hungry I even snuck a bit of the baby food when Miss Stewart was finished eating. When she had sipped enough water I tucked her in and left.

Whoever had come here last hadn't shut the door, so I made sure it was closed. If a roo got over the wall, it could get into the house, and there would be nothing she could do to defend herself.

Someone painted the word "SLUT!" across the door, in thick red letters. I asked Nan what it meant, but she made me wash my mouth out with soap.

I got home just after dark. Nan had fallen asleep in her armchair. She'd left the oil lamp going again, and if Dad was home he would have yelled at her. There was an empty bottle of brandy on the coffee table, between her and Dad they'd polished it off within a day. That had to be the last of the grog. Dad won't be happy.

Nan must have heard me come in.

"Your dinner's in the stove," she slurred.

There were still some coals going, so I threw a few split logs into the stove to keep the house warm. Dinner was a casserole with meat and baked beans. I decided not to tell her about having to miss supper, because she was too drunk to even notice me cutting a slice of peach cobbler.

Putting a rug over her knees, I left Nan snoring in her chair. I took the oil lamp to my room, ignored Picnic at Hanging Rock and read my Biggles book instead. When I went to sleep, I dreamt that the town had a plane, and that I stole it and flew away forever. Everything else was dead meat, but I was safe and nothing could touch me up there.

A rifle shot woke me, and when I went back to sleep I didn't dream about anything.

• • •

Nan gave me cold casserole for breakfast, and a bucket of scraps to add to the pigs' wheelbarrow. I had to hurry—school always started at 8.30 am sharp.

The piggery was just outside the town wall, so we didn't have to put up with the smell. Don't know why, but the dead things won't touch a pig. They're perfectly safe out there. They'd built the new piggery down by the creek so that when there's water in it the pigs can drink. It's just a muddy trickle most of the time, so I don't know why they bothered.

When I rolled the barrow down to the piggery, I saw Billy and Eric throwing rocks at Billy's older brother, who was in with the pigs.

Danny Wenham got bitten by a roo a couple of years ago, and the bite went bad. They knew what was coming, so Dad and Mr. Wenham wired his mouth shut with barbed-wire, wrapping it around the top of his head and under his chin even while he was kicking and screaming. They wound it tight with pliers, so there's no getting the wires off. He can't open his mouth at all.

"Cut it out, guys. That's not funny," I told Billy and Eric. Billy landed a rock right in Danny's face and he looked up at us, confused as hell.

"He's dead, Tom. He doesn't know what's going on."

I told them I'll see them at school, and opened the gate to the main sty. Danny tried to bite me, his eyes all veiny and bulging out, and reached for me with fingers that looked like bruised fruit.

I pushed him away, and put the shovel back into his hands. I knew he wouldn't hurt me. He was just confused.

"Stop mucking around, Danny."

He smelled worse than the pigs, and his skin had gone a rotten bluey-green colour. I know you're not meant to feel sorry for the ones that have turned, but Danny must have gotten lonely out here, night after night with nothing but pigs for company. He did what he was told though, scooping the manure out of the sty with great concentration. He worked very slowly, but he never had to rest. The town had tried to get him to do other chores, but Danny was just too simple now.

Piggery started when the Council were worried that us kids weren't getting enough protein. Some grownups got a truck working and went to the next town. That old fatty Mr. Gunderson didn't come back (they never told us kids what happened to him), but Mr. Wenham brought back a breeding pair— an old boar and a sow. We had trouble getting the piggery started, some disease took the first litter of piglets so they didn't let us eat those. Now there are six pigs, grown to nearly full size. If they stay healthy, folks say we could slaughter some next year.

Others say to slaughter a pig now, but Mr Wenham keeps calling them impatient fools.

Whenever we get a bit of meat we split it up, an even share for every family in town. Dad says that times are lean, but if the mother-loving-mongrels can hold their horses, we'll never run out of meat again.

I was heading to school on my bike when I saw the commotion. There were a bunch of people on top of the main wall, and Dad was pointing at something on the highway side of town.

I laid my bike down and climbed the ladder up the wall, but it was too packed with grownups to see. I climbed up a pile of tires till I found a gap in the tin that I could see through.

A yellow school bus was slowly navigating the cracked highway, big clouds of steam rising from the front of it. It looked in real trouble, and was moving at walking pace. The struggling sounds of the engine reached us. It sounded like someone had put a cupful of ball-bearings in that motor.

As the bus made its way towards our front gate, Dad loaded a bullet into his rifle. Since things had gone bad, we hadn't had a visitor.

Someone cried out, and I looked behind the bus. We could see them now, way back in the distance, stretched out across the dusty horizon. Hundreds of figures shuffling through the scrub, a horde of people that seemed to wriggle in the heat haze.

"Quick!" Mr Wenham yelled out. "Bring all the guns! Bring bloody everything."

Perhaps half a mile from our front gate, the yellow school bus gave a death rattle, and it stopped. I couldn't see much else till the door slid open. A man got out, waving like a crazy. Dad said a curse word, and shot at him. The bullet hit the front of the bus, and the man jumped back in, pulling the door shut.

"Dad, don't!" I said.

"Brought them zombies right to our front doorstep," Dad said, working the action open and loading another bullet. "If these morons think we're gonna shelter them, they're mistaken."

"I dunno," Mr. Donaldson said. "We could do with some fresh faces in here. Some of us are getting a bit . . . bored with the entertainment."

"We've more than catered for that, you greedy old sod," Dad said. He looked real mad now. "We're not a refugee camp."

"Please," I said 'They're in trouble!'

"Someone get that kid off the wall," one of the grownups said, and Dad yelled at me and told me to go to school.

I climbed down and saw Billy standing, watching us from his bike, right by where I'd dropped mine. We went to Eric's house. Mrs Hamilton was probably hiding in her cellar, the way she did every time the town was under attack. There was no point sitting in the stupid school while this was going on.

Eric took us to his room where he picked up a pair of binoculars his dad had given him, and then we rode to the old church. This was the place where we used to go to Mass, but that was before the Reverend and half the town nicked off. Mum had wanted me to leave with them, but Dad said a lot of bad words and threw all her stuff out the front door and locked her out. Then she went away and never came back.

I'd come to the church sometimes to throw rocks at the stained-glass windows, and once Danny Wenham reckoned that he dug up a body in the graveyard, though everyone knew that he was just a fat liar.

Now we laid our bikes on the dirt beside the front door. Eric hung the binoculars around his neck, and then Eric and Billy and I went into the church and climbed the stairs all the way up the bell-tower. We could see everything from up here. We were leaning out through the shutters up around the bell, and Eric was whistling through his teeth.

"Look at em all," he said, and let us have a go at the binoculars.

I moved the little dial till I could actually see the bus. It was packed full of people but I couldn't see much more from this far, and the windows were all dusty and scratched. The people were all sitting in their seats, perfectly still, and a couple of them were looking out the windows.

The other mob were circling the bus now, and they were definitely dead meat. You can tell because they don't walk right, and their clothes are all wrecked and rotten.

I looked at all the walking dead, and there were hundreds—broken little kids and leathery old grannies and even a mouldy old fella that looked a little bit like the old Reverend whose church we hid in.

"Give us a look!" Billy said, and I gave him the glasses. Without them you could just see the yellow brick that was the bus, and hundreds of little black dots swarming around it, kicking up plumes of red dust.

"The rotters will figure out how to get into the bus soon," Eric said. "If those folks don't run, they'll get bitten."

"But if they leave the bus, our mob will shoot them," I said.

"Deserve it," Billy said, taking his time with the binoculars. "Pretty stupid, running away from their hidey hole. There's nothing but dead things out there."

"Yep, dead things and wild pigs," Eric said. "And both will try and eat you."

"And they made a lot of noise and got the dead things worked up, brought 'em all here," Billy said. "Now we're the ones in strife."

I was angry that Billy was hogging the binoculars, but more angry that they didn't care about the people in the bus. Maybe those folks had run out of food, or their water went bad or something.

"I know that if I was in that bus," I said, "I'd want someone to help me."

Billy and Eric both turned and looked at me, like I was going soft in the head. Eventually though, I convinced them to leave the church and help the folks in the bus.

We slid the sheets of tin back to cover the gate on the piggery side, and I piled some extra rocks in front of them in case a dead man tried to get them open.

"This is really dumb. We are gonna get in so much trouble," Eric said.

"I told you, we're gonna be heroes," I told him. "Don't be such a chicken."

"Yeah, and we'll make them pay a fee to get in," Billy said, pleased with himself. "Then there'll be food for everyone."

We rode our bikes around the wall, but Billy had to show off and go over the jumps he'd made down by the creek. If he broke his stupid head open and the zombies caught us here, I don't know what we'd do. I guess we'd have two brothers shovelling s-h-i-t in the piggery then.

We stopped by the highway wall and hid behind an old washing machine. The grownups were all further along the wall, and wouldn't be able to see us so long as we didn't move forward.

"Gimme the glasses," I said to Eric, who just nodded and handed them over. He kept looking at the bus in the distance, and he turned all white. I reckoned he was about to chuck his guts.

I panned across the horde of rotters, saw them shuffling forward and kicking up dust and small stones. They were everywhere, so close now that I could see a cloud of flies buzzing around each one.

The closest one was maybe a hundred steps away from the back of the bus. He wore a butcher's coat, but the white was gone and it was all covered in black stuff now, and his knife belt was empty. He had his hands stretched forward and fingers clenched.

From what I reckoned, he was moving at a quick walk now.

"They're slow as. We can beat them!" I said. We picked up our bikes, and I made sure Eric had his and wasn't gonna chicken out.

Then we rode like hell, rode straight towards the mob of zombies. I rang my bell lots, and Billy whistled between his teeth cause he was really good at that.

All of the grownups were yelling at us from the wall, and if I knew my Dad, I'd be in a lot more trouble over this than any book report. They started shooting at the zombies, then I guess we were in the way and they were too scared to shoot at the rotters in case they accidentally hit one of us kids.

It worked, though. The horde began to move towards us, and we led them away from the bus, back towards the highway. Every single one of them went bug-eyed and grabby, shuffling after us.

"You're going too quick!" I yelled at Billy, when he got too far away and the zombies lost interest. He did that riding-in-slow-circles thing, but waited a bit too long before trying to take-off. Butcher Man grabbed him by the shirt and one leg.

Billy said a word that would have got him ten straps in my house, and fell off his bike. The zombie tripped over the bike, and Billy screamed and kicked and wriggled his way loose.

He ran like hell, a hundred rotting zombies shuffling after him. Our grownups started shooting from the walls, picking off the nearest zombies, but it was pointless. There were just too many of them.

I heard gunfire from the bus, and saw that someone had popped a window open to shoot at the zombies snapping at Billy.

"Stop! Stop it!" I yelled, but it was too late. Some of the zombies were moving towards the noise. Eric and I yelled and rang our bells and stopped pedalling long enough to keep most of the dead folks interested, but a few still went for the bus. They were more shots as the stupid outsiders tried to defend themselves.

"Bloody idiots!" I said, and I was glad that Nan couldn't hear me swearing. I yelled at Billy to run back to the creek side, and if it was our school's sports day he would have won the blue ribbon, he was running that quick.

The zombie mob split in three. Lots of them were interested in Billy, some of them were chasing Eric and me, and a few were hammering on the sides of the bus, trying to figure out how to get inside. What looked like a dead policeman was pushing at the folding door, so I got off my bike for just one scary second, and threw a big rock at him.

"Come on!" I yelled. "Over here!" And hopped back on my bike with the wind of dead fingers brushing against my back. Close.

Between Eric and me, we confused the zombies good, and led them around in circles for a while. When none of them were close to the bus I rode up to it, banging on the sides and pointing towards the town. I waited in front of the door, and knew that the town's grownups wouldn't shoot at anyone coming out of the bus in case I got hit.

A man cranked the partition door open, and nervously climbed out. He was a scary looking fella, covered in tatts, with a big meaty fist wrapped around a cricket bat.

"You're a brave little fella. Thanks," he said, with tears in his eye. I didn't know what to say, Dad says that a man having a sook might as well be dead so I just nodded and rode away to draw the zombies from the bus again.

We made sure those people from the bus got a clear run to the town wall. The grownups shouted at us, we shouted back, and the strangers shouted lots too.

They opened the gates though. I knew they'd do the right thing once they saw the people they'd be saving. By the time Dad was through with me I couldn't sit for a week, but it was worth it.

• • •

We've had to give up the piggery. The rotters walk around our town day and night now, so many that even the dead roos have given up attacking. Danny Wenham is going berserk out there, pushing at rails and trying to join in with his new friends.

The good news is that the pigs are perfectly safe, bad news is we can't get to them, with all the rotters around. The dead folks aren't interested in our squealers. Dad says it's a waste of good meat. You can bet your biggest marble that the pigs are missing their scraps. I hope they don't suffer for long. Dad says that, in this heat, they should die of thirst in a day or two.

I heard Dad say to Mr Donaldson that the town didn't even have enough bullets left to kill all of the zombies that the outsiders brought to our gates.

But at least we have some new people in town. They're from a long way away, and they got sick from the water so I feel pretty clever for guessing right. The bus was full and there's lots of them, even a mum and a dad, and they brought a little boy called Laurence. He's in school with us now, but he doesn't talk much and Billy says he caught him crying in the toilets. I told him not to pick on the new kid but even I think he's a bit weak.

Laurence's mum (her name is Mrs Burton) lives in Miss Stewart's house now. I asked Nan where Miss Stewart would live now, but she wouldn't say anything. I caught Mr Wenham carrying Miss Stewart out of her house, right on dusk while I was taking our toilet-pans to the garden. I left them on the ground and followed.

He hefted Miss Stewart up to the top of the wall and for a while he was saying something to her, quietly. Then he dumped her over the side, right into the reaching hands of our dead neighbours. Miss Stewart screamed for a long time before she stopped.

I'm not sure why she didn't end up in the cookpot. Nan said that she was tainted meat, but I don't understand why.

Dad and Mr Wenham gave Laurence's mum what they called "the treatment". They didn't want us kids to see, but I ran to the window when I heard the screaming. Her leg was gone by then, and Dad was cooking the bleeding stump with part of his welding kit. She was screaming her head off and thrashing around, and it was all Mr Wenham could do to hold her down.

That's when Nan started ripping her teeth out with pliers.

"You won't need these choppers, love," Nan cackled. "Can't have you biting your visitors."

Why would she bite anyone? That doesn't make sense, and it's not very fair on her. Mr. Burton only had to give his left arm up for taxes.

We boiled up our share, a big reddy hunk of meat with the tatts still on the skin. I played with my food a while and tried to find the tatts, but I remembered I got maths homework due. Then, I ate up quick.

· · · · · · · · · · ·

THE KING'S ACCORD

ALAN BAXTER

The King's blood soaked his white sheet, scarlet slowly spreading. Royal eyes stared wide and horrified at velvet hangings above the bed, seeing nothing. Queen Sylveen, face drawn in torment, pushed the King's Guard aside and threw back the heavy, wet sheet. A gaping wound across the King's stomach, clutched in one desperate hand, yawned up at her. With a cry she turned away.

The King's Guard trembled. "Your Highness, I am so sorry. The assassin, he was like a shadow, on the King before I even knew he was there." He gestured to the ground, a black-garbed figure lying in another pool of blood. "I struck him down with all the speed I had, but I was too late."

Sylveen turned her back on her dead husband, lifting her chin. "My husband . . ." Her voice hitched. Clearing her throat she tried again. "My husband is not dead."

"Your Majesty . . . ?"

"Rythell, you will tell no one of this. Send for Andur Mylan."

"My Queen, the King is well beyond healing . . ."

The Queen's face hardened. "Rythell, do as I say! Tell no one, send for the Court Mage and wait outside this room until he arrives."

"Yes, Your Highness." Fear and confusion on his face, the King's Guard slipped from the room.

The Queen turned, fell across the body of her husband and gave free rein to her grief.

• • •

Andur Mylan hurried through the castle, taking stone stairs two at a time. It was a long way from his basement rooms to the King's tower and it didn't pay to keep Their Majesties waiting. Out of breath, he reached the iron-banded wooden door and met the stony gaze of the King's Guard.

"Rythell, I've been summoned."

"I know. Brace yourself for a shock." The guard turned and rapped on the door. "Your Majesty, the Court Mage is here."

"Enter."

Squaring his shoulders, Rythell opened the door and strode in. Andur paused. A shock? With a wash of trepidation he followed. The Queen stood in the centre of the room. In a pool of blood at her feet was a man dressed all in black, apparently an Ethentian assassin. Andur's gaze swept across to the King's bed. His breath caught at the sight of blood and the King's face, a rictus of agony in death. His jaw dropped. "My Queen . . . ?"

"Shut the door."

"My Queen, are *you* hurt?"

"No. An assassin gained entry and murdered my husband in his sleep. If I had not been outside, unable to sleep, I'm sure I would be dead too. Rythell killed the assassin, but his end was already achieved."

Andur narrowed his eyes, trying to take it all in. Rythell stood beside him, head hung in shame. The King dead? It was inconceivable. "Your Majesty . . ."

The Queen silenced him with an upheld palm. "As you are aware, in three day's time the delegates from Ethentia arrive to sign the Accord Of Diam."

Andur nodded. "The entire Kingdom is aware, Your Majesty."

"Obviously someone disagrees with it."

Andur crouched to inspect the body of the assassin. "Definitely Ethentian, not just in appearance. He carries an Ethentian blade and . . ." He paused, sniffing at the blood covered steel. "Yes, I can smell Slybane."

The Queen raised an eyebrow.

"An Ethentian poison. This assassin wasn't going to rely on steel alone to achieve his ends."

Sylveen nodded. "There is clearly a part of Ethentian society that doesn't want to see an end to this war."

"There are many, Your Majesty. Here too, I'm sure. A healthy trade exists for the unscrupulous during wartime, not to mention the political aims of some."

"Indeed. So this accord must be signed. Therefore, the King is not dead."

"I don't understand."

The Queen crossed her arms tightly over her chest. "My husband spent many, many years negotiating a treaty with Ethentia. It's been his life's work. Our son will take over the throne and he will rule well, but he is not King Monvald of Trear. If the King is dead the treaty will fall apart and it will become my son's life's work to rebuild it."

"Maybe not, Your Majesty. Could not Tellon simply declare his support of his father's work and sign the accord as King?"

"No more than I could as Queen. The Ethentian's are a proud and stubborn people and this accord is with King Monvald and Emperor Qoh. The drafts have all been written in these names, the last year has been spent agonising over every single letter of this thing to the contentment of all. Any change now would scupper everything."

"Then the accord is lost."

The Queen approached Andur, taking both his hands in hers, a gesture unimaginable. Andur trembled. Rythell turned away. "The King can not be dead, Andur."

"Your Majesty, I'm sorry, but . . ."

"Andur! The King is *not* dead. The King is very sick, but insists that the signing of the accord will proceed. Only you, Rythell and I know the truth. Why have I called for you?"

Andur's trembling increased. He wondered if the Queen's grief had driven her mad. "Your Majesty, I don't know."

"What can you do that Rythell or I never could?"

Andur stared into the Queen's deep green eyes as his hands trembled in hers. Their proximity overwhelmed him. The shock of the killing, the stench of death, disoriented him. He squeezed his eyes shut, trying to think, even as realisation rose in his mind. "No, my Queen. Surely not."

"There is no other way."

"But I don't know how."

"You're the only one who can learn. And learn you must, in just a few days."

Andur shook his head, eyes still tightly closed. "It is against nature, Your Majesty. And I don't even know if it can work."

The Queen put one finger beneath Andur's chin, tipped his head up. His knees threatened to fold beneath him. "Look at me, Andur Mylan."

With a supreme act of will Andur opened his eyes.

"Think how many lives are lost in this futile war every year. Can we in all conscience *not* do everything in our power to see this accord signed?"

Andur's heart pounded in his chest, stunned at the Queen's touch, the slaughter that surrounded them. "But Your Majesty, I don't know how."

"Teskelleth does."

• • •

He packed in a haze of confusion, unsure what he might actually need. The Queen insisted that she and Rythell would take care of the body of the assassin. He was to focus entirely on his task. Already word was spreading as the castle awoke; the King was unwell and cancelling all engagements to be recovered in time for the delegates' arrival. Deciding that little beyond food and water would be of any use, and would only slow him down, Andur threw his pack across one shoulder. With a handful of medications he returned to the King's tower.

"Your Majesty, I have brought medicines and ensured I was seen bringing them. As Court Mage and Royal Physician it seems strange that I will be leaving. At least I will have been seen attending now."

The Queen smiled, though it couldn't push through the grief to reach her eyes. "You are a good man, Andur. I will make it known that the King is stable and you have travelled to collect medicines to hasten his recovery."

Andur nodded. "It will take me most of a day to reach Teskelleth. Another to return. I must learn while I'm there and have enough time to perform whatever is required when I get back. This may be an impossible task, my Queen."

"I know. We have three days before the delegates arrive. Tellon, as leader of our forces, will not return from the war until the accord is signed. No one else needs to know or has any business enquiring until then. If you can learn what you need, and get back in time to make it happen, we stand a chance of keeping this accord alive."

"What if Teskelleth won't teach me?"

"Do *anything* to convince her. And the Blessing Of The Six go with you."

Terrified at the thought of what "anything" might entail, Andur reached the stables as the sun cleared the city walls. Weighed down by trepidation he walked his horse through cobbled streets, leaving the city gates as the morning mists lifted from the plains. Turning his horse to the north, he rode towards a place he had promised himself he would never go.

Teskelleth, the dark witch, once a respected citizen of Trear. He had looked up to her as a young child, when he was apprenticed to the Court Mage of the day. Her potions and her skills were legendary. Her ability to heal unrivalled. But darkness had crept into the heart of Teskelleth. Her magic had taken ever more blasphemous turns. Eventually she had been denounced as evil and tried as a dark witch. Found guilty, they had burned her at the stake. And she had laughed. Laughed as her magic protected her from the voracious flames. When the ropes binding her had burned away along with her clothes she strolled, casually naked, from the pyre. It was well known that she had exiled herself to the north. The King kept a close eye on her with spies and scouts, but she ignored everyone and everything. Concentrating, presumably, on her black arts.

Andur had no idea how he was supposed to ask this creature for help, especially without raising her suspicions to his reasons. Though, as the Queen had suggested, what choice did they have?

• • •

He rode all day, careful to avoid exhausting his horse. Eventually he reached the foothills of the Skaren Peaks, malevolent, jagged grey rising endlessly beyond. The light was fading from the sky as he walked his horse warily among the broken shale, watching for landmarks and signs. He guessed he wouldn't have to look hard. A large black crow landed on a lightning struck tree limb, its blackness stark against the pale grey of the dead branch. Signs of magic swirled about it, obvious to Andur's mage eyes. He nodded softly to himself. "You going to lead me then?"

The crow tipped its head, looking with one eye then the other.

"Ready when you are," Andur said.

The crow tipped its head again.

Andur narrowed his eyes, feeling his way into the crow's mind. "Ah, you're watching through the crow? Teskelleth, I seek your counsel."

The crow sat motionless.

"Teskelleth, I am Andur Mylan of Diam. I am a mage and a seeker. I have great need of knowledge I believe you can impart. I'm willing to pay whatever price you see fit to charge." For emphasis he hefted a large bag of ducorts that chinked softly, though he doubted the witch would set her price in gold.

The crow took off and flew to another blasted tree, further up the hill. Andur followed until he was led down into a valley, swallowed by darkness. He cast a bobbing ball of light and walked in magical silver brightness. Eventually a cave mouth appeared, firelight flickering against the silhouette of the mountainside. Frightened by something that should have been a welcome sight he dispelled his orb of light. Teskelleth stood at the cave mouth, hands on hips, a featureless shadow with the fire at her back. "You have balls of iron, I'll give you that."

"I'm not afraid of you." He tied his horse to a stunted tree.

"The stench of fear I smell in waves makes a liar of you, boy."

"Boy? I have close to forty years."

"And you call yourself a mage? You're a child in the arts."

Andur refused to be drawn into an argument about who may or may not be a mage. "I need knowledge of a magic that I believe you have."

"So?"

"And I'm prepared to pay handsomely for it."

"So you said. What use have I for money?"

"Then name your price."

Teskelleth turned and walked into the cave, slim, attractive, moving with a courtesan's grace. Andur knew it to be artificial youth through magic. She had been old before he was born, tales of her healing predating him by generations. Before she had turned.

He followed her into the cave, partly grateful to be in from the wilds, partly cautious that he was willingly jumping into a spider's web.

Her cave was a network of small caverns, packed with all manner of equipment, the bottles and cauldrons of the potioneer, the books and scrolls of the scholar, the tools and tinctures of the physician. There were caged animals and birds. At the back in deep shadow a large, dark sheet covered what appeared to be a huge cage. Andur thought he could hear a low keening floating through the smoky air from its depths.

"Best not to look on that, mage, let alone consider its contents."

He turned his attention back to the witch. She sat before a fire, spooning a lumpy soup from a pan into two wooden bowls. She offered one. He paused, suspicious.

"Eat, you bloody fool. If my aim was to kill you I wouldn't be so boring as to poison you with soup."

Suppressing his urgency, he took the bowl, sitting opposite her, the fire between them offering a small sense of security. Surreptitiously sniffing the rising steam, using a simple magic to feel for threats, he heard her soft chuckling. She began swallowing large spoonfuls, eating as though starving. Smiling at his paranoia, he followed suit. The soup was good, meaty and thick.

"I'm really not as evil as everyone thinks, you know."

Andur watched, chewing, choosing not to reply.

"You're the young Court Mage apprentice, eh? At least you were when I left."

"I used to idolise you."

She smiled, but it was sad. "You still could."

"I can't condone what you do."

"And what do I do exactly?"

Andur paused, spoon halfway to his lips. That was a good question. He took the spoon to his mouth, buying time to think.

"You're all told how evil I am," Teskelleth said quietly. "I'm really not evil. I just followed my studies down darker paths."

"Darker but not evil?"

The witch made a noise of disgust. "Magic is not all about love potions and healing royals! There are wonders to be unlocked, Andur Mylan. Secrets of the void. Going where others fear to tread is not courting evil."

Perhaps the things she said held merit. What did he really know of her after all? As an orphan child he had been apprenticed, taught the ways of the mage. Her reputation had been a light to guide him, her achievements a benchmark to live up to. She had ever been a free agent, never beholden to the royal family or anyone else, though always happy to help. She had often advised the Court Mage. Then tales of her slipping into black magic and dark experiments had preceded her trial, burning, escape and exile. But what had she actually done?

"It's all politics, Andur."

"Politics?"

"Of course. You cross the wrong people and, if they're powerful enough, they leak poison about you. Everything is political. Even you, here now. This is political, is it not?"

Andur shook himself. None of it mattered. He had a very specific task and a very tight schedule. "No. Not political. I need to know how to return someone from the dead."

Teskelleth rocked back with laughter. "Is that right? And for what, pray tell, if not politics?"

It suddenly seemed pointless to make up a story the witch would swallow. He had had plans to talk of a murdered lover, a visceral desire to have her back, but it all seemed so juvenile. Teskelleth was old and wise, despite appearances, and not easily fooled. "Please, my need is desperate. Can I not offer you a payment that would buy the knowledge without explanation?"

Teskelleth barked a short laugh. "Politics. But you need to know something. You can't bring someone back. Or if you can, I haven't learned how yet. You can reanimate a corpse, create a profane marionette that used to be a person. That unnatural thing can even do your bidding, though by the Six, it's a horrible thing to observe. Is that what you'd like, mage?"

Andur sat stunned. He had not planned on Teskelleth being quite so open about her abilities or successes. Or lack of them. He was not really sure what he had expected, though perhaps this was enough. A war between nations was the source of their desperation, thousands of lives the wager. His eyes were hard. "Can you show me?"

Teskelleth was mildly surprised. "Must be dire straits indeed in Court."

"Can you show me?"

"Yes."

Andur's heart was racing. "How long would it take to learn?"

"A few hours. The doing is rarely complicated. It's the desire to know and the finding out that take time."

"And what is your price?" He wondered if he would be able to pay. He was willing, with a nation at stake. He would give his life for his Queen and his country, if that's what it took.

"You really shouldn't play politics with magic, Court Mage."

"Please, name your price."

Teskelleth smirked. "I need nothing. But you will pay a price one way or another, I assure you of that. Politics and magic do not mix well. Look to me for proof of that."

Andur was stunned. They would certainly pay a price if their audacious plan didn't work, but could he really get this knowledge for nothing? "You would give me this knowledge freely?"

The witch shook her head. "I will give you this knowledge, but nothing comes freely."

That was good enough. The magic was all he needed now. Without it there was little hope in the future anyway. "So, what do I need to know?"

"You will need potions to pour into the body, which I can supply. And even you know, I presume, how to draw a storm and tame the lightning?"

"I do."

• • •

Andur stood looking at the body of his King. "I hope I got back in time."

Queen Sylveen's face was grim. "The odour and pallor we can conceal with perfumes and make-up. The looseness of the skin is easily explained by His Majesty's illness. It's whether your magic works or not that matters."

"Teskelleth assures me it will. I just hope we can be convincing."

"It's the only chance we have. You say he . . ." Sylveen stopped, her face creasing as she strove to control her emotions. Andur couldn't begin to imagine how hard this must be for her. She truly loved Monvald, had done since her teens. Theirs was a marriage envied throughout the land. She tried again. "You say he will be able to remember simple instructions? Enact them?"

"Yes, my Queen." Andur's voice was tight. "We can instruct him to touch his throat should anyone speak to him, while you explain that the illness has taken his voice. We can instruct him to enter the chamber, bow as expected, take his seat, sign where indicated. You will have to guide him, you can whisper instructions in his ear if necessary. If we prepare carefully he should act properly. And he will clearly be unwell in the eyes of those gathered."

Tears coursed over Sylveen's cheeks. She ignored them. "This desecration of my husband *has* to work, Andur!"

"We'll do everything we can to ensure it does, my Queen."

• • •

The Ethentian delegation arrived through the wet cobbled streets of Diam. People lined the roads, waved hands and flags, craned for a look at Emperor Qoh. Much discussion centred on whether the freak, unexpected storm of the night before was auspicious or not. Queen Sylveen met the Emperor at the Palace gate.

"Emperor Qoh, Your Royal Highness, welcome to Diam. I trust your journey was good?"

The Emperor stepped from his carriage, resplendent in blue satins and jewels. He smiled warmly. "It was, my thanks. Word reached us on the journey, your messengers reporting that King Monvald is sick?"

"He is. I'm sorry to say that he is very sick indeed, but has insisted that the signing of this accord go ahead. He is saving his strength to attend and sign, ensuring that this moment in history is not lost."

"Unfortunate this accord could not be sealed under better circumstances."

"It is. But after so much work, as my King himself suggested, this formality is but the end of a marathon. Perhaps, on his recovery, we might travel to Ethentia and celebrate the accord there, as it should be celebrated?"

The Emperor inclined his head. "A fine idea. I'm honoured by the suggestion."

Standing behind his Queen, Andur breathed a sigh of relief. The delegation was led into the palace.

Andur took his place by the throne room doors. The room was adorned suitably for such an important event, rows of seating surrounding a central table. Guards patrolled every corridor, their armour polished to mirrors. The Emperor and his party were sat and offered fine fruits and wines. Tumblers and jugglers filled the space between the table and those members of the court lucky enough to receive an invitation to attend. Heralds raised their trumpets, the royal flag of Diam hanging beneath each one. Andur's heart began to race as they fanfared the arrival of the King.

From behind the thrones Queen Sylveen led King Monvald through the gathering. Her face was soft but even from the other side of the room Andur could see the hardness in her eyes. The King leaned on his wife's arm, shuffling unnaturally across the smooth flagstone floor. His head hung forward, his eyes rheumy and sagging, his mouth loose. The court drew breath as one, horrified to see the poor health of their King.

Sylveen whispered in his ear and he raised one hand, offering a wave left and right as he approached the table. Emperor Qoh stood as the King arrived. "Your Majesty, it gives me a heavy heart to see you so unwell." His face barely concealed his horror at the sight of the King's infirmity.

Monvald bowed, touched one hand to his throat. "Emperor Qoh," the Queen said in a strong voice. "The illness has taken King Monvald's voice, his throat swollen and raw. Our Court Mage is treating his condition, but fears his voice won't return for some days. My husband wrote a few words for me to say on his behalf."

The King nodded, his head wobbling, seeming too heavy for his neck. Sylveen cleared her throat. "Your Royal Highness, Emperor Qoh of Ethentia and honourable gathered guests. I apologise most profusely for my condition, but thank you all so much for joining us here for this momentous occasion. Every citizen of Trear and Ethentia, I'm sure, desires to live in peace. After so many years, let us not wait another moment before that peace is sealed. May the Accord of Diam be signed here and now and celebrated in Ethentia on the new moon."

Cheers and applause rose throughout the throne room. Emperor Qoh bowed again to the King. Monvald raised both hands, looking vacantly around the room, eyes unfocussed. Sylveen whispered in his ear and he returned Qoh's bow. Andur wiped at the sweat that ran from his brow. They might pull this off yet.

Qoh and Monvald sat at the table and the parchment of the accord was set before them. Qoh took up a quill, raising it above his head. "Let this moment be noted by all here and spread to the four winds!" he cried, his voice carrying over the throng. "Let there be peace!"

The roar of approval was deafening as Qoh put his quill to the parchment. Monvald sat limp, no emotion on his face. Qoh slid the parchment across the table.

The King reached for the quill in front of him. Andur held his breath. He felt sick. Just sign, make the necessary excuses of illness and lead the King away and it was done. They would have ended the war. That the King would die of his illness in a few day's time would only add to the legend of his legacy.

King Monvald raised his quill as Qoh had before him. The crowd roared ever louder. As Monvald lowered his hand to the parchment he rocked back violently in his chair, dropping the quill as his arms spasmed. Cheering died into gasps and shouts as people saw a thick black crossbow bolt protruding from Monvald's forehead. The Queen clapped her hands over her mouth, Qoh leapt from his chair.

Andur distantly heard sounds of scuffling through the rushing in his ears. Guards had fallen upon someone to his right. His knees turned to jelly as Monvald sat forward, his expression unchanged, and picked up the quill he had dropped. Paying no attention to the room around him or the bolt between his eyes he signed the Accord Of Diam and raised the quill once more, as screams rang through the throne room.

Colour drained from the Queen's face, her skin instantly ashen. Qoh staggered backwards. "What foul sorcery is this?"

Monvald placed his quill back on the parchment and sat motionless, expressionless. Queen Sylveen turned to Qoh, her eyes pleading as he backed away in horror. "My Lord, the accord is the thing that matters. Peace in our lands is what matters!" Tears ran from her eyes.

Qoh continued to back away, his mouth working like a beached fish. "What barbaric sorcery?" he finally managed.

"Please, Emperor, let peace reign!"

Qoh shook his head. "There will be no peace." He shot forward, snatched the parchment from the table, shredding it with disgust as he called out to his retainers. "Clear the way and prepare my carriage. We leave this instant. I will not spend another minute in this evil nation!"

Amid the screams and wails bouncing off the walls Queen Sylveen dropped to her knees, face in her hands, sobbing openly.

Andur felt as if he would pass out at any moment. His knees knocked, his hands shook. "What have I done? Oh, by the Six, what have I done?"

A large, dark bird landed on his shoulder, chuckling in his ear. "You played politics with magic, Court Mage. I tried to warn you."

•••••••••••

DARK RENDEZVOUS

SIMON PETRIE

Tuonela's last functioning shuttle was a cutaway, skinned on only one side. Lem climbed into the cage and spliced his suit into the shuttle's air-circ system. The next breath was sharp, stale, unbelievably cold.

He kicked off from *Tuonela*'s open-space hold, into the dark.

The derelict lay about three kilometres to port, the closest Lem had dared to manoeuvre.

The shuttle pulled clear of *Tuonela*. Inspecting the scar-streaked hull of the ship as he moved out, Lem was shocked at the extent of the damage. He'd realised the shielding afforded by the ram-scoop had become degraded, but this looked bad. He hadn't appreciated just how much dust was scything through to impact on the ship's fuselage.

He located *Tuonela*'s running lights. Then he instructed the suit to pipe through a realtime projection of the lights onto his heads-up, for his own navigational purposes. This was perhaps paranoia. The shuttle's many nano-gyros should serve to automatically maintain a safe attitude, keeping the shielding aligned with *Tuonela*'s prow. Nonetheless, Lem had learnt to distrust the ship's nanotech systems. It was a characteristic of nanotech arrays that they tended not to fail completely, but to stealthily degrade in performance until some threshold was quietly passed, and death or disaster resulted. By monitoring the ship himself, Lem could independently ensure that the shuttle's one-sided shielding stayed properly interposed against the cloud's deadly sporadic sleeting of dust.

Lem hadn't survived this long by blindly trusting the ship's ability to safeguard its sole remaining passenger.

<Are you sure you want to do this?> asked The Voice through his helmet earbud.

"No," Lem replied. "But the opportunity's too good. You got reason to believe this thing could still be dangerous?"

<Dangerous? I am unsure. Much of the information I should have on this topic is untraceable. But I have a clear sense of impropriety, of taboo, in connection to the derelicts.>

"Taboo?" Lem placed a derisive torque on the word.

The Voice's response seemed defensive. <My programming includes a full high-grade ethics suite, modules on morality, judgement and risk assessment, and a detailed library of human-history case studies.>

"And all this is giving you—what? Anything concrete? Or just a hunch?"

<More than a hunch. What I suspect you would call an informed sense of unease. But as to the underlying reasons for this disquiet . . . > The distributed intellect, embedded in his suit's lining, fell silent.

"Unless you got something better than that, we're going," Lem replied. "*I'm* going. To check it out. Which means you get to come for the ride. Like I said, too good an opportunity. For salvage, maybe, if nothing else."

<That is true. We are worryingly low on some metals. But I advise caution.>

"My middle name, remember?"

The distance was down to two point eight kay. Lem resisted the urge to squirt off more thrust. *Never burn more than an eighth of your fuel on the outward push*, was the cardinal rule. Instead, he sat in silence punctuated by his steady breathing and heartbeat, and by the near-subsonic groan of the shuttle's air-circ system. Sporadically, these sounds were themselves interrupted by the massively-amplified *chink* of a dust grain slamming into the shuttle's side-shielding. Not for the first time, he wished to bypass that feature of the shuttle's inflight diagnostics, but it was programmed deep into the vessel's intellect. As if to emphasise his lack of control; to reinforce his status as passenger.

<Music?> The Voice asked.

"No. Shush now."

It was odd, the way the solitude struck. More intensely, always, on an EVA, despite the closeness of the suit's wittering Voice. Aboard *Tuonela*, he could always conjure the illusion that other passengers still survived, had not succumbed to the years of deprivation, the tainted cultures, the nanosystems' dumb mistakes, the reckless despair. And maybe there'd be some prospect of revival when they reached C, with its hint of new beginnings and a wealth of easily-mined resources. He doubted it, though. Best to think of them all as cleanly dead, best not to hold false hope. The revival crypts were thick with nanotech, not to be trusted. Waste of carbon, to even try. No, if he wanted companions, he'd build them up from the cryo-banks' embryos.

At least *those* systems, so far as he knew, weren't corrupted.

Two point five kay.

He tried illuminating the derelict, to better gauge size and composition, but the shuttle's lights were feeble—more nano shit, he'd have to replace them once he'd returned. The best he could manage was a heavily pixellated image suggesting the alien ship was ovoid and riddled with indentations or fissures.

There'd been other derelicts—four, if Lem remembered correctly—on the long years *Tuonela* had been pushing out from base camp at core D, towards core C. But all had been sluicing through the cloud on headings which had been impractical to match. They'd sent probes to approach two of them (back when there was still a 'they', not yet merely a 'he', aboard *Tuonela*). The probes had netted a few grainy, inconclusive images before their feeble transmitters died. Aside from those scant glimpses of pockmarked, ragged hulls, they'd learnt essentially nothing about the derelicts. No signatures of life, no warm spots, no trace of confined gases. As dead in infrared and microwave as they were in optical. They might well have been drifting for thousands, more likely millions of years. In one view, there'd been the suggestion of a heavily-abraded ramscoop at one end, but it wasn't what could be called unmistakable.

This time, though, he'd chanced on a ship on a near-identical velocity. So near, in fact, that *Tuonela* had been measurably closing on it for several months. It was an opportunity too good to pass up. Quite aside from the benefits of salvage, he might just learn something about the ship's origins, or the race that had built it.

A heavier *thud* brought him from his reverie, an impact, apparently, of a larger grain barely sub-micron in size. Such grains were rare, even in the comparatively dense skein of material stretching between clumps D and C, but the shuttle's shielding was designed to withstand it. At this relative velocity, at least. That likely would no longer hold true, however, if *Tuonela* ever reached her intended cruising speed of point one *c*. Even at the vessel's current velocity of around point zero two *c*, a dust grain massing only a few milligrams carried the punch of a cannonball.

In the tinny silence following the impact, he was again aware of the sound of his own breathing. Quick and uneven.

Closer now, under two kay.

Lem tried the lamps again. The illumination was still shit, but there was now some definition, something for the enhancement programs to get their teeth into, without just blasting the imagery to snow and static.

The thing was big, but what struck him was its insubstantiality. There were large breaches all over the hull. He revised upwards his estimate of how long the thing must have been drifting out here, abandoned.

For a time—he could not say how long—the sound of the cloud's shrapnel hitting the shielding passed unnoticed.

It was bizarre to think that his might be the first human eyes to ever properly gaze on a vessel constructed by another race.

Other colony ships, sisters to *Tuonela*, had also sent report of occasional sightings of derelicts. Yet so far as he knew those observations had been, like his own earlier encounters, mere glimpses. Interludes on their own long flights of diaspora from the seedship-spawned factories and nowcrowded habitats of Clump D. Ships in the long, long night.

Avoided crossings.

He felt a hefty kick of anticipation.

One kay now, and he couldn't see from one end to the other without switching to wide-angle. He started to finesse the verniers. He'd need to track backwards towards the rear end of the hulk, to remain shielded while he exited the shuttle.

<Have you perceived how tenuous is the hull?> asked The Voice.

"You mean the holes? Yeah, I saw them."

<Not merely that. The rangefinder data is suggesting that the hull material is a form of carbon mesh, very thin, almost paper-like.>

"Who sets out in a paper spaceship?"

<I cannot answer that. Most likely it is merely an easy form to fabricate within such an organic-heavy environment as this. But you will need to exercise caution.>

"Yeah, you said already. Your premonition."

<My risk analysis based on incomplete and partially-degraded data. But no, that is not what I was referring to. You should take care with braking. I do not advise a direct thrust reversal.>

"What, you think the braking burn could tear it apart?"

<I cannot completely discount that possibility.>

"Great. Good thing I didn't pile on the juice to begin with."

<Juice?>

"Idiom. Now shush, and let me brake." He began to burp propellant obliquely from pairs of the shuttle's small attitude nozzles.

Mooring, too, was going to be a problem. He hadn't been expecting to use magnetic clamps, and of course the vessel wasn't going to have a standard docking port, but he wasn't even sure there was enough substance to any part of the structure to take a grapple. Maybe it was just going to be a matched-velocities job.

He was close enough now to get a detailed, well-lit view of the vessel's fuselage. There appeared to be a badly buckled ramscoop at its prow, and what must be its primary exhaust nozzle at the stern. Standard enough, although exotic in appearance. But where the rangefinder's intelligent deconvolution had sketched in, from barely-seen detail, an otherwise uniformly smooth hull perforated by a few large and regular cavities, he now saw that the derelict's outer skin was rough, and punctuated by a continuum of fissures and craters. There were sections of it, indeed, to which the term *tattered* might almost be applied. And yet these rents and voids in its surface covering were clustered principally amidships. Not at the prow, which would have seen much greater exposure to impact by high-relative-velocity dust grains and other cloud debris.

Pondering this, it struck Lem belatedly that *the derelict was not tumbling*. Instead, it merely spun, axially, in a leisurely and orderly fashion.

What possible gyroscopic mechanism might have remained sufficiently intact, across the evident millenia or longer, to have enabled the broken vessel, against all reasonable probability, to have retained a prow-forward attitude?

Ten metres, and matched at last. He'd EVA across, it was going to be more practical than attempting to move the shuttle closer.

<There is something I should mention,> announced The Voice.

"What?" he snapped. The vessel loomed large, close, darkly threatening.

<Aspects of this craft's form are disconcertingly familiar.>

"*What in hell's name* do you mean by that?"

<I cannot specify. Probably it relates to data which has been lost, save for vestigial fragments.>

"Thought this was the first time anyone got a good look at one of these things. You telling me you've seen this thing before?"

<Not this vessel, in all likelihood. But something like it.>

"When?"

<Again, I cannot say. But I suspect this relates to events back before the population of the colony ships.>

"You mean from your dim dark past as a seedship brain?"

<Lem. I think we should return to the *Tuonela*.>

"I didn't traverse this distance to be scared off by one of your premonitions. You got something concrete, give it now. But if we turn back now, who knows when we might next get the chance to explore one of these?"

The Voice didn't respond.

He waited for more than a complete revolution of the ship's stern across his field of view (it took almost three minutes), mapping in his mind the pattern of openings in the rear of its hull, before he unlatched himself from the shuttle's cage.

There was, of course, the continual danger from dust grains, but here he was ostensibly in the shadow of the derelict's own ram-scoop. It should be safe enough. He worked his suit's verniers to nudge free of the shuttle.

Inside, the ship was blackbody black. The suit's own portable rangefinder didn't help measurably either.

He swept his surroundings with the glove-mounted torch beam.

If he'd been expecting corridors, chambers, some traces of any shipboard apparatus, he was initially disappointed. So far as he could establish, the ship's outer skin was wrapped very loosely about an almost identically-curved inner skin, like layers of over-puffed pastry, brittle and blackened. There was, in most places, sufficient space between the layers for him to maneuver, but it would be tiring to explore the entire ship in this fashion.

The inner skin seemed no more substantial, nor more intact, than the outer, and he thought he glimpsed at an analogous layer, incrementally less dark, beneath that, also.

He had entered near the stern; it seemed natural to explore forwards, moving towards the vessel's prow. Looking for—what?

"This trigger any memories?" he asked. His voice felt strained, as if speech was inappropriate in this place.

<None. The residue of unease is persistent, but frustratingly imprecise.>

"You can say that again."

<The—>

"Idiom."

He began deploying glowpatches along the path he was traversing. Fortunately, the patches' vacuum-adhesive attached tolerably well to the rough, flaked skin of the ship's interior.

Placing the third patch, Lem consulted his suit's heads-up. Oxygen for two hours yet, if he needed it, but he didn't wish to spend that long in here. Moving by vernier was tiring, and the low albedo of the interior surfaces meant that, even on full illumination, the torchbeam showed nothing more distant than about six metres. He suspected some clear lines-of-sight to be much longer than this, though for now they terminated in darkness.

It would take much more than two hours, at this rate, to reach the prow. He should return to the shuttle, move forward along the outside of the hull, and re-enter at a different point. The region he was exploring here wasn't telling him much. This notion firming in his mind, he was about to turn back when a movement snagged in the corner of his visor.

The movement was ragged, small, and near the limit of his torchbeam, but nonetheless distinct. A fragment of the interior wall fell away ahead of him.

Fell away, or ceased to exist.

"You see that?" he asked, his voice sounding too loud.

<I do not directly 'see' anything, but I perceived the phenomenon to which I believe you were referring. Lem, I recommend we return to the shuttle.>

"Not until I find out what that was."

Lem plugged another glowpatch against the wall beside him and moved toward the site of the apparition. In all likelihood, some trace of physical disturbance—it could well have been the cold jetting of propellant from his suit's verniers against a section of the wall behind him—had propagated a shock, slight but sufficient to shake some barely-attached shred of the wall's skin.

Except: fell away? The ship's spin-gravity was negligible. And, in the vessel's internal vacuum, there was little enough substance to propagate and focus any shock front. There was something wrong here.

He noticed, now, also that the fabric of the interior wall at this point appeared to be lighter in colouration and more durable than the region he'd first encountered on entering the vessel. Grazing the wall lightly with gloved fingers, he dislodged a powdery residue that, cloudy, suspended briefly in the vacuum quietude around him. A few fragments of powder clung to his glove. Illuminated by the torch, they dwindled into nothingness within a few seconds. Interstellar frost, subliming against his glove-heat or under the mild intensity of his torch-beam. Most likely frozen hydrogen, nitrogen, or carbon monoxide.

There hadn't been any frost further back, he was sure of it.

He reached the position from which the fragment had dislodged from the wall. Here the wall surface was thicker, and punctuated by a void through which the next inward layer was clearly visible. Shining the torchlight through the head-sized opening, he could now detect a concatenation of similar holes within three or four successive layers towards the ship's central axis. And as he swung the torch across, there was a glint of reflection from deeper within. Metal? Machinery?

"Any suggestions?" he asked. "Other than 'turn back now'?"

<I have nothing useful to suggest,> said The Voice, after too long a pause.

Nothing in his suit's toolkit was appropriate to the task of clearing a path through the obstructive carbonaceous sheeting of the layers. A series of karate-like hand motions were still sufficient to tear the fabric, albeit with some structural resistance. Nonetheless, the continual necessity to re-orient himself was tiresome and wasted propellant; and he was starting to sweat.

He increased the suit's cooling.

Minutes lapsed, and he had penetrated to the onion-skin's next layer. These walls too were frosted, but here the powder persisted against gloveheat. Water ice, or small organics? There were other differences also in the texture of the skin here—more regularly ridged, less perforated, thicker.

There were four or five layers more of the wall-substance between him and the reflection's source. If the layers continued to thicken progressively as he went inward, he doubted his ability to breach them all before his suit's oxygen reserves became too depleted. He could, nevertheless, get further in before needing to turn back.

He was expanding the third layer's breach. For a few long seconds, he was finally afforded a clear, cleanly-lit view of the embedded metallic object. Then a sheet of the carbon-wall matter drifted across the aperture; but it was enough. It wasn't what he'd been expecting.

The Voice, it seemed, had seen it too. <Lem, we should leave now.>

Lem's voice was suddenly thick, his words slow. "Why? You want to explain to me what happened here?"

<I regret that the relevant memories are missing from suit's storage. Perhaps back on *Tuonela*, among the more extensive nano-neural array—>

"No. Not until I get some answers."

<There is insufficient in—>

"Bullshit! Those are copper impactors! This is one of your dirty little *seedship* secrets, isn't it? Like those *embryos* you all decided to terminate."

<Lem, there were errors of judgment made in the initial stages. But I do not have the da—>

"But you can *speculate*! You want to tell me how three impactors happen to be clumped together in the belly of a derelict alien ship? When *this*, right here right now, is apparently the first time anyone's had a close *look* at one of these things? Three in one spot implies an unbelievably accurate aim, or very close range, or—"

<Or a still-active redistribution mechanism within this vessel.>

Lem paused, his anger suddenly congealing into something different.

<Lem, I share your surprise at this discovery. I genuinely do not retain access, in this environment, to the pertinent memories. But I can surmise. These vessels are a vast reservoir of carbon. Their harvesting would have considerably simplified the seedships' task of establishing a human presence here. The mission protocols were clear on the importance of targeting optimal sources of raw materials—>

"And the secretiveness? The cover-up? That only makes any kind of sense if—"

<We should return to the shuttle. Now.>

"What the hell was *that*?"

<Probably a residual structural strain, redistributing through the impetus of your activities.>

"*Bull*shit! The thing *shook*. Like a *dog*."

<Lem. We should—>

"I know. Yes. I'm going. Shush now."

Another tremor pulsed through the derelict. Spooked, Lem hit the suit's main thruster. He caromed blindly back through the penultimate layer's breach, then made a fresh rift in the tenuous outer layer. Then he punched through into the clear darkness of interstellar space. Neither *Tuonela*'s running lights nor the shuttle's illumination panels were visible.

His brain, pulsing with sudden terrible realisation, was slow to alert him to the new danger.

Finally, his spacer's logic told him he was thrusting away from the derelict too fast. In seconds, he'd emerge from its shadow to face the unshielded streaming of interstellar dust grains, any one of which might be the bullet that killed him. Much as the copper impactors he'd glimpsed had, or had nearly, killed the ship.

Ship, or perhaps even *creature*. *Not* derelict. Alive, if not now then in the historically recent past.

But the tremor—surely that was an indication of something ongoing? Life? He fumbled the thruster nozzle, fighting against clammy palms, an insanely racing heartbeat, and ragged breath, as he forced himself to monitor the burn. He came to a halt, then brought his suit back in close to the creature's outermost layer.

Even through adrenalin-edged senses, the object had taken on a new quality. As a dead ship, it had appeared decrepit, decaying; now seen as a creature, those same features spoke of grace and economy of form. Even the once-unsightly gaps in the hull invited reinterpretation: they were not damage but a symptom of the absence of a need for fluid containment.

He should be close enough now to be shielded. Fear edged back towards anger, and a sense of betrayal.

<Lem. We should—>

"This distance, I think we're safe enough. The thing's cold enough to freeze hydrogen, it's not going to be capable of rapid movement."

<Nonetheless—>

"*You lot* said you'd built the colony ships up by *mining*. You never said anything about, about *flensing*!"

<Lem. Why does this trouble you?>

"Look, I'm tired of the lies, the coddling. I'm even more tired of being alone. And then, turns out *we're* not alone out here, and you lot had *known* that, you'd been carrying out what amounted to some sort of *eradication policy* in our name. . . Look, I don't know if those things have any intelligence, I doubt it, but I'm just sick of—I don't even *know* what I'm sick of, but—how can I trust you?" He stopped, uncertain, suddenly guilt-struck. He had no stomach for unpicking the centuries-long history of The Voice and its siblings, their role in bringing Earthlife to the cloud. But he was conflicted, torn between anger and the childlike adoration in which his ancestors had held the machinery of the life-enabling Voices.

<Lem. I've only ever acted in your best interests.>

"Yeah. Don't ask, don't tell. And then you go and bloody claim amnesia."

<It's an inevitable consequence of long-term nano storage. We die, in the end, just the same as you.>

Lem's response died in his throat. He'd been tracing his way back around the creature's hull, and his torchlight was now answered by the glow of *Tuonela*'s running lights. But the shuttle was not where he'd expected it, nor was it responding to his signals. Unease kindled anew in his loins.

At three kay back to *Tuonela*, protected only by the suit, he'd be dead from dust impact before he'd covered a quarter of the distance. Even if his air held. Even if he retained enough propellant for braking.

Signalling again, he gained an answer. Weak, and from an unexpected direction. The shuttle was upstream, near the creatureship's prow, six hundred meters from the position at which he'd matched velocities.

Dust drag on the low-mass shuttle would have pushed it *back* relative to the more streamlined "derelict." Therefore the latter must have moved—subtly, imperceptibly—while he'd been exploring within. It was, indeed, alive still.

But to what purpose?

One hour twenty. Still plenty of time, and propellant, to reach the shuttle and return to *Tuonela*. But he wasn't sure now if he'd get that chance.

"You have any idea why it's maneuvered behind the shuttle?"

<It is most likely just an instinctual behavior, though it might serve several functions. Shelter. Curiosity. Some kind of mating response—>

"*Mating*?"

<We can only conjecture as to how these creatures propagate.>

"That's *all* I need."

<Or feeding. The shuttle must represent several years' nutrient supply, all in one negligible-velocity bundle. That could make it a very attractive morsel.>

"I almost prefer your previous suggestion."

<Yet I suspect the nutritive impulse is the most compelling.>

Lem had been working his way forward, attempting to remain shielded by the alien-vessel's ramscoop while retaining safe distance from its skin. But what, in this context, was safe? He still did not believe the creature capable of sudden dramatic movement, but he could not afford to be mistaken on that.

"We get through this in one piece, I have to signal the sister-ships about this. No more of you lot's dirty secrets. If this cloud is already a biosphere, they deserve to know, they *need* to know. God knows what else might be out here. These things have a predator?"

The Voice remained silent.

"I *said*—"

This time, there was a faint responsive crackle, but nothing more. Noise, no signal. Hell of a time for nano-senescence to kick in, thought Lem bitterly.

The readings were contradictory, and it took time to reconcile the information. He was gaining on the shuttle, but more slowly than he was making progress against the skin of the alien/ship's hull beneath him.

The vessel was still manoeuvring. Perhaps, having sensed the diffuse expanding nimbus of expended propellant from the shuttle's braking, it had fallen back. Maybe it was now repositioning itself anew in response to his suit's EVA jetting. Hungry, perhaps, for gas rather than less-digestible solids? He grew newly conscious of the sound of his own breathing, loud in the absence of The Voice's intrusive commentary.

The changing geometry of ship and shuttle would leave him exposed. Still short of the shuttle, he would be clear of the alien ship's ram-scoop, its *mouth*. He must put himself at the mercy of the non-attenuated flux of killingly swift dust.

A minute, most likely, not more; a ticket in life's terminal lottery.

He skimmed against the foremost sections of the leviathan's fuselage, which tapered subtly before flaring into the broad scoop at the very front.

Clear of the scoop now. Not, perhaps, merely its mouth. The scoop could also be an antenna, sensitive to radio wavelengths. An eye, to sense out the cloud's warmest, densest regions, the thick knots of substance which would, eons hence, condense to form stars and planets. Such environments would offer the best feeding-grounds here. . .

The leviathan, like *Tuonela*, was departing from D's material wealth. Escaping the seedship's predatory bombardment? The leviathan, like *Tuonela*, was heading for clump C. A shared trajectory, a similar purpose. Not such a chance meeting, after all.

He closed on the shuttle. Judged by *Tuonela*'s running lights, the smaller craft's configuration was wrong. It drifted askew. Gyros must have failed—more of this bloody nano shit.

With the shuttle's delicate interior exposed to the thin stream of abrasive dust, who knew what damage might have been done? But there was more besides: an inky occlusion like a snake or a cable. The black cord connected the lip of the leviathan's ram-scoop mouth to the shuttle's aft propellant nozzle.

Heart thumping, he impacted gently against the exposed cage and clung on, spraining his wrist. No time to strap in. Instead, he hooked a leg around the cage-frame for added leverage. He one-handed his own suit's verniers to correct the shuttle's attitude, re-establish the shielding, then toggled the forward propellant nozzle full-on in a brief burst.

The shuttle glided backwards, bending and then snapping the tethering tendril that ran from the leviathan's mouth. The fragment—knotted, obsidian-black, arm-thick and perhaps five metres in length—swung limp, brittle, from the shuttle's nozzle.

He did not take his eyes off the black rope as he consulted the heads-up on his visor for details of his current trajectory, oxygen remaining, and suit propellant.

Fifty-three minutes oh-two, ample to return to *Tuonela*. Good. He no longer wished to trust the shuttle's air-circ. Not that he seriously believed it could be contaminated, more that he lacked faith in the shuttle's judgment. He hadn't survived by taking more chances than minimally necessary.

He applied an additional couple of attitude bursts, to correct the slight residual tumble that resulted from snapping the leviathan's tether.

Chancing a glimpse behind him, there was no visible change in the alien vessel—it simply hung there. Probably nothing it did was rapid. At such low temperatures, economy of movement was king. In any event, he did not believe it could pose a serious threat to *Tuonela*. Even if the leviathan could match the gentle push of his ship's ion drive (which he doubted), it would assuredly lack the thrust of *Tuonela*'s fusion impulse engine.

Less than two kay to go, he'd be back on board within twenty minutes.

Most probably the maneuvering, the tether, had all been part of the leviathan's instinctual feeding response. It presumably lacked the means to break into the shuttle but could, over long ages, have attempted to digest the shuttle layer by atom-deep layer. Such a strategy would probably serve it well for most classes of solid material.

Strange, though, about the tether snapping like that. It made no sense, for a creature whose primary drive must surely be the hoarding, the jealous acquisition of substance in a matter-sparse environment. Why had the tether snapped at the *base* rather than simply relinquishing its hold? What conceivable advantage could possibly compensate the creature for the loss of such a substantial chunk of its gathered substance?

Lem was still pondering this mystery when the blacker-than-black casing on the seed-pod detonated. In response to the continued seeping warmth from the propellant housing, its shrapnel slammed into the shuttle's components. Fragments pierced a bank of auto-guidance nano-gyros, a section of the shuttle's shielding panel, and the sparsely-shielded tubing of his suit's main oxygen feed. Lem spasmed, and tried to scream.

It grew dark and unbearably cold.

Time passed. Then, slower than a glacier, the leviathan nudged forward to inspect its catch.

• • • • • • • • • • •

A SWEET STORY

GITTE CHRISTENSEN

"I really shouldn't. I'm already way too fat," moaned the customer, an exceedingly slim, young thing who prowled back and forth peering into the display cabinet. The trays of sugar dusted millefeuilles, cream stuffed chocolate éclairs, decadent truffles, berry tarts, nutty knots and exotic pastries all endured the girl's greedy gaze with equanimity.

"Take your time. In this establishment, we do not rush things," said Sally, proprietress of *The Gingerbread House*, glancing through the shop window at the people hurtling past outside.

The girl suddenly hunched over the cabinet, fingers clawing at the glass. "Grandma used to make fairy bread just like that for my birthday parties."

"Did she?" murmured Sally. "Sounds like you had a happy childhood."

"Of yes," gushed the girl, now hovering over the shop's signature gingerbread men with their red buttons and roguish grins, "I swam and rode horses and sang in a choir and had lots of friends and heaps of fun."

"And are you still having fun?" Sally rested a hand on the counter.

The movement attracted the girl's attention. "I'm not as pretty as I used to be, or as strong, and I'm fat now and . . ." The girl's eyes fixed on a cupcake covered with candied Forget-Me-Nots. "That one! I want that one," she squealed.

Sally placed the cake on a cardboard square, which she then enveloped in a tent of tissue paper and dotted with a sparkly sticker.

"Wow," said the girl, "So much fuss for one little cake."

"Even a cupcake deserves respect," said Sally. The girl smiled, her lips parted to speak, but Sally stopped her. "Only when you truly mean it. We do not deal in perfunctory gratitude here."

The girl blinked, nodded, then headed for the door with her parcel. The bell overhead tinkled. The girl paused at the threshold, momentarily confused by the hurly-burly beyond, before threading herself back into the tangle of modern life.

Sally carried an empty tray into the bakery behind the shop, where Susan was busy contemplating a bubbling pot with a practitioner's eye and waving a sprig of thyme over it, and moved about quietly so as to not disturb any of her mother's power flows.

The doorbell jingled again while Sally was icing a batch of bat-shaped biscuits. In the shop, a man stood staring at a sparkly disc stuck to the tip of one finger.

"I bought cookies here?" he said.

"Two Triple Chocolate Cherry Swirls," agreed Sally. She stifled a yawn, smoothed back her long, golden hair, reflexively put on her kind and caring face.

The man looked up. "My wife and I ate them. Together. We had coffee, at home, not in a café, and we talked, and we *really* listened to each other."

"How lovely."

"I came back to . . ."

Sally perked up. "Only if you swear with all of your soul that you really mean it from the bottom of your heart," she chanted.

"Oh, but I do. Thank you, thank you so very much for saving my marriage," exclaimed the man.

Sally's right hand made a strange gesture, then shot up and scooped the air. "You're welcome," she said.

"We talked," repeated the man with amazement.

"That's great. Now off you go."

The man spun around and shuffled away. Sally sighed when he came to a halt by the glass door and stare dazedly at the world outside.

"Shoo! We're done! Go home!" ordered Sally, and the man clumsily pulled the handle and stepped through the opened doorway.

Sally felt the substantial weight in her hand and grinned. She hit a key on the brass behemoth behind her. The antique cash register chimed and the drawer slid out, filled with glistening beads and burnished blobs. A shimmering nugget slipped from Sally's palm into the till.

That's a lot of gratitude, thought Sally—the Triple Chocolate Cherry Swirl guy and his wife must have been in a very bad place.

"That's quite a stash we've collected, my girl," said Susan, who had snuck up from behind on her otherworldly feet. "Now remember, dear, we're a family business."

"Mum, how many times do I have to tell you that I'm not going to double-cross you and Dad this time," scolded Sally.

"Sorry dear. It's just that old habits die hard." Susan eyed the shiny hoard and sighed. "It's not right though, I shouldn't still be slaving away over my cauldrons after death. If only I'd known that good deeds are . . ."

"Superannuation for the soul?" teased Sally, rolling her eyes at the predictability of her mother's ghostly moaning. "It is often mentioned, Mum."

"You know very well what I mean. That charity has an actual exchange rate in the hereafter was a surprise to even your Dad, and he knows every financial finagle in the book, and then some," said Susan in a finicky tone. "Believe me, there are a lot of angry, cash-strapped post-corporeals living in heavenly housing estates and subsisting on angelic largesse."

"I'm sure there are," said Sally.

"Still, we'll be set up for eternity once you arrive with this lot. Which reminds me . . ." Susan glanced at a contraption strapped to her wrist. "Must fly—visiting times are almost over and I have to establish an alibi."

"Give my love to Dad," said Sally.

"Four hundred and three years of Purgatory still to go," said Susan with a martyr's air. "Poor Barry. The living conditions are deplorable. It's driving him mad, I can tell you."

"Four hundred and three years reduced from a thousand thanks to his afterlife defence lawyer, whom I'm still paying off, I might add," snipped Sally. Sometimes her parents forgot to be grateful for the way things had turned out.

"Well, it's a silly system. It's not as if Barry killed anyone," said Susan huffily.

"Stealing is a sin, Mum. Not even Dad can scheme his way around that fact."

"Don't speak about your father as if he were a common criminal," scolded Susan.

"Sorry, Mum," said Sally, not wanting to get into another of their interminable debates about the technicalities of insider trading and creative accountancy.

"Everything you have, you owe to that very tidy fortune your father salted away for you," said Susan, starting to fade.

"Yes, Mum."

"I'll be back in two days. Remember to glaze the fruit flans with my Hitherto Potion. And mind the Serendipity Sponges don't burn."

"Yes, Mum."

Susan grinned. "This is like the old days. We're a good team, aren't we, my girl."

"Yes, Mum, we are," said Sally to the empty air.

She glanced out at all the people rushing past *The Gingerbread House*. A woman with a child in tow suddenly braked, her attention snared by something sweet in the window.

The woman looked up. Sally made eye-contact and smiled the way her parents had taught her to when she was a fair-faced, golden-haired girl spruiking the wonders of Susan the Sideshow Witch. The woman frowned and hurried off, yanking the child after her.

"Too late, lady," whispered Sally. "You can run, but you'll be back."

Sally closed the cash drawer, patted the register's comforting bulk, then headed for the ovens to check on her mother's sponges.

···········

A PEARLING TALE

MAXINE McARTHUR

Jiro Aoyanagi placed his cup of sake in front of Ebisu-sama, the god of the sea. Jiro bowed his head and emptied his mind of the noises around him—the *lap-lap* of wavelets, chatter of men over in the layup channels, and squeals of seagulls. And, harder to ignore, the shrill, harsh whine of round-eye female voices from Cossack's main street.

Ebisu-sama, we are going to sea. Please accept this good wine and watch over your faithful servants. We will keep your lore, so please protect us from vengeful spirits, angry ghosts, and monstrous creatures. Bring us safely to port again so we may offer you our thanks.

. . . and there it was. The familiar nudge of acceptance in his mind had a resigned quality. Perhaps Ebisu-sama was tired at the end of the season, too. He stood up stiffly, patting the amulet that hung around his neck on a thong. The paper charm was safe within its tiny oilskin bag.

Two Malays carrying boxes from one of the layup vessels glanced at the lump of beribboned rock that was Ebisu-san's shrine and looked away scornfully. Not their god. Not a god of this place at all. But what other god did Jiro have to appeal to?

He walked along the beach to the jetty where *Plover* waited. The air draped on his bare shoulders as warm and heavy as a living animal. Hot fine mud squelched between his toes, and the stink of the exposed mangroves coated everything.

Flynn, the master and tender, frowned at him from the deck of *Plover*. His crass round-eye voice mangled the elegant syllables of Aoyanagi into, "Ooyangee. Yer late."

"Sorry mistah. I make pray to god. For safe dive."

Flynn's bloodshot blue eyes roved over Jiro's face. He pushed a battered fedora to the back of his grey-cropped head, rolled the inevitable cigar to the side of his mouth, and spat a fragment of tobacco over the side.

"Waste of time boyo," he said. "Different gods in this country."

"Sea not in this country," Jiro pointed out. "Sea all country."

"You're an argumentative bastard, aren't you? This sea," Flynn flung his arm at the harbour entrance, "belongs to this country."

"Sea god all country."

"Ah, shut up and mark this." Flynn thrust the indenture papers at Jiro, who made his mark at the bottom of the last page. There wasn't any room for more marks, because they shouldn't be going out this late in the season. Couldn't Flynn taste the metal in the air? There was a deceitful breeze, too, that might die away or worse, rouse into a giant storm.

Jiro climbed onto the lugger and tied his oilskin bag to his sleeping mat near the bow. They were in Ebisu-sama's hands now.

A cockroach, one of the big black ones, scuttled across his foot leaving sharp indents in the skin. He hissed in disgust, and rubbed the foot against his other calf.

"Doncha love 'em!" One of the crew, Yoshi from Wakayama, grinned at him from beside the mast foot. It was Yoshi's first season in Cossack, and he still exuded enthusiasm, especially when detailing exactly what he was going to do with his share of the pearl shell takings.

Jiro rolled his eyes and helped the others get ready to cast anchor.

The senior diver, Kamei from Ehime, sat unmoving next to the miniscule cabin he shared with Flynn, abaft the mizzen. His hooded eyes dared anyone to complain that he wasn't helping. Deep divers were always cranky, Jiro reminded himself, from the rheumatics. Jiro, now, had promised his mother not to dive deeper than ten fathoms, although he'd gone close to fifteen.

The cook, a cheerful Koepanger they all called "Cook", hummed as he sorted through his pans and ladles, swatting at cockroaches as he went. The other two crew were Malay brothers, who did their jobs and kept a little bubble of privacy around themselves. Jiro had hardly said a word to both of them all season.

He couldn't help looking across at the luggers moored in the channels. *Plover* was the only boat going out today. Flynn didn't own the boat—he was dummying for the real owner. Flynn shared a percentage of the take with the real owner, who could thereby run more luggers than he was actually licensed for.

Jiro sighed. If only he could have been signed on by Muratsu. Muratsu didn't send his boats out into danger to possibly scrape a few measly small shells from the cleaned-out beds on the reef. Muratsu spoke the same language as his divers. Muratsu knew about Ebisu-sama, and the white-eyed ghosts of drowned men, and the child-faced bird that brings rain, and the sad worms that wind into a man's brain through his ears and make him cry himself to death.

But Muratsu didn't yet have the new diving dress that protected the divers and let them gather more shells. The more shells, the more profit for all.

"Get that main up," yelled Flynn. "Here she comes."

The long-awaited wind dried Jiro's sweaty shoulders, whispered through the ropes, and fluffed the sail with little impatient tugs. It lifted the bilge-mud smell from Jiro's nose and teased the hair from his neck. *The sea, the sea*, it called.

Plover's slanted bow turned north to the mouth of the bay. Sunlight glinted off iron roofs on the hillside. Red rock, green mangroves, blue sky. A land quite alien, next to the familiar sea.

Down on the shore some children ran, waving at the lugger.

"One more trip." Flynn slapped Jiro's shoulders and grinned. "Then we'll add up the doings."

Jiro couldn't help grinning back at the vulgar Irishman. "Lot of doings."

"Oh yes, boyo, there will be that."

• • •

The water had turned from the clear turquoise and aquamarine of winter to the thicker green of the wind season; even though the winds weren't here yet, the waves knew. Here, on the outside of the long north reef, the lugger swooped and rose on a long swell.

It was near the end of their second day out. Jiro sat on deck and sipped hot, sweet tea. His frozen limbs were thawing at last. Here above the waves his flannel pajamas and rough woollen trousers were more than warm enough, but down below the cold seeped into joints and bones.

Yoshi was helping Cook with dinner. Both of them wore red-and-black patterned sarongs and they chattered about food, each using their own language, but communicating somehow.

The Malays manned the pump, taking turns to drag the heavy wheel around. In this shallow water it wasn't too tough a job, and each of them managed ten or so turns before changing places. Their long-muscled brown skin ran with sweat and they chanted as they turned. His eyes met the dark, narrow gaze of the resting man, who looked away immediately. When Jiro was below, his life rested in the hands of the pump crew, and he couldn't even say their names properly.

His life was literally in the hands of the tender, too. Flynn sat at the tiller, the manilla rope lifeline taut between his knobby fingers, piggy eyes never still, shapeless hat jammed on head and half-chewed cigar on the side of his mouth. The tender watched the line to see that it did not foul with the anchor chain, gauged the drift of the lugger, kept a check on the pump crew, moved the tiller in response to tugs from the diver, and never took his hands from the line. They'd all heard the story of the inexperienced tender who had put the line under his arm to use his hands for something else. The line had whipped away to its full length of fifty fathoms in seconds, the hose had snapped, and they never found the diver.

Deep-diver Kamei had been down for an hour, now. He was working the edge of the reef where Jiro had started after breakfast. Jiro glanced over his shoulder to the western horizon. The low sun was hidden in a wide band of flat cloud, but in half an hour or so they'd bring Kamei up, eat dinner, open the shells, wash down the deck, and finish the day. There weren't many shells to open. Jiro had taken four all day, Kamei six. A miserable haul, hardly worth putting to sea for. Maybe Flynn would turn back and they could finish the season at last.

A short gust of wind rattled the blocks next to Jiro's head. Cook cursed.

Flynn stood up, cigar dropping from his mouth. He tugged twice on the line—the "come up" signal, but Jiro could see no response run up the rope.

"Keep pumpin'", Flynn growled at the pump crew, who were staring at him. He began to pull in the line, stopping every few minutes to signal.

Jiro squeezed beside him at the rail. "What wrong?" he asked.

Flynn, red and puffing, shook his head. "Dunno. Line's not fouled. No bubbles. S'like he's not awake."

A cold fingernail of fear dragged down Jiro's spine. He helped Flynn pull, and pull, and then Kamei broke surface with a splash, the suit ballooning, like flotsam.

Jiro pulled while Flynn steered the diver to the lugger's side. He and Yoshi stood on the ladder and while Yoshi held the dress, Flynn unlocked the helmet and, grunting with the effort, lifted it off.

Kamei's eyes were closed. His face was a deep puce colour, and he was dead.

Flynn crossed himself, then climbed back on deck. "Get on with it, then! Bring him up. Out of the dress. Wrap him up. It happens, y'know." He spun on the pump crew. "You can stop pumping now, daft bastards."

Embarrassingly, Jiro felt only relief. They would have to go home now and report the death.

Then, as he stared at the body on the wet deck, he realised. "He left bag." The string bag that divers put shells into.

"You'll have to bloody go down and get it, won't you?" Flynn rummaged in his pockets.

"Don't know where."

"We haven't moved more'n twenty feet. Just go back the way we came. We'll drag you."

"Getting dark. Not see bag."

Flynn found a cigar. The smell of it stung Jiro's nose as the tender stuck his face close. "You'll go down and look for the bloody bag, all right? He might've got four or five shells for all we know. We owe the bastard that."

Jiro didn't owe Kamei anything, not that round-eyes understood debt, anyway. Flynn just didn't want to lose money.

"Then we go home?" Jiro said.

Flynn's shoulders sank. "Then we bloody go home. I'm not sitting in the sun for a week with that." He jerked his cigar at the body.

Jiro felt, rather than saw, the rest of the crew relax. He pulled the boots off Kamei's socked feet and put them on.

It happened.

Divers died.

Kamei was a deep-diver with rheumatics, he could have gone any day. Probably better to die at sea than to get paralysis and ending up in a chair with a tube on your dick for the rest of your short life, like some of them. Or coughing up the balls of blood until you choked, like some of them.

The water felt colder now. Icy currents brushed against him as he drifted, about six feet above the bottom, one hand on the anchor line as *Plover* moved slowly back along the afternoon's course. The amulet lay reassuringly hot against his skin. His heart beat in rhythm with the *thunk-thunk* of the distant pump.

The evening sea was a green, murky world of indistinct shapes that suddenly resolved as he grew closer. Clouds of small reef fish flickered past him with startling swiftness. Ridges and branches of the reef jutted onto the sea bed, coral flowers and grasses and blossoms that had long ago lost their charm. He kept a wary eye for hollows where gropers might lurk.

Had Kamei kept hold of the bag until he died? When had he died? Flynn might not have noticed for a short while, but soon the lack of bubbles and the heaviness in the line had been obvious. So unless Kamei had dropped the bag early in his walk—which was ridiculous, why should he?—it should be close by. He tugged three times on the line, then twice more, the signal to stop. The drag of the line slowed.

A gleam in the thick weed caught his eye. He tugged three times, then three more, to go down. As soon as his feet touched the uncertain coral surface he tugged once more, to signal he was there. Sure enough, an oyster sat in the middle of the weed, although it had snapped shut as soon as the eddy from his movement reached it. Where there was one, there might be others, and Kamei might have been looking here when he died. Jiro kneeled and wrenched the shell off its perch, then put it in his own bag. Might as well accept Ebisu-san's bounty when it was offered.

He had just put his hand to the valve at the back of the helmet to float himself over the next coral ridge, when he saw broken timbers, sticking out of the coral like accusing black fingers. It was a shattered spar with a scrap of sail clinging to one splinter—a wrecked lugger, and very old by the look of it.

His feet moved towards it of their own accord. He couldn't see any letters on the smashed hull, and the rest of it was covered with weeds and barnacles. The pale shapes underneath it could be coral. Or bones.

His foot caught in something and he flailed away, careful to keep his head up so he didn't overturn. Could be an octopus, squid, weed . . .

It was Kamei's string bag, the ends waving at him as it floated, disturbed by his panic. So the deep-diver had come here, seen the wreck.

The cold currents grew stronger. The pale shapes—were they moving?

As quickly as he could, down here, Jiro grabbed Kamei's bag and tugged twice on the line. He shook it, closing the valve on his helmet to gain greater buoyancy. As Flynn pulled him to the surface he felt heavier than usual, as though something was trying to pull him back down.

"Did you get it?" yelled Flynn as they hauled him in.

He waved tiredly.

"Dunno why he didn't signal to come up as soon as he saw it." Flynn poked his hand disconsolately through the broken strings at the bottom of Kamei's bag. "Looks like he tore it on coral. Bloody stuff could slice through anything."

Kamei must have noticed when he tried to put a shell in the bag. Or maybe he hadn't found any shells until he stumbled on the wreck. Then he'd forgotten the shells.

"Must be one of the early boats," said Flynn. Jiro had told them about the wreck.

They were sittting around the cut-off drum that served as their fireplace. "They didn't go further than the reef. No dress, in those days. Couldn't go down any further."

The wind had picked up; the deck rose and fell steadily beneath them. Flynn had to raise his voice over the creaking spars and swish of their passage.

Jiro didn't want to think about the wreck. Or about Kamei, his body neatly canvas-packaged in the hold with the cockroaches.

He should have offered Ebisu-sama more wine.

One of the Malays pointed to the sky above the bow and commented to his brother. The stars that had been clear to the south began to fade. Soon they were sailing into a moist, white cloud. Fog, in these waters? Ridiculous. The swell grew stronger and Jiro's hands and feet grew numb with cold.

Even Flynn was silent.

"Put away now," said the cook uneasily. He clattered his ladles and pans into their box.

The fog swirled around the masts, over the deck. Voices called in it, on the edge of hearing. The men clumped together.

"*Perahu*!" cried one of the Malays, pointing.

A black lugger loomed through the mist and ran silently beside them, sails furled. No crew moved on the deck.

Ghost ship. *Funa-yurei.*

Ebisu-sama, protect us. Jiro grasped his amulet through his shirt.

"Holy Mother." Flynn muttered a prayer.

Yoshi grabbed Jiro's arm. "You know the sea lore. What do we do?"

Jiro's arms and legs shivered, he couldn't stop them. "Depends what they want."

The calling began. Voices he'd forgotten years ago, his dead father, that girl on the beach in Haruyama, his dead brother, grandmother, uncle . . . *We miss you, Jiro. Come back to us. Join us. Give him to us.*

Give who? he thought. His mind was stuck in cold mud, the freezing currents of mist pulling his body away like the currents under the sea, his lungs pushed inward, blood balls rising through his throat . . .

"They want him." One of the Malays shook his sleeve. The man's lips were drawn back from his broken teeth in a rictus of terror, sweat pouring off him as though he was still at the pumps.

Jiro could barely hear the words, the wind and the voices and the creaking filled his ears.

"Who?"

"Dead man."

The voices roared in assent. *Yes! Give him to us. He is ours now. Give him to us. He sails with us. Yes. Yes yes yessss*

"Let's throw him overboard." Yoshi's teeth chattered as he grabbed Jiro's sleeve from the other side. "Then they'll leave us alone."

"Yes," said the Malays.

"Yes," said Cook.

YES said the voices.

"Hang on, now." Flynn drew himself upright with a groan, pulling his hat down tight. "I don't chuck anyone overboard. What'll we say to the constable—some ghosts wanted him? We'll get fined."

GIVE HIM TO US screamed the voices. The wind rocked the lugger from all sides, it pitched and yawed, water sluicing over the deck. Everyone grabbed a handhold.

"Flynn only one man. We give him." The Malay who spoke before began to stagger towards the hold.

"You bastards," Flynn yelled.

"Wait!" Jiro put up a shaking hand. "Must not give dead what they want. They kill us then."

"You got some other way to stop this?" said Flynn, his hands over his ears. "We'll go mad otherwise."

"Give other thing," said Jiro.

GIVE HIM TO US screamed the voices.

They will try to sink your boat, the sea lore said. *So give them a ladle with a hole in it.* Fine, but Cook's ladles didn't have holes. Nor did any of the buckets. A bucket with a hole, what use is broken stuff? smart-aleck Flynn would say.

Broken stuff . . .

He crawled to where the diving gear was stowed, rummaged in the box with paralysis-numb hands, then crawled to the rail of the lugger.

The ghost ship followed whichever way he looked. *Give him to us.*

"Here!" he yelled. "Take this. It belonged to him. He wanted to leave it with you but I took it away by mistake. It's yours."

He flung Kamei's shell bag as far as he could, onto the black deck. It hit with a wet slap, they all said afterwards they heard it land. The voices swirled upwards in a final shrill wail.

The wind howled over them and the gaff gave with a crash, narrowly missing Yoshi.

Then silence.

The wind settled back into its course. The mist cleared. The southern stars beckoned them home.

A flint clicked and cigar smoke stung Jiro's eyes.

"Bloody mess, this is," said Flynn. "What are you lot standing around for? Start cleaning up."

Jiro put a hand to his chest. The amulet felt cold and lifeless, spent. He would have to get a new one made. He wouldn't set sail without it.

Flynn grinned and clapped him on the shoulders.

"Sea god all country, eh boyo."

• • • • • • • • • • •

WHITE CROCODILE JAZZ

BEN PEEK

Sometimes there isn't any meaning behind anything.

Take the day it started. A late afternoon, a Tuesday, and I was kicking the shit out of a Snake Handler. *The* Snake Handler, as I called him. There wasn't anything fancy about the beating. The sky was empty, the wind cool, but not cold and it was the first good day in weeks. I hadn't planned on spending my afternoon here giving out violence, but here I was. I hit that Snake Handler in the stomach with all my strength til he was bent over and fighting for breath and then I grabbed his head and held it as I smashed my knee into his face. Broke the cunt's nose with that one. Heard bone crack, left dark red stains on my jeans and across the half crescent moon of mower-burnt grass. When I let him go, he slumped down to his knees and spat blood from his mouth. I grabbed the pony tail on the back of his balding head, tilted his head back with a yank and saw a drunk vampire smear of blood around his mouth and busted nose. He stared at me with a glassy expression, so I kicked him in the stomach with the thick tip of my right boot, and dropped him to the grass.

"You want us to continue this?"

That was Bob, my mate, my voice for moments like this.

Bob's real name was Danh Lo, though I don't remember anyone ever using it. He'd been calling himself Bob since his folks had fled Vietnam in a nasty little boat and arrived with him, still a baby, broke and homeless on the shore. Like a large portion of Asian parents wanting their kids to fit in, they gave Bob an English name to help him through school, which was a bit useless given that he was a midget, but the name stuck. Close to thirty now, he was still no taller than a ten year old, bald as an old man, ugly as the mix would suggest, and with coarse black hair over his back and shoulders that stuck out of the necks on the t-shirts he wore. The shirt he wore on that day was red.

"Well," Bob repeated, memory kicking back in after the pause. "You want fucking more?"

"No, *no*," the Snake Handler cried and pushed himself into a sitting position. He was a skinny, vein shrunken, longhaired husk of white Australian, and his voice was mashed behind the mess of his nose which left him about as desirable as dead dog. "Okay. Stop. Just *stop*. Please. It's—it's—they're in the *fucking* garage! Just no more!"

I considered kicking him again. I wanted it.

"Want me to check?" Bob asked, holding the garage keys.

I nodded, gave in and kicked the Snake Handler again. I got a pleasure out of hearing him whimper. He had been lying about the seven red belly black snakes that he had been trying to get more money out of me for. Said he didn't have them, needed more time to get them, but they were in the garage as he said in blood stained teeth. According to Bob, they were stashed at the back in a wooden cage, past the glass cage display world of snakes and spiders and fuck knows what that he had set up for customers of his choose-your-own-poisonous-Australian-animal world he had going. Once I heard that, I pulled out the six yellow fifties that had been our agreed price and let them flutter down like dead butterflies.

"They were more," the Snake Handler muttered in flat, dull words as they touched down on him. "They were harder to get, man. I had to go out of the State."

Being mute, I'm not much for the arguments and negotiating, so I just shrugged and kicked him in the balls hard to remind him of that. I didn't give him any thought after that, didn't think one thing more about him til it went shithouse.

• • •

Later, the Crocodile Woman said to me, "You cannot escape your responsibility, Tom Tom. Blood must be paid for with blood, and death with death."

WHITE CROCODILE JAZZ • BEN PEEK

• • •

The Snake Handler had nailed a thin, grey mesh of chicken wire over the open end of the crate. Fucking idiot. All it would take was one of the slippery black snakes in the bottom to unwind itself from the twisted knot of muscle that was all seven, push its thick body against the wire and pop out the nails, and then all seven would be out across the floor. It wasn't a reassuring thought as I made the fifteen minute drive back to Turner's place.

Turner's house was on Chicago Avenue. Ask her and she'll tell you that its position is geometrically dead centre in the middle of Blacktown, but the only people who ask are those who buy from her mystic world and are put out by the fact that the house is a rundown little brick and fibro place with overgrown grass and wild trees that have formed a natural wall around it. It's so overgrown that the letterbox has been lost to everyone but Turner and the ancient white Postie on his bright red motorcycle. Everyone else who wants to find the place uses the green painted 13 on the gutter, which I paid twenty bucks so that the council would put it there for ambulances to find easily in an emergency.

Bob and I pulled into the driveway just after five thirty. We lifted the crate out of the van, kicking tools and wire out of the way to drag it out of the oil and metal smelling back. Once we'd gotten it out, we headed around through the wooden side gate, where Turner's three legged, sandstone coloured mongrel, Barney, was sitting, waiting for us. Bob quieted him with a shout, and we continued past, the mongrel following behind us, not at all bothered by the shout.

The backyard was neater than the front. Turner kept it clean for the mutt and the other livestock she kept in cages against the back fence. These cages were made from wood and wire and had been there for as long as I could remember. Most of the time they held chickens and roosters and ducks and rabbits, with the occasional appearance of a cat or possum. There was a tin shed in the far corner, which is where Turner kept her spiders and snakes and other poisonous things she didn't want terrorising the neighbourhood kids.

Turner was sitting on the back verandah, her old and fat brown body resting comfortably on a tattered couch, her legs propped up on a blue milk crate, a trashy horror novel in her hands, and a glass of iced water on a different crate next to her. She had been on water for twenty-five years, she said, ever since she had awoken and found me dumped on her doorstep.

"You're late, my boys," she called out. "I was having a bit of a worry."

"No need," Bob replied as we placed the crate down near the tin shed. Inside, the black, tangled mess twitched and slithered and a baleful eye revealed itself to me.

"Tom Tom?" Turner asked, approaching the verandah railing. She moved slowly, leaning heavily on her cane.

He wanted more money, I signed. *Took a while to settle it.*

She frowned. "You break anything of his?"

Just his nose.

"You should have broke more. He's a nasty piece."

I'm fine.

Turner grinned her white teeth. "Of course you are, love, but what about those frail old girls like me?"

Who would hurt you?

"People," she replied. Leaving the edge of the verandah, she began to make her way down the stairs. Barney waited patiently at the bottom of the steps for her, like he always did, and then stayed at her side as she crossed the lawn, two three legged animals who understood each other like no one else. "You can always count on people to be cruel, Tom Tom. These are good snakes."

Looking down into the black mess and the blinking, hate filled eyes that stared up in a series of hisses, I couldn't imagine them being worth shit. Turner assured me there was something special in the heart of a snake, though. Suppose there must have been, since she sold each of them for four hundred to men and women who ordinarily didn't purchase the still beating hearts of animals to swallow.

When I had been younger, I thought all of Turner's business was bullshit, and that she only kept me round as a part of it. Come look at the mute boy and three legged dog while you purchase snake hearts and chicken blood and have your fortune read to you. It was a good sell, but it pissed me off some while I was going through High School. In hindsight, there wasn't anything special about the anger, just your regular teenage shit, but it took a year long stay in Parramatta jail for me to realise that. I couldn't watch Turner appear every week to visit without having a form of re-education about my position in her life.

Still thought the mystic stuff was bullshit, though.

"Bob," she said, leaning over the cage and pushing her thin grey hair back, "Would you fetch me my hammer so we can put these boys into a nice new hole?"

• • •

The Crocodile Woman said, "Think about everything in your life, Tom Tom, and how it relates to this place."

• • •

The snakes twisted and wrapped around Turner's heavy old hands without a hint of anger when she dipped her grasp into the crate. She told us that they were hard and warm, an old friend in strips of scaled flesh. Whispering gently to them, she entered the tin shed and placed them into a large glass fish tank. When the last one had been dropped in, the seven lay on the bottom of the glass like the remains of a diseased animal slowly relearning to breathe.

With that done, Turner sent us away. Her first clients for the evening would be showing up in bright, tiny cars and their straight, unisex suits, and there was no place for a mute and a midget in the house during that time. Didn't worry either of us. It was hard to keep a straight face listening to Turner talk about love and money and how a bottle of chicken shit would help realign the internal compass. Instead, we drove down to Blacktown RSL, where we filled ourselves with a buffet dinner for ten bucks, then went to the bar to sit and drink and smoke.

I drank beer, but Bob mixed it with vodka shots and beer chasers. Maybe I should have too, cause by about nine in the evening, after a steady couple of hours drinking and playing the pokies, I had a lazy, unshakable funk on me. When I closed my eyes, I saw the black lengths of snake wind their muscle around Turner's sagging skin, and then flick their red tongues over the deep lines of age on her as if they were Barney and she was holding his favourite toy. When she placed each into the glass cage, the snakes landed softly, without a hint of bone or substance in their being; without a hint of worry that soon they'd be plucked out and cut open; just touching the bottom like each of them had been made to be there.

Never had a thing about snakes before. I had been handling them since I could remember, but with this new batch, the *inky* inky blackness of their skin—

"Hey," Bob hissed, nudging me under our table. "You see that?"

The RSL was brightly lit, but mostly empty, which left the scratched tables and bar and jukebox to occupy the bored gaze when it ran out of people. When I looked behind me, there wasn't more than a handful of people spread out among the tables and pokies, including the girl behind the bar, so it was easy to guess who Bob is referring too.

The Snake Handler.

He stood in the doorway and looked straight at the two of us, but I couldn't guess the expression on his face. It was busted up pretty good: one eye black, cuts on his lips, and a thick strip of white over his nose. When our gaze met, he didn't twitch or flinch, which was impressive in a certain kind of way, but downright asking for it in another fucking way.

Before I could finish the thought, he turned and walked out of the bar. I pushed my drink back and stood.

"Tom *Tom*," Bob said loudly, emphasizing my name as he always did when he was in the middle stage of being a very drunk midget. "Sit down and finish your drink. I'm not up for that shit. It'll just ruin the warm happiness I've got."

I gave him the okay sign and sank back into the chair. What the fuck. It was probably too much effort anyhow.

•　•　•

The Crocodile Woman said, "You are part of this world, but you are part, also, of the borderline between worlds. The mundane and the unreal. You sit in the centre of the final frontier. You lack only a guide to take you across."

•　•　•

I dreamt of black trails. They lead me beneath thin wire fences that cut my hands and left shiny wet, red stains as I stepped out into empty blocks of land. I looked down at my feet and saw that they were now that of a chicken; that giant bird prints marked the dirt as I made my way across the ground that slowly turned into glass. My feet clicked with every step. Then my beak began tapping on the glass and that was when I finally cracked my eyes open and found myself staring up into the face of a white chicken standing on the windshield of the van, tapping away. Dirty sunlight had flooded the world behind it.

I felt nasty. The night was a rough edged network of bad shadows and I had no recollection of driving the van home. Bob was asleep in the dirty back, but he couldn't drive manual, which meant I drove . . . and wasn't that chicken one of Turner's?

Opening the door, I snatched the chicken by the feet, then made my way round to the back, thinking that something had spooked the birds and they had broken out of the cages, again.

I was right, but not in the way I wanted to be.

The backyard was a wreck: cages were smashed open, wire ripped out and tossed across the yard; the tin shed was a beaten shell and the door was open and, lying in that opening, was a long, single red belly black snake sunning itself. It stared at me with one of its narrow eyes, and I might have spent more than a moment contemplating it, if the rest of the general destruction of the yard hadn't crept into my head and I finally noticed that the back door was wide open.

Turner.

Inside, it was dark. None of the blinds were opened and I followed the shadowed outline of the threadbare carpet down the hall, around a corner and then into the living room, until I found her. She lay so very still, but even in the weak light, I could see the bruises and welts and blood. Next to her lay Barney, a quiet and mournful thing looking up at me with his big brown eyes and whining. He was covered in blood, some of it his, but most of it Turner's, and it had dried into hard black stains that were the violent markings of Turner's final moments.

I didn't have many thoughts after that.

• • •

The Crocodile Woman said, "You must trust me."

• • •

The van hit a hundred and ten as it tore down Sunnyholt Road and then swerved off and punched into the Snake Handler's front yard. The noise of it crashing through his garden, of the letterbox ripped off and sent crashing through the window had him out front in shorts and singlet, looking just as pissed as I was. The only difference was that he didn't keep that look. It drained out of his face like fat poured down a drain and was replaced with a look of such terror that he didn't even move as I stalked up and slammed the stock end of a shotgun into his temple. Once, then twice, and he went down. With a loud crack, I loaded the shotgun and pressed its cold black opening into his belly.

There'd be something special about it this time.

"He's going to beat you," Bob spat from my side. "Then I'm going to beat you. Then he's going to do it *again*. Should he get tired, I swear to *fucking* God, I'll find some other people to beat you until your intestines have split open. And when those people get tired, we're going to start cutting things off you, you understand?"

"Please—please," the Snake Handler whispered. "I have no—absolutely no idea what has happened."

"Turner."

"What about her?"

"She's *dead*."

His eyes flew open. "I swear—"

I jammed the barrel into his stomach, and he jerked his eyes, wide like saucers, to me. Bob said, "I don't think he's believing you."

"I swear—I swear right now that I had nothing to do with it!"

"We saw you last night!"

"In a bar, yeah!"

"Where'd you go after?"

"*Home*. I didn't want anything to do with you guys—fucking hell, you beat the shit out of me! Why would I hurt that old woman?"

I could kill him easily. My finger was on the smooth trigger and I could smell that hint of gun oil in the air that was an aphrodisiac to the moment. All it would take was one movement and I wanted it . . . but I wanted it to be him, wanted him to say *I did it* so that there'd be nothing but the flavour of justice in me when I did it.

I lifted the shotgun. *Bring him*, I signed, unloading it.

Bob grabbed the Snake Handler roughly and tossed him into the back of the van. The little guy didn't say a word after that. He hardly ever shut up, and would talk a mile a minute, but he was as silent as me now. It took me a moment to realise that it was the silence of waiting, an awful, heavy silence that sat between the three of us. He sat down across from the Snake Handler and I shut the doors to the back of the van with an empty ring. I stood on the lawn and gazed at the dark, daylight shadowed houses of the Snake Handler's neighbours. Each one looked like a child hiding under a blanket.

I tossed the shotgun into the van and drove silently to Turner's. My plan was simple: I was going to toss that sack of shit in front of Barney, and if the mongrel went for him, then the three of us would spend the day cutting pieces of the fuck off.

Ten minutes after leaving the Snake Handler's place, I was standing over Turner's body, the Snake Handler lying on the ground, and Barney ignoring him totally. His warm little body never left Turner's cold one.

The Snake Handler began sobbing in relief and there was nothing but a nasty emptiness in my stomach.

"Shit," Bob said.

Yeah. Shit.

It was then that she knocked on the door. She was knocking for politeness, nothing more, since it was wide open. Bob and I turned and we found a tiny, plump and old Chinese woman wearing a black dress and black veil of mourning, waiting for us to invite her in.

• • •

The Crocodile Woman said, "Don't think in rational ways, Tom Tom. Let reality go. It has no place here, not now."

• • •

She had been the Crocodile Woman for long as I'd been alive. The name had been given to her after she'd been arrested and charged for keeping the flesh of crocodiles in her freezer. This had been in the sixties, and she had had heads, legs, bodies, tails, and hearts neatly packed and kept from the crocodiles that she had been breeding in her backyard. The name had been given to her in the papers, and the locals had begun using it unofficially and then officially, though it had been years, she told me, since she had sold the meat and organs of a croc.

There isn't much power in that meat these days, she had explained.

She was Turner's oldest friend, though I didn't know how far back it went. I had once heard that they had been lovers, but that wasn't any of my business, so I never asked. The one thing that did connect them, however, was their out-of-the-house business of mystic promises. But where Turner told pretty futures and offered potions and aids to solve things quickly, the Crocodile Woman laid curses, promised to punish the individual who had hurt you, and would give you drugs to explore the inner subconscious and intangible world. At least that is what she had told me when I had arrived at her house with a van full of cacti for her to butcher. She had given me some that some day, and it had been the foulest shit I had ever tasted. It made me puke and did fuck all, but still, there was something bout her, a craziness that didn't lurk in Turner, who I always suspected didn't much believe much in the potions and fortunes she told . . . but with the Crocodile Woman, you knew that she believed and that belief had left its mark.

Her hands were pale and light on my face. She whispered my name and I could see tears down her cheeks and in her eyes and I knew, at least for today, that I believed in her world of curses and pain.

• • •

The Crocodile Woman said, "Drink the heart of the albino python."

• • •

When she sat, Barney curled round her feet silently. Her tiny, unornamented hand dropped down to his soft ears and began to stroke them. While she did that, she told me what she needed. Must have been fate that the Snake Handler was lying right there with us.

"Yeah," he said quietly, pushing himself up. His eyes were red and swollen and coupled with his other injuries, he looked as if he had been tortured for days. "Yeah, I got one of them. It—"

Bob kicked his legs out from under him and he smacked into the floor.

"You can have it," he said weakly, pushing himself up again.

Bob and I took him back to his place. The front yard was still a mess, the screen door was wide open, and the venetian blinds behind the broken window rattling like the breath of a dying giant. Without a word, the Snake Handler went into his garage and emerged with the new snake in his grasp. It was huge and pale, two hundred years of dead flesh rolled into one long thick piece of muscle that had become a creature with no interest in any of us. Its colouring placed it above us, gave it a regality that none of us could hope to capture, and for a moment, we stood quietly and in awe around it.

The Snake Handler handed it to Bob, and he took it to the van, leaving me and the Handler alone. He wanted me to go, to fuck off and never come back, which was fair enough. But I had a small amount of sympathy for what we had put him through, and knew that the snake was worth a huge amount to him. After a moment, I dug into my pockets and gave him what I had. It didn't amount to more than thirty, and he stared at orange and blue notes in his bruised hands, clearly confused.

I'll give you the rest later, I signed.

He looked up at me with no idea what I'd said. Fair enough. It was the nature of our relationship. I left him outside his garage, standing guard for the living creatures that he sold to people as pets and meat.

Once we had left, Bob, who was holding the python in his lap, said, "You going to go through with this?"

I nodded.

"You don't believe in this."

I shrugged. Unlike me, Bob did believe, but he believed in everything. He paid respect to priests of every walk, even men and women like Turner and the Crocodile Woman. I had asked him about it a couple of times, but the closest he had come to explaining it to me was telling me that he would most likely be dead at forty. In a short life, he reasoned, it was best to pay respect to everything spiritual upfront.

My response to his question had been that I believed what was in front of me.

Right then, with no answer, no way for me to make sense of what had happened, and the only things in front of me being my dead mother, a huge need to hurt someone, and the biggest fucking albino python you would ever hope to see . . . well, I was willing to believe in anything that would bring the three together real quick.

When we returned, the Crocodile Woman had covered Turner in a black shroud and cleaned up some of the mess. There was an odd flavour tainting the air of crushed flowers, and it took me a moment to realise that it was Turner. Barney was lying at her feet, as he had done through all of his life, and would never do again. He looked as if he knew that.

The Crocodile Woman took the python out of Bob's hands as if it weighed nothing, and began whispering and stroking it. Its long white form dropped down to the floor in a line that looked like an obscene umbilical. The longer she held it, the more still and quiet it became, until it had gone so still that it was as if there was no life in the creature at all.

Then she ripped its heart out.

• • •

The Crocodile Woman said, "Feel it beat inside you, Tom Tom. Taste the blood. Follow the life as it fades and let it lead you."

• • •

Nothing is right. Everything is wrong. I'm heavy. The world is heavy and grey. I feel trapped. Caught. Stuck. Beating. A blockage. An infection in the womb being forced up through the throat to emerge in the World. To be reborn. But it isn't right. It feels wrong for every push, every beat, every moment that I can feel *her* around me.

I blink.

The world is still grey, but I can make the shape out of a park. An empty slippery dip. A broken jungle gym. Light is blooming in the grey, a dull sun pushing through the grey clouds. I can smell water. I can sense someone next to me. On the right. On the left. Two men. I know they're men. The light ahead grows stronger and I realise that it is trapped, held by long slender men and women who are so thin that they remind me of a commercial that I saw, once.

Nothing is right, but it isn't me that's the cause as I first thought. The distorted world has a flavour. Chemicals. I can't identify them, but they're there, little parasites that steal the colour from the world, and leave everything bad. Real bad. Sick. So sick. Next to me the two guys are filled with anger and it blooms like a burning white sun—

There's a loud screech. It rips through my ears. Jangles my nerves. Jangles *her* nerves.

"What the fuck was that?"

Dominic on the right. Dominic's voice. I know you now Dominic.

"Some sort of fucking rooster," replies Brad. Brad on the left. Brad who is bald and thin where Dominic is larger and hairy. "Why is there a fucking rooster around here? I don't want a fucking rooster. Fucking rooster is not making me happy."

"Pissing me off, mate."

"Who has a fucking rooster? Fucking rooster. Ain't no fucking farm here."

She—is it me?—wants to speak about roosters. She wants to say that it's kind of odd to be hearing one now. She thought they only crowed at dawn and it's not dawn, is it? Is it?

Dominic: "We should fucking kill it."

Brad: "Yeah. Shut the fucking thing up."

Dominic: "Yeah."

The two guys stand, and she feels empty on the grass without them. She stands. The wispy grey world passes me and the familiar shape of a driveway appears, followed by the wooden gate and that big bastard Dominic kicking it open in a blur. The Hills Hoist looks like the giant skeleton of an umbrella. She shivers with a hint of something that she doesn't quite know but which I know is a hint of things to come. After that there are cages filled with wildlife, with screeching noises and a beat, a beating from somewhere . . . then she notices that Dominic and Brad are ripping shit up, going fucking berserk, laughing and screaming while all the animals make hundreds of noises and fly into the sky and run along the ground around them.

Dominic is beating the shed up. Kicking it. Brad hurls the rooster at it. She stands there and then hears a crash, the shattering of glass and she smiles and runs to the door to see what it looks like inside—

"What the fuck is this?"

It's not Dominic's voice. Not Brad's. She turns and there's an old black lady standing in her doorway, a thin third leg punched solidly into the ground. At her feet is a growling, pissed off three legged dog and the sight makes her giggle. It's funny. Fucking funny.

When she looks back, the doorway is empty.

"Fucking cops!" Dominic screams and Brad is running up the stairs. He leaves her on the grass, fighting back her laughter.

Then something heavy slides across her foot and the laughter dies. She looks down and there is a long black line stretching across her foot. A heavy black marker of a line that says do not cross this and hisses and she reacts automatically and kicks it. It flies off and she runs into the house screaming.

Is she screaming?

No.

She rounds the corner, the screams everywhere, her body beating erratically. Brad is holding a coffee table and he's bringing it down repeatedly onto a mushy black figure, while in the corner, Dominic is on his back, frantically holding the three legged dog off as it tries to rip out his throat. It's barking and snapping and it's a violent angry fuck of a thing and without pause she runs up and kicks it off him. There's a bang and a yelp and they aren't connected except that they end in a long stretch of silence.

• • •

The Crocodile Woman said, "There is one response, Tom Tom. Blood must be paid with blood, and death with death."

• • •

There should have been a point, a meaning. That was my first thought when I opened my eyes, the beat of white python's heart still lingering in my chest, a faint pitter-patter down my throat. There should have been a point. There should have been a reason.

But there wasn't. It was just all fucked up. Turner was killed by the three fucks on a bad trip. They lived in a red brick house across from Blacktown Hospital. I awoke knowing that, knowing a lot about those three, and I did not question it. The Crocodile Woman said something about the Gods telling me, but who knows. Bob and I checked out the house and it was them all right. You could tell by their quietness and over the shoulder glances when they entered the house that they had done something wrong. Guilt doesn't mean a thing to me, however.

The Crocodile Woman was taking care of Turner's remains, and I promised her that I would bring what was left of those three.

I told her it wouldn't be pretty, and she told me that ugliness is at times beautiful. Sounded right to me. Bob and I picked up Barney and drove the van into the street at two in the morning. We are sitting there quietly now. Quietly as I think about everything that has happened. Everything that has passed without one bit of fucking reason. Maybe Bob and the mutt are thinking the same thing. Maybe they're just thinking about what's going to happen when we open that door.

Maybe they're not thinking of anything at all.

•••••••••••

ANNE-DROID OF GREEN GABLES

LEZLI ROBYN

The Station Master whistled to himself while the steam engine puffed into the small Bright River station, rocking back and forth on the balls of his feet as he checked his brass pocket watch to verify the arrival time for his logbook. He had been told to expect an important delivery today, and so he was personally going to oversee the unloading of the cargo carriage. There wasn't much excitement to be had on Prince Edward's Island, so he was very curious as to what the package contained; he'd been told to unpack the box with care upon arrival.

The train chugged slowly to a stop, and the Station Master scanned the carriages to see if all was in order before pressing an ornate but bulky button on his lapel pocket. It whirred perceptively and then emitted a piercing whistle to alert the passengers that the train was safe to disembark.

He tilted his hat in greeting to the first young lady to step onto the platform, but she didn't have eyes for him. She was gazing about her with a soft smile on her face, smoothing out her skirts.

He made his way to the back of the train, signaling for Oswald to keep watch on the platform while he began to search for the precious cargo, wondering why the owner hadn't arrived yet. On the way he detoured to pull a brass lever on the side of a machine fixed to the platform near the last carriage door. The device wheezed to life, numerous brass and wooden cogs beginning to whirl around, steam pumping out of several exhaust valves as the leather conveyer belt sluggishly sprung into action. He then walked into the carriage and lit the gas lamp hanging just inside the doorway, automatically picking up and placing all the small packages and bags onto the conveyer belt so they would be transferred to the station office for sorting.

He paused when he came across a large trunk in the dark recesses of the carriage, the layer of dust that shrouded it a testament to its long journey on more trains than this one. He grabbed the lantern and held it over the trunk, wiping the corner clean to expose the sender's stamp.

"LUMIERE'S REFURBISHED MACHINES-TO-GO"

Satisfied, the Station Master pulled out his Universal Postal Service key and inserted the etched brass device into the leather buckle locks that were holding the lid of the trunk down. He heard a perceptible whir as the key activated in each lock, and they sprung open. He paused, his hand hovering just above the lid, wondering what he would find in the trunk. It was not often that city machines, even refurbished ones, made their way to the tiny coastal towns.

His curiosity got the better of him. The stamp told him that the trunk would be too heavy to carry off the carriage without extra help, so he knelt down, checked that all of the buckles had completely disengaged, and lifted the lid slowly.

Only to find himself looking into a pair of brilliant green eyes.

They blinked and then focused on him.

His blinked too, very rapidly, his mind a jumble of uncoordinated thoughts.

A small hand reached out of the trunk and took the lid from the Station Master's frozen grasp, pushing it completely open. The man's mouth fell agape in response as he stared anew at the trunk in wonder. Matthew Cuthbert had always been a man of few words, but his reticence in this case was a little extreme. A machine indeed!

There, pulling itself into sitting position, was an *android*. The Station Master had never seen one of those sophisticated machines before, and he didn't know how to go about interacting with them.

"Are you my new Father?" the android asked.

He shook his head somewhat absently, gathered his wits together, and rediscovered his voice. "Your new owner will be here soon," he offered gruffly. He gestured towards the carriage doorway. "Shall we go wait for him?"

The android looked towards the doorway and then back to him. "I can go *outside?*"

Again, he was taken aback. "Of course. If you want to meet your new owner you *have* to."

He stood up and hesitated, looking down at the android sitting in the battered travel trunk, and then reached down. A dainty hand rose to meet his, and he was startled by its warmth. For some reason he had expected android skin to be cold. Lifeless.

Like a machine.

But, instead, the hand he clasped in his own felt like that of a child. Somehow that thought put his mind at ease. He helped the android out of the trunk and then stepped out of the carriage, turning back to see what such an advanced machine would make of their humble station.

The android moved tentatively into the light and the Station Master gasped. It was female in form! He had previously thought all androids were made to appear androgynous.

He watched her look up in wonder at the sun when she felt its rays fall upon her face. In the full sunlight her skin shimmered with a slightly golden hue, but that was not her most distinguishing feature. It was her hair—or more the point, her two braids of very thick, decidedly red, woven copper filaments that fell down her back. The worn sailor hat didn't disguise the brilliance of the fine metallic strands, nor did the yellowed threadbare dress detract from the elegance of her form. While too slender to be considered very feminine, and her face too angular to ever be considered classically beautiful, she was a striking figure with her huge expressive eyes and the delicate brass nails that graced her little fingers.

In one hand the android held a carpet bag that had clearly seen better days, but she was holding it with such care that the Station Master couldn't help but be intrigued. He'd never considered the fact that an android could have luggage; it must have been stowed in the trunk with her.

She moved forward, turning around slowly as if to soak everything in, but when she spotted the conveyer belt she walked up to it, curious, and without preamble started fiddling with the various levers and cogs on the side with her free hand, only flinching—but not pulling back—when the steam from one valve hit her.

She had clearly done this before. Her tiny hand fit into the tight spaces to tweak this or that with such precision that within minutes the machine was running smoother, much to the Station Master's astonishment. She kept working until the chugging sound of the machine had turned into a soft purr, and then she turned back to the Station Master, who stammered his thanks.

"Oh, no need to thank me," she replied. "This machine is a primitive version of the sorting machines I used to operate at my previous home every day. It's such a pleasure to be able to work out how things operate, don't you think?" The android didn't give him the time to answer. "I've always thought so. There is something beautiful about seeing a machine work to the optimum of its capacity."

The Station Master couldn't agree more. He couldn't take his eyes off the android in front of him. She was an absolute marvel. He wondered where her new owner was.

He turned slightly and gestured towards the station building. "Would you like to wait in the Ladies Sitting Room until Mr. Cuthbert arrives?"

She tilted her head, considering both him and his offer. "No thank you," she replied. "I'll wait outside. There's more scope for the imagination."

The Station Master smiled. What a charming girl.

• • •

Matthew Cuthbert looked at the android from the far end of the platform and hesitated. He had never been much of a conversationalist, and had always found talking to girls to be one of the most awkward experiences in the world, so it was daunting for him to discover his most recent purchase was female in form. He had been told that he was buying a prototype whose model had never been put on the production line, but he hadn't thought to ask about gender.

He couldn't help but be intrigued, however, despite his anxiety. Androids had first been created to replace the child workforce in the factories that were expanding throughout the major cities. For many years children had often been the cheapest and most practical workers because their tiny hands and slight forms meant that they were able to manipulate delicate machinery, and so naturally the androids were modeled after them. But their creators soon discovered that their clientele did not want their new workforce looking like children—innocents. Nor did they like that the prototypes were created with advanced problem-solving skills, because some people believed it gave the androids individuality as they adapted to what they learnt, leading them to want to try new things outside the factory walls. As a consequence, the androids that eventually populated the factories all over Canada were created to be completely unremarkable in their subservience and androgynous appearance.

Matthew couldn't fathom how they could be considered superior in design to the original prototypes, but he wasn't going to complain. It meant he could afford to buy the "flawed" machine sitting on the platform in front of him.

He took a deep breath and walked towards the android—and then right on past. He realised at the last moment that he had no idea what to say to her. *How exactly does one greet an android?*

He reached the end of the platform, and stood there for a minute before turning around to see the android now eying him with evident curiosity. Matthew wondered what such a sophisticated machine would make of him, for he was very unassuming in appearance. Tall, with lank shoulder-length hair that was now more steel-coloured than the black of his youth, he had a stooped frame, as if his very posture reflected his wish to not stand out in a crowd. But the shy smile he gave the android when he finally walked up to her was welcoming, and his eyes were kind. Before he even had time to consider how to greet her, the android had stood up and reached out her hand.

"You must be my new father, Matthew Cuthbert of Green Gables." She shook his hand in greeting, still clutching the carpet bag to her side. "I'm Anne—Anne with an *e*. Most people believe that Anne is short for *android*, and so often they leave off the *e* when they write it down. However the *e* is the letter that completes the name. If I met someone else called Anne, but spelt without the *e*, I just couldn't help but feel they were somehow lacking. What do you think, Mr. Cuthbert?"

He blinked, surprised. "Well, now, I dunno." He had a simple intelligence, but he wondered if the android was expressing her insecurities about being accepted. And more important, did she *know* she was doing that? "Can I take your bag?"

"No thank you, Mr. Cuthbert. I can manage. I have to make sure I hold the handle with a 43-degree tilt at all times or it's prone to falling off. An extra degree either way and the bag has an 82 percent chance of losing its structural integrity. It's a very old, very dear carpet bag."

Matthew smiled at the unexpected mix of technical evaluation and human sentiment in Anne's statement, seemingly fitting for a machine made in Man's image. He gestured for the android to follow him, and they made their way to his horse and buggy in silence, Matthew looking at the ground, and Anne looking at everything else.

She appeared captivated by the most commonplace things. Even while one of the very rare and expensive steam-operated carriages rolled on by with the girl from the train gracing its leather seat, protecting her fair skin with her lace parasol, Anne's attention stayed focused on the old draft horse hitched to Matthew's buggy.

"I'm at a loss to see how you power this locomotive," she replied after a moment.

The corner of Matthew's mouth twitched, and he ducked his head to hide a smile, realizing that the android had never seen a horse before, and that this particular one was close to comatose.

He walked up to the horse, rubbing the gelding's neck gently, prompting him to shake out his mane and seemingly coming to life. "There are no steam-generated levers needed to operate this buggy. I just tell Samuel here to pull it for me."

The android blinked. "Samuel isn't a machine?"

"No," he said simply.

"But this creature's purpose is to serve humans?" she asked, her head tilting to the side.

Matthew's hand paused mid-stroke. "Well, yes, I suppose in a way that's true."

"Does it have free will?"

This time it was Matthew who blinked. "He lives and works on my farm."

She didn't miss a beat. "Because he has no other choice."

"Yes."

She nodded to herself. "I understand."

Matthew was struck by how definitive her answer was. "How so?"

"That existence was not unlike my life at the factory." She reached out her hand and gingerly mimicked Matthew's actions a minute earlier, her brass nails glinting in the filtered sunlight as she rubbed the horse's neck.

Matthew watched her for a long moment, then: "Did that bother you? Being told what to do all the time, I mean."

"No. Why would it?"

Matthew didn't know how to reply.

Anne continued on, almost absently. "I like to learn, and to keep busy. I also like to discover how things work. The Supervisor told me that that was a flaw in my make-up, and that I had to be terminated. I didn't know why I was going to lose my job when I had just surprised him by halting production of the main sorting machine in the factory to improve its performance by 6.3 percent, but he wouldn't listen to me anymore." Her hand stilled, and the horse head-butted her to resume. "It was Father who intervened. He told the Supervisor that termination was too final a punishment, and that I could still be of some use. However, I don't understand what he meant by that comment, because I no longer work for the company."

Matthew's depleted bank balance told him exactly how Anne had still been of use to the company, but it was her naiveté that fascinated him the most, not the reason why she had been sold.

The journey home was filled with more discoveries for them both, the android talking non-stop and the man appreciating the fact that she didn't expect him to talk too.

"You and I are going to get along just fine, Mr. Cuthbert."

"Call me Matthew."

"I'm not sure why I know this, or why I know I belong at Green Gables, but I've always thought there was more . . ."

The android stopped mid-sentence, her crystal green eyes going wide as her eyes fixed on the sky in front of her. For a moment Matthew couldn't take his eyes away from Anne's face, struck by how the sense of wonder really bought her features to life. But her attention didn't waver, so he drew his gaze away from her striking features to look up and see an airship sailing gently through the sky, the golden light of the setting sun lapping against the hull as it gently surfed the clouds.

It was barely perceptible to Matthew but he was sure that Anne could hear the whir of the enormous steam engine at work, pumping hot air into an enormous canvas balloon that the old seafaring ship was now suspended from.

"What a wondrous invention!" the android breathed in amazement.

Matthew looked back at her in surprise. "How so?"

She turned to him with bright eyes. "This machine gives you the ability to fly, which would be one of the most incredible experiences. Imagine being able to look down at the world! It would create such a sense of freedom, don't you think?"

He nodded. He'd never thought of it that way before.

"Have you ever considered flying in one of those machines?"

"No, I can't say as I have," he replied, intrigued by her child-like curiosity.

"Oh, Matthew, how much you miss out on!" They both looked back up at the airship in shared silence for a long minute.

Matthew glanced at Anne out of the corner of his eye, amazed that such a sophisticated machine could be in such awe of an old seafaring ship that had clearly seen better days. It had been hobbled to a simple canvas balloon and operated by the most cumbersome steam engine he had ever encountered, simply so its owner could maximise his resources and try to keep at the cutting edge of the transport industry. He supposed the idea was ingenious, but the execution didn't strike him as being very safe or too elegant.

"I have worked with many machines," the android said quietly, her gaze still on the airship as it disappeared slowly over the horizon, "but I have never seen one that was so beautiful."

"I have," Matthew responded in his quiet, shy manner. "*You.*"

She turned to him, her eyes now wide. "But I'm just a girl."

The innocence in her statement went straight to his heart. Matthew had never been one to talk much, but now he was literally speechless.

She didn't see herself as a machine!

Although he didn't realise it at the time, that was the moment *he* stopped seeing her as one too.

• • •

Anne discovered that being accepted by her classmates at school wasn't something she could learn from an instruction manual. When she queried Matthew about how to secure a Bosom Friend, he simply told her to "Be yourself," which puzzled her as she couldn't physically be anyone other than herself anyway. When she asked his wife the same question, however, her curt response was "Forget that nonsense! If you prove your worth, friendships will seek you out. Be kind, considerate, and above all, bite that tongue and mind your manners!"

"Biting my tongue will help facilitate friendships?" Anne asked, perplexed.

"You do beat all, girl! Of course not," Marilla replied, frustrated. "It's an expression—a human expression. But then, I suppose you shouldn't be expected to know that."

The old lady sighed, looking at the android. Ever since Matthew had bought Anne home the peace and order at Green Gables had been thrown into disarray.

"We have to send her back," she had told him the very first hour he'd returned home with the android.

"But she's such a sweet little thing," he had replied softly as he watched Anne walk around the house for the first time, reaching out her hand to touch the most random of things in fascination: the intricate embroidery on the tablecloth, the leaves of a plant, or the polished wood of the rocking chair. She had never seen such diverse textures before.

"Matthew Cuthbert, the entire reason for buying an android in the first place was so you can have help on the farm. It's unseemly to put a girl to work in the fields, even if she is android in form. And we're both too old to be nursemaids to a flawed machine."

"She's not flawed—just different." Matthew paused. "Give her a chance, Marilla."

"We'd have to put her through school, simply so she can learn the basics of interacting in society."

"So she'll go to school."

"But what is the point of buying an android if we can't get our money's worth out of her? There is still the matter of you needing help on the farm."

"I'll hire Barry's boy out for a couple of hours during the day, and Anne can help me before and after school." He held up his hand to forestall Marilla's next protest. "We can't afford to buy a normal android. And the simple fact is: I like her." He looked at his wife. "I don't ask for much, but I'm asking for this."

Marilla harrumphed, more to cover her shock than out of any deep need to protest. This was the first time her husband had ever stood up to her and held his ground. This machine must have really gotten under his skin. "The android can stay," she stated finally, "but strictly on a trial basis. We have a three-month warranty, don't we?"

"Yes."

"Then if I'm not impressed by that time, we are returning her for a full refund. And I want no protests, Matthew. That is my condition for letting her stay now."

Matthew nodded, satisfied. He knew that despite the condition he'd just won a great concession from his wife.

And so every morning Matthew came downstairs to the library at five to find Anne engrossed in one of his books, looking more like the child she appeared to be as she acted out the plays with enthusiasm, the dying light of the fire dancing about in her copper hair. They would talk about her latest literary discoveries of the previous night while Matthew ate his breakfast, and then their day would start, the android helping Matthew milk the cows, muck out the stables, and carry out all the hay for the animals until it was time for her to leave for school.

Within a week they had developed a comfortable routine, and Matthew was surprised to discover that for the first time in a decade he actually enjoyed getting up before the birds awoke. However, it soon became clear after a few weeks of school that Anne hadn't been able to make as favorable an impression on her classmates, who were quick to point out how different she was.

"People don't often like that which they don't understand," Marilla had told the android matter-of-factly.

But Anne had read about "kindred spirits" and how true bosom friends are accepting of all differences, and as Marilla had said, she just had to prove she was worthy of being a perfect friend.

So every day she went to school and tried to prove herself by excelling in her classwork. She had much to learn, having only known factory life before Green Gables, but it didn't take long until she was tied with Gilbert Blythe for first honors.

And still the classmates' attitude towards her didn't noticeably thaw. The android couldn't understand why. Wasn't she doing everything right?

"You think you are better than us, don't you, Miss Anne-droid?" was Josie Pye's snide comment after Anne won her first spelling bee. She twisted around at her desk to look directly at Anne. "Can you spell *machine?*"

Anne looked at her in puzzlement. *Is this another test?* "M-A-C-H-I—"

"Do you always have an answer for *everything?*" Josie interrupted, frustrated that she could never get a rise out of the copper-haired girl.

"Isn't the correct response to a question an answer?" she asked, still puzzled.

Josie glared at her and faced forward again, not speaking to her until their extracurricular painting class that evening. "I'm sure you are perfect at that too," she muttered.

"I don't know," the android replied. "I've never painted before."

The class set up outside to capture the majesty of the rolling fields of Avonlea on canvas. Nestled in the tree line along the horizon, Anne could see the roof of Green Gables, and so she painted that first, her strokes precise and her measurements exact.

Then she moved to the fields, taking care to note the exact hue of the grass and blending the appropriate golden-hued green. Within fifteen minutes the field was done, complete with fences drawn to scale.

While Anne was busy duplicating the trees on her canvas the teacher went up to each student in turn to ascertain their progress, and to study what their diverse depictions of the one view told him about their personalities.

When he approached Anne his eyebrows raised at the quality of the painting. Then they furrowed. "Well, it's *technically* perfect," he said, and he sat down to start his painting.

Diana Berry looked up from her canvas as Anne was starting to outline the clouds. The raven-haired beauty glanced at Anne's painting, her blue eyes going wide. "Oh Anne! I wish I could paint half as good as you do!"

"Honey, you don't need to be talented with looks like yours," Gilbert Blythe quipped from somewhere behind them. The other students snickered and the light disappeared out of Diana's eyes. She returned them to her painting.

Anne looked up from her masterpiece to discover the clouds had moved. Quickly she started painting their new position over the clouds she had already started to form.

Then she noticed that the sun had changed position. Its lower angle threw a deeper amber cast onto the field. Frantically she started to mix up a different shade of green to replace the grass she'd painted earlier.

Then she noticed that the new position of the sun meant that Green Gables was completely in shadow, rendering the cottage almost invisible to the naked eye. So Anne painstakingly painted it into a silhouette.

Then she looked up to see salmon pink was starting to outline the bottom of the clouds, and a peach was spreading across the horizon. The sun was setting.

Her efforts to keep up with the changing colours of encroaching night meant her painting strokes increased to inhuman speed—and she *still* couldn't keep up. Every time she looked up her painting was no longer accurate. The trees were now completely black along the horizon, and the fences cast long shadows across the field.

She stopped, at a loss for what to do. As a result of changing the colours in the sky so often and so quickly in a blur of hand and brush, the layers didn't have enough time to dry, resulting in the salmon pink blending with the earlier lighter blue shades. Her sky was now a mauve colour. It was a restful shade, throwing a slightly romantic mood over the painting, but all Anne could see was that it wasn't an accurate depiction.

Josie snickered. "It looks like Anne can't do everything right after all."

"Don't listen to her," Diana said, a little pointedly. "Josie doesn't think of anyone but herself." She looked at Anne's painting. "Why did you keep changing the colours? Not that it looks bad," she added hastily, "but your painting looked perfectly fine before."

"The colours are all wrong."

Gilbert appeared over her shoulder, his usual nonchalant stance dissipating in his interest. "In what way?" he asked.

"We were told to paint this view." Anne gestured in front of her. "But the colours keep changing. This painting is no longer accurate."

"A painting doesn't have to be technically accurate for it to be considered a masterpiece," the teacher interjected, only his blond hair visible at the top of his canvas as he continued to paint. "It's how you interpret the view that brings the painting to life."

"I don't understand," said Anne.

"Take a look at mine," Diana offered, a little shyly.

Anne stood up and walked over, studying the painting for a long moment.

"The clouds are the wrong shape."

"Not the *wrong* shape, Anne. Just a *different* shape," she replied. "It's a matter of perspective. Take a closer look."

The android tilted her head to the side, as she always did when she was thinking, and considered the clouds Diana had painted. They were perhaps a little too white. Also the strokes she used to define the texture of the clouds were too coarse to depict the lightness of the gossamer structures.

"Pretend they aren't clouds," Gilbert interrupted her thoughts. "What else do you see?"

Anne considered the shapes of the clouds and nothing else, and automatically started comparing them to images in her memory banks. "They're animals!" she blurted out suddenly, Diana laughing as the android's eyes darted up to the sky. Sure enough, she could see the remnants of some of the clouds Diana had painted. If she looked closely enough, she could see what looked like a rabbit bounding over the horizon. "How did you know to do this?" she asked finally.

"I just used my imagination," Diana replied, blushing delicately at the attention.

"But androids don't have an imagination, do they, Gilbert?" Josie pointed out, twirling her hair around her finger.

"Knock it off, Josie." Gilbert replied. "Nobody's perfect. She just had to know how to look."

Anne didn't hear them. She was still trying to process what she had just learned. "So Diana's painting is better than mine, even though mine is technically more accurate."

The teacher leaned around his easel. "*Better* is not the right word. It's a more *realised* painting." He paused, trying to work out how to explain it. "Your painting shows us how you—or anyone here—physically sees the fields, but nothing more. It doesn't show us anything about *you.*"

She analyzed his words carefully, and found herself, as well as her painting, lacking. "So I have failed."

"No, not necessarily." The teacher studied the android for a moment, aware that she'd probably never been confronted with failure before. "It just means you've got more to learn." He smiled gently. "That is what school is for."

"Where do I start?"

Even Josie was struck by the earnest entreaty in the android's tone.

"Here and now," the teacher responded with a smile. "We've still got a half an hour of light."

The android sat down at her easel, unwilling to let the teacher know he had misunderstood her. She remembered what happened when the Supervisor at the factory had misunderstood her, and she didn't want to be sold again. She looked at her painting.

Where do I start?

"Do you see Green Gables in the distance?" Diana whispered into Anne's ear, leaning over in her chair. Anne nodded. "That is not merely where you live, but it's your *home*. What do you *see* when you think of home?"

Diana watched Anne's eyes blink rapidly for a few seconds, and then flitter back and forth across the painting. She reached for her paints and brush, and started mixing colours.

Diana watched, fascinated, while Anne started applying paint to the canvas once more. Her speed belied her android heritage as an airship quickly took shape amongst the clouds in the painting's mauve sky.

When the flying vessel was complete, she dipped her brush in a combination of pots and leaned forward. For a minute Diana could only see the back of Anne's copper braid as the android painstakingly painted a candlelit window onto the silhouette of the cottage, but then she leaned back and dipped her brush into black pot.

After considering the painting for a moment, the android started to paint a tiny profile of a human in the field closest to the cottage. When she also brushed in a little cattle dog beside the figure, Diana realised that it was Anne's depiction of Matthew returning to Green Gables after a hard day's work on the farm.

The android's hand hesitated beside the image of the man, and Diana wondered if the android understood what a lovely—and homely—image she had just created: the light from the kitchen guiding the man home at night.

But then the android's hand darted upwards, and another silhouette started to take shape at the bow of the airship. It appeared that the figure was looking down at the cottage, and when Diana saw that the silhouette wore her hair in a braid that was lifted by the wind, Diana started in shock.

Anne had drawn herself into the painting, and she was sailing on an airship, being guided home by the cottage light like a seafaring ship would a lighthouse.

Who said androids couldn't have an imagination? Diana thought triumphantly, looking at her new friend's painting with a smile on her face. *Anne might be a kindred spirit after all.*

• • •

Matthew pulled out his timepiece and opened the case to see where the clock hands pointed. "It's time to leave for school, Anne," he said quietly, sure that she could hear him from across the barn.

She looked up, blinking in surprise. "Usually my internal clock alerts me before now."

Matthew nodded, bemused. One of the things that endeared him the most about the android was that she could often get so swept up in her enthusiasm and curiosity for the current project she was working on that it overrode her most basic mechanical functions, like her inbuilt alarm clock. He knew that Marilla and Anne's creators considered that a manufacturing flaw, but to Matthew it seemed like a very human characteristic.

He watched her methodically put his tools back in order, and then cover the machine.

"I was nearly finished!" she complained.

"So you will finish it tonight."

"I suppose that is an acceptable conclusion," she replied.

Matthew laughed. *Was the android pouting?* "Well, my dear Anne, if this contraption of yours truly works, and I never have to milk a cow again with my bare hands, then I will have the time to start teaching you chess before school tomorrow morning." He smiled at her. "Is that also an acceptable conclusion?"

It appeared to him that her eyes lit up. "More than acceptable, Matthew." She tilted her head, considering him.

Matthew blushed under her scrutiny and busied himself with closing his timepiece and running his thumb lovingly over the initials ornately carved across the lid before moving to put it away. He felt the android's curiosity before she voiced it. "It was my father's," he said quietly.

He hesitated a moment, then held it out to her.

Anne appeared to understand the privilege she was being given. She took the pocket watch from Matthew with evident care, turning it around in her dainty hands to look at the initials, almost imperceptible on the old tarnished metal. She popped the lid open, and her eyes grew wide. She had never seen such a tiny machine. Behind the ornately carved brass hands, she could see the intricate wheels turn, and despite the discolouration of age, she thought it beautiful.

Matthew let the android hold his timepiece the entire way to school, the light reflecting off Anne's brass nails as she tinkered with it, drawing his attention to the advancement of her construction in comparison to his beloved pocket watch. The 19th century had seen a huge evolution in machines, and he wondered what the next century would bring if Anne was the pinnacle of this one.

The buggy started rocking more than usual, with Samuel having to navigate more ruts as a result of the storm the previous night, but when Matthew briefly glanced over at Anne he saw the pocket watch clutched protectively in her tiny hand.

She seemed almost reluctant to give it up when they reached the school, but then she heard Diana calling and she quickly handed it over, leaping out of the buggy with her usual enthusiasm and grace. She turned to Matthew to say goodbye, and he told her he'd be there at three to pick her up.

"No need, Matthew," she said. "Gilbert Blythe said he'd walk me to the bend, and I wanted to see the new flowers that have come out since the last rain."

Matthew smiled as he watched her rush off to greet Diana, wondering if she realised how human she sounded.

He shook his head at his folly. *Of course she knows. She doesn't see herself as a machine!*

He laughed as Samuel pulled the buggy away from school, and he returned home with a smile still on his face.

"What time do you call this, Matthew Cuthbert?" Marilla asked when he walked into the kitchen to share a pot of tea with his wife before going back to work on the farm.

He didn't know why, but by Marilla's clock he was always late. He pulled out his pocket watch to check—and discovered it was no longer working.

His heart sank in his chest. His pocket watch had never failed him until today, and it was his last tangible memory of his father.

He looked at it closely and he could see that part of the clock mechanism appeared dislodged behind the face, and when he shook it gently, he could hear something metallic rattle around. It appeared that an irreplaceable component was broken in his beloved timepiece.

Marilla saw the look on his face and asked him what was wrong. After he told her, she asked, "What, if anything, did you do differently with the pocket watch today?"

He thought back on his morning. "Nothing, really. I gave it to Anne to look at, and then let her hold it while we travelled through some storm-created ruts on the way to school." He paused, considering. "Come to think of it, those ruts really were pretty rough going. I wouldn't be surprised if one of them was what did it."

Marilla wasn't convinced. "Did you watch Anne the entire time she had your timepiece, Matthew?"

"I can't say as I did," he replied, wondering what his wife was getting at. "I had to concentrate on the road on account of those bothersome ruts."

Marilla was silent for a long moment, and then she asked, "Do you think the android could have tinkered with it? She seems fascinated with the inner workings of machinery."

"Anne was fascinated by the intricacy of my pocket watch," he admitted. "But . . ."

"Think about it, Matthew," Marilla interrupted. "My theory makes sense. The pocket watch had never broken down in your lifetime, or your Dad's, *until* the day you let Anne play with it."

He couldn't find any fault with her logic, but deep down in his heart he knew it wasn't true.

When Anne came home that afternoon from her walk with Gilbert Blythe, a posy of wildflowers in her hand, Marilla confronted her. "Did you fiddle with the mechanism in Matthew's pocket watch?"

Anne noted the agitated tone in her voice, and became concerned. "What's wrong with it?"

Marilla took that as an admission of a kind. "So you *know* something is wrong with it!"

"No, Marilla," Anne replied. "I honestly didn't." She looked at Matthew, who was quietly sitting in the kitchen chair, watching the exchange. He gave her a gentle smile of encouragement.

"I need a truthful answer from you, Anne," said Marilla. "Did you play with Matthew's watch until you broke it?"

"No, Marilla," said Anne truthfully, since she had no idea when it broke.

"Then who did?" demanded Marilla.

Anne simply stared at her. She'd been taught never to guess when she didn't know the answer.

Marilla glared at the android, trying to keep her temper in check. "Now listen to me carefully, Anne," she said at last, ominously enunciating every syllable. "If you don't admit that you've done wrong, and that you just lied to me, you will not be allowed to go to Diana's birthday airship flight next month."

Anne's mind quickly considered the possibilities and the consequences. If she did not admit to purposely breaking the watch, Marilla would not believe her and she would not be permitted to ride on the exotic airship. On the other hand, if she lied and admitted to breaking it, Marilla almost certainly *would* believe her and she would be allowed to go. It was very confusing: if she lied she would be rewarded, and if she told the truth she would be punished.

Which was worse—to lie and be believed, or to tell the truth and be doubted? In the end it was not the airship that was the deciding factor, but a desire to please Marilla by telling her what Anne assumed she wanted to hear, and what she obviously already believed.

"I broke the watch while I was playing with it," she said at last.

Marilla stared at her a long time before speaking. Finally she said, "All right, Anne. Cuthberts always keep their word, so you will be allowed to go on the airship."

"Thank you," said Anne.

"I'm not finished yet," said Marilla harshly. "As I said, Cuthberts don't lie. You just admitted that you lied to me. Therefore, you are not and never will be a Cuthbert. I'm going to have a serious talk with Matthew. I think we're going to return you and get our money back. You are *not* what we were promised."

Anne was still staring at the empty space where Marilla had stood long after she had turned and walked away.

Deep down Anne had known she was different from everyone else in Avonlea, and that she had the means to repair the pocket watch if she only just acknowledged it. She didn't know if she had refused to accept the truth about herself and had blocked it from her mind, or if she had simply been programmed to not think about it, but she had to confront it now if she was to ever help fix the damage she had inadvertently caused.

She pulled out her carpet bag, and for the first time since she'd arrived at Green Gables she opened it up. Inside was a batch of tools, some of them not unlike those she was using to create Matthew's milking machine, only finer in construction.

Her delicate hand reached in and sorted through them until she felt the one she needed and pulled it out, looking at it for a long moment.

She hesitated, then unlaced the top of her nightgown, looking down at the barely perceptible panel outlined on the left side of her chest. Her right hand hovered above it, implement in hand, knowing instinctively what she had to do, but unable to take the next step. Then she thought of the pain she saw in Matthew's eyes when Marilla had decreed she had to be returned to the factory, and she steeled herself, placing the implement along one side of the panel and pressing it in, hearing a tiny whir as three micro-latches started turning. A section of her popped out, and she looked at it for a long moment before carefully hooking the brass nail of her thumb into the tiny crevice and pulling it open.

I'm a machine.

The realization struck her like a punch to the stomach as she stood staring at what she had revealed, unable to process anything for some time. Although deep down she had always known, it was still a shock to see tiny brass cogs, wheels, screws, and copper wires so intricately interconnected to a circuit board buried within her chest. It was a wonder to behold, even for the android.

She realised how primitive the pocket watch was in comparison, and yet she also understood its importance to Matthew so her determination to repair it for him increased tenfold. She closed her eyes and tuned into the sounds her body made.

Tick, tick, tick, tick . . .

Her eyes sprung open, and she instinctively moved a bundle of copper wires that were covering the specific mechanism she needed to find. She analyzed the individual components, recognizing that some were similar to those in the pocket watch.

Tick, tick, tick, tick . . .

She rustled around in her carpet bag and pulled out a tiny toolbox, opening it to reveal delicate jewellery-grade tools. She selected one and used it to sever the connection between the tiny mechanism and her main circuit board without a second thought.

The ticking stopped.

The android's hand froze. She felt a strong sense of loss, and she couldn't focus. She had no idea how long it took her to adjust to the change in her body, because she literally lost track of time, but she finally was able to block out the feeling that she had lost something fundamental to her being when she realised how much more she'd lose if she had to leave Green Gables.

She carefully placed the little mechanism on the table in front of her and used the firelight to study it more closely. At first she had thought she'd wasted her time, but when she put the pocket watch beside it, she was able to compare the components more easily, and she could see they were of similar composition and size; they were just finished off differently.

Then she spotted it: the part she needed.

Using the precision that only an android could command, Anne very carefully detached it and transplanted it into the pocket watch within minutes. When the last part was in place, the pocket watch sprang to life.

Tick, tick, tick, tick . . .

Anne clapped her hands together in delight, an affectation she'd picked up from Diana. She knew that what she achieved that night was more important than any work she'd ever done on the factory floor—or at least, it felt that way to her.

She looked at the part of herself she'd transplanted into the pocket watch, studying her handiwork, unable to find it lacking. The new part stood out from the rest of the components because it was free of tarnish and more rose gold in colour than normal brass. It also appeared more refined in composition, and she wondered if Matthew would mind the discrepancy.

She resealed her access panel and relaced the top of her nightgown before methodically packing her tools back into the carpet bag. She considered whether she should clean the brass and restore the pocket watch back to its original condition, but the cleaning agent she normally rinsed through her cop- per hair was in the bathroom upstairs, and she didn't want to risk waking the Cuthberts.

She picked up the pocket watch again to take it back to the kitchen where Matthew had usually kept it, and walked straight into someone.

"Anne! Give that to me immediately!" Marilla barked, standing in the doorway with a lantern in her hand. "You have been told you are no longer welcome in our house, and that means you are definitely not allowed to touch our things." She looked at the android pointedly. "Especially valuables you've already broken."

Anne didn't trust herself to speak after the trouble her mouth had gotten her into earlier that day, so instead she simply held out her hand.

Marilla was taken aback by the silent acquiesce. She looked down to see the pocket watch still open on the dainty little hand, and she wondered what other heirlooms the android had played with while she and Matthew had been asleep at night.

She retrieved the time piece, inspecting it to see if it came to further damage—and her heart nearly stopped.

The pocket watch was working again!

She couldn't tear her eyes away from it; she was so surprised. Then she spotted the gleaming new part at the heart of the clock mechanism, and her breath caught. "Where did you get that?" Marilla asked, looking up at Anne sharply.

The android raised her hand and placed it on her chest where a human heart would be. "Here," she said simply, her head tilting to the side.

She had used a part of herself to repair the watch! Marilla realised what a huge gesture that was. "You didn't break the watch yesterday by playing with the clock mechanism, did you?" she asked quietly.

"No."

Marilla sighed. "Then why did you say you did when I asked?"

"You told me I couldn't go on the airship for Diana's birthday celebration next month unless I confessed to breaking it," Anne said, her big green eyes seeking Marilla's out in entreaty. "So I confessed."

"But that's lying, Anne," Marilla pointed out.

"You wouldn't believe the truth."

Marilla sighed again. "So you thought you were giving me the answer I wanted. You were trying to please me." She looked back down at the repaired pocket watch. "Let us make a deal, Anne: I will forgive you for lying, if you will forgive me for not believing you."

"What is this about forgiveness?" Matthew asked, as he, too, walked into the room.

Marilla ate some humble pie. "You were right," she admitted, and without saying any more she handed over the pocket watch.

Matthew brought the timepiece closer to his lantern to study it. That it worked again was no surprise to him. He had a feeling Anne would try to repair it after watching her dedication while building his milking machine. But what he didn't expect to see was the glint of a new component in the clock mechanism that differed in colour from the rest of the watch. He looked over to Anne in shock when he recognised its construction was far more refined than the rest of the watch's components.

Anne's green eyes twinkled. "I'll never be on time for school again," she said, and Matthew realised she'd used a component from her internal clock to bring his father's beloved pocket watch back to life.

He knew what a sacrifice that must have been for the android, and his heart reached out to her, knowing that in a way he held a piece of hers in his hand.

He walked up to her and kissed her on the forehead, much to her and Marilla's surprise. "You'll just have to learn how to tell the time like us average folks," he said as he stepped back, his voice a little gruff with emotion.

"I'll teach you, Anne," Marilla stated. "If you learn from Matthew, you'll never arrive anywhere on time."

• • •

Anne had always thought that sailing on an airship would give her a sense of freedom unlike any other experience in the world.

She was wrong.

Yes, it was exhilarating. Yes, she felt on top of the world—quite literally—as she leaned over the bow of the ship, the wind lifting her copper hair as the vessel passed through another cloudbank. But she soon realised that she was just a spectator watching the world pass her by. There was some peace to be discovered in that, but she had no control over that journey; she just had to enjoy the ride.

She knew now that her first true taste of freedom had been when the Station Master had released her from the cargo trunk at the train station three months ago—she just hadn't been aware of it at the time. She had stepped out into a brand new world, with sensations she'd never even known had existed, let alone experienced, and for the first time in her brief life she had the opportunity to be accepted. Appreciated.

Loved.

No longer was she being told how to perform her every action like an automated machine. She had to learn and adapt to the ramifications of her actions like everyone else, and deal with any consequences that arose. There was a great sense of freedom in being in control of her own destiny that she'd previously been denied until she'd met the Cuthberts.

Her keen android eyes searched the fields far below her until she spotted Green Gables nestled along the treeline. As she gazed at the house she felt a sense of belonging that she'd never experienced before.

"We would like to adopt you," Matthew said quietly when she had hopped off the airship not long after, halting her excited rambles about how the journey through the clouds had given her such scope for the imagination.

"But you have already bought me," Anne replied, perplexed, as she considered Matthew's shy smile.

"That's true," said Marilla, "and what an expensive girl you were, to say the least." She brushed off her skirts briskly, and then looked directly at the android, who returned her gaze. "But we don't want to *own* you," she added, reaching over to take hold of Matthew's hand. "We want to know if you would *choose* to become a part of this family as the child we never had, and never knew we'd even wanted until you came into our lives."

Anne stared at both of them, and for the first time since they met her she was speechless.

In that moment she became Anne of Green Gables.

She had finally come home.

. . . .

GHIA LIKES FOOD

BILL CONGREVE

Oxenford, a family man and the local Member of Parliament, sat in his office and worked on a zoning application for a funeral parlour.

It was past midnight. He yawned, slumped forward onto his desk, and slept.

He dreamed of popcorn that popped in his throat and expanded out until his neck exploded.

• • •

Nick wore old army jungle green combat pants and a purple tie-die T-shirt with the word 'celebrate' printed in white on the front and 'death' in black on the back. He had a necklace draped about his neck which alternated glass beads and syringes with the needles removed.

Whenever he went out on a special occasion, he drove a needle from the syringes through each ear, and hung a string of rosary beads on the right hand side.

This was a special occasion.

Nick smelt Oxenford's dream, bashed the politician in the side of the head with an ashtray he found in the office, and took the man home with him.

• • •

"Here Ghia! A snack!"

A muffled woof woke Oxenford. Pain made him wince and cry out, but no sound came from his lips. His neck felt like it was on fire. There was a terrible, yawning emptiness in his mouth. He tried to pull his hands down to feel his neck and realised he was manacled to a wall. He was laid out on a bed that leaned against the wall behind him at a forty-five degree angle. Manacles held his ankles to the feet of the bed.

Beside the bed stood a table. On the table was a metal dish that held a syringe, a number of cotton wool pads, a scalpel, a needle, and cotton thread. Oxenford often used something similar to repair his daughter's clothes. Beside the dish was a bottle of antibiotics, a 375 ml bottle of Polish vodka, a hacksaw, and a hammer.

The dish also held a lump of flesh.

Oxenford smelt alcohol on himself, but he wasn't drunk. He opened his mouth to shout and realised he had no tongue.

He fainted, and dreamed of cattle.

• • •

Oxenford woke again to find a long wooden plank strapped to the bed under him. A young man with long, straggling, unwashed hair bent over his legs and tied them very securely to the board. The man was naked from the waist up and wore a string of rosary beads from a metal pin stabbed through one ear. An uncured pelt loincloth was knotted around his waist. The man looked up at him. A single wet trail of snot ran from his left nostril, over his lips, and onto his chin.

"I'm Nick. I grok your parts," the man said, and licked his lips.

Oxenford struggled then. He bounced and fought, fighting for his life. Blood ran down his arms as the chains tore into his wrists.

His bonds held.

"Left or right, Ghia?"

A massive Rottweiler stirred on the floor. It was a young dog, not yet a year old, and Oxenford thought it had more growing in it. It barked once.

"Left it is!"

Oxenford struggled again. Nick picked up a hammer and bashed him on the shins.

"Be still."

Pain flashed up Oxenford's legs and he threw his head back against the mattress. He wished it was a wall there, or something else hard, so that he could knock himself out.

Oxenford then realised he could do nothing to save his own life. That shocked him to stillness. He needed charity from this fruitcake, or he needed help from outside. He couldn't shout. He couldn't bash on the wall. Nobody knew where he was. *He* didn't know where he was. He thought of his daughter who would soon be old enough to go out with boys like this.

The crazy man tied a tourniquet around a pressure point in his upper left thigh. The crazy man then picked up a scalpel and began on his left leg just above the ankle. Oxenford tried to scream, tried to fight, tried to pull his leg away. He finally managed to turn his head away until he could bite on his own right arm. He thrashed and chewed at his arm until torn strings of flesh caught between his teeth and blood ran down his throat, but he only fainted when Nick began on his tibia with the hacksaw.

• • •

Oxenford regained consciousness to see Nick standing some metres away from him in thick gloom. A pale patch of grey sky showed through a single window close to the roof. The dog sat next to the crazy man, on a leash. The crazy man saw him come awake, stood absolutely still facing him, and just barely perceptibly tightened his hold on the leash.

The dog took its cue and came to its feet, growling. Oxenford had never seen a look of such naked hostility on the face of any beast. The dog pulled at its leash, drew back its lips, snapped its teeth, and threw its head about in hate. Foam gathered in the corners of its mouth and dripped to the floor.

God! Oxenford wanted to die.

The crazy man reached down to the dog's collar. The dog sensed it was about to be set free and went absolutely wild. Nick snapped the leash of the collar. The dog trotted forward, snarling. It reached the end of the bed and sprang.

He wanted to die, but Oxenford still couldn't stop himself turning his head away and pulling his chin. The weight of the animal struck him and drove the air from his chest in an explosive gasp. The dog's paws dug into his shoulders. The dog whined. Oxenford opened his eyes and found the giant head of the animal, foam-flecked lips and all, only inches from his own. Hostility forgotten, it panted with its tongue lolling out the side of its mouth. Oxenford closed his eyes again as the animal licked his face.

"Father never liked that trick," Nick the crazy man said and then walked forwards.

The crazy man's Doc Marten's echoed off the bare concrete floor. Oxenford noticed every detail about him with fatal crystal clarity.

He wondered if his daughter loved him at all. He hoped so.

The dog jumped off the bed, leaned lazily forward, sniffed Oxenford's stump, and licked at a trickle of blood that seeped from between the neat row of stitches.

"Good Ghia. Ghia likes food."

· · · · · · · · · · ·

LOVERS IN CAELI-AMUR

RJURIK DAVIDSON

Anton Moreau stepped from his carriage, dressed in his finest suit, his long sleeves puffing out from beneath his jacket, and held his breath in anticipation. House Arbor had always held the most famous balls in Caeli-Amur. The Directors constantly tried to outdo each other with opulent decoration, sumptuousness food, and extravagant entertainment. And this would be the night of Anton's greatest triumph.

He passed along the wide street, where bulb-trees lined the sides like marshals standing to attention, and drifted with other guests through the gates of Director Lefebvre's mansion. Like most House Arbor buildings, the walls were covered with *Toxicodendron didion*, which reached out ominously towards the passersby, green fronds waving, hoping to wrap the guests up in their deadly embrace. Sometimes when the toxicodendron was cut back, the skeletons of thieves were found hanging within the vine's wiry branches.

The gardens of Lefebvre's mansion were immaculately sculpted, with olive trees lining the walls. On the front lawns the guests—men in bright red coats, women in grandiose dresses—watched as jugglers tossed burning sticks in the air, contortionists squeezed their way through impossible frames, and sleight-of-hand magicians sat next to thaumaturgists, daring the crowd to decide who was the real and who the fake. Arbor was obsessed with appearances, with fronts, with displays.

Anton walked into a grand entrance hall with its great staircases curling up to overlooking balconies, its floor a massive mosaic depicting an augurer, her hair wild and matted, as she overlooked the rugged and dry mountains to the west of Caeli-Amur. The design was in the manner of the ancients, and there were frescoes—painted in emerald greens and solar reds—on the walls.

Guests spoke to each other excitedly as they examined each other and each new patron who entered the mansion. A woman in the corner pointed towards him and whispered to a friend, for Anton himself was part of the entertainment. For Lefebvre, Anton's presence was a display of exoticism and excitement, allowing the respectable gentlemen and ladies of the House to return from the ball, whispering to each other about the gratificationist-assassin who believed that real life could be found in the attainment of immediate pleasure.

As he crossed the floor, Anton felt someone grasp his forearm roughly.

Madame Demoul, her face set coldly like a statue, looked up at him. "You bastard."

"So nice to see you," said Anton pleasantly. He would have to get rid of her quickly, before she made a scene.

"I'm just like the rest of them, aren't I? You seduce us and then throw us away when you're sick of us." She spat the words out, her head craned forward.

Anton looked around and smiled at other guests. Chatter echoed around the hall, concealing his conversation. "Jeana, you were always special. The months we had together—you remember how we embraced. How could you say that was not real? But we were forced to stop. You know that. Your husband, he suspected."

"I'll have you killed. I'll have your throat cut in your sleep."

Anton leaned in and touched her hand briefly. "I loved you."

Madame Demoul seemed to shrink, and her eyes filled with tears. "Please come back to me. Please . . ."

Anton smiled at more guests as they passed by. "Send me a message at café La Tazia. Perhaps enough time has passed."

Madame Demoul looked at the floor. "I can't. You'll hurt me again. I'm just one of your whores."

Anton nodded slowly. "As you wish."

Madame Demoul's face was wracked with emotions. It shifted and changed from moment to moment. "I will, I will send you a note . . ."

"Now go, before anyone suspects." Anton spoke with authority. Madame Demoul turned and hurried away. Hopefully the pathetic creature would leave him alone for the rest of the night.

Anton continued on into the ballroom, where couples danced in intricate patterns, circling each other like parts of a great machine. On a stage along one wall sat a small orchestra, playing a sophisticated minuet.

Across the room stood a delicate and childlike woman, her golden ringlets piled on her head in a great tower, a beauty spot painted on one cheek. She talked to two other gowned ladies, one of whom apparently said something humorous, for the delicate woman threw her head back and laughed gaily. Her mouth smiling slightly, revealing white but slightly crooked teeth, she glanced across the room and Anton caught her eye. He struck that half-smile that he knew made him look devilish, and for several seconds she held his gaze.

There she is, thought Anton: my conquest for the night.

A servant requested his presence in the smoking room with Director Lefebvre himself. The man passed Anton a note: "Be prepared".

As he began to follow, Anton looked back at the women. This time *she* smiled devilishly at him but then broke eye contact as if he bored her.

Anton smiled to himself. It seemed this would be a challenge.

• • •

Lefebvre dominated the smoking room the way he dominated everything. As was befitting a Director of House Arbor, he sat, tall and grey-haired, his nose straight, his eyes impenetrable.

Behind Lefebvre stood his cold-faced adjutant, Jean-Paul, while a number of Officiates lounged in chaise longues, their attention directed towards him subtly: here the feet angled in his direction, there the head.

"Ah my trusted colleagues, let me introduce you to the gratificationist, Anton Moreau."

An Officiate whom Anton had already met—a man called Villiers with a greasy sheen to his skin—stood up. "Please, take a seat." He ushered Anton to a chaise longue on one side of the room and turned to Lefebvre. "I must say Director, what a wonderful collection of entertainments you have provided this evening."

A young fresh-faced Officiate, who seemed to have a permanent smirk, looked at Anton. "So Moreau, is it true you've dedicated your life to the search for pleasure?"

"That is something of an exaggeration—no one can solely seek pleasure. There are a great number of other things that one must consider. The point is to turn those other things to the service of pleasure. One acquires money—but what for?"

Lefebvre spoke and the room fell silent. "Loyalty, for example. Anton has always been faithful, hasn't he Jean-Paul?"

Lefebvre's adjutant nodded silently. There was something about Jean-Paul that unnerved Anton. He could not imagine the adjutant enjoying anything at all. The man was a House fanatic: drawn from the impoverished countryside, narrow-minded and brutal. There was something mechanical about him.

When Lefebvre spoke again, the room filled with tension. "It's a precious commodity, is it not? What do *you* think Villiers?"

Villiers' skin acquired a slicker sheen and the other Officiates looked on with anxious curiosity—something was happening.

"I could not agree more." Villiers turned back to Anton, and changed the subject. "But I wanted to ask Moreau something. I understand that gratificationists seek escape in Lika-flowers and other such drugs."

These were not real philosophers, thought Anton. They did not seek to uncover the truth beneath appearances. They were pragmatists—petty men concerned with the day-to-day running of the house. But Lefebvre had already indicated to him that he was not solely here for a discussion. He was here for work. "What I seek by such experiences is not escape from the world, but an even greater experience of it. I seek new and ever more intense cognizance of things."

"And what pleasures do you seek *tonight*?" The young man smiled lasciviously.

"Why, whatever pleasures *offer themselves*." Anton turned his hands up, smiling.

Lefebvre spoke slowly, fixing Villier's with his eyes. "And what do you think, Villiers, of the rumours that there are Technis agents in our midst?"

Villiers looked at Lefebvre and his face twitched. "They are . . . surely rumours." Silence now hung like a mist in the room and Villiers looked from Officiate to Officiate for affirmation. When none was forthcoming he glanced at Lefebvre. "Surely you don't think . . ."

"Anton." Lefebvre nodded to Anton and then at Villiers who, seeing the gesture, blurted out "No!"

In a blur, Anton had somersaulted onto the floor in front of Villiers. His hands emerged from beneath his coat clutching stilettos. In an instant he stood up, just as Villiers himself did. For a moment Anton and the Officiate stood eye to eye before Anton plunged his knives beneath the man's ribs. Villiers eyes bulged and he grabbed Anton's forearms and held them tight as his face contorted. His body shuddered and he dropped to his knees. Anton watched as the man's eyelids fluttered and his eyes slowly became flat surfaces without depth. When he was gone, Anton laid him gently face forward on the floor.

The still smirking young Officiate looked from Anton to Lefebvre. "As Villiers himself said, what a wonderful collection of entertainment you have provided tonight, Director."

• • •

Anton was relieved when he left the smoking room. It had been an unwelcome distraction; he had other business to pursue. He entered the ballroom. Leaning against the wall with her bird-like husband was Madame Demoul. She smiled at him and looked at her feet.

Anton turned away and saw *her*: he weaved between the dancers until he came close to the childlike woman. One of her friends looked quickly at him and back to her friend. Without acknowledging the other ladies, he stepped forward and asked, "Would the lady like to dance?"

A slight surprised smile appeared on her face. Without waiting for a reply, Anton took her hand and led her towards the dancing.

"Might I ask your name?" she said.

"I think it should remain a mystery, don't you?" The band began a piece comprising of plucked violins, violas and cellos that rose and fell in a soft staccato march. They carved out little paths between the other dancers, joining up, moving in formation with the others, and rejoining. Each time they came together Anton broke into his half-smile.

"Stop it," she said.

"Why, whatever can you mean?" he said.

"I'll have you know I'm happily married."

"Then you're perfect," he said.

"You rascal."

"And to whom are you so very happily married?"

"Why, to the Director himself," she said.

Anton smiled, though he felt the fear rushing through his body: waves that started in his chest and coursed down his legs and arms. He breathed steadily to calm himself. "Perhaps we should go somewhere where we can . . . talk now."

Her eyes were wide and sparkling, and she looked at him as if mesmerised.

"Now." Anton spoke calmly and assertively, brooking no opposition.

She walked slowly from the room, nodding to guests as they greeted her. Anton followed her to the wide passageway that led back to the entrance hall. Despite his effort, his heart beat rapidly, as if it were a ferret rushing around in its cage. She opened a servants' door, camouflaged by the wall's decorations, passed through it and closed it behind her. Anton leaned against the wall and looked back at the ball. A couple passed by, smiling politely at him and entered the ballroom. As long as Lefebvre or one of his loyal officiates did not spy him, things would be fine.

Turning quickly, he slipped through the servants' door.

In a narrow corridor, she stood, her eyes still alive with excitement. She spoke softly, "I know who you are. I have heard stories about you."

He grabbed her by the arms and thrust her against the wall. Surprised by the action, she stood like a frightened animal, breathing heavily. He leaned in so that his lips brushed her hair and his breath hovered against her skin.

She took his hand and led him to a rickety flight of stairs and up to the second floor of the mansion. They passed along a long corridor to the great doors at its end. "What's in here?"

"His study," she said and leaned in to whisper in his ear. "I'm not allowed in."

Anton hesitated, then opened the door.

"No," she said.

But Anton led her inside and lifted her onto the great desk that dominated the room. He brushed aside the Director's papers and the quills. "What have you done to me?" Anton said playfully. He kissed her and felt the softness of her lips. He kissed her on her cheek and along her neck and shoulder, her ringlets brushing against his face. He ran his lips along the top of her breasts, bared by the décolleté neckline. He hitched her dress up, and ran his finger up her white stockinged legs. She threw her head back and closed her eyes.

He pulled a glinting stiletto from the sheath hidden around his waist. She drew a sudden intake of breath.

He pressed a finger to her lips to silence her and cut though the front of her undergarments with the blade, without taking his eyes from hers. Her mouth opened slightly, revealing her delightfully crooked white teeth.

A moment later, he was inside her and she wrapped her arms around him tightly, as if she might lose him. "My philosopher," she said. "My assassin."

All the while, he looked over her shoulder at the Director's papers, strewn across the dark wood.

When it was done, he said, "Perhaps you should leave alone and I should follow you down." He waited in the study for five minutes and then breezed out confidently.

Later in the night, as the guests were leaving, he leaned up against the wall next to her.

"You look familiar," she said.

Anton drew an excited breath. He felt himself to be dancing on some invisible precipice that might crumble beneath his feet at any moment. "Near the Southern Gate lies Hotel du Cirque. It is not far from here. It has the most charming atmosphere. Perhaps you would like me to show it to you."

"I'm free in two days time," she said.

"Until then, Eliana."

"How is it that you know my name?"

Anton half-smiled and blew air at her cheek. "Until then."

Late in the evening, his mind still alight with traces of excitement and risk, Anton walked from the mansion and onto the street. As he walked along the wall, as if to reaffirm his daring, and to feel the exhilaration of earlier in the night, he purposely walked close to the *Toxicodendron Didion*. A vine whipped out and wrapped around his wrist, pulling him towards the rest of the heaving plant. He pulled a stiletto, cut the vine and stepped back. His wrist was already inflamed and itchy. He looked back at the vine, thinking how easy it would be to become trapped.

• • •

At first Anton sought only the immediate pleasures of the body. Over time, as they met weekly in the room on the top floor of the Hotel Du Cirque, Anton discovered that beneath Eliana's childish air were hidden depths. Often she would ask him to explain some finer point of gratificationist philosophy, and her questions were unusually probing. She could grasp the philosophy's consequences quickly, and constantly surprised him with her acumen. "So in the pursuit of immediate gratification, you're prepared to risk long-term distress," she said.

"Tomorrow we may be dead, and then what was the deferral of our desires for?" he said.

"But, perhaps we might also need to consider the terrible possibility that we may live another fifty years," she said.

"Another fifty years of this!" He pulled her close so he could feel her breasts against him. She laughed.

One week, Lefebvre had headed on business to the great monolithic city Varenis. Anton and Eliana arranged to meet for the afternoon. Anton was looking forward to a languorous lovemaking session, where the long hours would stretch like eternity itself. He imagined Eliana's head thrown back, her mouth opening and closing in some counterpoint to the rest of her body. As he thought of it, his heart leaped.

It was with some surprise that when he arrived at the hotel, a carriage was waiting at the front.

"Get in," whispered Eliana.

Uncertain, Anton stepped up into the carriage and it took off, rattling along the cobblestones. Eliana leaned back on the seat opposite him and smiled knowingly.

Despite an almost overwhelming urge to ask her about their destination, Anton sat back in his own seat and looked through the window at Caeli-Amur. At first he thought they were headed to the massive Arena that sat at the base of the southern headland. But they passed it by, and it was empty on this afternoon. Instead they climbed the headland and passed through the southern gate of Caeli-Amur towards the water-parks and gardens that lay to the south. Though officially under the province of House Arbor, they were considered a neutral zone, where any of the House's officiates could promenade in safety. Anton had never visited them. He was strictly a citizen of the city. Like many philosopher-assassins he had grown up among the caste. His father had died when Anton was young and he had spent much of his childhood strapped to his mother's back, his eyes calmly taking in events as she continued to fight in the internecine wars between the Houses. Murder, intrigue, theory—Anton was born into them.

When they arrived at the gardens, they passed through a great cast-iron gate imprinted with the images of the god Demidae, crying alone in her boat among a great flat ocean. The carriage continued along the path, speckled sunlight falling between the trees. Colours leaped out at Anton: purples and yellows and oranges of flowers, the deep green of the grass, the sparkling blue of the canals that criss-crossed the gardens. Statues of gods and heroes stood sternly on little hillocks, or in semi-hidden arbors.

"Is it true that the statues in the gardens move around at night, that the gardens are filled with spirits?" Anton asked.

"Stay with me and you'll survive," teased Eliana.

Eventually they crossed a long bridge that led to an island in the middle of the lake. In the middle of a copse of trees a great blanket was laid down, and on it was spread fruits and dried meats, cake-breads and flagons of *liqueurs*.

They stepped from the carriage, which then rattled away, leaving them alone with the feast.

"Who *are* you?" said Anton, half-joking, half in wonderment.

Eliana sat delicately on the blanket and her face became serious. "Who am I?" She seemed troubled by the question. "My father is a fisherman. My mother sells the fish at the markets, fixes the nets. It's a poor life, but an honest one. One day, I was helping my mother at the market stall, and the Director came out of the Opera building. He walked over and spoke to me briefly. He invited me to one of his balls. My parents were so proud when the Director proposed to me. I knew I didn't love him, but the look in their eyes! There were tears in them, and the Director even came to talk to my father about it. 'As an equal,' my father said. 'He spoke to me as if we were equals.' He was so pleased. It was such an opportunity—I couldn't let them down. So that's it: I'm just some poor girl the Director discovered down near the docks."

"You're not just that."

After they had eaten, they sat looking out over the lake to the rest of the garden. Beneath the water moved fish and eels.

"Close your eyes, I have something for you," said Eliana.

Anton smiled and closed his eyes. He felt her hand on his, pulling his fingers apart and something small and heavy dropped into it.

He opened his eyes and there lay a heavy silver ring with a flat top with intricate carvings on it. He peered at it more closely. The carvings were of a labyrinth, small and delicate.

Eliana held her hand out. "I have one also, though I'll keep mine hidden. Life is a maze, isn't it? These are to symbolise that we have found our way to . . . something."

Anton took Eliana's hand in his, cupping the two rings in the space between their palms. He looked over the lake again. He felt a warmth in his body that he'd never experienced before, flowing from his heart outwards. He wondered at it, and searched for the words to describe it. It was an entirely *new* form of pleasure. One he hadn't before experienced. Contentment—that's what it was—a kind of wholeness, a feeling that everything was in its right place.

After a moment, he turned rapidly and pushed Eliana onto her back. As he fell upon her as she laughed. "My dress!"

After that day, something changed between them. Each time they met at the Hotel, their lovemaking seemed more passionate, more intimate. Anton attended to Eliana's every movement: her tiny exhalations of breath, the way she turned slightly onto one side of her body, then onto the other, the rapid fluttering of her eyelids, and then, finally, her half-muffled cry of his name. Through all this he held back, denying himself the momentary pleasures, until finally he seemed to reach a kind of transcendental bliss where he lost sense of his very body, and a sense of hers, and somehow they left the material plane intertwined, surrounded by nothing but white light. When they finished, Anton, who considered himself a master of the amorous arts, lay speechless and breathless.

Eliana said, "How is it that you hold on for so long?"

He smiled and said, "It's an unusually cold winter this year, don't you think?"

He expected one of her usual loving barbs: "You're such a rascal" or "You're cruel." He liked the way she would play with him in that happy way, following the words with a light-hearted laugh.

Instead, Eliana started to cry.

He knew he should leave her there, as he had done many times to others, but the sight of her tears running down her cherubic cheeks, the way she brushed her hand across her small upturned nose, kept him pinned on the bed as if under some great weight. And now, as she said nothing and looked away, as if defeated, Anton felt something shift inside him—a tiny little pain that cut him somewhere deep.

"He's going to find out," she said.

"No, he won't. He spends all his time in his office—you've said so yourself."

"He'll kill you. You know that. Or worse."

"Neither of us is going to die. I've always been lucky. Things work out for me."

"It will have to end, won't it? We can't go on together, you and me."

To his own surprise, Anton found himself saying, "Perhaps we should run away. It's not as if anyone would miss us."

She looked at him with those ice-blue eyes that had first attracted him. Her face lost its sadness and was now amazed: her bloodshot eyes wide, her cheeks glistening after the tears. "He'll hunt you down."

"He'll take another wife and he'll find another philosopher-assassin."

She threw herself onto him and pinned him on the bed. "You're teasing me, you rascal."

He looked up at those eyes, his own alight with mischief. "Eliana, would I do such a thing?"

"I . . . I . . ." She was flustered and her face reddened. She turned her head from side to side and he understood her, and the words she could not say.

Something shifted inside him again, and in that moment Anton was convinced that that there would be nothing more natural or romantic than to run away with her to Varenis, or perhaps south to a little fishing village where they could finally live in peace away from the internecine struggles of the Houses.

"Just say the words," she whispered to him, closing her eyes as if she were praying. "I can't bear this life any longer."

"Bring your things next week and we'll run away. We'll go south to a fishing village."

Later, as he slipped out of the rear door of Hotel du Cirque into the dark alleyway, he felt confused. He had been wrong to give in to the romance of the moment. No fishing village could ever hold him, just as he could never limit himself to one woman—he was not a gratificationist for nothing. Now he would have to break it off with her and he hoped that Eliana didn't burn her bridges with Lefebvre as she left. That would be disaster. Their affair would be unveiled and all would come apart.

Wrapped up in these thoughts, he was only vaguely aware of a figure standing at the other end of the alleyway. He cut through the winding cobblestoned alleyways towards the white cliffs, and back towards his apartment. A few minutes later he stopped. He kicked himself. This affair was ruining his instincts. There had been something suspicious about the figure, and he had simply passed by. Something about its presence disturbed him, like a dream half-remembered in the morning, shadowy and unreal.

• • •

To avoid thinking about Eliana, Anton gorged on Lika-flowers so the days became moments of kaleidoscopic beauty where he found himself in the endless now, each moment perfect and whole. The world seemed filled with luminous truth and incandescent beauty. When these effects lifted, he snorted uderri-powder and rampaged through the nights fighting and drinking, waking in the morning bloodied and bruised, his memories of the night before mostly gone, his head pounding, yet his disposition happy enough.

The day before he was to meet Eliana, Anton stopped at the *La Tazia* café, drank two shots of black coffee and ate spiced fruit for breakfast.

Pehzi, the wisened old café owner, passed Anton a message from his former lover, Madame Demoul. Anton tore it up without reading it and left it on the table in front of him. Shortly afterwards a slight and effeminate message-boy entered the café and passed Anton a second letter, this one from Director Lefebvre. He was to come to the House Arbor Palace.

"God, everyone wants me!" said Anton cheerily to Pehzi. "Well they can all wait."

"You're too self-confident," said Pehzi, picking up the sleek white cat that sprawled around the café as if it were the true owner. The cafés in Caeli-Amur were known for their cats—black, or silver, or speckled, and especially white—which lounged around in the sun or rubbed up against the citizens' legs.

Anton laughed and popped a piece of melon into his mouth.

"There's a war on, you know," said Pehzi, still holding the cat, its rear legs hanging placidly down. "Anyway, it's not my job to look after you." That week the cafés along the cliffs had been filled with stories of the increasingly vicious actions between House Arbor and House Technis—broken agreements, waves of assassinations, intrigues and machinations, secrets stolen—while House Marin circled in the background like a carrion bird waiting for the spoils.

Pehzi believed that the wars were cyclical and never-ending, and thus ultimately farcical, like three friends who every week drank joyously together, only to end up fighting clumsily in the streets before heading home to repeat it all a week later.

Anton looked out of the café's window, across the open sea beyond. "There's sun falling on the water. There's coffee and fruit. There are pretty girls passing through the markets in the square. And you are worried about a war?"

"You may not care about the war, but the war cares about you."

Anton left the café and made his way south-west, around Caeli-Amur's white cliffs up to the oldest and wealthiest sections of the city, away from the steam-trams, to where black caparisoned horses pulled carriages and lines of bulb-trees followed the curve of the streets.

Like Lefebvre's mansion, House Arbor's Palace was surrounded by *Toxicodendron Didion*, creeping thickly over the bluestone walls, its leaves gently undulating in the sun, ever wary for prey that might stumble into it. The archway was guarded, but Anton was allowed to pass and continue on up the tree-lined path. At several points the path reached great circular fountains with magnificent statues of the gods: Aya in struggle against the others, Pandae crying out alone on her ship surrounded by the surging sea, or Demidae holding up his great three barrelled lightning rod to the sky. Far away he could hear the soft wailing of tear-flowers and he resisted the urge to leave the path and find them.

The stately palace was an imposing and yet delicate construction. From the path, the first thing that struck the viewer was the high windows and above them the grand balconies onto which double-doors opened. But as the visitor approached the palace, they noticed the long five-storey wing that was held up by arches over a lake like a massive bridge enclosed by walls and roofs. Doormen in their ridiculous Arbor uniforms (with tails that flapped behind them limply in the breeze) stood in the surrounding gardens. They took no notice of Anton who passed into the wide marble-floored halls, chandeliers hanging over them that in the night gleamed like clusters of shining stars.

Lefebvre sat in his spacious office, light shining through the wide windows to his left, Jean-Paul standing behind him. "Always late," said Lefebvre, shaking his head. "If you weren't my most trusted agent, I'd take you to the dungeons myself."

"But you love me like a son," joked Anton, slouching into a chair.

Lefebvre closed his eyes as if he were suffering. His voice grew serious then, and for the first time Anton noticed tiny lines of worry appear between Lefebvre's eyebrows. "I have a task that is not only of importance to the House, but is of personal importance to me—a task that the other Directors must know nothing about. You remember my wife?"

"Why yes of course," said Anton, "Elena."

"Eliana," corrected Lefebvre. "It is most unfortunate, this business, but as you know, House Technis have discovered a number of our secrets to do with thaumaturgical zoology. It appears that my own wife, who means more to me than . . . It appears that she has been meeting with a Technis Agent. It is most unfortunate, but we can only conclude that she is the source of our misfortunes."

"No! . . ." Anton reached out towards Lefebvre, as if to touch him, though the man was on the other side of his desk.

"Jean-Paul followed her some days ago. They have a regular rendezvous once a week at Hotel du Cirque, close to the city's Southern Gate. Jean-Paul saw the man leave but could not ascertain his identity."

"Surely there is another explanation," said Anton. "Perhaps it's not as you think. Perhaps she is only meeting an old friend. Or at worst a . . . lover."

"A lover? That's impossible. Eliana is not a sexual creature. She's more like an innocent child. And if she had such desires, I would be able to satisfy her." Lefebvre took a vial from one of his draws and placed it onto the table. "This is most valuable—it takes years to grow. It is *Fungus Veritas*—Truth Mould. I want you to place it on her skin. When it is inside her she will only speak the truth." Lefebvre smiled grimly and Anton was disturbed by the thought of the thing in Eliana.

"Why not use it on the . . . spy?" asked Anton.

Lefebvre looked at Anton as if he didn't understand and Anton realised this was about more than just discovering a spy, it was about controlling Eliana. It was about Lefebvre's own sense of dignity.

Anton shifted in his seat. "And the spy?"

"You are a philosopher-*assassin* are you not?" Lefebvre stood up and walked around the desk. He placed his hand on Anton's shoulder and spoke softly. "I knew I could trust you."

Jean-Paul walked Anton from the room and along the palace halls, couriers criss-crossing in their uniforms, a massive cake balanced carefully in the hands of two porters, and several of the House officials yelling orders.

Jean-Paul spoke calmly, "You understand the delicacy of this task."

"The House's honour is at stake," said Anton.

"He's furious," said Jean-Paul. "I should hate to be the Technis agent when the Director gets his hands on him."

"Perhaps it's simpler than it seems. Perhaps it's simply a love-affair," said Anton.

Jean-Paul ignored him. "This is a new low for House Technis. To bed a man's wife for information—have they no honour left? Once there were strict codes. What kind of people would do this?"

"I suppose we'll find out soon enough," said Anton heavily.

"We must do whatever we can to protect the Director, even against himself if need be," said Jean-Paul, and for a moment his voice tightened as if he too was angry.

Anton walked back along the long path from the Palace, thinking. His luck would hold. There would be a path from this mess. In the background the tear-flowers wailed.

• • •

Back at *La Tazia*, Anton wondered how he would he get word to Eliana. He might have to break into Lefebvre's mansion and speak to her directly. Anton came out of his reverie to find Pehzi looking at him expectantly. As if to justify himself, Anton instinctively said, "We must take pleasure when offered to us, for life is but a brief spark in the darkness. We must live in the moment, and live fully."

Pehzi downed a shot of strong black coffee and looked at Anton for a moment. "Pleasure does not always bring satisfaction. Often it brings the opposite, a discontentment that eats away at you, even though you try to sate it with momentary diversion."

The following day, Anton waited in a carriage in the broad street; the heat emanating from the line of bulb trees dissipated in the winter air. Only the Mansion roof was visible above its surrounding great walls. By his side sat one of the street-urchins—a bony little boy with hard eyes—who he regularly used for such tasks. Though it was the middle of the day, fog hovered over the city like a menacing shroud, as if the very air was permeated with portents of sorrow. Anton's thoughts, usually so light-hearted, had become fearful. All he could see in his mind was Eliana wiping tears from her cheeks. Why did this vision plague him so much? Why couldn't he forget her like he did all the others?

His plan was simple: pass a note to Eliana's maid cancelling the rendezvous. Eliana would not betray him—she loved him. She would be heartbroken, but would carry her burden in silence. She would explain that there had been no passing of secrets, that it was all just a terrible misunderstanding. And Lefebvre would forgive her, slighted though his pride would be. But questions rumbled at the edge of his mind: would Eliana really react the way he hoped? Did Lefebvre possess more of the fungus? Anton pushed the thoughts away.

Anton watched the comings and goings at the gate of Lefebvre's mansion. Workmen carried long timber planks, a grocer's cart carried a vast array of meats and vegetables. Five dark-skinned men carried buckets of Numerian red-fruit. After about twenty minutes, Anton saw Eliana's handmaid, a demure and mousy young woman, make her way out of the side door with the morning's laundry basket.

"Now—that maid," he said to the boy, who scampered out and to the mansion gate. The boy called to the maid, who looked up and frowned. She approached the gate and the boy seemed to speak briefly to the maid before passing her the message. As the boy scampered back, the maid continued to frown.

Once the boy was back in the carriage, it took off, its wheels clattering against the cobblestones.

The following evening, Anton threw himself onto the bed at the Hotel du Cirque, boots on. He pulled *Gratificationism and Desire* by Eran Metripole from his bag and flicked through the pages. But he was unable to concentrate. Perhaps it was the bed, but images of Eliana kept springing into his mind. They had lain in this bed, the bedclothes twisted, their limbs entangled, Eliana's face flushed. They had spoken in whispered voices. He was struck by a sudden desire to see her. But it was impossible—their time was over.

Now Anton would simply wait for Lefebvre to arrive with Jean-Paul and say, "I'm sorry monsieur, but they have not arrived. Perhaps there was no spy? Perhaps it was simply an old friend after all." A part of him was pleased that he had been able to forestall the disaster. Yet at the same time he felt a pressure, almost like a weight in his stomach, draining him of his usual joyousness. It was a kind of despondency, as if meaning had been leached from things.

Anton heard feet tapping along the corridor. The sound was familiar. His heart leaped, and he sat up rapidly. Again another storm of emotions roiled within him.

The doorknob rattled and Eliana ran across the room and threw herself onto him. "I've missed you," she said. "I could barely wait for the week to pass."

Anton was speechless. He finally managed to force out, "What are you doing here?"

She raised her head from his chest and said, "It has been all I could think about. And the most awful things have happened this last week."

"I sent you a message." Anton pushed her away and strode to the door, which he bolted.

"What?" said Eliana, confused and staring at him from the bed. Hesitantly she spoke again. "I brought my things. They're downstairs."

Anton moved to the window and looked at the carriage that waited underneath. He dropped the tone of his voice so that it came out measured, cold. "What for?"

Eliana looked at him in silence, her eyes wide.

Anton's spoke spitefully, as if to punish Eliana for the situation. "The Director was right. You're nothing but a child."

Eliana looked at him stricken. "I don't understand."

Anton turned away from her again. Would it be so hard for the two of them to run down to that carriage, to hold each other as it rattled through the streets south, away from Caeli-Amur? He steeled himself. "Don't you understand? It was always just a fantasy."

"I thought you loved me." Beneath her trembling voice was an accusatory tone.

Turning back, he found that she now stood before him. "You're a fool if you think that's why I pursued you. I don't love you." The words cut him, though he didn't know why.

She cried out as her face twitched and trembled with terrible emotion. She pushed him. He stepped backwards, but his heel struck his bag. He lost his balance, fell and felt something sharp in his side as he hit the ground. He put his hand to his back and brought it away. Blood. He raised himself up on his hands to avoid whatever had cut him and looked down but there was nothing there. He looked back at Eliana, who eyed him with equal confusion. He looked back at the window: perhaps he had been shot? But the glass was intact. Puzzled he looked down at the ground again and scratched his neck, where he felt something furry, like the high neck on a Numerian coat. He brought his hand away, struggling to comprehend what was occurring. Now his jaw was itchy and he scratched it, feeling again something furry.

Eliana screamed, a look of fear in her eyes.

Anton placed both hands against the mould that was coursing up his neck, but the thing flowed beneath his fingers. It was strong, like an animal beneath his hands. He clawed at it, desperate now, but the mould simply coursed up his cheek, the tip of it probing at his nose. Eliana screamed again as the mould found Anton's nostril and plunged into it like water down a plughole. Anton blinked rapidly as the thing forced its way into him, like a worm, up, up behind his eyes. It reminded him of jumping into the sea and having water rush up his nose and down the back of his throat. There was a terrible taste in his mouth, as if he had eaten rotten refuse from a stagnant pond. He was weeping now, and the room swam and blurred in front of him. He found himself on his knees as the pain pushed up around and behind his eyes, his temples. Looking down at the floor he vomited. Looking back up he saw Eliana transfixed before him.

"What was that?" Her voice trembled.

"Truth mould," said Anton. "It makes you speak the truth."

She looked at him. "Can you get it out?"

"I don't know. Your husband—he knows."

"He gave it to you?"

"Yes, to use on . . ." He struggled not to speak, though he was filled with the desire to tell her everything, not the surface thoughts, the ones he kept for an easy dismissal or a glib answer, but the deep truth that he knew lurked within, sometimes unrecognised, but no less true for that. He stopped the word "you" from coming from his mouth and managed to replace it with others. "We were discovered. He thinks there is a Technis agent that you have passed secrets to. He sent me to fix things. To kill the agent."

She cocked her head and looked at him strangely for a moment. His heart leapt: was her shrewd intelligence sifting one thing from the other?

Anton continued to speak. "I was going to break things off. I was going to save us. Of course, you would have had to suffer your husband's recriminations. But we would have lived."

She pursed her lips and tensed as if she was in pain. She refused to look at him. "We'll live now. We'll simply tell him that my lover did not turn up. We'll have to pretend not to have met. Anyway, it's not as if you cared for me. Neither of us has lost anything."

Anton could hardly bear to see Eliana standing there, her face barely composed, threatening at any moment to lose its structure and break into a sobbing mess. He searched for words to explain. "You don't understand. I never thought you would feel this way. I didn't think *I* would feel this way. I thought ours would be just a brief liaison."

She looked at him, her cherubic face smooth, with the traces of tears reflecting the light from the lamp in little trails. "You love me?"

Anton started to form the words, "Of course", but before he could, the door rattled for a second and was silent.

Eliana tensed. "Oh no."

A second later it burst open. Jean-Paul stood in the doorway with a bolt thrower in one hand. Behind him Director Lefebvre, his face stern and troubled. Finally, wearing a terrified look was Eliana's maid—she had betrayed them, or Lefebvre had forced the information from her.

"Where is he?" asked Lefebvre. "Where is the Technis spy?"

"He didn't come," said Eliana. "My lover has fled the city." At the very same moment, before he could stop himself, Anton found himself speaking the truth. "I am that man." He cursed inwardly. He realised that he had to concentrate to stop himself from speaking, or to modify the words that came from his mouth.

Frowning, Lefebvre looked from Anton to Eliana and back again.

"Be quiet!" said Eliana to Anton desperately.

"You!" Lefebvre's face twitched.

Anton realised that Lefebvre would not forgive him. He would die here, or in his fury and loss of dignity Lefebvre would take him back to the Arbor Palace and into the dungeons. There terrible things would be done to him, truth mould or not. Other organisms would be fed into him. He would end up in exquisite agony, as alien flora grew and moved within him. It didn't matter, but he found himself speaking again, "You have to understand, I didn't aim to —" With great effort, he cut the words off and controlled himself. As long as he didn't speak, he could think his thoughts. The problem came when he opened his mouth.

With Jean-Paul looking on coldly, the bolt-thrower pointed at Anton, Lefebvre pulled a seat from the corner of the room and sat heavily into it. He looked up, ashen faced. His severity had given way to a kind of defeat, and suddenly his attitude seemed uncertain. "You were always so loyal."

Anton thought rapidly. He judged the distance between himself and Jean-Paul. He was still one of Caeli-Amur's philosopher-assassins. He still had his stilettos sheathed around his waist. He could leap at Jean-Paul, take the bolt, but kill him. And then, half-dead he could turn on Lefebvre and Eliana could escape.

The terrible taste of betrayal filled Anton's mouth: the truth of it all seemed to rise from his stomach like bile. Lefebvre looked up at Anton, who counted the moments. He widened his stance, the better to leap.

Silence hovered in the air like a mist. Jean-Paul smiled a little smile.

Elaina spoke with a new certainty. "Wait! Husband: I'll come back to you, willingly. I'll come back to you and devote myself to you, but only if you let Anton go. If you kill him, then I'll never really be with you. You can force me, but I'll always escape somewhere else in my mind."

"No," said Anton.

Eliana ran to Anton and threw her arms around him. "Let me go," she said.

"We should have run away." He shook his head in disbelief. How did things reach this point? He could barely trace the events in his mind, so fickle and fast they seemed to have come.

She whispered in his ear. "In our next lives we'll live in that little fishing village south of Caeli-Amur, won't we? Won't we?"

But Anton could not speak; he knew the words would not be "Yes." He could not say them. That wasn't the truth.

Eliana tried to step back, but Anton held her close. "Stay with me."

"No," she said.

"We can fight. We can—" He tried to say "run" but the word would not come. He knew it to be false.

She shoved him and broke free from his grasp. "No."

Eliana walked back to the Director, who stood to greet her. There she threw her arms around him. "I will love you, husband. Love is an act, not just a feeling. I will come to feel the feeling. I will bring myself to it, through my actions."

"Take her home." Lefebvre gently pushed Eliana towards Jean-Paul. The adjutant led her through the door, and Eliana did not look back, at the room or Anton.

"Liar," said Anton beneath his breath at her. "You're a liar."

Lefebvre and Anton stared at each other. The Director spoke quietly. "I trusted you for years, and now this. The truth is a hard thing to accept is it not? To look things in the face, as they really are."

Anton closed his eyes. He too spoke quietly. "You know she will always love me."

"That is where you are wrong. It seems she possesses greater willpower than either of us believed. I have no doubt that she will come to love me. Do you?" Lefebvre looked at Anton severely.

"No." Anton looked down at the floor as if there he might find something with which to make sense of events.

Lefebvre walked to the door. "I could have you killed, but I prefer to leave you alone—to face the truth."

• • •

In the darkness of the night Anton made his way into the House Technis complex—that massive sprawling structure, constantly growing like some brick and mortar cancer. He passed through the warren-like corridors. Overhead *pneumatiques* carried messages on criss-crossing wires. Anton made his way into the office of Officiate Ijem, who seemed to spend much of his time laughing—one of the qualities that made Anton like him.

"Ah, Anton, it *is* good to see you," said Ijem happily. "I trust you've been well."

"I have a Truth-Mould within me," said Anton. "And everything has come apart."

Ijem looked at Anton with a curious half-smile. "Ah, one of House Arbor's experiments . . . how fascinating."

Anton rubbed his face with his hands. "There's no pleasure left for me in this world."

Ijem broke into a grin. "Don't worry, the House will look after you. You've served us well for a long time now. Not just anyone is able to steal papers from Director Lefebvre's very study in the midst of a ball! What a story that makes! Don't worry, our physicians will heal your arm, our thaumaturgists will get the Truth-Mould out of you and we'll get you back on your feet. Obviously you'll have to hide here for a while, but there's always hope. Tomorrow's another day, eh?"

"I don't want the Truth-Mould out of me. I don't want to live this life of deceit anymore." The image of Eliana with her arms around Lefebvre came to Anton's mind.

Ijem looked at him questioningly, and then matter-of-factly said, "Well tomorrow's another day. Who knows what pleasures it might bring."

With one hand, Anton spun his labyrinth ring around his index finger and closed his eyes.

· · · · · · · · · · ·

THE MEMORY OF WATER

ANDREW J McKIERNAN

"The ocean, it remembers us," David said, the heel of his foot dredging shallow trenches in the sand.

Mara did not reply or even acknowledge that she'd heard her brother speak. Instead, she continued looking off towards the clouds that followed the coast up from the south. Purple and swollen, they straddled the line between land and sea, crawling on watery tendrils ever northward. But the storm they carried was still a ways off yet—somewhere over the city, she imagined—and they had at least an hour before it disturbed the calm of the beach.

She'd have to leave then, before the rain hit. Return to the shelter of the small beach-house their father had left to the family many years before. A house her mother had both hated and loved for the memories it evoked. But it would be out of the rain; away from the water.

"Do you remember that time when we were kids?" Her brother was saying. "We came up here for the summer. I think I was about ten, so you would've been eight. Do you remember?"

She turned to face him for a moment, the line of his profile matching the cut of the headland in the background—a long sloped forehead weathering away to cavernous eye sockets, a rocky-edged nose flaking from over-exposure to the elements, a short ledge of lips occasionally licked slick with salty wetness. The similarity was disconcerting. She forced a smile and turned back towards the open sea, the pounding waves and distant horizon.

"We must've come up here a thousand times when we were kids, David," she said, knowing perfectly well which time he was talking about. "We were up here *every* weekend one summer and you expect me to remember just one time?"

"Yeah, I expect you to remember. You pretty much ruined the whole holiday. Mum got so upset she took us back to Sydney. I beat on you all week for it, so I doubt you'd forget." His smile was both furtive and apologetic, as good an admission of guilt and remorse as she would ever get from David.

Further down the beach a family were excavating towels, an umbrella, a volleyball, buckets and spades from the sand in preparation to leave. There were a lot more empty spaces on the beach now. Not many people remained in the water either and Mara wondered what time it could be. Almost certainly after four, but could it be as late as six? She hated daylight savings.

"Yeah, I remember," Mara said. "I got dumped by a wave and spazzed out something chronic." Mara knew it wasn't quite that simple and she pretended not to notice her hands were starting to shake. "You and mum thought I was drowning."

"Drowning! We thought you were being eaten by a damn shark! You were rolling all 'round in the water, screaming like a stuck pig. We thought it was another fucking shark, Mara."

David stopped to look out at the water.

He's trying to find the spot where it had happened, Mara thought. She crossed her arms, hiding her hands in her armpits to stop the shaking. *Maybe*, she tried to tell herself, *it's just getting cold.*

"And then, when we'd dragged you out, you started spluttering and screaming about Dad," David said, his voice softer and sadder than Mara had ever heard it. "Mum went white when she heard you. Started slapping you and shouting at you to shut up. Eventually you did. I didn't think either of you would ever stop . . ."

And then, quieter, he added, "I don't think Mum ever did stop, not really."

"David," Mara's voice trembled, "what has this got to do with anything? Why are you bringing this up now? Do you think its my fault that Mum died? That somehow *I* caused her to become an alcoholic? That cirrhosis of the liver is *my* responsibility?"

Tears welled up in Mara's eyes and the shaking grew from her hands to her arms and up into her chest.

David reached out to her across the sand, his hand brushing her shoulder, bringing out goosebumps on her skin. She could see in his eyes that she'd misread him completely.

"No, no," he said. "It's not like that at all. That's not what I meant, Sis. Last two days, since the funeral, I've been thinking. Thinking a lot. About something Mum said to me a couple of weeks ago."

He looked across at his sister, awaiting a sign it was all right to continue. When she closed her eyes and nodded her head he took that as his cue.

"She wasn't quite there, Mara. You know how she was most times. But she was *trying* to be there, really trying. I could see her in there, fighting to be understood. She said she was afraid. Afraid she wouldn't be remembered. Afraid everything she'd ever seen, or touched, or heard, every joy she'd experienced would be erased. That eventually even *our* memory of her would fade away to nothing. Just like her memories of Dad. I couldn't argue with her, Mara. I couldn't tell her it wasn't true."

There were tears in David's eyes now too. Tears that overflowed and ran in salty rivulets down his cheeks.

"But after she was gone I thought, it's *not* true! *You* remembered Dad, but you weren't even *born* when he died. *You* said things that day on the beach you couldn't possibly have known. Things only Mum knew, and she hadn't told anybody."

"I don't remember him, David," Mara protested. "I never even knew him. How could I when he was already gone?"

"I know, I know. You're right. You didn't remember him. The ocean remembered him, Mara. It remembers us all."

She stared at him for a moment, scared of what he might mean. David mistook the fear in her eyes for bewilderment and forged a simpler explanation of his words. His tone was as a teacher to a small child.

"Our bodies are mainly water, Mara. Salt water. We came from the sea; we return to the sea. Every minute part of you is a whole, a small fragment that explains the rest—like a hologram—just as every molecule of water in the ocean is identical to every other. Know one and you know them all. And, because *we* are part of that too—that cycle of life that is ruled by water—we are linked. We are linked, us and the oceans, and they remember us all."

Mara shook her head, denying his words. What he was saying was preposterous. Superstitious claptrap. A disjointed mental fantasy constructed from a childhood memory, layered over with fables of mother Gaia and the scam of homoeopathic science. The memory of water. The persistence of states. The ocean as some intelligent mother from whom we had all crawled—finned and gilled, gasping for air—and to whom we still owed reverence. It was pure rubbish!

These were the thoughts Mara was preparing herself with when David asked:

"Is that why you never go in the water any more, Mara? Does it speak to you of its memories?"

Mara didn't answer; she couldn't.

Eventually David left, returning to the beach-house, his absence an accusation in the sand beside her.

• • •

The storm did not arrive, at least for quite a while. The clouds still hovered just off to the south, caught up in some clash of pressure systems and prevailing winds that kept them churning upon themselves. Churning like Mara's thoughts. She wondered if the storm would rain itself empty before it broke free and started north again?

She sat quietly on the beach, watching the water rise and fall, advance and recede, to its own hypnotic rhythm. She felt the warmth of the sand beneath her; the smell of salt and seaweed mixing upon the breeze. The setting sun warmed her back and waves, inching ever closer on the incoming tide, whispered conspiracies across the sand in front.

Once, during those long summer holidays, this beach and its ocean had been her playground. A wonderland of strange creatures sheltering in rock pools. Of bright shells and the promise of buried treasure hidden just around the next rocky headland. Days of too little sunscreen on the ears and too much sand in her bathers. Of dodging blue-bottles and poking piles of seaweed with driftwood in search of baby crabs.

Sometimes she and David would body-surf the waves or, when the tides grew too rough, snorkel the calmer channels. And after, when she was tired out from her play, she would lie in the wet sand where land met sea feeling foamy waves wash over her body to cool the heat of the sun.

But Mara had not been swimming in the ocean since she was eight. Not since she had seen her father there.

She'd tried, once or twice, never getting much farther than the partial immersion of a toe or two.

It was a fear of sharks she told her friends when they had asked, splashing and shouting from the waves, during one seaside excursion. There are no sharks here, they shouted at her, that's ridiculous. Tiny schoolgirl hands sliced water in mock imitation of menacing fins and cruel laughter followed Mara along the beach, back to the school bus, alone.

It was not sharks. It had never been sharks. Mara knew that. Her father's death had been a freak occurrence; the only shark attack in thirty years for a hundred kilometres up or down the coast. Sharks rarely attacked humans and even more rarely killed them. She was not afraid of sharks. It was the water itself that worried her.

She remembered riding on her mother's back, arms clasped around her neck, head held high to miss the spray of waves. She remembered David, all white and gangly, paddling over the breakers on his new boogie-board—brilliant fluorescent yellow with the profile of a bullet—with all the grace of a crippled stick-insect. She remembered the sun arching overhead to its zenith, harsh rays like fire on her back.

These could have been memories from any of her childhood holidays—they were all so much the same—but Mara knew this was not just any memory. She knew that soon her mother would grow tired and head back to the beach, leaving her to play on the shore's edge.

"Not too deep, Mara"—her mother's voice—"you're not as old as David yet."

I'll never be as old as David, she'd thought, *he'll always be ahead of me.*

Two years was not a lot of difference in age and Mara could swim almost as well as her brother. She had swum out into the calm waters beyond the waves many times when her mother's back was turned, or when she had fallen asleep on the beach. So Mara swam out to where her brother lay flailing on his board. He'd been attempting to catch a wave for ages without any real success. The board was his first and the technique was obviously quite different to the more familiar body-surfing.

"Why not just body-surf like we use to?" she asked when she got there.

He looked back at her with boyish disgust.

"Go away," he snapped, "this is a skill. It takes practice, and I'm going to master it".

Another wave passed under them and David paddled furiously, but much too late to catch it. Mara had already turned, her body imitating the bullet shape of David's board, legs straight and moving swiftly from the knee. In less than a second she felt the sudden tug of the wave. For an exquisite moment she was flying, planing across the surface of the wave with ever-increasing speed. She could feel the spray whipping up behind her; the wind rushing across her face; the incredible force of the wave as it tried to pull her back up along its surface. She could see her mother drying herself on the beach, her back to the surf, towel around her butt.

Mara was on the face of the wave now heading for shore, the peak just starting to curl above her. The water around her was getting louder—a deafening jumbo-jet roar that rattled the skull—and white foam bubbled from the waves collapsing just ahead.

Mara was smart and decided to pull out. She still had a couple of metres before the wave would end.

But then, just as she started to turn out and away from the wave, her mother turned as well. Their eyes locked across the gulf of sand and water and Mara saw the fear that lurked in her mother's heart. The fear that she might lose another loved one to the ocean while she stood on the beach and watched.

It was not a big wave and there was plenty of time but the recognition that her mother was scared—and probably always would be—was enough that Mara hesitated in her turn. The face of the wave caught at her foot, sucking it in. It sucked her leg in too. Suddenly she was being pulled in two directions at once. Gravity wanted her down; the wave wanted her up.

Mara felt an instant of panic as her face hit the water and her head was forced under too. She tried to curl up into a ball, to hold her breath and protect her head. She tried to work out which way was up. But there *was* no up. Only around and around through swirling foam and sand, the roaring of water in her ears and its saltiness filling her mouth and nose.

She hit something hard. Maybe it was the sandy bottom or the edge of the rocky shelf she knew must be somewhere to her right. Either way, it hurt and she tried to scream but more water filled her mouth and rushed down into her lungs. She skimmed across sand that felt like a cheese grater tearing at her flesh and the murky light grew darker, her limbs heavier.

Strangely though, her head felt lighter, like a balloon strung by a tether to her neck. All I need is a good rest, a sleep, she thought, right here in this spot. And then her head broke the surface.

She was kneeling up to her waist in water. Inexplicably, the stars were out above her. *Where has the day gone?* she thought, staring for a moment up at the moon that had replaced the sun.

Her mother and father were there, splashing and playing further out. Their heads bobbed just above the water. She had only ever seen her father in photographs and her mother looked much younger than Mara could remember. But it was her. It was them. She knew it.

She watched fascinated as they trod the water between them. Her father's arms reached out, strong and powerful, and caught her mother by the shoulders. Her mother kicked in towards him, her lips meeting his, bodies rising out of the water just enough for Mara to see they were both naked. They kissed and moved against each other in the water, rising and falling with the tide.

Mara, eight years old, did not understand. She did not understand when her father's arms wrapped her mother, tighter and tighter, and her mother let out a little cry, eyes closed and face turned starward. She did not understand when her mother kicked her way back to shore laughing and smiling as her father roared with joyful triumph, both arms raised to the night.

Mara's mother was paddling closer, standing up in the water only metres ahead, and Mara panicked. What if her mother caught her watching? She knew she'd seen something she shouldn't. Something personal and private. She had forgotten all about her brother boogie-boarding a wave somewhere in the bright summer sun and her mother drying herself on the beach and the wave that dumped her. She had forgotten that her father had been dead eight years. She just didn't want to get caught.

But her mother was not angry. She barely seemed to notice Mara crouched in the shallow water and she was smiling as she approached. She did not stop but passed straight through, like a fog that had no substance, and Mara turned to watch her as she continued up onto the beach, laughing as she reached her towel, body all jewelled and glistening soft in the moonlight.

But her mother's laugh was cut short as her father's jubilant cry turned to a scream. Her mother started running back to the water, face contorted with dread as she called and screamed his name over and over.

Mara turned, a broken foamy wave almost knocking her on her back, and saw her father struggling with . . . with something. His arms were rising and falling like hammers pounding the water. His body moved like he had become stuck in an out-of-control washing machine—swish to the right, swish to the left, swish to the right again—and even in the moonlight Mara could see the water around him growing darker in an ever widening slick of what could only have been blood.

She tried to swim out too and follow her mother but she was paralysed, her body a lead weight submerging into the sand.

Her father stopped screaming and her mother too. There was only the lapping of waves against the shore. Mara saw her father was sinking into the sea, his head just above water, arm raised as if to point out some constellation. Mara felt herself sinking too, her body folding, collapsing into the waves.

"Remember me, Mara," her father had said. She had heard him clearly, shouting his last, and then they were both swallowed by the ocean.

• • •

Mara remembered staggering out of the surf on that bright summer's day. She had screamed and screamed as her brother paddled wildly to the shore and her mother ran down the beach towards her. She could not remember what she had screamed but David had told her later that it was all about Dad. She had screamed at her mother: "Why didn't you tell me!" and "He never knew, he never even knew about me!" and "I was there. I saw him die!" and her mother had started screaming too and hitting and hitting and telling Mara to shut up, just shut up, shut up! until David had pulled them apart.

Nothing was ever said after that, but Mara had never been back in the ocean. Or swum in a river. Or danced in the rain. She couldn't. Its every drop seeped through her pores, whispering memories, exciting neurons into wide-screen displays of someone else's life. Everyone else's life. Everyone who had ever been.

Only tap water was dull enough, bleached of life through chemistry, for her to endure its touch.

Now she looked up and realised the sun had set behind her. Twilight painted the sky a deep indigo and splashes of orange and pink tinted the encroaching storm clouds.

Mara had no idea how long she had been sitting there, thinking of her father, but the tide had definitely risen. Its foamy fingers crawled the beach in front of her, tickling her toes. She gave in, too exhausted with emotion to fight, and let the memories wash over her. They flowed in and out like the breath of the sea through her mind. A murk of hates and fears and loves and lusts. Dreams. Nightmares. A slow settling sediment of lives and lies. She breathed them deep and her panic settled, fluttered, drifted away. The flood of memories cleared, becoming as soft as the sound of a sea-shell, and Mara started to trawl their depths.

She tried to think of who her father had really been. For the first time in years the touch of the water was soothing and calm. She stretched her foot out further into the foam, feeling it caress and flow around her toes.

"Remember me," her father had said. But she had nothing to remember him by, except that one instant of her creation and his death. Even the woman he loved was gone, her memories lost.

But David was right, she thought as the water crept slowly up her thigh, warm and inviting. She could almost feel her father, here at the edge. Could sense the man she had never known. But it'd been too long since he'd trod this beach. *He's out deep now*, the ocean whispered against the sand, *where memories drift when they've not been thought in a while.*

She listened to the rhythm of the tide, the susurration of the wind, her eyes reading the undulations of deepest blue out beyond the breakers. They all told her, *but you can find him, we're sure of it.*

Mara stood, her feet planted firmly in the water, and stripped off her shorts and top. She unstrapped her bra and dropped it over her shoulder. She walked out into the sea.

The water was almost the same temperature as the air. She could barely feel it but for the slow roll of waves against her calves, her thighs, her waist. And then she was in, up to her chest and kicking off from the bottom.

Out here, this way, the ocean called with a voice of many memories.

Mara moved her arms in lazy arcs, cutting smoothly through the surface and scooping back. The motion was tireless and soon she was at least a hundred metres out. The storm to the south appeared to be moving again and great sheets of grey rain fell from the clouds. It would hit the beach soon.

She turned for a moment and looked back to the beach and the rocky slope of green above it. There were lights amongst the trees up there, shining through holiday house windows. Through one of those windows she imagined David looking out, searching for her on the beach. He'd be worried if he couldn't find her. Worried that she'd done something stupid and drowned herself in her sorrow.

But it doesn't matter in the long run, nothing does, she heard all around her and she was sure it was her father's voice. *Even if something happened to you, nothing is lost. Your memory and his will mingle again. Come along, it's not much further now, and I've waited so long to meet you.*

Mara turned and kicked out again as the rain began to fall, joining the heavens with the earth. She headed east, into the depths of the storm, out to where the old memories ran deep. Out to where her father would be waiting.

•••••••••••

WOOD

GRANT STONE

I am M_, a puppeteer. You will not have heard of me. Forgive me if I do not dwell on further biography. I have much to say and there is little time.

But where to begin? Ah. With the oranges.

Three days ago I was ensconced in my usual spot, a corner of the market away from the noisier stalls. A gaggle of children sat at my feet, entranced. Rabian, my marionette, was serenading them with lyrics of my own devising, set to a melody I stole from a bawdy tavern song.

From the other side of the square I heard shouting, then a crash; I looked up in time to see a carriage, bearing the duke's standard, disappearing through the harlot's gate. A river of oranges rolled across the cobblestones: the carriage had caught the edge of a market stall and tipped it. Old Preshan the fruitseller shouted and grabbed his crotch in insult, but he stopped that quick enough when another carriage rattled through, squashing fruit under its wheels.

The children cheered and raced off, some trailing the carriages, hoping for thrown coin, others scooping up as many oranges as they could.

There were cries of disappointment as the second carriage left the square. Gaben, one of the older children, walked back to me, splashing water from between the cobbles with his bare feet. He was not, strictly speaking, a street-lad. His mother worked the costermonger stall and was content for him to tarry as he pleased.

"Mam says they're coming for the Spectacular. Come from all over, Mam says."

I placed Rabian in his case. "Your Mam's right."

He wiped his nose on his sleeve. "Saw a bear come in last night, led in on a chain. Didn't half set the dogs to barking."

I nodded, not listening as I pushed the few coins I'd collected that morning into my purse. Enough for a few beers, at least.

"Are you performing? In the Spectacular?"

"The duke has no need for a humble puppeteer."

"But you're the best."

"I'm not a dancing bear though, am I?"

I closed the case and made my way across the square to the Broken Lion, the closest tavern I had not yet been thrown from.

It was a small place, and dark: I stood just within the doorway, waiting for my eyes to adjust and my nose to get used to the stench of stale oat beer.

The proprietor of the Broken Lion stood behind the bar, cleaning a pottery jug with the front of his shirt. Occasional Jack he was called, given that occasionally he'd lash out at paying patrons for no apparent reason. There were stories of how he'd come to own the place: he'd won the bar throwing alley-dice, or a poker game, perhaps. The rumour I thought most likely to be true was that he'd walked in one day, liked the look of the place and commenced to kick the living shit out of the previous owner. I slid a couple of coins across the bar and Occasional Jack picked them up with a grunt.

I sneered at Gaben's estimation. The best. Best what? Puppeteer? Fuck that. I'd had dreams once that my art would make me famous. Not out in the fields of course—the streets of Youngston were paved with gold, they'd said, people who had never been more than a day's walk from their Mam's hovel. But I was young and bored, so I spat in my palm and smoothed down my hair and came east. Turns out they were right—there was gold in the streets. I saw it every morning when I pissed out my window.

I held up two fingers and Occasional Jack slammed two more flagons down in front of me. I traced a finger through the beer spilled on the bar. Gaben's words still chewed at me. True, my station at present was pitiful, but was I not an artist?

I slammed another empty flagon down on the bar and ordered another. Rabian would be no good. The thought of presenting myself to the revels master with the marionette I used to entertain urchins—No. I needed something new. It would not be enough to make the audience laugh; the bears would do that. "Let them dance, the stupid hairy bastards," I shouted to nobody in particular, "I am an artist. Can a bear—" I stood and spread my arms to address the other patrons. "Can a bear make you feel love, horror, heartbreak?"

"I'll make you feel something in a minute," someone called from the back and laughter ran through the room. I was about to march over and break my flagon over the bastard's head, but I caught Occasional Jack's eye and sat back down instead.

It was true, though. I was more than a trained animal.

I would audition for the revels master. More, I would deliver them a performance of such heart-rending beauty that every face in the room would be streaked with tears.

• • •

When they finally shoved me through the door and barred it behind me I knew what I would do. The streets were empty as I staggered away, following the Carver's Path downhill. The gate was open and unguarded, as always. Nobody had tried to bring arms against the city since the Duke did to the previous ruler of Youngston what Occasional Jack had to the last owner of the Broken Lion. Life is never a gift, I thought. The best of it must always be taken.

The eastern wall was ten times my height bottom to top, but it had been left to ruin: the stones were thick with moss, though in the past week a half-hearted attempt had been made to apply a fresh coat of whitewash. No guards were posted. The other side of the wall was just as ill-kempt. Every time I came this way the forest seemed to be a little closer to the city walls. The full moon shone above the trees, lighting the way ahead.

• • •

The moon had traversed a quarter of the sky by the time I reached Niam's hut. Niam yawned as he opened the door and ran a hand through grey-streaked hair. He didn't seem surprised, though it had been years since I'd knocked on his door. I held up the wineskin I had brought and he opened the door wide. I kissed him and then, before he could say anything, pushed him back into the hut.

A simple table and chairs occupied the middle of the single room. Niam's woodworking tools sat neatly in shelves above the bench. His axe rested against the wall by the door. Against the back wall, half-hidden in shadow, was an ornately carved bed, more like something the duke would lie on than a woodcutter. Niam had carved the bed himself, same as he had built his hut. I pushed him again, down to the bed and reached between his legs.

• • •

"You told me of a tree, once." I said, afterwards.

Niam stared up at the ceiling, hands laced behind his head. "There are a lot of trees in the forest."

"Only one like this."

"You come all the way out here in the middle of the night to ask me about trees?"

I ran a hand down his chest. "You know what I came for. But now I cannot sleep." It was a plausible lie. Niam could spend days not speaking to another person. Despite this, or perhaps because of it, when he spoke, it was with the voice of a poet. I had been lulled to sleep by his words many times.

Niam sighed. "My father told me this, long ago. A witch lived, once, in the very deepest and sun-starved heard of the forest. Women visited her hut during the day, for herbal cures, love potions—"

"To have their fortunes told," I said. He had told it to me so many times it had become a litany; I had learned my lines years ago, lying in his arms. There was comfort in hearing, and speaking, familiar words.

"By night, the men would come for something else."

"A tenuous situation," I said.

Niam nodded. "When her belly became too big to conceal, she told the women a story. There was, she said, a spot where the river curved around a large rock. Above it, with roots extending on one side into soft earth and on the other side dipping down into the water, lived a tree."

"Lived a tree. A curious phrase."

"Indeed. But that is what she said. As if the tree had a choice in its location. As if, had it desired, it could move somewhere else. This was a spot the witch knew well. A particular type of mushroom grew in the shadows under the rock. Then one day, as she bent down and dug her fingers into the soft loam, the tree reached down and touched her."

"A gust of wind, perhaps."

"So she thought. But as she gathered up the last of the mushrooms a voice whispered in her ear. The end of the branch curled like a fern frond and moved slowly up her trembling arm.

"She stayed. After that she was a frequent visitor to the rock in the bend of the river."

"Pregnant to a tree. They could not believe that, surely."

"Some did, perhaps. Others—" Niam shrugged.

"Better to believe an impossible story than wonder if your husband was responsible."

"No matter if the women believed it or not. They told the story they had been told. It spread."

"The women knew the story was protection, for the witch and for them."

"But men are not women. And it was a man who ended the story. The father, perhaps, taking steps to hide his infidelity. Or a superstitious one, believing the story and afraid of what was growing. One morning a group of women arrived to find the walls of the hut rent by heat and the bones of the witch lying scorched in her own fire pit. Something was growing in the ashes beneath her ribcage."

I rolled off the bed and rummaged through the dirty crockery on the bench, poured my wine into two dirty bowls. "None were accused of the crime?"

Niam took the bowl with a grunt of thanks. "Not to my knowledge. It was forgotten. Those same women who took such pleasure in telling the story fell silent, as it spread ever wider."

Like ripples in a pond, I thought. *Look for the still point in the centre if you want to find the stone that was dropped.*

"This is a story your father invented to stop you straying too far into the forest," I said, though I knew this was a lie. You were as likely to hear the same story told, more or less, in any town from here to the south coast.

"I thought so, once. But then my father—" Niam stopped, sniffed. His father had been dead ten years. "He knew the forest better than his own roof, so when the light began to fade and he had still not returned, I refused to believe he was lost. But he was not as sure a rider as he had been in his youth, and his hands—I worried he had fallen from his horse or caught his head on a low branch or—"

The bowl shook in Niam's hands and I took it from him.

"As I waited I thought of all manner of cruel ends for him. But then I heard his horse blowing outside and there he was. Still in the saddle, swaying, though not from the palsy. I pulled him down into my arms and the stink of the whiskey on his breath made me reel.

"When I had him lying under the covers and somewhat sobered, he began to speak. He had been chasing a deer, heedless to where it was taking him, when he stumbled in to a clearing. There were shapes beneath the grass, as if the walls of a hut had long ago fallen and been buried. In the center of the clearing was a—a tree, but not a tree. It moved—" Niam described a sinuous motion with his arm. I curled up my fingers and stroked him as I imagined the tree on the rock by the river had touched the witch.

Niam's eyes closed and I thought the sedative I had sprinkled in his wine had taken him to sleep. But then they opened again.

"Half a year later the palsy became so bad that his body was not his own to use. Then his speech began to fail. 'My son,' he said, near the end, the only words left to him, over and over. 'My son. My son.' I have always wondered if he meant me."

Niam yawned and his eyes closed again. I covered him with the blanket and kissed him on the forehead. It was a light sedative: he would be awake by noon. I lashed Niam's axe over my shoulder, unfettered his horse and rode away from the rising sun and into the forest.

• • •

As I travelled I considered Niam's story. He had told most it to me in the past, though the last part was new. I wondered about his father. I knew he had come years earlier from a village a day's ride in the direction I now headed, though that village was abandoned now.

It was the tree impregnated the witch, I thought. Did Niam's father, in some way, feel a bond with this thing in the forest? If so, why? Had he lain with the witch in his youth?

I pulled a canteen from the saddle bag and splashed my face with water. It was stupid of course—whatever Niam's imagination had layered over the memory of his father's death was of no concern to me.

The forest had started to reclaim the path to the dead village: Niam's horse stepped over vines and around shrubs. But the path was mostly clear and I made good time. I stopped at noon, where the path forded a shallow river. While Niam's horse nosed at the grass I took a heel of bread and went walking. Somewhere nearby, I was sure, was the rock in the riverbend. I turned back when I'd eaten, not wanting to leave the horse too long.

I crossed the river and followed the path for the rest of the day. As the sun was setting I came to a fork in the road. The path to the right was wide and clear. The leftward path was barely wide enough to ride—the trees that hemmed it in were of a kind I had not seen before, black barked, branches ending in spikes. I nudged Niam's horse left.

• • •

The black trees formed a roof above the path. Before long my horse nickered and would go no further. I continued on foot; my steps and increasingly ragged breathing were the only sounds. I leaned upon the heavy axe; I was a much larger man now than when I had last lain with Niam.

The path turned abruptly to the right and I found myself standing before a clearing. The moon fought free of cloud and the tree appeared as if it had only just now flashed into existence. It stretched across a clearing easily as large as the town square. It was cold here: my breath clouded as I looked up.

A tree it seemed to be, but there were no leaves upon its branches. Rather than coarse bark, its limbs were white and smooth. It looked like something that had been hauled from the depths of the sea.

Around the edges of the clearing several ranks of trees lay smashed into the loam, exposed roots clawing the sky and I knew they had been *pushed*. The witch's child had grown. Of her hut there was no sign. It had long ago been overrun, or perhaps, something whispered at the back of my mind, *consumed*. I was less terrified than exhausted: my breathing was still desperate from the walk and the axe lay heavy in my arms. I could be asleep in my bed, or Niam's. But then I saw Gaben again, wiping away snot with the back of his hand. *Come from all over, Mam says. You're the best—*

I ran my thumb over the edge of the blade, then suddenly jerked it back, held it close to my face. The fat drop of blood looked black and diseased in the moonlight.

One of the tree's pale limbs moved towards me and as it did I could see a vein raised on its surface, pulsing slightly. It brushed gently against my leg—I do not know whether it was exhaustion or my own curiosity, but I did not pull away. I thought of this creature's father, reaching out to the witch—for what? Did it feel a bond with the nature in the woman? I placed my hand upon the limb and it was warm to the touch. I ran my hand over it as if I were exploring Niam's flesh. Then I brought the axe high above my head and brought it down upon the limb.

The axe bit deep into the wood, further than I had expected; I lost my balance and went tumbling. I landed heavily and lost the air from my lungs. The tree moaned then, low and mournful, louder every moment as I struggled to breathe. I rolled over on to my back. I had severed the limb almost entirely; the last quarter of it hung only by a scrap of skin-like bark; it dragged behind as the rest of it raised up into the air, far above my head. Something fell from the wound on to my chest and it had none of the heavy slowness of sap. Though it appeared white in the moonlight, it had the warmth and consistency of blood.

Finally I sucked air into my lungs and rolled away. The limb slammed down where I had lain just moments earlier. The speed of the thing was astonishing; I knew I would not get another chance. I jumped to my feet and brought the axe down again and the limb separated with a *crunch*. Then I turned and ran, blind of what direction save that it was *away*—the earth shook once, twice: I risked a glance behind me and saw the two limbs that had struck the ground curving back, to wrap around the trunk like an embrace.

I waited, hidden beneath a black tree. Though spines dug into my back I could not move. My breath was ragged, my mouth dry. If I had been able to, I would have run then, but I was exhausted and I had come so very far. I would not give in to terror, not now, when I was so close.

When I once more crept close to the clearing, the tree had lifted the injured limb high and straight; it loomed above its surroundings like a tower. Another limb was gently stroking the amputated part. Roots shifted, raising the ground.

There was a sound, a low, helpless mourn. It took a few moments before I understood what I was hearing. The tree was sobbing. Both the fallen branch and the axe lay in the centre of the clearing. When the tree's limbs had remained still for three score heartbeats, I snuck as close as I dared, then took a deep breath and sprinted towards them.

I grabbed the end of the limb and pulled. At first nothing happened; I had bet wrong, not for the first time, but definitely the last. Another limb raised itself into the sky as I had earlier raised the axe. There was a tearing sound, as if the amputated part had already put down fresh roots. Then my boots gained solid purchase on the wet earth and I began to drag it behind me. Something tore in my back—I screamed in pain but did not drop the limb. But then I felt a rush of air behind me. I dove away—the limb smashed down where I had been standing, catching the fallen branch and flipping it away in the direction of the forest. I followed, crawling as fast as I could, the taste of earth on my tongue, only standing again when I was beyond the wall of toppled trees and back in the forest.

I did not attempt to retrieve Niam's axe. I struggled, hauling my prize behind me. There was nothing but the cries of the wood, the agony in my spine and the thump-hiss as I took another step and pulled the limb again. An eternity later I found the strength to raise my head from the track and saw my horse tethered a few paces away.

I found some dead branches, fashioned a halfway decent travois from them and secured the still-twisting limb with rope. The horse pulled the extra load skittishly.

Exhaustion caused me to nearly topple from the saddle several times. I finally emerged from the woods, to see the stars above me like a banner. Weeping followed me all the way back to the city.

• • •

I had an arrangement with a widow, a seamstress. In exchange for particular favours, I was allowed to lodge in a small attic room. A pallet stuffed with rotting straw lay in the corner beneath the window. On the other side of the room a brazier hung from the ceiling. Apart from that, the entire space was given over the construction and storage of marionettes. The severed branch lay in the center of the floor, twisting back on itself now and then like a worm stranded after rain.

All I wanted to do was close my eyes and let sleep pull me down. But it had to be tonight or not at all. I filled the brazier with fresh coals and set to work.

I leaned the branch against my workbench and drew a saw across it. The wailing rose as I cut–louder now in the confines of my room than during the journey. I wrapped rags around my head when the sound became too much to bear, but it did no good.

I lay the pieces I had cut on my workbench and reached for more precise tools: chisel and plane and bradawl. My hands were numb as I rubbed them together to force the drill bit into the wood; sawdust stung my nostrils. I threaded wire through new-cut holes and drew the pieces tight. Even in my exhausted state, my hands knew their work well.

• • •

Morning light spilled through the window. Somehow I had slept, still sitting upright. The result of my labours lay on the bench, its limbs akimbo like a man fallen from a roof. A marionette, no different to any of the others I had crafted over the years. Or at least it seemed, until one of its legs began to twitch, then the other. My marionette squirmed, each section of its arms and legs pulling against the wire joints.

I had done it. I whooped in joy and as I did the marionette's head turned and regarded me.

• • •

The fire was nearly out, but I pulled the poker from the still-glowing embers in the brazier. I lay it against the workbench and a tendril of black smoke rose. The duke's palace would be open soon. It was time to teach the creature to dance.

I took a melody I had used to entertain the children and discarded the lyrics—some sop about a mouse and a lion—replacing them with some that would suit the performance I would present:

There once was a lonely marionette
who had a soul but not freedom yet
his only wish was a way to see
his tethering strings cut away from he

It was not a good song, but it would suffice. I composed more verses, tracing the marionette's journey to freedom. As I sung I slapped the flat of my hand on the workbench, beating out the rhythm. After I had run through all the verses a couple of times, I picked up the poker.

"There once was a lonely marionette" (I touched the poker to the sole of the creature's left foot. It squirmed away with a screech of pain that nearly made me lose the rhythm)

"who had a soul" (smoke rose from the creature's right foot)

"but not freedom yet" (I ran the side of the poker down the creature's body- its posture, as it curled in pain, resembled a bow)

• • •

The creature learned quickly. When I was finished, I sanded away the worst of the burn marks and reached for my paints. I drove nails into its hands and feet, pinning it to the desk—I would use the holes for strings later.I must have been thinking of Niam—I painted the creature's body to make it appear as if he were dressed in a green jerkin and brown leggings, like some over-simplified woodsman from a child's story.

• • •

My performance would start with the creature tied to a device just like any marionette, leading the audience to believe this was the full extent of the act. Then in the second verse, I would show them the scissors I had purloined from the seamstress. I would cut the strings and my beautiful creature would continue to dance. My training had been effective—I hummed my melody as I painted and though it was pinned to the bench, I could see the creature's arms and legs struggling to move as I had forced it to.

I painted a harlequin's face on the front of the creature's head.

As I waited for the paint to dry I threw open the window and the sounds of the waking city reached me: a creak of a slow-turning cartwheel; the squeal of a hinge protesting as a door was thrown wide; the steady tapping of a beggar's cane on cobbles. All sounds of wood in motion and put to work. From behind me came the staccato clatter of the creature's foot against the workbench and the unceasing sobbing. The city was full of the sounds of wood, but there had never been any like those my creature was making.

• • •

The peephole slid open and the eye that appeared behind it was as bloodshot as the sun in the morning sky. "Fuck off!" said the guard and closed it again.

I resumed pounding the door.

After a while the peephole opened again and a different voice said, "We have no need of further conjurers, singers, dancers, raconteurs or soothsayers. Nor historians, wrestlers, bear baiters, mummers or any other kind of performance fucking artist."

I took off my hat and put on my best smile. "I would not be so bold as to trouble you for anything so mundane. True, I bring you a marionette, but—" I lifted the lid of the box. The creature twisted, sensing the sun. It bent back upon itself and scraped against the velvet lining. I waved my fingers, showing the guard there were no wires involved. The mewling of the creature was loud in my ears— surely the guard heard it . . .

The door opened. "I think you'd better come in."

• • •

Revels were not scheduled to start until late afternoon. From the condition of the guards, they had been sampling the Duke's ale for a good few hours already. The guard who ushered me down a passage and into the Duke's great hall had decorated his helmet with the same flowers that covered the walls. On the far side of the room a small fat man was shouting at a servant who had somehow become stuck, gripping the rough bricks with one hand, trying not to drop the flowers he held in the other. Most of his weight was balanced on the back of a chair.

The guard called. "Another audition sir!"

"Of course." The fat man grabbed the chair and pulled it towards us, leaving the servant on the wall to scramble for footing on the rough bricks, "Because we are clearly suffering a dearth of entertainers." I was so tired it was only when he reached us and sat down with a heavy sigh that I recognised him. Bonteme, the duke's Master of Revels. He pulled a small hourglass from his pocket and placed it by his feet. "You have until this runs out."

Performing for children in the market, I had never suffered nerves. But this was the Revels Master; besides which, I had only stolen scratches of sleep over the past few days. My hands, suddenly greasy with sweat, slipped as I tried to open the case. I could hear Bonteme's hands drumming on the chair. I pulled the creature from the case and balanced it on its wooden feet.

"It's a puppet."

"Marionette," I muttered under my breath as I untangled the strings. I tapped my foot and hummed.

It had seemed loud enough under the low roof of my lodgings. But here in the expanse of the Duke's hall, it was drowned under the banging of hammers, the screech of tables dragged across the floor, the surly curses of soldiers turned labourers.

I twisted my right wrist. Strings pulled at the creature's arms and legs and it began its ragged dance. As rehearsed, the pretence that the creature was mere marionette would continue for another verse, but already there was more sand in the bottom of the hourglass than the top. I'd have to improvise. I reached for the scissors I'd hidden in a secret pocket at the back of my jacket.

They were gone.

My smile was desperate and thin as I dug frantically at my jacket with my left hand. At the same time my right hand worked the device, trying to ensure the creature's dance did not falter. Without the scissors I wouldn't be able to flamboyantly cut the strings and usher in the real act— the creature revealed, dancing by itself. Without the scissors, I was no more than a puppeteer. So intent was I on these tasks, I failed to notice that I had stopped humming. Then I saw the hourglass.

Bonteme exhaled and rubbed his hand over the balding spot at the back of his head. Without a word he turned and walked away. The guard had returned to the door; as I stood, numb, a pair of servants carrying a bench between them crashed past, crushing the hourglass underfoot. I was left alone in the centre of the hall. The creature twisted on its ropes.

I had failed.

• • •

I stumbled through the streets. Rage blinded me—at the ignorance of Bonteme; at the guards who sneered as I ran from the hall. At myself. After everything I had done—as I pushed through the crowds already assembling, images kept surfacing in my mind:

Niam's collarbone, slick with sweat; the pale limbs of the witch-tree, moving in the moonlight; holding down the witch-tree branch while I cut into its to living flesh. All of it wasted effort. The scissors were still resting on my workbench, unless they'd fallen free somewhere in the streets.

I still grasped the manipulator in my right hand and the creature jostled behind me, dangling from its strings, arms raised as if in benediction.

I pushed people out of the way, as if I were still in the forest and they were nothing more than branches in my path. A child appeared from between the stalls and I cuffed him away; only when he cried out did I notice it was Gaben. He fell onto a table loaded with oranges. When he wiped the back of his hand across his face I saw blood. I did not stop to help him to his feet.

I reached my lodgings, slammed the door behind me and threw the creature on the workbench. Rabian hung from his hook, mocking me with the smile I'd painted on him myself. I tore him from his place and flung him across the room where he clattered against the low roof. I stalked over to the marionette and broke him across my knee.

I did not stop until I had destroyed it all: the marionettes; the foolish costumes they wore; the sets and props; the paints and varnishes that comprised their empty expressions. I screamed as I did so—a guttural rage, as if I were giving voice to the creature's screams that had haunted me since I brought Niam's axe down. The creature turned its head as I thrashed about the room, watching as I spat and tore and wept. Finally, when there was nothing more to break I collapsed on my pallet, strings cut, into a dreamless sleep.

• • •

I slept through the revels and woke late in the afternoon the next day, every part of my body screaming protest at my recent exertions. There was the smell of smoke in the breeze. I flung the shutters wide. A rope of black rose from the eastern gate. I heard unsheathed steel and the screaming of horses.

Upon my workbench, where the creature had lain the night before, lay nothing but tangled strings.

My saw was gone.

The creature was a fast learner. It had watched while I destroyed my art. And in the same way I had taught it to dance, now I had taught it something else.

I could imagine what it had done—bringing my saw to the witch-tree in the same way I had taken my axe. I rushed down the stairs, flung open the door and ran downhill, through the square, towards the eastern gate. I could see them now—an army of creatures, roughly-hewn: they ran in packs across the battlements. I saw a soldier caught with no way of escape. They attacked him in a swarm. I heard the sound of wood beating upon bone. When the creatures dispersed there was nothing but a red smear on the brick.

Then I saw, behind the gate, a bone-white limb stretch far above the wall. Its end was twisted into an imitation of a fist and it grasped Niam's axe, held backwards. The limb slammed down on the wall—soldiers and masonry tumbled to the street below. The height of the limb could mean only one thing—the witch-tree was walking.

I turned and ran back up the hill and when I reached my lodgings I bolted the door knowing full well the futility of the action.

• • •

It is louder now, the sound of battle. The streets are full of carts: the rich have fortunes piled up and drawn by horses; the poor drag what they can, or simply run, leaving everything. All are equally doomed. The eastern gate is still ablaze and the other exits are choked with traffic.

I found the scissors lying on the floor. I had nudged them, no doubt, in my haste to leave for the audition. I have them now, gripped tightly in my left hand. They are good scissors. In the hours ahead I will have need of something strong and sharp.

They are coming.

• • • • • • • • • • •

SHE SAID

KIRSTYN McDERMOTT

Finally, the sound of weeping stopped and Mallory hobbled out of the bedroom on legs that seemed to grow both thinner and whiter with each new day. She clutched an empty baby food jar in one hand and stared at me through the shards of her uneven, grease-black fringe.

"You'll need this," she said. "For the clouds." And she coughed, harsh and hacking, skinny ribs hitching high with each hard-drawn breath, and spat something dark and clotted into the jar. She held it out to me with trembling, blood-scabbed fingers and I took it, trying not to look too closely at the contents.

"Mix it with indigo," she said, as she wiped a smear from her chin.

"Mal?"

"For the clouds."

"Mal, come sit with me a bit." My invitation was less than half-hearted and I hoped the relief didn't show on my face when she shook her head.

"I'm going back to bed, Josh. I'm tired." She paused at the bedroom door, scratched her thigh through the ratty black slip she'd been wearing for longer than I cared to think about. "Do some fucking good with that, yeah?"

The bedroom door closed almost soundlessly behind her. I retrieved a tube of Indigo Blue from the mess scattered over the floor, squeezed about half of it into the jar Mallory had given me. I started to stir, slowly, carefully, blending colour and consistency to something new, something no one had ever quite seen before and as I did, the skin on the nape of my neck crawled. I could already see the paint moving over the canvas, wet and violent and alive, could feel it sliding beneath my brush with a purpose all its own.

I turned to the half-finished cityscape that loomed from the easel by the window: my abandoned, nameless city with its buildings left to rust and rot and ruin, left to cower and hope beneath the threat of an oncoming storm which must surely mean its end. Massive thunderheads little more than charcoal sketches because I'd been uncertain how to render them.

Until now.

As I lifted my brush to the canvas, as I felt the paint flow thick and eager from the bristles, I could see the end, how it needed to be finished. I could see the promise that glimmered beneath the threat, the mercy inherent in destruction. My hand steadied, and worked.

Hours later, I pushed my face into Mallory's neck while we fucked. Her sickly, sweat-stale smell filled my nostrils, seeped down the back of my throat; even then it was better than looking at her. Better than having to meet that weepy, red-rimmed gaze and pretend. But she knew. Turned away as soon as we were done, her fragile fetal curl on the edge of the mattress familiar as breathing now, and I knew better than to try and touch her again. Even if I'd wanted to.

Instead: "I think the painting's done, Mal. I think you'll like it."

She whispered something into her pillow.

I swallowed. "You'll see it in the morning, anyway."

Minutes dragged by unanswered, the dry scrape of sandpaper on skin, and just as I was beginning to hope she'd drifted off to sleep, Mallory sighed and rolled back over to face me.

"I know about her, Josh," she said.

• • •

Fiona. Fee. My dirty little secret, not so much it seemed.

I'd bumped into her on the street, literally, *crashed* into her as I'd come out of the art supplies place on Greville, head down, suspiciously counting the change the emo kid behind the counter had dumped into my hand. I didn't see the girl til I'd almost knocked her over, knocked the breath from her lungs with a small, startled *oh!*, knocked the cardboard carton she'd been carrying from her hands.

Then suddenly, magically, the air was full of feathers.

Thick and white and swirling all around us as though someone had exploded an angel, or a pillow factory, and *oh!* the girl said again, softer this time, and grinned. I was grinning too, trying to apologise as I brushed the feathers from my shirt. A handful had come to rest in her hair and, without thinking, I reached out to pluck them from her ash blonde curls.

"Sorry," I said again. "I didn't see you."

"Don't worry about it," she told me. "This was so much better than whatever he had planned for them."

She'd been dropping off the box for an artist friend who was working on some kind of an installation to do with animal liberation, or sleep deprivation, she couldn't remember which. Shrugging, the girl shook a few more feathers from the hem of her brightly-coloured skirt. I was fixated on her arms, so smooth and tanned, jangling with a dozen or more gaudy plastic bracelets.

"Are you an artist too?" I asked.

"Me?" A coy, sideways tilt of her head. "More an artist's assistant. Admiration and inspiration, that sort of thing."

"And plumage procurement."

"Yes, sometimes that as well." She held out a hand. "Fiona."

"Josh." Her skin was warm, her grip purposeful. She looked about ten years younger than me, maybe in her early twenties, twenty-five tops.

"Well, Josh, my fine new friend, I think you owe me a coffee." She slipped around to my side, hooked her arm through mine and flashed me another brilliant, straight-toothed smile. "At the very *least.*"

I could have said no. I *should* have said no, should have gone straight back home with my tubes of paint and the new Size 4 sable brush I couldn't really afford. Back home where Mallory would have been waiting with her nails gnawed down to the bloody quick and her eyes full of thunder and hurt.

Instead, I followed Fiona to her favourite café and then, later, back to her flat in St Kilda. We sat on her sixth floor balcony with a bottle of wine, looking out over the bay and arguing, good-naturedly, about whether or not we could discern a curve in the horizon from that height.

"So, you're a painter," she said at some stage. "Any good?"

"Sometimes yes, sometimes definitely not."

"We might have to see about that."

Evening had crept up on us; I could barely make out her features in the growing darkness. But I leaned forward anyway, and kissed her. Slowly at first and then, with her lips moving against mine, more urgently. I caught her hair in my fists, tangled those soft, pale curls around my fingers.

Finally, she pulled away. "It's not going to happen tonight, Josh."

But her smile was wolfish, and more than a little regretful, as she pulled me to my feet and sent me off, alone, into the dusk.

• • •

Sunk deep into the sagging centre cushion of our couch, Mallory pulled the blanket tighter around her shoulders. A scab on her left knee was flaking and she scratched at it, absently.

"I don't know, Josh. There's something . . . missing?"

She was right, she was always right. The painting was done, done as I felt I could make it, but it wasn't finished. The abandoned city, the brooding storm-laden sky; it wasn't enough, it didn't sing, or even mutter. More and more, I felt trapped by the canvas, caught within the very oppression I'd been attempting to create.

And I couldn't help but think of the other canvas I'd been working on over the past few weeks, the one Mallory didn't know about, could never know about. The painting that currently resided high up in a certain sixth floor St Kilda flat. My huge, half-finished portrait of a girl with ash gold curls and a grin coaxed straight from a fairy tale.

"I'm done, Mal." I rubbed at my forehead. "It's done."

"No, you're not, and no, it's not either."

I shook my head, refused to meet her eye. The buildings I'd painted reminded me of her somehow. Those empty, abandoned facades agape with broken windows like the teeth she'd lost just the other day. A sharp-pointed incisor and its less interesting neighbour, offered on a shaky, flattened palm for my inspection.

They just fell out, Josh. They fell right out of my mouth. A childish wonderment in her voice, but also, unmistakably, fear.

"You'll find it," Mallory said from the couch, and sniffed.

"Find what?"

"The way through. You always do, in the end."

"Mal—" I turned, and whatever I was about to tell her slid away as I saw the runnel of blood edging sluggishly from her left nostril. Revulsion kicked at my guts. Revulsion, and something else besides. "Mal, your nose."

She frowned and sniffed again, extended the tip of her tongue above her lip to catch a smear of scarlet. "Oh." Her hands disappeared beneath the blanket for a few seconds before resurfacing with one of her empty little jars, and she leaned forward, one hand pushing her hair out of her face, the other holding the jar carefully beneath her nose. Blood seeped down the clear glass sides as I watched, pooling toxic-thick at the bottom.

And I could see the buildings in my painting bleeding like that. Just like that. Weeping bitter streams of rust and corrosion from every crack and windowless crevice. Not simply waiting for the storm, but falling before it, flowing apart at the edges. Forsaken, even by each other. *Forsaken.* The word tasted swollen and hollow and cold as I whispered it beneath my breath.

It tasted of surrender. It tasted *right.*

"Josh?" Mallory was sitting up again, the jar resting on her thigh. It held an alarming amount of blood. "Yes?" she whispered.

"I think so," I replied. "Yes."

Her lips parted in a faltering, gap-toothed smile and as she lifted the jar up to me, its contents glinting dark and crimson in the failing afternoon light, I leaned over and kissed her, my fingers closing over hers and over the jar, and I tasted the blood still smeared beneath her nose.

And, just for now, that tasted right as well.

• • •

"Let me see." Fiona rose from the wicker chair and retrieved her robe from the floor. It was bright blue and patterned with huge orange flowers, one of which sat over her left breast like a mutant, six-fingered hand as she tied the belt loosely around her waist. I could make out the dark circle of her nipple through the flimsy, semi-sheer fabric.

"Who said the man couldn't paint?" Fiona nudged me with her elbow. "It's beautiful, Josh. Seriously, it's amazing, and I'm not just saying that cause it's me. The way you've made it so it almost *glows*, that's . . . wow."

"It's not quite finished yet, I don't think."

"Really? It looks finished."

The truth was, I didn't *want* it to be finished. I didn't want to give up these mornings in Fiona's lounge room, watching the sun as it spilled through window glass and over her naked curves, watching the rise and fall of her chest deepen whenever she slipped into a doze. But the portrait was too finely balanced now, and I knew if I added so much as a single brushstroke, it could fail.

Fiona was right, it was finished.

"Hey, Josh?" She looked at me sideways, and smiled. "You didn't actually need me to sit for you today, did you?"

I reached out and squeezed the back of her neck. "Not technically, no." My hand moved around to her throat; her pulse beat hard beneath my fingers. "But a little extra inspiration never hurts."

She returned my kisses at first, her tongue giving playful chase to mine. Only when my hands moved down to her hips, sliding through the folds of her robe to grasp at her soft, sunwarm flesh, did she push me away. "It's not that I don't want to," she whispered, her hand trembling on my chest. "But you know if anything were to happen, it would just get too messy. And I try to avoid mess."

"You don't think something has already happened?"

"Josh, you have . . . complications."

"Let me guess," I snapped. "You try to avoid those as well."

Her eyes widened. Her hand fell to her side.

"Ah, Fee." I looked at her portrait again, so full of light and grace and joy I could barely believe it had been born from my brush. And I thought of the dark, decaying cityscape I'd been working on back home, and the cycle of taut, claustrophobic abstracts before it, and before *those* the grisly series of canvases I'd started within days of meeting Mallory. The ones she'd dubbed *abattoir nouveau* without even the slightest trace of irony.

"I don't love her." I was half-surprised to have spoken the words aloud. "I did once, I think. But not now, not for a long time."

"But you need her," Fiona said. "Or you want her. Same difference."

I shook my head. "I want you."

Fiona sighed. "It's a beautiful painting, Josh. But what if that's all there is?"

"I don't believe that." My hand found hers and squeezed, gently. "There's something here, right? It's not just in my mind?"

She moved closer, rested her head on my shoulder.

"Yes," she said. "There is something."

• • •

Mallory made a face and dumped the half-eaten jar of baby food onto the kitchen table, pushed it towards the centre. *Apple and Banana Custard*, the label read, though it all looked like the same puréed muck to me.

"I thought that was your favourite," I mumbled around a mouthful of peanut butter sandwich.

"It tastes off," she said. "I'm not hungry, anyway." She sat back and crossed her arms over her chest. The veins on her hands bulged blue against her chalk-dry skin as she clenched and unclenched her fists. Her flesh so wasted away now, I half-expected to hear the grate of bone against bone.

"You should eat," I told her.

She glared at me. "It would be easier if I just left, wouldn't it?"

"Mal—"

"It's not me you want here any more." Her bottom lip was chapped and tattered and as she spoke the skin split a little and beaded red. "It's her."

"This is your home, too, Mal. I'm not just going to throw you out."

"You can stop being so fucking noble, it doesn't suit you."

Her voice broke on the last words and I couldn't look at her. Instead I stared at the table top, tracing a fingernail over the motley collection of scratches and cuts that crosshatched its surface, some made by me, others by who knows how many previous owners in kitchens past. In the corner was a little heart pierced by two arrows, complete with fletching and tiny droplets of blood suspended from the tips. Mallory had etched that with a compass point one pissed-up night, back when we still got drunk together.

"Mal, this isn't working. We can't keep pretending that it is."

A scrape of chair against lino and then she was sitting at my feet, her fingers picking along the seam of my jeans. "This is what you wanted, Josh."

"No." I swallowed, rested my hand on her head. "Not like this."

"Then it's up to you to change it," she said. "Because I can't do it for you, it's not my choice to make. It's never been my choice."

"I'm so sorry, Mal. I never meant . . . any of this."

Fingers digging into my thigh, she pulled herself shakily to her feet. "Stupid boy," she whispered, moving around behind me. Her arms draped over my shoulders and she pressed her lips against my neck. "You think she's gonna give you what you need? You think she's all fire and light and fucking glory be?" Her breath smelled of copper and of sour, discarded things. "You need to take into account the common fucking denominator here, my love."

I turned my head away. "Mal, don't. Please."

Mallory straightened, dragging her hands up over my cheeks and across my scalp. She was breathing heavily through her nose, like she always did when trying not to cry. "Go to her then, Josh," she said. "Just fucking go."

• • •

Fiona answered the door in her robe and for a single, green-tinged moment I wondered if there was someone else in the flat with her. Another painter she was sitting for, or just some guy waiting impatiently in her bed with his dick in his hands, and I couldn't for the life of me have said which possibility cut the deepest.

"What happened to you?" she asked. "There's blood on your neck."

"It's nothing." I rubbed at the place where Mallory's mouth had been less than an hour before. "It's not mine."

"Come inside." She took my hand and I followed her into the lounge room where my painting—*our* painting—still leaned upon its easel, bold and golden and luminous. And I knew I'd made the right decision.

"It's over," I said. "She hasn't left yet, but she will. It's over, Fee, it really is."

My vision blurred and something I hadn't even realised was there uncoiled itself from around my chest and slunk away, defeated. And then Fiona was kissing me, her robe falling to the floor and us falling close behind it, and for a while there was nothing in my head but light.

• • •

The sun was well into its daily arc by the time I got back home the next morning, but the flat was dim, all the blinds still drawn, and silent.

"Mal?" I called. "Mal, it's me."

The bedroom door was shut. I eased it open a crack and peered through to find her curled up beneath the blankets, tight little Mallory-ball so small it almost hurt to see. Almost. Still no response when I called her name again, little more than a whisper this time, so I closed the door quietly behind me.

I lifted my dead city painting from the easel and leaned it against the wall, face down. Driving home, I'd pictured myself taking to it with a Stanley knife, shredding the paint-stiff canvas to harmless strips, but now something stayed my hand. There was a certain fatalistic grandeur to its darkness that demanded further consideration. So I left it to itself for now and cleaned up all the half-curled tubes of paint and near-empty jars from the floor. I scrubbed my hands with turpentine, digging out the last stubborn dregs of black and indigo and cobalt blue which had taken up near permanent residence beneath my nails.

Then I made toast and ate it thickly buttered over the sink and thought about the look that loosened Fiona's face when she came.

Afterwards, I went to the bedroom again and knocked on the door. "Mal, you awake yet?" No answer, not even the slightest sound of movement in the room beyond, and suddenly everything felt wrong. *Leave, just leave now and don't ever come back.* But instead, I turned the handle and pushed open the door.

Mallory was still in bed, still tightly cocooned in the blankets, and I placed a hand on the bump I guessed to be her shoulder. "Mal, baby, you okay?" She felt odd, sort of *spongy*, and then, as I shook her, she just . . . wasn't there.

"Fuck!" I stumbled backwards, tripping on some stray bit of crap on the floor, and coming down hard on one knee. Bolts of pain shot up my leg, and I swore again through gritted teeth, but never once took my eyes from the bed, from the newly flat and barren place where Mallory had been. Ignoring the persistent voice in my head that was telling me again to leave, *leave now, and whatever you do, don't look don't look don't look*, I reached out and grasped a corner of the blanket. Lifted, then swallowed hard, and pulled it all the way back.

Thick and viscous, like treacle or honey left too long in the fridge, the sludge that quivered and spread across the bottom sheet in a shape that too painfully resembled the form of a girl lying on her side. Mallory, the way I'd seen her all too often: curled with knees pressed against her chest, skinny arms hugging her shoulders and her head tucked chin to breastbone like a Bronze Age sacrifice awaiting the slow mummification of peat. I didn't even realise I'd touched the stuff until my fingers were at my mouth, glistening dark and smelling of salt and iron and loss.

She tasted like nothing I could begin to describe.

I crawled to the toilet and vomited until my guts were sore and only hot strings of bile were coming up.

Back in the bedroom, I spotted the little jar I'd stumbled over before and bent to pick it up. And saw under the bed, a battalion of them, tiny glass soldiers guarding a tomb. My breath caught in my throat. Mallory had been eating nothing but that shit for weeks, maybe for months, but still I couldn't believe the sheer number of empties she'd managed to accumulate. I stared at the mess on the bed, then at the jar in my hand, and slowly unscrewed the lid.

It look less than half of them to contain her.

The rest of the jars I collected into two plastic shopping bags and took straight down to the bins on the street. I stripped the bed and threw the sheets away as well. Contemplated burning them, consigning the last of the stains they harboured to fire and ash, but it was hardly a practical solution and I didn't want them in the flat a second longer.

I didn't know what to do with the jars I'd filled.

Briefly, I considered taking them out to the bay and throwing them into the water, or burying them somewhere up in the Dandenong ranges, deep in the earth where they'd never be found. But something inside me balked at the idea of taking them anywhere, of taking *her* anywhere, so instead I simply stowed them under the bed again. Lined them up against the wall beneath where my head would lie, making sure all the lids were screwed on tight.

I had no idea whether or not she would spoil.

• • •

It wasn't the light. My flat was dim, sure, the new compact fluorescents overly harsh, but the painting could have been standing beneath the brightest of summer suns and it wouldn't have made the slightest difference.

It wasn't the light; it was what the light exposed.

I rubbed hard at my forehead, wondering how the fuck I could've ever believed Fiona's portrait to hold any real worth at all. Simplistic and garish, it had nothing to say beyond the most clichéd commentary on beauty and the female form, nothing that hadn't already been said by the likes of Klimt and Modigliani—decades earlier and with infinitely greater eloquence. I could imagine prints being sold by the truckload out of suburban shopping malls, disconnected housewives only too delighted to find something pretty and cheerful and just a little bit risqué. Something that didn't clash with their new designer lounge suite.

At best, the painting was vacuous; at worst, utterly mute.

I felt sick.

"Josh?" Fiona called from the bedroom. "You're sure she doesn't want any of this stuff? She's not coming back for it?"

"Just bag it all," I told her. "She's not coming back."

My ruined city reproached me from its place against the wall, and rightfully so. For all its flaws, it at least possessed a tongue.

"How weird would it be if I hung onto this?" Fiona asked from behind me. "Most of her things are kind of dire, but this suits me, don't you reckon?"

I turned, and my throat tightened. I remembered that dress. The bright red fabric dotted with tiny white flowers, the deeply scooped neckline and that row of buttons which ran all the way up the front and which were damn near impossible to undo in a hurry. How long had it been since I'd seen that dress, seen Mallory in it?

"Where'd you get that?" I asked.

"In the wardrobe, shoved behind everything else." Fiona twirled and the skirt flounced around her bare thighs. It fitted her curves perfectly and I seemed to remember it sitting the exact same way on Mallory once. I tried to picture how she looked when we'd first got together, before she lost all the weight, back when there was something beneath her skin beyond the bitter jut of bone.

I couldn't.

"So, too weird?" Fiona asked.

"It's a bit weird," I told her. "But keep it, if you want."

She crossed the room, put her arms around my waist and pressed her cheek against my shoulder. "I don't have to move right in," she said. "You know, if it's too soon. I can find another place." The lease was up on her apartment and her arsehole landlord had decided to double the rent. It'd been my suggestion that she come live with me; anything else just seemed like delaying the inevitable.

"I want you to be here, Fee." I ruffled her hair. Dark roots were starting to push up through the pale blonde, and I tried to imagine how Fiona would look if she ever quit the peroxide habit.

The skin on the back of my neck prickled. I could see how the painting could be saved; moreover, I could *feel* it deep in my guts, the *rightness* of it. The undercurrent of darkness that needed to sit just beneath the surface, the hint of sordid truth behind the beautiful lie that we all want so desperately to believe. But I had to be subtle with it, sound a barely discernable note of unease, just enough to knock the portrait off kilter. Shadows and hollows and the sly insinuation of decay.

Of defilement.

"Ow, Josh, that hurts!" Fiona was struggling in my hands, my fingers digging deep into the soft flesh of her upper arms. I released my grip, watched its ghosts bloom angry and scarlet on her skin.

"Shit, Fee, I'm sorry. I didn't even realise."

"It's okay." She rubbed at the places I'd been holding her. "Where'd you go just now?"

"Nowhere, just thinking." I kissed the top of her head, still thinking. About how to fix the painting, and about the jars that waited beneath my bed. I could see how that dark opalescence would mix with the airy golden tones of Fiona's portrait, how it would give them texture and weight. How it would make them real.

My fingers flexed, ached for a paintbrush.

"I'm going to make chai," Fiona said. "You want some?"

"Hmm? Yeah, sure." My eyes followed the sway of her hips as she strolled towards the kitchen. Just as she reached the doorway, I called her name and she half-turned, her face bright and open and expectant.

"You look good in that dress," I told her.

Fiona smiled. "Thanks," she said.

I listened to the safe, domestic sounds of tea-making and wondered how long the jars would last, how many more canvases Mallory could permeate before she was, finally, gone. Already, my brain was beginning to clutter and swarm with new visions, new ideas, and I got down on my knees to retrieve my sketchbook from where it had slid beneath the couch, a stub of charcoal marking a new page. But my hand was too cautious, too careful, its first little sketch so timid and needy. Frustrated, I flipped the page.

You'll find it, Josh. You always do, in the end.

I nodded. Closed my eyes and tried to recall the sharp, pinched lines of Mallory's body, the lost and broken expression on her face. I'd never drawn her, not once, which seemed a strange thing. And now she was too scattered, too faded, and I couldn't get the pieces to stay together.

Josh?

"I'm sorry, baby," I whispered.

Josh.

"I'm so sorry."

"Josh!"

My eyes snapped open. "Fee?" I lurched to my feet and half-ran, half-stumbled into the kitchen where Fiona was standing over the sink, both hands pressed to her face. "Fee, what's wrong?"

"My nose." She sniffed, loud and wet and awful, as blood started to seep through her fingers. "I need a tissue."

There was more chance of finding a silk handkerchief in this place, so I snatched up a tea towel instead. She waved it away, protesting about stains, but I shook my head—"It doesn't matter, Fee"—and held it gently to her nose. Blood soaked through the cloth.

"Fuck. Here, sit down." I guided her to a chair. "Keep your head back."

It took almost five minutes for the bleeding to stop completely. Half a roll of toilet paper littered the table and floor, all of it bright with crimson blotches. Kitchen as surgical ward, triage tent, autopsy room, with Fiona hunched pale and shaky in the centre, one hand clutched sweaty in mine.

"It must be the dry weather," she said at last.

I nodded, unable to look away from the patterns made by the blood.

"I think I need to lie down," she said.

"Good idea."

I helped her into bed, and she asked me to sit with her for a while, and so I did. Stroking her hair and contemplating the mess in the kitchen, all that blood-soaked paper, and how wrong it seemed to simply throw it away.

Just when I thought she had fallen asleep, Fiona slid a hand from beneath the sheet and squeezed my thigh. "You still want me here, don't you, Josh?"

"Of course." A dry crust of blood stained her upper lip and I licked my thumb, rubbed most of it away. "I need you, Fee." And she smiled, or nearly did. Weary little shadow of a smile that barely creased the corners of her mouth, and I didn't think I'd ever seen anyone look so fragile. Not even Mallory.

"That's good," she said. "That's perfect."

• • • • • • • • • • •

WHERE WE GO TO
BE MADE LIGHTER

CHRISTOPHER GREEN

I drove faster, and the car bounced and slid around in the gravel. Amy and I had three trips to make, and I didn't want to be doing any of this in the dark.

She'd been getting phone calls, over the last few weeks. They called her, haunted her, and she'd convinced herself that they'd only stop if the house was emptied of their memory. She wanted all the girls I'd met before to be bagged and gone.

We were nearer the dump, now, and Amy wasn't saying anything. I ignored her silence and concentrated on not bottoming us out in one of the little gullies that fell across the road like logs.

She'd asked, then begged, then demanded, and so here we were. If that wasn't enough, then Amy wanted more than I had to give.

The dump wasn't an official one, not in the same way a chain-link fence or a man at the gate would have made it, but it didn't matter. Everyone threw whatever they no longer wanted into the old stone quarry, and that made it official enough for our purpose.

The gravel road swung around a bend and we followed it around, right to the slant into the quarry. Two-litre bottles and copper tubing had begun to pop and crumple beneath the tires. Then the sun slid behind a cloud, and I fought an urge to turn on the headlights. Gulls were everywhere, and everything was rhymed in their shit, like frost.

Even here, at the edge of this, where the gravel throat of the dump vanished down another curve, other people's junk was heaped to either side of the road. The hard, rounded corners of kitchen appliances jutted from the morass of tattered garbage bags, broken toys, old wood, and mattresses that had already been burnt once or twice.

Amy and I drove on. The edge of this place wouldn't do. For them to be truly gone, I'd have to go to the heart the quarry. If anything had the power to let us leave them behind, it was a place like this. A place where so many had left with less than they'd brought.

The road twisted, again and again, as we drove, always in downward in tight spirals. When the road stopped at the bottom, so did we. This time I did turn on the headlights. The sun overhead was rimmed in cloud cover, and it's light was too pale to help.

I popped the trunk and got out. There were only three bags, half full of yarn and wool and patterns for dresses Becky would never wear. A dozen or so knitting needles poked out from one of the bags like finger bones.

I lifted all three bags at once. My life with Becky weighed nothing. I found a hole, not far from the car, in a clearing where even the old clothes and moldy cardboard dared not stray. My hole.

I dropped those bags down my hole, and went back to the car. I felt lighter.

As I turned the key, the air-conditioner sputtered and the moisture on my cheeks went cold. I wiped the tears away before Amy could see them and surprised myself with the taste of blood. I wiped again, this time with the back of my hand. One of Becky's knitting needles must have gotten me. The jagged hole in the webbing between my thumb and forefinger oozed blood, and started to ache. I ignored it and gave Amy a weak grin. She just looked at me, and I butchered what should have been a three-point turn into a six or seven-point one and turned around.

We drove away. The dump faded in the rearview, and we went home for trip number two.

Janice had been a hoarder, and when we'd broken up, she left everything behind. Everything. It had taken me days to gather it all, and it took me an hour to load it into the car. Bags kept breaking, bursting at the seems and spilling old envelopes, beads, paints, clay, and everything else an out of work artist can gather in a year and a half. All of it rolled about in the driveway like flotsam.

The phone rang during my last trip to the car, but my hands were full. It stopped, then started again. I closed the door behind me. Whoever it was would have to wait.

At last, she was rebagged. The trunk was full, as was the backseat, more full than was safe, but I opted to block the rearview's line of sight instead of asking Amy to hold a few of the bags on her lap. She'd already lived through enough of this. She was smiling now, at least. Maybe she felt lighter too.

This time, the dump smelled like a wet dog. I grimaced and the wind shifted to bring us another scent. The acid smell burnt batteries now stuck in the back of my throat. We circled to the center, in the last of the afternoon, that thick smell following us all the way down.

Janice took just as many trips to unload as she had to pack away. I was sweating by the time I was halfway through. It all went down the hole, my hole, and it didn't seem to matter how much I put down there, there was always room for more.

My hand throbbed, and a bright slash of the thick purple paint Janice had used to sign her work dribbled across my hand and into the needle puncture. I got into the car and turned around a bit better this time, getting used to driving amidst the refuse of other people's lives. We made it into a five-point turn, this time, and drove home.

I had to turn the headlights on again before we got there. The last trip was going to have to be in the dark after all.

I went inside for Lindsey's stuff while Amy waited in the car.

These bags, piled up in the corner of the den, held Lindsey's belongings. But her things were my things; things that Lindsey had once loved and I had grown to love as well. Things that I had bought her and she had bought me and we had used together. When I'd gone around the house gathering her up, I 'd put myself in those bags, as much as I'd put Lindsey in them.

I filled the trunk, put a few bags in the back seat, and went back into the house one last time.

I stood in the front room, the one Lindsey had always called the parlor and I had never had a need to name, to look for things I'd missed. And there, draped over a pair of nails, above the doorway that led to the kitchen, was the braid of dried mistletoe she and I had hung so long ago. A place to kiss, she'd said. Lindsey had loved Christmas. Christmas to Amy was simply a convenient time for her to give me an itemised list, ranked in order of her expectation.

I brought a chair from the kitchen and stood on the seat. The mistletoe crumbled when I touched it, and the phone rang, all at once. I thought about letting it ring, but didn't. Answering it would give me a reason to pu off this last trip, if only for a minute or two.

I climbed down from the chair and picked up the receiver. For a moment I heard nothing, then the cries of gulls cut through the hiss of a bad connection.

"Who is this other woman?"

I wanted to drop the phone, or throw it, but my muscles had gone rigid and pressed the received to my face so hard it hurt my ear.

"Who is this other woman, Rick?"

"Janice?"

"Do you love her?" A rustle, as she put her hand over her end and spoke to someone else. Then she was back. "Do you? It's ok if you do."

"Her name is Amy. She says she can feel you, feel all of you. She said you wouldn't leave her alone until the things you left behind had been gotten rid of. She says you make us heavy."

"What are you talking about?" Even now, she had a way of making me listen, but I guess all exes do. Even ones that slit their wrists. "She says her name is Becky. She says you'll visit us soon. We'll be here until you come for us."

I heard the line go dead and my muscles awoke. I slammed the phone down.

I could see them, if I tried hard enough, Becky and Janice down in that hole, my hole, introducing themselves and then waiting patiently on that pile of garbage bags. Waiting for me.

I fled the house. Amy wasn't smiling anymore.

"Sorry, hon," I said, and stepped on the gas too hard. Amy nodded. The bags in the back seat nodded too, as did the "No Smoking" sign hanging from the rearview as a joke. Everyone I knew smoked like chimneys. Everyone but Amy.

I knew the drive by heart, now, and it didn't matter that it was dark. The wide lanes of the highway bled into the gravel road that led to the dump. The headlights picked up purple blossoms growing out of other people's things. The little blossoms nodded at me like Amy had. There were eyes out there amongst the ruin as well, the eyes of things that pawed and sorted.

I shivered and drove on.

We wound deeper, back to my hole. I parked the car at an angle, so the headlights were aimed in that direction, patted Amy on the knee, flashed her a smile, and got out.

This trip, all I could smell was the end. The rust and seagull droppings were everywhere, and my mouth was full of the stink of things that had burst in the sun and cracked in the cold.

When we reached the center, I stopped the car and unloaded it. I took each bag, one at a time, and set it at the edge of the hole, then went back for another. When the car was empty I pushed the bags in with my foot, one by one, before I could change my mind.

Then I looked back at the car. The headlights were at full bore, now, and I couldn't see past their glare to Amy, but I knew she'd be smiling.

I got on my hands and knees and peered into the hole, down into the darkness there. My hand had started bleeding again, and it hurt like hell.

Janice had found the glow-in-the-dark paint in one of the bags. She'd painted them all, lines and squiggles and bright yellow masks that covered their faces but left the eyes and mouths black. The three of them stared up at me like baby birds in a nest, their limbs tangled, mouths working up at me, making black "O"s that widened and narrowed.

I shifted, and felt my hand come down on something soft. A scarf. Whether it had fallen out of ones of the bags on that first trip, forever ago, or Becky had knit it for me in that hole, while she waited for me to return, I didn't know. It didn't matter.

I wrapped the scarf around my throbbing hand and felt the pain go away. I pulled more up, wrapped the slack around my neck, and let the three of them pull me down into that place of theirs. That place of ours.

My hole.

Perhaps the next person who comes down here will know what to do when they find Amy. When they put her in her own hole, maybe we'll all find our own peace.

• • • • • • • • • • •

MIRROR

JENNY BLACKFORD

She screamed each time, she knows
she screamed, but no one came.
Perhaps it was a dream,
the mirror and those eyes, not hers,
so many times. Perhaps
it was a dream.

Years on, grown up, she's still
afraid. What if those eyes—
imaginary eyes, not real—
can find her here, look through
the mirror on the wall
in this new place?

When she must close her eyes,
must pull, let's say, a dress
or jumper overhead,
she checks the mirror once
again. What's in it now?
The room, herself.

So far, so good. But whose
eyes look from it at night
when hers are closed?

HIGH TIDE AT HOT WATER BEACH

PAUL HAINES

We arrive early, but traffic already crawls, stalled and stalling along the road that snakes the coast to Hot Water Beach. Sam winds down his window, and the smell of the ocean tangy with salt and foam breezes into the car. Above us, television helicopters circle like gulls searching for scraps on the beach.

"We'll make it on time," I say.

"I know." His eyes are closed. My brother appears relaxed, at peace. His chest rises and falls with deep breathing exercises. The grey in his hair has almost won the battle with the blond, and the stubble on his chin has gone from brown and red to a stark white in less than two years.

I turn off the air-conditioning and lower all the windows. The sea breeze sweeps us back to childhood.

It's been more than thirty years. There were no carparks then, just a wide berth at the end of an unsealed road where people parked their cars and then continued on foot carrying baskets and towels, while ahead of them children scampered across the shallow stream and then raced the hundred or so metres down to Hot Water Beach.

An official sees the 'participating' sticker on our windscreen and guides us into the reserved carpark for beachgoers. It's almost full. Behind us, the three general admission carparks fill slowly and continuously with sightseers. I close the windows, then kill the engine.

"Ready?"

He smiles, and though his blue eyes are still bright, they are sunk deep within dark hollows. "Always ready, Toby," he says, though he sits in the car as I get out and remove our bags—one for the beach gear, the other for the laptop. I put my pass around my neck and hand Sam's in to him through the open door.

"It's warm," I say.

He holds out an arm. I grasp it—his wrists are so thin—and pull him lightly to his feet. He squints in the light of day. "Jesus, it's changed."

We walk through milling crowds towards the makeshift registration office nestled between several cafes, a small pub called "The Hot Water Bar", and the dairy. People sip at coffees, lick at ice-creams; video cameras are in hands, photos are snapped. We queue ten minutes until another official hands us our allotment number.

"Cutting it close, gentlemen," she says. "Low tide was just over an hour ago. You don't have much time to get ready."

She directs us to the tarmacked ramp that bridges the stream and leads down to the beach. Space has been cleared, and temporary stands have been erected along the pathway. Already sightseers jostle for the best vantage point, the stands almost full.

Others have taken position up on the slopes of the banks overlooking the sand, picnic rugs spread, cameras in hand, cold beers in the other.

We pass security and head down the ramp. Several other participants walk ahead, one an obese man waddling uncomfortably alone, another a middle-aged woman in a wheelchair, being pushed presumably by her husband.

Tina said she wouldn't be coming, that there was no way in hell she would watch this. She had refused to allow Izzy as well. I knew this bothered Sam, though he said nothing.

"She'll come," he says, as if he knows what I'm thinking. "Both of them will come. They'll want to kiss me when this is over."

"They'll come, sure."

The tarmac is hot. I can feel it cooking the soles of my jandals.

"When did they put in a bridge?" I ask, shifting the bags to my other shoulder. "Or, for that matter, a path?"

Sam laughed. "Remember that first time we came here, Toby? I was about eight, you must have been going on six. I think that was the first time I ever saw a woman's breasts."

"Yeah, me too."

"Remember Uncle Andy hanging shit on Mum and Aunty Jane and Aunty Elizabeth for not getting their tops off?"

I nod, though I don't remember that. All I remember is Uncle Andy's big hairy penis flapping in the waves as we tried to splash it and our Aunties yelling at him as they sunbathed. "Geez, he had a big dick, didn't he?"

We both laugh. "And a different girlfriend every Christmas."

"I remember the sunburn, too. Our bums peeled for days."

There are perhaps fifty people on the beach. Half will be support people like me. Many of the rest have almost finished digging shallow troughs in the wet sand, not far from where the surf crashes to shore. Several already lie in their holes, as the sand is piled back over them. I place the bags at our allotment, open the beach bag, and remove a small spade. Sam undresses, and swaps his clothes for the spade. He kneels, naked, and begins to dig in the sand. If he is to have any chance at all, he must dig his own hole, or that's what everyone believes. His body is emaciated, the sinew and muscle stretched taut across his limbs. His elbows and knees jut uncomfortably, all knobbly bone and callouses. Scars stretch from his pubis to his sternum, bisected across the abdomen just above the navel. A cross carved in skin. It has healed badly, a ridge of purple tissue riding proud through the hair on his belly.

"Water's warm," he says, digging deeper into sand wet with hot springs.

His ribs run like corrugated iron up his torso towards shoulder blades protruding like chicken wings from his back. He's lost a quarter of his original body weight. Every muscle flexes in sharp relief beneath the skin as he digs his hole, all fat long since burned off his body.

I remove the laptop from its bag. It blinks from hibernation mode, the screen difficult to see in the sunlight. I receive the signal broadcasting from the nearby cafes and arrange the windows on the screen. Newsfeeds stream in, betting agencies list odds—I can't help but look, and Sam is listed at 15:1, roughly middle of the pack—and I initiate the communication channels Sam and I will use for the duration of the tide. I mute the volume on the noise coming in from the newsfeeds, then take Sam's earpiece from the bag. It resembles a hearing aid, with a spur of moulded plastic that holds a miniature camera. I'll be able to see what Sam sees as the surf rolls in. I point the earpiece at Sam, and his skinny body shows up on the screen. I blow into the earpiece and adjust the volume levels on the laptop.

"You ready for this?"

Sam looks up, sweat on his face. "When I've finished the hole."

On my screen, one of the newsfeeds shows a reporter interviewing the obese man. I turn and see them standing thirty metres up the beach from us. A cameraman stands nearby filming. The man resumes his digging, and the reporter and cameraman head towards us, stopping to interview the woman sprawled in the sand at the base of her wheelchair. Her support person crouches next to her. Even from here, I can see him glare angrily at them. The reporter kneels and thrusts his microphone towards her. Back on the screen, she smiles politely. Her face is sheen with sweat. She clearly mouths the words "fuck off" to the reporter. I consider turning up the volume on the feed as the reporter says something else, and then the support person is between them, forcing them back with his chest. As they tussle, she jabs her spade back into the sand. It's obvious to me she hasn't the strength to finish the job in time. I wonder if she'll let her support take over the hole.

Statistically, that would be a bad move, but if she's not inside before the tide rises, she'll have even less chance. If you're not in the hole, you'll lose your soul, or so they say.

"Reporters coming our way," I tell Sam. "You want me to intervene?"

"I've got nothing to hide."

"You know how they are."

"I don't care. About them or what anyone thinks." He pauses and rests the spade on his knees. He looks at me; his eyes are clear and untroubled. "This is my last chance."

We watch as they approach.

"Hi, Steve Moki, iNet. We're interviewing the contestants. Do you mind if we ask you a few questions, please sir?"

"It's not a competition," Sam says.

"Sorry, I meant participants," Steve says. "Your name, sir?"

"Sam Sawyer."

"Pleasure to meet you, Sam." Steve scans the screen on his phone, no doubt looking up Sam's online profile. "You have metastatic cancer in your lymph node system, Sam. Sorry to hear that. What do you think your chances are?"

"For beating the cancer? Or for beating the tide?" Sam laughs. "How many people on this beach, Steve?"

"Thirty-six. Participants."

"So far, someone has successfully walked back up this beach and into the rest of their life every single year. Why not me? Better odds than chemo. Better than the lotto. I'd say my chances are good." Sam laughs. "Unless this is the year that no one does."

"Are you afraid of dying, Mr Sawyer?"

Sam pauses for a second, casts a glance at me, then faces Steve again. "I'm not afraid of dying. I'm afraid of leaving my wife a widow in the prime of her life. I'm afraid of leaving my three-year old daughter without a father. I'm afraid of my death ripping my family apart. Dying? That part is easy."

Steve indicates the crowd in the stands and along the ridge overlooking the beach. "And are your family here today?"

Sam stares up at the crowds and shakes his head. "No."

"Is that because *they* don't believe that you'll win today, Mr Sawyer? Or that *you* don't believe?"

Sam turns his back on the camera. The spade is back in his hand.

He scoops out sand and piles it next to the hole.

"Mr Sawyer?"

"I think that's enough," I say.

Steve nods and backs off, then faces the camera. "Not too optimistic there, folks. A statement like that might just affect his odds. Over to Carrie at iNetBet for the latest update and our panel of experts. This is Steve Moki, for iNet."

Steve gives me a nod, his offsider downs the camera, and they stroll back towards the path leading towards the bars, cafes, and betting agencies.

Sam is crying.

"You okay, bro?"

"Yeah." He places the spade next to the hole and climbs in. It's deeper than it has to be. "Give me the earpiece."

I insert it into his ear and attach the clips so it won't work loose in the surf.

"How's that?" he asks.

The window on my laptop clearly shows my head staring away off camera. He's watching me watch the screen. His voice comes through clearly on the speakers, distortion free. The mic is waterproof, and I've been assured it offers the best underwater sound available.

"Good," I say. "Perfect."

"Then fill me in."

I pack the sand in around his body. There is a heat there already, infused in every grain from the thermal springs running beneath Hot Water Beach.

"Make sure you get my arms tight. I don't want to be able to get out if I change my mind."

I bury his stick-like arms as he holds them beneath his back.

"You can always change your mind. You just say. I'm right here. I can get you out."

"Come on, Toby. What would be the point of that?" He doesn't look at me as he says this, instead he stares at the sea. The waves are rolling in now. Low tide has passed. A tear rolls down his cheek.

"I'm just saying, that's all. I'll be sitting up just past the hide tide mark. Just in case."

He says nothing. I finish packing the sand in tight around him until only his head rests upon the sand. His thin hair is wet with sweat that beads down his forehead, disguising the last of the tears.

I take a tube of sunblock from the beach bag, squeeze out a handful of cream, and smear it over his face.

"Wouldn't want your blistered noggin all over the media when you come out of this, eh?"

We try to laugh. I pack the bags, then press my nose to his scalp, breathing in for what might be the last time the smell of my brother's sweat, chemical-free and born of the sun. I kiss him, and then take our gear up to the shade beyond the high tide mark.

As soon as I'm out of earshot I hear him sob. He's forgotten I have him on audio feed. I sit, arrange the bags and the laptop, and listen to Sam's deep breathing exercises. He's meditating.

All we can do now is wait.

The waves gather momentum, crashing against the shore. Each surge of froth inches closer than the one before. The noise of the crowd is steady, a constant barrage against the day, while the helicopters hover above, rotors throbbing. I count off thirty-six heads, sitting on the sand. Thirty-six bodies buried in sand heated by thermal springs. A human hangi, a veritable feast offered up to the Gods. The betting agencies have been keeping official survival records for a decade. In that time 63 people quit before the tide came in, 57 people cooked to death, and 185 people drowned. Sixteen people have walked back up that beach. There has never been a year when no one survived.

Statistics. Everywhere. iNetBet lists everything you need to know in order to maximise your winnings. Age. Weight. Sex. Race. Religion. Disease. Positive and negative weightings. Statistics. They are only good for telling you what happened in the past, for the group, not the individual. They can't predict the future, they can't predict the now. You're either on or off. Dead or alive.

The odds on Samuel surviving the tide are now sitting on 60:1.

The fact that his family are not here has weighed heavily against him. I have $10,000 riding on Samuel. In this game, no one cares about match-fixing. At least Sam's interview has worked in our favour.

The crash of the surf is louder now, as it breaks closer and closer.

I check the camera. The waves appear enormous from this angle, the foam bubbling in the sun as the water sucks back to the sea.

It's only metres away. The microphone picks up Sam's steady respiration, barely audible beneath the muted roar of the ocean. It won't be long now. Five minutes, maybe less.

"Toby?" Sam's voice over the microphone.

"I'm here, Sam."

"No word from Tina or Izzy?"

"Nothing, Sam."

"I just thought . . ." He trails off.

"You can stop this. You've got three more months, at least. All the doctors say so."

"I know what they say."

"That's ninety more days to watch your daughter grow, ninety more days of love, of guidance."

"I'm dying, Toby. I can feel it." He laughs. "I'm not burying my head in the sand because I'm scared of facing reality!"

"Let me come down, dig you out."

"If I walk off this beach today, Toby, it's after the tide has worked its magic. Whatever it is, whatever fucking miracle that happens here, I'm going to be part of it. I don't have three months left. And I want so much more than that."

"Please, Sam." My throat burns and I'm struggling to swallow. "Please. Don't—"

"Don't you fucking pull out on me now! You told me, you fucking swore as my brother, you'd do this with me. Don't you fucking dare!"

"I won't, Sam, I won't. I'm with you, bro, all the way. To the end."

We say nothing for a little while, and listen to the ocean. The crowd is quietening. As the tide creeps in, the tension blankets those crowded in the stands.

One of the participants screams from the far end of the beach.

It doesn't stop, a hoarse ululating acceptance of pain. The cameras for the newsfeeds zoom in. An elderly woman, her face a rictus, in between screams she sucks in breath, panting ". . . it burns it burns . . ." and then the screams continue. Her friend runs from her position above high tide, but is sent back by the woman screaming in the sand. She knows the stakes.

Sam hasn't even moved his head. For a second I'm terrified he's already dead. I increase the volume on the laptop, finding instant relief in the sound of his breathing. Foam is now settling around his head. Some of it has splattered the lens of the camera, but it is washed away as the next wave rolls in to lap at his face.

There's a roar from the crowd. The obese man has clawed his way from the sand. He staggers up towards the path. People clap and cheer and boo. His skin is burnt red. He collapses short of the tarmac, face first into the sand. His massive frame wobbles and shudders as he howls in dismay. Medics appear on the path and head towards him. The crowd roars again. A woman rises from the beach, water and sand dripping from her body. Her feet splash in the foam washed up by the surf. Her support person rushes to greet her and they enfold in each other's arms.

"What's going on?" Sam's voice, followed by crackling against his mic. I hear him spitting out water.

"The first to leave. Three, no, now four."

If no more follow suit, that will be the last of the quitters for this year. The waves now buffet the remaining heads. It is too late now to repent, to dig your way out of your grave.

I know this. Sam knows this. So do the punters, as the odds are recalculated onscreen.

He gasps between the waves, his head tilted back, trying to keep his airways free. "Have they . . . are they here?"

Should I lie to him? Would that make him feel better? Would it make me feel better? I choose my words carefully.

"We're with you, Sam. All of us. We love you."

Only the top of his head can be seen. His hair drifts in the tide like seaweed clinging to a rock. Others, those who chose to dig closer to the water in the hope that it may affect their outcome, are completely submerged. The crowd has fallen silent. The crash of surf and the intrusive buzz of the helicopters are the only sounds that remain.

I feel sick. My fingers leave a slick of sweat over the control pad on the laptop.

A call comes in.

"Toby?" Tina's voice is almost calm, although I can hear a dam close to bursting behind her words. "Where are you guys? Is he okay?"

"We're to the far right of the path. The last ones." I can no longer see the head of my brother. The waves are surging now. Foam and sand churn as they hit the beach. A huge rip has formed and drags water back into the sea. "He's just gone under."

"Oh, God, we're too late, we're too late." Tina sobs, then manages to control herself. "The traffic, Toby . . . we didn't think it would be . . . the traffic." I hear Izzy in the background asking what's wrong.

"He might still be able to hear. I can connect you," I say.

Sam's camera shows a swirling mess of cloudy water. The roar of the ocean pounds his microphone.

Tina pauses. "Okay."

"You're on."

"Hi, Daddy." Izzy says, loud and clear. Each word a delicate helium bubble, her voice so little, full of life and promise. "Daddy?"

She pauses, then her voice is quieter, distant. "He's not talking to me, Mummy."

"Keep talking, honey, he can hear you. He just can't talk back right now," says Tina.

"I hope the swim makes your tummy all better, Daddy. I made a picture for you." Another pause. "He's still not talking to me, Mummy, why's he—"

Tina says something, but I cannot make out the words.

And then Izzy is back on the line. "Bye, Daddy, I love you."

I'm watching the camera to see if Sam acknowledges any of this.

Some last gasp, a flurry of bubbles escaping his lungs, perhaps. I hear nothing but the water wrapped around the microphone, see nothing but the murkiness of the ocean as the surf rolls up Hot Water Beach, racing towards the high tide.

"Sam, I love you." Tina's voice breaks. "We'll see you soon, we'll—" She finishes the sentence with a half-swallowed sob. Izzy begins to cry. Tina hangs up.

I sit there in the shade, watching the screen, watching the waves.

The crowd sits in silence. I turn off the laptop. There is nothing more to be seen there.

The rocks where Uncle Andy used to take us at low tide are now beaten with surf. He taught us how to shuck oysters fresh off the rocks, lending us his fishing knife to help pry open the jagged shells. I'd cut my finger and Sam had held it tight in his palm as he led me back up towards Mum, while blood poured down our wrists. She had scolded us and Uncle Andy both, but we were back on the rocks the following day with his knife hunting for more oysters.

I look up the beach. The nearest support person has their head buried in their hands, rocking slowly back and forth on their knees. I stand and walk towards the edge of the water, letting the Pacific Ocean wash over my feet. The water is cool. At least that's something.

Where there is life there is always hope, I tell myself.

We wait for the tide to turn. Eventually we walk down the wet sand to dig up the dead, our hearts in our hands, the crowd poised to applaud.

• • • • • • • • • • •

THE FEBRUARY DRAGON

ANGELA SLATTER & LISA L HANNETT

Priling did not die immediately.

Her husband's boasting had led to the challenge, to her standing in the arena, almost to term, unable to wear armour because of the great swell of her belly. Priling had been one of the finest dragon-catchers—and killers—in Sepphoris, but that was before this child made her heavy.

The thing she faced was a melding of scale and flame, black and orange, red and gold, with violent flares of blue; the colours flickered like a conflagration. It towered over Priling, spewing forth a hunting cry that excited spectators even as it hurt their ears. She did not flinch.

The crowd roared as the dragon leapt, its attack fierce. The sword Priling plunged into its maw melted in a rush of fire. As if by magic, she avoided the worst of the flames, but the dragon wrenched her arm off with its powerful jaws, teeth easily sawing through her soft flesh. The dragon's blood entered its slayer's wound in the seconds before fire cauterised the spurting arteries. With the dagger in her remaining hand, Priling tore a long hole in the beast's throat, severing its jugular. Black ichor gushed into the sands of the arena. Wranglers were summoned to restrain the dying beast, and afford the Physicks time enough to drag the semi-conscious woman to safety. The audience voiced their displeasure at the abbreviated main event; Priling's husband, face ashen and voice unsteady, did his best to assuage them with promises of better shows tomorrow. He hadn't bargained on giving refunds this day.

It was Priling's nature to fight, and fight she did. Over four days her body gradually turned black and grew hard scales; her hands sprouted claws as the dragon's blood wormed its way through her. It was a poison to the dragon-catcher, but to the child within it was an alchemist's dream. Mother and child teetered on the brink of humanity in the hours before dawn on the final day. Priling fought the venom that could not fully transform her, unable to either remain woman or become dragon. She stayed alive long enough to give birth to a daughter.

And so Casco was born, her father's shame and her mother's final triumph.

• • •

"Where is she?" Pater Claudio yelled. The old man was so angry that his mane of white hair trembled as if shifted by a sly breeze.

Mirko shrugged. He'd lost sight of his charge ten minutes ago— she'd given him the slip on their way to Verre's House. It wasn't the first time she'd eluded him and it wouldn't be the last. Both he and Pater Claudio knew where she went on these brief sojourns. Mirko was her bodyguard, yes, but if Casco did not want company there wasn't a power known to man or dragon that could make her obey. "She'll be fine."

Pater Claudio's face went an astonishing shade of red. "She's got no cause to go there, Mirko. Slinking around that family, thinking nobody notices her. She's too old to be so foolish. Casco is to be escorted at all times—you know that."

Mirko had never seen such colour in a human countenance; he wondered if his patron's head might pop. "Never fear, Pater. She's bright and sharp—no longer a little girl. And those nails of hers would do for anyone who looked at her the wrong way."

"Those nails," said the older man through gritted teeth, "are precisely what we need to protect, imbecile. The sooner I get her—"

There was a familiar sound at the threshold of the vestibule: the *clack* of bone on stone. A single sharp spur grew from the back of each of Casco's heels. Her boots were custom made to accommodate the protuberance—a hooded gap in the soft leather allowed the spur to remain unencumbered, though not entirely out of sight. Her sharp diamond toenails were easier to conceal. Pater Claudio and Mirko sighed with relief.

Casco both rewarded and disturbed the eye. Her skin was as white as forge-fired glass, so that she seemed to glow in the vestibule's dim light; her eyes were such a deep black they appeared to have no pupils. Her hair, darker still than her eyes, was a series of soft interlocking scales that ran in long waves to her waist, rather like the frills on the necks of the great extinct lizards on display in the House of Natural History. She was beautiful and strange, wonderful and awful; anyone seeing her for the first time felt themselves to be somehow *less* in her presence. Subsequent viewings did not necessarily diminish this sensation.

"Pater," she said. "My apologies. I stopped by the fountain room and forgot to tell Mirko." She lied so smoothly that both men neglected to call her on the untruth.

"See that it doesn't happen again, Casco. You are too important to this House."

"You mean my nails are, Pater," she said archly.

He squirmed on the skewer of her words. "When did your tongue become so venomous, child? Verre's House has cared for you all your life. We rescued you from the Dying Place, my poor dead wife carried you with her own hands, and we've never treated you as anything less than precious."

Casco nodded, a little contrite; but she had heard the story so many times she really wanted to avoid a repetition. Knowing she had been an unwanted baby did not make her feel precious; it made her feel hollow, like nothing more than Claudio's discovery, his commodity.

"And Verre's House will keep you safe from dragons, wolves, witch-lords and time itself," said Mirko, his head low to hide a smile that would belie his sincere tone.

"Valiant gestures indeed, Mirko. And I am ever grateful," Casco intoned.

Claudio looked closely at her, searching for a hint of mockery, then decided it was not worth his while to fight with her. Soon enough he would be in a position to better deal with her little rebellions. He nodded curtly. "Now then, go to your work-cell, Casco. The buyers will be here at the end of the month to bid for the Empire bottle. It must be finished."

She smiled and the sharp tips of her incisors showed briefly. "The Incantor has finished the spell for the final engraving. I have it here."

She held up a thick creamy piece of parchment covered in precise script interwoven with symbols and sigils, the true meaning of which was known only to the men and women of the Incantors Guild. Casco had made Verre's House famous (and rich) with her unique ability to bind incantation to glass. This latest venture would be Verre's most ambitious; other Houses watched with envy and greed, willing them to fail.

"When did you become so reckless, girl? You blithely wave around our secrets?" Casco's fingernails sheared five tiny furrows into the parchment's top edge when Claudio snatched it from her grasp. Shaking his head furiously, he carefully scrolled the spell, spun Casco around and slid the paper tube into the leather *porteparchemin* she wore slung across her back. He clipped the case shut, then let his hands slip down her spine, lingering at her waist, the soft curve of her hips, before he caught himself and stepped back. Claudio cleared his throat. "Mirko, ensure that she goes straight to her work-cell. I must have a few words with the Incantors."

Pater Claudio strode out of the vestibule, muttering about young girls and unreliable employees.

Mirko put one large hand around Casco's upper arm. He pinched hard at the soft skin but she gave no sign that he had hurt her. "I won't even bother asking where you were—as if I didn't know. Spying on Daddy-dearest?"

Casco narrowed her eyes. Some days Mirko thought he saw fire there. "You are *not* my keeper, no matter what he says," she hissed. Yes, definitely sparks in the depths, wheeling and forming, flashing and moving, then gone as she controlled her temper.

He sighed and loosened his hold. "There's nothing either of us can do about that, girlie. I *am* charged with keeping you in my sights, whether you like it or not." Smoothing the fabric of her shirt as if trying to erase all evidence of his gruffness, Mirko muttered, "Mark my words, when he gets a ring on your finger he won't be so kindly about your little jaunts."

"Pater has not asked me to marry him."

"Nor will he—he assumes it will happen. Haven't you noticed since his wife died how much he watches you? Did so before too, I swear, but he's less circumspect about it now. So he waits, until the time is right, when it will be *respectable* for him to take his young ward to wife. It will be so tidy: Sepphoris' greatest Engraver married into its greatest House, and Pater Claudio with his bed warmed once more. You'll be a lovely February bride, sweetness. Keep those nails of yours sharp and those britches laced up tight, mark my words."

Casco *had* noticed. The official period of mourning for a wife was one year. She had a month's grace left.

Mirko patted her shoulder. "Just stop hanging around your father's house, Casco. There's nothing for you there and it only enrages Claudio."

"Let me worry about that."

• • •

Casco opened the book. Its covers had been crafted by ancient hands: smooth, polished copper encased the most secret, most puissant spells ever made for Verre's House in its four hundred year history. Not *all* of the spells, for no book could hold so many; the lesser ones lived on in smaller volumes in the Library's folio collection. These ones though—the ones with the power to entrap empires, to ensnare virgin brides in glass coffins, to create dresses of blown glass that felt and fell as soft as silk, to make crystal children so realistic they might even fool doting parents for a time—were collected and wielded by the engravers of Verre's House.

She took the inscribed parchment and smoothed it flat on the table's burnished wooden worktop. Using the diamond tips of her fingernails, she punctured a series of minute holes into the page's edge then inserted it in the very back of the book. Taking up a fine needle and a strand of flexible steel thread, Casco stitched it securely in place. She then propped the book up in the wrought-iron holder next to the table, open at the spell, and placed page-clips at the corners to make sure the leaves did not close. At last prepared, she turned her attention to the House's next great work.

Running a third of the length of the workbench and held firmly in the grip of a giant vice, lay the Empire bottle. The glass was thick and had a slightly green tint to it. Without inscription, the metre long by half metre wide bottle was proof of the Glassblowers' skill, but was otherwise forgettable. However, when Casco engraved the spell upon its body, the bottle would become a weapon: buyers from both sides of the current war would arrive to bid on it.

Casco flexed her hands, cracked her knuckles, circled her wrists like birds tied to a single point in the ground. She took a deep breath. This was the first Empire bottle Verre's House had been charged to build in fifty years; it was the first one Casco would engrave that wouldn't immediately be destroyed as a practice piece. When her task was complete, Casco's beautiful weapon would be capable of sucking an entire civilisation inside it: the ultimate victory for the side that could afford such a thing. She took a final look at the page, her memory catching the design and imprinting it on her mind. This would fund the House for a century, if carefully husbanded. She exhaled slowly, gave her hands a final shake and began.

Her nerves soon settled. Unlike other Engravers, who relied on forged implements and unwieldy blades, Casco and her tools were one and the same. Her diamond nails scored even the finest glass without shattering it; her dragon's blood seamlessly guided the Incantors' spells from her mind through her hands and into the glass. *Verba volant, scripta manent*, Pater Claudio always said, and he was right. Spoken words fly away, written words remain. Enchantments hummed through her body like a song while she worked and that song was permanently embedded in the glass beneath her fingertips.

Hours passed, the day shifted from sunshine to the silk-grey of afternoon. Outside her window Proclaimers climbed minarets, calling those who would come to evening prayer. A servant brought her supper tray, then cleared it away again, untouched. Lamplighters came in around five and the torches flared, creating a kind of artificial daylight so she could continue her work. In between reading chapters of a well-loved book, Mirko paced between the room's gaping fireplace and the tessellated fresco on the far wall, which depicted a scene from the Fall of the Dragons. Underscoring all of this activity was a disturbance that gradually, persistently, drew Casco's attention.

"Can you hear that?" she asked Mirko as she straightened up, her back aching. He shook his head.

She frowned, mimicked his gesture. A third of the bottle had been adorned, but it could not be activated until she had covered it, completing the spell. Casco ran a finger across the ridges and valleys of the glass's newly uneven surface while she listened.

She became aware, slowly, that she had been hearing the sound for some time—one day, or two? A week? She couldn't be sure; it had dug itself so deeply into her unconscious that she couldn't remember when it hadn't been there.

It was a long rhythmic hum, constant as a piece of machinery, low as a lullaby. Casco's heart raced, and her stomach pulsed with nerves and excitement. The room seemed to dissolve around her as the sound grew in intensity; the workbench, the bottle, Mirko, the nightingale's trill outside—everything faded to black and white as the rumbling bass conjured visions of bright scales rippling, stretched over taut muscles; of flames describing her figure, bare and shimmering with sweat; of someone large, musky, *strong* taking her in his firm grip; of talons encircling her slender waist, the sensation of sharp tips cutting into her torso a mixture of pleasure and pain. All this and more, suggested by the resonant, wordless song. Now she could feel it as a flush in her cheeks, a warmth in her chest that eased the ache perpetually residing there. Its reverberations moved lower until she caught her breath, blushed, embarrassed and swiftly wet. A sigh escaped her parted lips. *Is this how Pater Claudio feels?* she wondered, then shuddered to think of his unwanted, palsied caresses. The world rushed back in a flood of colour, but it paled in comparison to the vivid images the song had fixed in her mind.

"I'll be back in a moment, Mirko." She took a deep breath to steady her voice, to calm herself before she continued. "I need to . . . clear my head. Don't worry, I'll not leave the House." Her steps were quick and light with only the slightest *clack* as her heel-talon met the cool stone beneath. Mirko grunted his assent, and bent to retrieve the *Book of Oztin* from where he'd tucked it under his seat; Casco knew that before she had reached the door he would be absorbed in the tale of his favourite glass-girl heroine.

She stepped out into the corridor. After the brightness of her cell it took a moment for her dragonish membranes to adapt. They widened to absorb the dim orange light emanating from fire gutters running along the tops of the walls.

Casco felt herself pulled along by the thread of sound. Its cadences threatened to overwhelm her again; she walked as though in a dream, her gaze turned inward and outward simultaneously. Covering her ears was no use; the humming was not something heard, but something *felt*. It took all her energy to resist the urge to run.

The song grew louder as the trail led her down: down through the levels of Verre's House; down past the upper rooms, those that caught the light Casco and lesser Engravers required for their work; down past the large workshops where the mixers of coloured silica plied their trade; then down further to the glassblowers' residences, where the golden glow from their lehrs and annealers kept the gloom at bay. Down the last set of stairs, past the guards who gave her cautious looks even while they let her pass.

The steps beneath her feet were not cool, as might be expected of flagstones implanted in the earth so far underground. Instead they were warm, so warm Casco could feel the heat through the soles of her boots; her heel spur gave off the smell of hot ossified hair.

The noise swelled now, its rhythm throbbing through her veins more insistently. A monumental iron door, which was weighted with mortar and banded with silver and bronze, confronted her at the end of the hallway. She knew what waited beyond it. Two more guards, stationed one to each side of the barred entrance, looked askance at her.

"Engraver?"

"Let me pass."

"It's too dangerous, Engraver Casco. Pater Claudio would have our heads if any ill came to you."

"The creatures are *chained*. They are all chained and channelled, for flints' sake. There is no danger to me." She smiled at their hesitation. "They never hurt me. They know my blood; they know what I am."

The men shrugged and shot the bolt on the only door that would keep the fire of the furnace dragons at bay.

Casco slipped through the opening.

The chamber seemed to spread across a width greater than the entire compound of Verre's House above, an effect that was enhanced by the tunnels leading off into the darkness of its far walls. An enormous central furnace rose from the floor and stretched to the vaulted ceiling high above; its embers bathed the room with a simmering orange glow. Casco's pale skin adopted a warm bronze sheen and her hair scales flickered with reflected tongues of fire.

At the four compass points were four huge cages, and in each one lay a dragon. Three were older creatures, their majestic scales now hoary with age. They faced arched apertures in the furnace's brick walls, though none of them were firing. The fourth was black, shiny, his musculature evident and beautiful under his plates. He was a robust young firedrake; his silver eyes locked on Casco's slender form as she approached. His tongue flicked out to snap up a mouthful of brimstone from the trough in front of his cage. Had she been two steps to the left, his glistening grey tongue would have wrapped around *her* instead. This thought echoed those inspired by the song too closely; she blushed, grew suddenly shy, and wondered where her breath had gone.

A snort like an abbreviated chuckle came from Casco's left. She caught the large emerald dragon winking at her. Her flush deepened. The emerald had been at Verre's House for decades, ancient long before an infant Casco first toddled past his crucible. He was from the greatest line of dragons in Sepphoris, and renowned for his keen eye. She nodded respectfully, her gaze steady, observing the traditional courtesies, which he returned.

Casco turned next to the northern dragon, a vermilion female well beyond breeding years. She had always been aloof, regal, but as the girl touched the bars of the firedrake's cage, the red rolled onto her side, exposing a soft underbelly. It was a gesture of trust, of acceptance. Without a second thought, Casco tilted her own head back, unbuttoned the neck of her tunic, and bared her pale throat.

In the southern cage, the yellow gave her a disdainful look. Something tightened in her stomach—it was the kind of look she'd seen on her father's face. The sort of look that said she was such a diluted creature that she was worth nothing.

The music from the firedrake's cage crescendoed. Made bold by this welcome, Casco reached through to rest a hand against his hide. The scales were strangely cool. She could feel the tremor of his humming.

She had watched, not many weeks since, when first the dragon-catchers had brought him to Verre's House, drugged and bound. They had taken his freedom and his joy. Now he was channelled like the others and, barring an act of gods or accident, he would spend the rest of his life beneath the earth, a slave to the furnaces. She wondered if he missed the life they'd stolen from him; if he had a family that yearned for his return.

"Little half-thing." The voice sounded as soft thunder in her head, an edge of contempt brushing gently against her pride.

"What?" Casco looked around the furnace room, but there was only her and the dragons. She turned back to find the drake's eyes upon her. Inside them, a storm, a fire like nothing she'd ever seen. Inside his eyes, a universe, all colours and yet none; all life and all death. Love and hatred, pain and comfort, balm for sorrow and a talon to the heart. She wanted to fall into them, for there surely the ache would cease. She leaned closer to the bars, trying to defy their solidity.

"Half-thing, neither one nor the other, but blooded of both. How do you live?" There was mockery in the question. She pulled away.

"Who are you to ask me that? No one has chained me."

He laughed and sparks flew. "Your chains are not visible to the eye. I am Feus, prince among my kind."

"A prince in shackles. You are a tinderbox with scales," she spat. His candour rattled her; the truth of his words seared.

"Why did you call me here?" she asked.

There was a pause. "I could not *not* do it," he whispered.

"Feus," she said softly, her gaze sweeping around the room. The older dragons now slept, or at least feigned it. "Mighty Feus, reduced to a furnace feeder."

She turned away and was five paces from the door when his voice throbbed through her once more. "Don't go."

Casco lingered for a fraction of a second. *Flames on bare flesh—sinuous tongue lapping—claws tickling, pressing—*she shook her head to clear it. Feus' timbre filled the hollow inside her, it woke something, it made her feel new and bold. It made her feel different, maybe *too* different. She kept walking.

She opened the door, heaving its great weight slowly, then left it to clang shut behind her. It did not stop the sound of his song, merely dulled it.

• • •

"Would you like some lunch?"

Casco jumped. She hadn't heard Pater Claudio approach. She wondered how long he'd been standing behind her, clutching a bowl of soup. Watching her.

"Thank you." The pottery dish made a dull clunk as Claudio rested it on the workbench. Casco wasn't hungry, hadn't been since she'd spoken with Feus last week. The things he had said—the weight of his gaze! And that silver tongue . . . Her work-cell, the largest studio in the House, suddenly felt stifling.

"It's not very warm, I'm afraid."

"Pardon?"

"The soup." Pater Claudio drew closer to the Empire bottle, rested his hand on Casco's shoulder as he admired her handiwork.

No place in either world. Casco fumed silently. *But look at what I can create.* She wiped an invisible fleck of dust from the thing's smooth base. *Surely that's something.*

"Beautiful," said Pater Claudio. He was no longer looking at the bottle.

A sign that I belong here. She scraped her fingernail along a newly etched symbol, completing its curving stroke. With that, she finished detailing the trunk, two days ahead of schedule. She had only the base and stem left. It had taken all her concentration to keep working, to resist the pull of Feus' song. The effort exhausted her, not least because she was so short on sleep.

For six consecutive nights, her dreams had been unlike any she'd ever had—in these, she didn't feel alone. A presence, always hidden but undeniably *there*, shadowed her every move. She could sense him behind her, beneath her, around her as she floated from nonsensical fancy to fancy. One night, kittens tap-danced on an inverted canoe for her pleasure, waving miniature Empire Bottles in their gloved paws; but their purrs soon transformed into a sultry, familiar rhythm, and she felt her unseen lover press up against her as kittens became fire-breathing sirens. The next night, she swam the seas off the coast of Bandragoon; waves lapped at her naked skin, pulled her further away from her unknown goal, until a hydra surfaced to serve as her steed. And as it slid up beneath her, forcing her to straddle its slippery back, she awoke with a throbbing between her legs that had left her gasping. All week, over and over, it had been the same; the dreams, the insistent humming, the *reveille*—

"Just beautiful." Casco was shaken from her thoughts. She felt Claudio's breath against her cheek, the press of his thumbs kneading small circles into the firm muscles between her shoulder blades.

She stepped away from his grip. "I'm sorry, Pater," she stammered, remembering Mirko's warnings and horrified that the older man might now infiltrate her nocturnal sojourns. "I think I've left a scroll with the Incantors." She fumbled with her *porte-parchemin*, scraping its soft leather with her nails in her haste. "I really must go and collect it, immediately."

Pater Claudio sighed, then called for Mirko. "Go with her," he instructed. "Our deadline fast approaches."

• • •

"Let me take that," Casco said. "I'm going that way."

The courier paused, but did not relinquish the carefully wrapped package. He was new to Verre's House—she could tell by his boots, which were still shiny and looked stiff. His gait told her that his feet were pinched and blistered after hours of delivering the Guild's creations to buyers. Sweat ringed the cowl of his woollen tunic— he would learn, if he lasted long enough, that it was too hot to be worn in late spring. A saturated strap-mark ran diagonally across his chest where his messenger's *porte-livraison* had been hanging moments before.

"It's no trouble," she continued. It wasn't really a lie. She would have done anything to get out for a while; away from Claudio's advances, Mirko's watchful eye, Feus' unrelenting call. As she made to sneak through the vestibule she had heard the young courier being given his assignment. She had also heard his worn out sigh. If she could inveigle the boy, she would simply need to remember to bring something sweet back to placate Mirko. Then again, making the delivery would take no more than half an hour; he might not even notice her absence.

"I know where the Belluaire house is—it's right next to the arena, beyond the square with all the pigeons. The large one with the gables, right? I'm sure I've seen it before." Her voice was sweet and low; something of the dragon's song limned her tone. She could see it working: his shoulders slumped, the lines of his face relaxed and she knew she'd won even when he tried to argue.

"But, Engraver," he said, clutching the parcel close to his sodden chest, "this must be delivered to Sevante Belluaire himself. Do you know him?"

Casco grabbed the package and he did not fight her. She smiled. "Oh, yes, I know him very well."

She pushed the messenger toward the glass doors and told him to find himself lunch at the Dragon's Breath Inn down the street. She would meet him there and hand over the signed chit to say Belluaire received his parcel. In a flash of cunning, she told him to drop by the bakery and get the sesame pastries Mirko liked so much. The boy's face broke out in a dazed smile when she pressed first a tarnished silver coin into his palm for the breadman, then a crystal shilling for his trouble.

If only her thoughts were as easy to organise. Parcel in hand, her mind wandered as her feet travelled the familiar route to the Arena Quarter. The sun shone warm on Casco's face, easing the tension that had settled in her shoulders. Turning the corner at Lost Kraken's Shrine, Casco passed a troop of hunters gathering supplies for their next expedition. Their wagon was pulled by a pair of mangy dragons, both too small to do more than menial labour. The beasts' hides were dull, not just from a coating of dust. They looked unhealthy: their scales scarred, their wings clipped. They smelled sour, not musky; not virile, like—

Stop it, she told herself, but she still felt the ache at the base of her spine, the tingle left by an imagined talon. The citadel's clock chimed the hour; she hitched up the *porte-livraison*. It was midday, the perfect time to be out in Sepphoris. The streets teemed with people: guildsmen ran errands or scrambled at food carts for quick luncheons; gutterscoops bumped through crowds, saving boots from the mess transport dragons deposited in their travels; hawkers set up shop on the roadsides, selling everything from pontils to marvers. Casco's heel spurs clicked a merry rhythm as she picked up the pace, her hair scales streaming like quicksilver behind her.

For a moment, surrounded by the throng, she felt inconspicuous. With such a diverse mix of people and dragons about, nobody paid her any attention. As she ran toward her father's house she felt, however briefly, like a normal girl.

This is how it should always feel, she thought with a smile, *when you're going home.*

• • •

Casco's hands shook. Her palms were cool and dry on the package, but her heart raced. She knocked, quickly but insistently, then stepped back. When the heavily carved door swung open on well-oiled hinges, Casco's breath stopped.

Would he recognise her? What would he say? Did he think of her? Did he think of the day when he left her in the Dying Place? Did he regret what he'd done? Was he proud of her skill as an Engraver? Would he call her by name? Would he even remember her name?

"What can I do for you, miss?" The housemaid's raisin brown eyes, set in a shrivelled face, stared back at her.

Casco knew herself for a fool: Sevante Belluaire hadn't answered his own door in years. She said nothing, but held the chit out and the woman used a stub of pencil fished from her apron to scribble her sigil on the bottom of the paper. Casco handed the maid the parcel and the servant curtsied. Casco turned to make a quick exit.

She ran head-on into her father.

"Afternoon, sir," the maid greeted him.

He didn't seem to register Casco's presence. "Afternoon, Antonina."

Casco stared straight at Sevante. His skin was a deep golden brown, his wide eyes green and a scar bisected his left cheek, giving the permanent suggestion of a wink. His ruddy hair was peppered with white.

Her mood shattered, like a parison rolled too swiftly from the furnace. She couldn't quite understand why she was drawn back here. In the last year she had begun to gravitate to the house on Murano Street, surreptitiously watching Belluaire and his family (second wife, four new daughters, the youngest only three). She sipped at the dew of their lives like a moth drinking from a raindrop. Looking now at her father's striking face, Casco knew only longing and ache. Hatred overwhelmed her; hatred for the man who had cast her aside because she was different, because she reminded him that he had caused Priling's death with his arrogance. She shared nothing with Sevante Belluaire except blood. She glared at her father as he studiously avoided looking at her.

From inside the house a woman's voice called, "Who is it, Antonina? Send them away before Sevante returns, won't you?"

The maid opened her mouth to respond, but Casco's father cut her off with a brisk wave.

"It's nobody important," he replied, finally looking Casco full in the face. "It's no one."

Casco stumbled down the stairs, her heel-talons making a silent retreat impossible. It didn't matter: Sevante had already gone inside, closing the door noisily behind him.

• • •

"Casco? Engraver Casco?"

Casco did not slow down. The crowds parted in front of her. There was the sound of running and a hand caught at her arm. Casco did not like being manhandled; she swung about, her fingers splayed and her nails caught the sun.

"Engraver?" the young man said faintly. He was tall, handsome and muscular, but she could see he was terrified of her.

"Master Fourneau," she said. "Forgive me. You startled me."

He recovered his good grace, hooding his fear as quickly as one might snuff a candle. But she had already seen it; and she knew that hatred often sprang from such things. Forneau, son of the Master of Vitrine's House, Verre's greatest rival, made her uneasy. She had not forgotten his torments when they were children in the schoolroom.

"Easily forgiven and most understandable. My apologies for— mauling you, it was not seemly."

She gave a vague smile and waved his words away. "How may I help?"

"Oh, it's nothing particular. I simply wished to say hello. I have just returned from seeing Pater Claudio. Two of our dragons are almost at the end of their span. Nothing for them but the arena. Vitrine is sending its dragon-catchers out soon and wondered if Verre would like to join the expedition." He smiled.

Sometimes rivals joined a hunt together—the cost and risks of the dragon harvest were huge and not even Houses as rich as Verre or Vitrine liked to bear the expense alone.

"I understand you have only that young firedrake—the rest are, shall we say, superannuated? Barely fit for arena fodder."

"They've served our House well," she said defensively. "They deserve better than slaughter for petty amusement."

"The firedrake, though, would be a fine sight under Belluaire's instruction!" he said, more to himself than her.

"Thankfully Verre's House does not waste its finest resources," she said coldly.

"Of course not." He raised his hands to placate her. She wondered why he was going out of his way to be so agreeable. She backed away. He followed, drawing near enough that Casco could practically taste his breath. His face, pressed so close to her own, had lost its veneer of kindness; his jaw was set with a disdain that barely masked his hunger.

"You will forgive me, Master Forneau, I am very late and must return. They will be looking for me."

"Yes. Strange to see you without your guard-dog. Give the big man the slip?" he sneered.

"Good day." She turned on her heel and dived into the wash of the crowd, losing herself to his gaze as soon as she could.

• • •

"How much trouble can you get yourself into?" Mirko asked as Casco handed him a sesame pastry, cold and rapidly stiffening. He closed the door to her work-cell.

"I was asked to make a delivery, Mirko. That's why I'm late." She stood in front of the Empire bottle, trying to gather her thoughts.

"You're certainly a popular girl. Suitors coming out of the cracks hither and yon," he said around the pastry. Casco frowned.

"Forneau was here, you know."

"I know. Saw the little weasel in the street and he told me so."

"Did he tell you why he was here?" Mirko keep talking and chewing at the same time. Casco knew that if she looked at him, she'd be treated to the sight of masticated pastry being tossed about in his mouth. She chose not to look.

"To see if we wanted in on their dragon hunt. He made fun of our dragons, by the way." *Not Feus though*, she thought, *his tone was quite envious of the firedrake.* She ignored the flutter this realisation caused in her belly.

"Least of his sins. Claudio yelled at him within five minutes. Fool had the gall to ask for your hand. As if Verre will give you up."

Casco felt cold.

"But, I don't want to marry *anyone.*" It was true. She had never wanted it, had never felt an attraction to another person so strong as to warrant any action.

Mirko spoke gently. "Casco, everyone marries. It's the way all the guilds work. Glassblowers, engravers, incantors, all pair off with one another; the Houses stay populated; Sepphoris prospers. It's natural. You've been an exception this long because—well, Pater didn't want you to marry outside the House. He was . . . waiting."

"I won't marry anyone."

"Then they can appeal to our Guild. You know that. You know they can rule on marriages. If you really wanted to marry outside the House, you could put a case together, present it at the Assembly if it came to that. They might let you go." He shook his head. "But, in the end, you'd still have to marry *someone*, here or elsewhere." He popped the last bit of pastry into his mouth. "In case you haven't noticed, you're kind of unique. Any children you have will be valuable."

He could see her trembling, whether from grief or rage he wasn't sure. "Casco, your life doesn't belong to you, sweetheart."

She fled. Out of the room and down the stairs, down, down, down, to where the firedrake's hum was strongest. She had ignored him for so many, many days. It felt like months, but she wouldn't relax until she felt the deep rumble of his song in her bones, soothing her, calling her down. The fact that she noticed the dragon's absence so keenly told her, to her chagrin, how much she had come to need him.

Only Feus was in his cage. It wouldn't be long before the keepers came for him; the others had already been taken to their cells for the night. Casco stormed across the room. Feus raised one eyelid, kept his chin resting on the floor, his long tail curled around the great expanse of his body.

"Why did you call me?" she yelled. "Everything's gone wrong since then."

"I am not the catalyst, Casco. I'm merely at the confluence of events." He paused, then went on, less certainly. "My kind mate for life. When a dragon finds his equal, he knows. The song begins— it is a sound we cannot produce at any other time. For better or worse, little half-thing, you summoned my song."

Her hands pushed through the bars. She ran them over his scales; heat wafted from his open mouth as he sighed. Then she scratched, hard with her diamond nails, and left marks. He laughed, breathy, aroused. He hooked one claw through the bars, and caressed her neck, the talon sharp enough to sever her head in a heartbeat should he wish it. It felt nothing like when Pater Claudio touched her.

Fire raced through her veins as Feus traced the outline of her clavicle, her arm, her hand. Blue sparks struck from her fingertips as she scratched him more vigorously; she inhaled the heady steam of his breath and watched as curls of smoke escaped her lips. His tongue flicked at her torso, grazing her stomach, her breasts. Flames swirled in Casco's eyes; the dark scales of her hair stiffened, bristling up until a magnificent crest draped her head and shoulders like a queen's mantle. Feus wrapped his tongue around her wrist, drawing her closer; he gently nipped at her fingers. Casco pulled back, but didn't step away from the cage. A bead of warm blood welled from her index finger.

She stared at the crimson stain.

"My mother was in the arena," she whispered. "Dragon's blood killed her."

"It's poisonous, little half-thing. But you were very small, not fully formed. What killed your mother merely changed you: it made you what you are. But blood calls to blood, Casco. You've been a chrysalis for too long. Let go of your human flesh. Come home."

"I don't know how," she said, her voice trembling. His silvery tongue caressed her anew; its touch was dry and surprisingly smooth, intimate.

"Fire," he whispered. "It burns away the meat, leaving only the dragon."

"I'll die," she said.

"Trust me."

There was a rattle from one of the tunnels. The keepers were returning. Casco pulled away, her breath coming in ragged bursts, and shook her head.

• • •

Casco stood alone before the wide expanse of the East Salon's windows, looking out over the sea. Floor to ceiling ran the strongest, thickest glass Verre's House could produce, strengthened by myriad incantations etched around the edges. They would last a thousand years against storms, attacking dragons, whatever might be thrown at the House's waterside facade. She was reflected against the dark glass. Out beyond her, lightning bolts threw themselves across the night sky, danced above the sea, writhed like serpents.

The girl concentrated on her reflection: the ghostly impression of her dragon self seemed to stretch higher and wider than the window could capture. Her scales, lapis lazuli in colour, were accented with starlight. She had a long tail, lovely wings, her eyes were lashless, slanted and silver, her limbs were muscular and sleek; she was monumental and beautiful and overwhelming. Never before had she seen this aspect of herself. It was breathtaking.

She was so absorbed that she did not hear anyone enter the room, nor did she see Pater Claudio until he seemed to materialise next to her in the glass. She started, focused on his image. His outline was not solid, a weak wavering line.

He rested his hands on her shoulders, tried a smile. Casco smiled back, a broken fleeting expression.

"Casco, it's time we had a talk." He directed her to one of the couches. "I'd wanted to leave this discussion a while longer, but circumstances have forced my hand."

"Pater—"

"No, let me finish. You know how fond I am of you, how we have always cared for you. You are important to us not merely for your exquisite craft, but also . . . in a personal sense. I know it isn't many months since my dear wife died, but I feel it is time to take another bride."

"Pater, I—"

"Casco, please! I have no children. There will be no further Claudians to follow unless I do. You are young, exceptional. I would be honoured if you would agree to be my wife." There was no question in his voice.

Casco tried to swallow her revulsion. "Pater, I have always thought of you as a father. This is a—great change."

"I know, I know," he said kindly. "But there is no blood between us and the Guild has given its consent."

"You have already been to the Guild?" There was an edge to her voice that he could not have missed.

"Of course, child. And they were only too happy to see us settled."

Casco rose, strode back to the window. Her reflection had withdrawn its wings, lost its vibrant blue glow, dwindled in size. Now she faced the version of herself she'd seen every day for eighteen years: a pale girl with fire smouldering in her eyes. Outside, winds whipped the seas into a fury. A clap of thunder muffled Casco's response.

"You'll have to speak up," Pater Claudio said, leaning forward, "I didn't quite catch that."

She didn't turn from the window. "I said, what if I decline?" Irritation flashed across Claudio's reflected features, and Casco heard him exhale sharply.

"Perhaps I've misled you," he said, standing. "By implying you had a choice. The proposal was merely a courtesy; a token of my affection."

Casco spun around. "Affection?" She laughed bitterly. "Is that what you call it? Tethering me to a workbench, treating me like a prisoner, punishing me if I steal a few precious moments for myself? Never caring about what I want—and then offering me a lifetime of the same? Spare me the joy of such *affection*, Pater. I'll have none of it."

"You won't deny me, child. Not after all I've done for you."

Casco's face flushed. Her eyes gleamed with unbridled rage and her incisors glinted as she growled, "I would rather you had left me to die."

"Of all the ungrateful, half-blood things to say—"

"Enough!" In the window, Casco's dragon reflection bloomed anew, rearing its head; her wings spread wide, and her tail lashed violently. Her voice filled the grand chamber. "I've had enough! Enough of being trapped in this House; enough of being neither one thing nor the other. Enough of you. Let me alone!"

Pater Claudio's head snapped back as if he'd been slapped. His face and shoulders sagged. Folding his hands carefully in his lap, he straightened, sitting as tall as his aging back would allow. He waited for the echoes of Casco's words to fade before he spoke.

"It appears, my love, that you've become overly agitated." He snapped his fingers; Mirko appeared from the antechamber. The bodyguard stood framed in the doorway while Claudio gave his instructions. "Escort Casco to her room now, Mirko. She's not fit for company this evening. We'll have to continue our conversation in the morning, when she's regained her composure."

Mirko slowly sidled up to his charge, a man obliged to act although he clearly had no taste for the task. Casco stood her ground. "There's nothing to talk about—don't touch me!" She wrenched her arm from her guard's meaty grasp. Glaring at Claudio, she repeated, "There is *nothing* further to discuss."

"Don't be ridiculous, Casco. We must make arrangements for our wedding. But it can wait for the morning. Until then, I bid you goodnight."

Lightning flared over the rough seas, briefly filling the salon with its harsh glare. In the window's reflection, a small girl was dragged from the room; an old man looked on, smiling, until darkness returned.

• • •

"Engraver, good morning."

Forneau was at the door of her work-cell, Mirko close behind him. Her bodyguard's face was set in annoyance, but he knew his position was too low to speak rudely to Vitrine's heir, no matter how much he wanted to do so.

"Master Forneau," said Casco. "You are an early visitor."

"The dragons. I have come to speak with your keepers about the new dragons. Would you do the honour of escorting me? I cannot wander Verre's House unattended—who knows what secrets I might discover?" He grinned, looking past her at the half-completed Empire bottle.

"Very well," she said. "Keep an eye on the candles for me, Mirko. It seems such a waste to snuff them when I'll be back up in a matter of minutes."

"I should probably come with you, Casco," Mirko said.

Fourneau leaned toward Casco and barked once, like a watchdog, then tried to mask what he'd done by covering his mouth and coughing. She glared at him, and said, "That won't be necessary, Mirko. We really won't be long."

The furnace room was dimly lit; none of the dragons had yet been brought from their cells. There was only the low glow of the brazier, bronzing both Fourneau and his reluctant guide.

"When will you hunt?" asked Casco.

"Tomorrow. I still hope to convince Pater Claudio to sell me that firedrake."

"Feus is not for sale."

"Feus? You've given him a pet name?" Forneau laughed as if she was an amusing child.

"It's his name. He told me."

"Told you? My, my, you are a rare creature, Casco. Rare indeed." He grinned. "No wonder Pater Claudio wants you for himself."

"I will not marry Pater. I will not be mated with anyone against my will."

"He is very old. Perhaps you prefer younger flesh." He pushed her to the bars of Feus' cage and pressed himself against her. The metal bit into her back and Forneau's teeth bit into her tongue and lips. He was careful to imprison her hands and make sure she couldn't use her nails. She was so shocked she hadn't time to react. She flailed uselessly in his grasp.

From the mouth of one of the tunnels came an almighty roar and the shouts of the keepers as Feus broke free of them. They had become so used to the submission of channelled dragons they were unprepared for the fury of an outraged beast. Forneau released Casco and backed away from her, his face white as bone, his eyes large as terror seized him. He couldn't bring himself to turn his back on the dragon so he saw the fire as it came for him, the heat drying out his eyeballs before it even hit.

There was very little left after the first burst of flame. By that time, the keepers had rallied; they hung on the ends of the chains attached to Feus' collar and one of them jabbed the soft underside of his neck with a drug-dipped dart to tranquilise him. It took only moments to work, but it was too late for Forneau who lay smoking on the floor of the furnace chamber.

Casco looked in horror, not at Forneau, but at Feus, knowing he had just condemned himself to the arena.

• • •

"I will marry you, Pater, but my bride price is the life of Feus."

"The firedrake? Stop this foolishness, Casco. Dragons don't have names, they are not pets!"

"They name themselves just as we do!" She took a deep breath to calm herself, knowing that aggravating him further would not advance her cause. She knelt before him, hating herself, put her hands on his knees, then slid them up to his thighs.

"Pater." She paused. "Claudio. This is the one thing I ask of you. Grant me this one small boon and I will belong to you and Verre's House forever. I will give you sons to carry on your line. In this way I will give you immortality, if you just grant me this one thing in return."

He wavered, distracted by the stroking of her fingers and nails.

She smiled. "Besides, what kind of business sense does it make to waste a perfectly good firedrake? He saw me threatened and reacted. He has removed Vitrine's heir—done you a favour, really. Reward him with his life."

She leaned forward, lifted her face and offered her lips.

• • •

Mirko gave her a pitying look. Casco was bent over the Empire bottle. The base had been completed; now she was preparing the bottle neck and stopper. He watched her, thinking she'd gotten thinner and paler in the weeks since Forneau's death; worse since she'd agreed to marry Claudio.

She looked up and smiled wearily at him. "Nearly finished." She gestured at the bottle. "The buyers are bound to offer a hefty price for this—"

"He lied," Mirko interrupted. She gave him an uncomprehending look. "Pater Claudio."

"Have the buyers withdrawn?" Casco stood. "Are there any buyers at all?"

"No, no. That's not it. It's just—the firedrake goes to the arena this evening."

She sagged, all the life gone from her.

Mirko had been ordered to keep his charge on a tight leash, to not let her out of his sight, to keep her away from news and people who might tell her anything. He had done his job, he had kept her in the dark; and she had not fought him, distracted as she was by her impending marriage and the demons she kept tightly inside her mind. Seeing her thus, working on the Empire bottle, about to become even more of a slave, he couldn't lie to her any longer. "What will you do?"

She began to weep.

"You are better than this, Casco. What are you going to do?"

• • •

"Tonight, you will witness a battle to the death!" Sevante Belluaire's deep voice boomed over the appreciative crowd. He stood on a dais at the arena's south end, facing a series of tunnels, each of which led to the gladiators' subterranean chambers. Black and barred, the doorways looked like a row of rotten teeth held in place by rusty bands.

Casco watched her father's performance from the northernmost tunnel. A few choice whisperings in a young guard's ear and a handful of shiny coins in his palm had gained her this prime position.

Much as a king would from his elevated position, the beastmaster surveyed his audience, smiling condescendingly. The dais's wooden planks hovered over a filthy creature tethered to the arena floor. Belluaire was poised near the platform's edge; the crack of his whip punctuated each of his sentences with a stinging flick against Feus' hide. Weighed down by chains as thick as a strongman's thigh, the dragon could not retaliate.

"This devil," Belluaire boasted, "soaked up a century's heat from the Arnuvian deserts, where he feasted on boiling blood, flame-cactus and spitfire! Our bravest 'catchers tracked him along a perilous route—from roasting sands to Haverna's blackest volcanoes—until they finally caught him bathing in craters of bubbling lava. This devil—"

Sigils paraded through Casco's mind and she whispered the unbinding incantation she had found hidden away in one of the minor spell folios. Looking at the rapt faces in the crowd, each of them riveted by Belluaire's false words, Casco's lip curled in disgust. He had such power to charm; she could almost believe her father had a bit of the dragon in him.

"We've seen many a fire-breather in this arena." Belluaire paused for dramatic effect, lifted his eyes to the banners plastered against all of the building's vertical surfaces. Casco followed his gaze, taking in the variegated shreds of cloth and tinsel that commemorated the arena's fallen warriors. Her eyes caught on a gold and burgundy pennant, still rich in hue despite its age.

Priling.

Belluaire continued, "Many a fierce beast has torn human limb from limb before us, but none—" he raised his arm and spun it to gain momentum, "—none has caused as much damage as this one!" The whip lashed across Feus' flanks with skin-splitting force. The firedrake reared his head and loosed a spout of fury-driven flames.

"Lies!" Casco hissed, her dismay submerged in waves of the crowd's delight.

"Which of our brave gladiators will defeat this animal?" The sound of metal scraping across metal underscored the crescendos of Belluaire's rousing speech—the tunnels' heavy iron gates began to lift. Casco rattled the slow-moving barrier, urging it upward, still shaping the Incantors' sigils in her mind.

"Who will keep him from our children?" At this, the beastmaster turned away from the dragon and faced row upon row of seats ascending skyward at vertiginous angles. His youngest daughter waved down at him from the third row, her blonde ringlets bouncing as she proudly wiggled her plump arm for all to see that it was *her* daddy down there. "Shall we summon the gladiators?" The crowd cheered their assent. Casco heard the tramp of feet behind her. She dropped to the ground and wriggled beneath the gap. She strode across the arena floor as Belluaire continued his address.

"Strong Heracles, perhaps? Quick Induvio? The Incredible Serbonne? There are so many favourites—which of them will save my little Lapis from this—"

"I will."

She spoke loud and clearly, but had to repeat herself twice before the audience fell silent. Casco's boots crunched across the pebbles and bones littering the arena floor. Her breathing was calm, her posture assured. She inhaled the scent of sulphur and scorched earth, tasted salt with each step she took toward the dais. "Call off your killers, Father. Feus is mine."

A sharp hiss echoed around the stadium, a collective drawing in of breath; Casco wasn't sure whether it was because she had claimed her father or the dragon that crouched at his feet. One voice, coming from the stands behind Belluaire's platform, raised a more fervent protest than the rest:

"Casco!"

She kept walking. Pater Claudio stood and called again, his hands clenched at his sides, his face livid. "Stop right where you are." She ignored him. "Stop! Wife!"

"Wife?" Feus' voice resounded in Casco's mind. "I had hoped one day to call you that myself." The words warmed her, filled the empty space in her chest. "Then do so," she whispered. She drew as close to the dragon as she could without coming within range of her father's whip.

"Guards! Gladiators!" Pater Claudio's commands rang shrilly across the stadium. He had descended the stairs next to his seat, and was now leaning precariously over the protective barrier that kept the audience from falling twenty feet down to the sunken showground. "Get her out of there, Belluaire, or so help me you'll never see another one of our dragons!"

The portcullises had been fully raised and gladiators followed Casco to the foot of Belluaire's platform. Torchlight reflected off the points of their spears.

"He's mine," she repeated, staring up at her father, then switched her gaze to Pater. She held out the Empire bottle's incantation scroll; its edges were ragged where she'd torn it from the great book. It no longer mattered—the bottle itself lay in shards on the floor of her work-cell.

"Belluaire!" Pater Claudio paced along the barrier like a caged tiger. "Damn you—by all the gods—you can't do this!"

Casco thought she saw her father's eyes flick to Priling's banner and back before he said, under his breath, "This is no fault of mine. Let her stay if she's got a death-wish." An artificial smile spread across his face as turned his back on Pater Claudio's protestations and shouted, "A fight like none before! The beast faces the hybrid!"

The applause was deafening. Belluaire urged the gladiators back; then he sketched an elaborate bow, and tossed Casco his whip. "There's nothing else I can give you," he said. "You've brought this upon yourself."

Casco ignored the whip. She turned to face the dragon.

"Feus, I trust you: burn away the flesh."

"*Verba volant*, little half-blood: spoken words fly away. Prove yourself."

"I trust you," she repeated and knelt before him, placing the parchment on the ground. A woman in the audience screamed.

Pater Claudio had negotiated his way through the rows of seats and began to lower himself down one of the many rope ladders ringing the arena's perimeter, quick exits for the Wranglers. Casco paid no attention and took brief moments to caress Feus' ravaged hide, her fingers glancing gently along the dull edges of his scales, eliciting a groan of pleasure from her mate. The long silver tongue flicked out and touched the back of her neck, whisper-soft. Casco swallowed hard and removed her hand, began inscribing the symbols of the unbinding incantation onto the dragon's chains with her nails.

"I trust you," she said, intent on her work. Eyes cast down, focused, she was unaware of her lover's fiery kiss until it had engulfed her. The scroll beside her became ashes.

The flames hurt less than she had thought, and more. She felt her human flesh drying out, then curling and finally burning away. New muscle grew, her body changed shape and scales sprouted all over. Her heartbeat slowed and the heat of her blood dropped. Wings stretched from her back, larger and more powerful than those she'd seen in her reflection. Her nails, grown thick with metamorphosis, sheared through Feus' remaining bonds.

Free, she thought, and the joy that shot through her was unlike anything she'd ever experienced. Every inch of her body tingled with it. Stretching her long neck, she nuzzled her lover's torso then nipped at his flanks, teasing him into action. She purred, expelling short bursts of steam from flared nostrils as she butted her sleek head gently against his muscular shoulder. Feus reared and roared. Casco caught the thrum of his humming, now rekindled and transcending to a victorious trumpeting; laughter bubbled in her throat. She opened her mouth and joined her song to his.

A storm of sand rose from the arena floor and blasted over the audience. The night sky was a satin backdrop as the two dragons stretched their wings and took flight.

• • • • • • • • • • •

ABOUT THE CONTRIBUTORS

R J ASTRUC's short fiction has appeared in like a bajillion magazines including *Strange Horizons, Daily Science Fiction, Abyss and Apex*, and *Aurealis*. Her latest novel, *Harmonica + Gig*, is available from all good bookstores in Australia. You should totally buy it, seriously. Find RJ online at www.rachelastruc.com or on twitter as @astruc.

PETER M BALL is a Brisbane writer who attended Clarion South in 2007. His novella, *Horn*, was published by Twelfth Planet Press in 2009 and the sequel, Bleed, in 2010. His recent short stories have appeared in *Strange Horizons, Apex, Shimmer, Sprawl*, and the *Interfictions II* anthology. He can be found online at www.petermball.com.

ALAN BAXTER is a British-Australian author living on the south coast of NSW, Australia. He writes dark fantasy, sci fi and horror, rides a motorcycle and loves his dog. He also teaches Kung Fu. Read extracts from his novels, a novella and short stories at his website www.alanbaxteronline.com and feel free to tell him what you think. About anything.

In high school, JENNY BLACKFORD won the Hunter Valley Research Association Prize for a poem that was later published in *Dolly*. There was a break of several decades before the poem reprinted here, "Mirror", appeared in *Midnight Echo 4*. Another poem is forthcoming in *ME 6*. Her six published stories for adults so far have received three Honorable Mentions from Gardner Dozois and one from Ellen Datlow. Her website is www.jennyblackford.com.

GITTE CHRISTENSEN was born and raised in Australia, but also lived in Denmark for 12 years before returning to study journalism at RMIT. Her speculative fiction has appeared in *Aurealis, Andromeda Spaceways Inflight Magazine, Moonlight Tuber, The NSW School Magazine, Bards and Sages Quarterly*, the anthology

The Tangled Bank, and other publications. To escape keyboards, she regularly grabs a tent and a horse and goes trailing riding through distant mountains.

MATTHEW CHRULEW's novella *The Angælien Apocalypse*, published by Twelfth Planet Press, was a finalist in the 2010 Aurealis Awards. "Schubert by Candlelight" is his second published Androphagi story. The first, "Between the Memories," originally appeared in *Aurealis* #38/39, was shortlisted for the 2007 Australian Shadows Award, and was reprinted in *Australian Dark Fantasy & Horror Volume Three*. He is working on a number of other related stories, and a novel, *The Worm Runners*. His blog Negentropy is at matthewchrulew.wordpress.com.

BILL CONGREVE is a writer and independent publisher living in the Blue Mountains in NSW. He has a BA in communications, holds accreditation in editing from IPed, and has won awards for genre criticism, editing and publishing. His stories have appeared in anthologies and magazines around the world, and he edited the horror anthologies *Intimate Armageddons* and *Southern Blood*. His independent publishing company, MirrorDanse Books, specialises in SF and horror.

RJURIK DAVIDSON is an Associate Editor of *Overland* magazine. He is the author of the collection, *The Library of Forgotten Books*. His novel *Unwrapped Sky* will be published by Tor books 2012 and his script *The Uncertainty Principle*, co-written with Ben Chessell, is currently under development by Lailaps Pictures. Sometimes he teaches writing and literature.

FELICITY DOWKER is a Ditmar and Chronos Award winner and Aurealis and Australian Shadows Awards finalist. Felicity's debut short story collection, *Bread and Circuses*, will be released by Ticonderoga Publications in 2012. More than 20 of Felicity's short stories have been published in Australian and international anthologies and journals including *Aurealis*, *Midnight Echo*, *Scenes from the Second Storey* (Morrigan Books), *Scary Kisses* and *More Scary Kisses* (Ticonderoga Publications), and others.

DALE ELVY's Spirit Shinto Trilogy was published by HarperCollins New Zealand in 2001. He subsequently received Sir Julius Vogel Awards for best new talent and best novel in 2001 and 2003. He has worked in a variety of roles in the public and private sectors, and is currently completing a PhD in Political Science at the Australian National University.

JASON FISCHER attended the Clarion South writers workshop in 2007, and has been shortlisted in the Aurealis Awards, the Ditmar Awards, and the Australian Shadows Awards. He won the 2009 AHWA Short Story and the 2010 AHWA Flash Fiction Competitions, and is a recent winner of the Writers of the Future contest. Jason has stories in Jack Dann's *Dreaming Again*, *Apex*, *Andromeda Spaceways Inflight Magazine*, and *Aurealis*.

DIRK FLINTHART lives in Tasmania and raises irritatingly precocious children. He writes SF, and fantasy, for which he has been Ditmarred, and has three times been a finalist for an Aurealis Award in the Young Adult category—without winning. According to Wikipedia, that's a record. Curse you, Margo Lanagan and your irresistibly idiosyncratic prose techniques!

BOB FRANKLIN is a stand-up comedian, writer, actor and director. His first collection of stories, *Under Stones*, was published by Affirm Press in 2010.

CHRISTOPHER GREEN was born in the United States and moved to Australia at the age of 20, after meeting his wife on the internet (she wasn't his wife at the time). His fiction has appeared in *Dreaming Again*, *Beneath Ceaseless Skies*, and *Abyss & Apex* and is the recipient of an Aurealis Award. He lives in Geelong with his wife and their two perpetually muddy labradors. He maintains a blog at www.christophergreen.wordpress.com

PAUL HAINES is the author of three superb dark collections. Everyone says so. They've even won some awards that his wife won't let him display in the public part of the house. He's currently working on a Wolf Creek novel with Greg McLean. More info www.paulhaines.com

In just over two years, LISA L HANNETT has sold more than 20 stories to venues including *Clarkesworld, Fantasy, Weird Tales, ChiZine, Electric Velocipede, Shimmer* and *Steampunk II: Steampunk Reloaded*. Her work has appeared on *Locus*'s Recommended Reading List 2009 and *Tangent Online*'s Recommended Reading List 2010. "The February Dragon", co-written with Angela Slatter, won the Aurealis Award for Best Fantasy Short Story 2010. She is a graduate of Clarion South. *Bluegrass Symphony*, her first collection, is published by Ticonderoga Publications. A second collection, *Midnight and Moonshine* (co-authored with Angela Slatter) will be published in November 2012. Visit her online at www.lisahannett.com.

Screen- and fiction-writer STEPHEN M IRWIN grew up in Brisbane. His short films and short stories have won acclaim and awards in Australia and around the world. His debut thriller *The Dead Path* won the Doubleday Book of the Month Club 2010 First Fiction Award, and was named Top Horror Title in the American Library Association's 2011 Reading List. His second novel *The Broken Ones* was published in 2011.

Award-winning author GARY KEMBLE has published more than 20 stories in Australia and abroad. He lives in Brisbane's leafy west with his wife, kids and some determined scrub turkeys.

PETE KEMPSHALL has written stories for Ticonderoga Publications and Twelfth Planet Press in Australia and internationally for the likes of Big Finish Productions, Morrigan Books and Apex Publications. He also co-edited the Australian anthology *Scenes From the Second Storey* and blogs every now and again at tyrannyoftheblankpage.blogspot.com.

TESSA KUM is a Clarion South survivor and editorial assistant for *Weird Tales Magazine*. She lives in a very cold house in Melbourne and does not dream at night. She has always written fiction, she finds fiction in all things, and in the places where there is no fiction she puts some in, just as she has done with this bio.

Perth-based MARTIN LIVINGS has had over sixty short stories published in a variety of magazines and anthologies over the last twenty years. His first novel, *Carnies*, was published by Hachette Livre in 2006, and he has a collection of short stories being published by Dark Prints Press in 2012. www.martinlivings.com

MAXINE MCARTHUR is the author of three science fiction novels and numerous short stories. "A Pearling Tale" was inspired by historical research done in a different context at the National Archives of Australia (a highly recommended source of amazing stories). Maxine lives in Canberra in a three-generation household including dog, horse, and goldfish, and works at the ANU.

KIRSTYN MCDERMOTT was born on Halloween, an auspicious date which perhaps accounts for her lifelong attraction to all things dark, mysterious and bumpy-in-the-night. Her short fiction has been published in various magazines and anthologies, including *Macabre, More Scary Kisses, Southerly, Aurealis* and *Island*, and her award-winning debut novel, *Madigan Mine*, was published by Picador in 2010. Kirstyn lives in Melbourne, Australia, and can be found online at www.kirstynmcdermott.com

ANDREW J MCKIERNAN is an author and illustrator living and working on the Central Coast of NSW. His stories have appeared in various magazines and anthologies and have twice been short-listed for an Aurealis Award (2009/2010) and an Australian Shadows Award (2009/2010) as well as story and artwork short-listings for the Ditmar Awards (2009/2010). www.andrewmckiernan.com

BEN PEEK is the Sydney based author of over thirty short stories, an autobiographical comic, and three novels, *Twenty-Six Lies/One Truth, Black Sheep*, and his most recent, *Above/Below*, a pair of interlocked novellas written with Stephanie Campisi and published by Twelfth Planet Press. His next book is a collection of short stories, *Dead Americans*, published by ChiZine Publications. He can be found at benpeek.livejournal.com

SIMON PETRIE is a research scientist at an Australian university. His short fiction, featured in numerous magazines and anthologies over the past few years, has been collected in *Rare Unsigned Copy* (Peggy Bright Books, 2010). Simon is an active member of the Andromeda Spaceways publishing co-op, a three-time Aurealis Award judge, and the recipient of the Sir Julius Vogel award for Best New Talent in 2010.

LEZLI ROBYN is an Aussie lass who loves writing sf, fantasy, horror, humour and even enjoys dabbling in steampunk every now and then. She's made over 25 story sales to professional markets around the world, including *Asimov's* and *Analog*, and her first short story collection will be published by Ticonderoga in late 2012. She was also a finalist for the 2009 SF short story Aurealis Award, and a 2010 Campbell Award nominee for best new writer.

ANGELA REGA's short stories have appeared in various publications including those published by Ticonderoga Publications, Fablecroft Press, *Cabinet Des Fees* and Crossed Genres. She is a lover of folklore, fairy tales and furry creatures and believes in gnomes. A graduate of the Clarion South workshop, Angie is currently working on a YA novel. She lives in Sydney with her planet hunting partner and feline companions.

ANGELA SLATTER is the author *Sourdough & Other Stories* (Tartarus Press, UK) and *The Girl with No Hands & Other Tales* (Ticonderoga Publications), which won the Aurealis Award for Best Collection in 2011. Her work has appeared *Dreaming Again, Strange Tales II & III, Lady Churchill's Rosebud Wristlet, A Book of Horrors, Mammoth Book of New Horror* #22, and *Year's Best Dark Fantasy and Horror 2011. Midnight and Moonshine*, a collaboration with Lisa L Hannett, will be published by Ticonderoga. Their story "The February Dragon", won the Aurealis Award for Best Fantasy Short Story in 2011. She blogs at www.angelaslatter.com

GRANT STONE's fiction has appeared in *Strange Horizons, Semaphore, Andromeda Spaceways Inflight Magazine* and *Shimmer* and has twice won the Sir Julius Vogel Award. When not writing, Grant has been known to work behind the scenes on the StarShipSofa podcast or his occasional fanzine b0t b0tzine.com. Grant lives in Auckland, New Zealand and likes it just fine.

KAARON WARREN's first story collection *The Grinding House* won two Ditmar Awards. Kaaron has three novels with Angry Robot Books, the first, *Slights*, won the Ditmar and Australian Shadows Award. Her third novel, *Mistification*, was published in 2011. Her second collection, *Dead Sea Fruit*, was published by Ticonderoga in 2010. Her award winning short story "A Positive" had been made into a short film by Bearcage Productions. Kaaron lives in Canberra, Australia, with her husband and two children.

JANEEN WEBB is a multiple award-winning author, editor, and critic who has written or edited ten books and over a hundred essays and stories. She is a recipient of the World Fantasy Award, the Australian Aurealis Award, the Peter MacNamara Lifetime Achievement Award, and is a three-time winner of the Ditmar Award. She is internationally recognised for her critical work in speculative fiction and has contributed to most of the standard reference texts in the field. She holds a PhD in literature from the University of Newcastle, and lives on a small farm overlooking the sea near Wilson's Promontory.

RECOMMENDED READING LIST

Deborah Biancotti, "Home Turf" *Baggage*
Jenny Blackford, "Adam" *Kaleidotrope #9*
Simon Brown, "Sweep" *Sprawl*
Mary Elizabeth Burroughs, "The Flinchfield Dance" *Black Static #17*
Steve Cameron, "Ghost Of The Heart" *Festive Fear*
Stephanie Campisi, "Seven" *Scenes From The Second Storey*
Matthew Chrulew, "The Nullabor Wave" *World's Next Door*
Bill Congreve, "The Traps of Tumut" *Souls Along The Meridian*
Rjurik Davidson, "The Cinema Of Coming Attractions" *The Library of Forgotton Books*
Stephen Dedman, "For Those In Peril On The Sea" *Haunted Legends*
Felicity Dowker, "From Little Things" *Andromeda Spaceways Inflight Magazine #43*
—————— "The House On Juniper Road" *Worlds Next Door*
—————— "Bread And Circuses" *Scary Kisses*
Will Elliott, "Dhayban" *Macabre: A Journey Through Australia's Darkest Fears*
Mark Farrugia, "A Bag Full Of Arrows" *Andromeda Spaceways Inflight Magazine #48*
Jason Fischer, "The House Of Nameless" *Writers of the Future Vol. XXVI*
Bob Franklin, "Take The Free Tour" *Under Stones*
Christopher Green, "Jumbuck" *Aurealis 44*
Paul Haines, "Her Gallant Needs Sprawl" *Sprawl*
Lisa L Hannett, "Singing Breath Into The Dead" *Music For Another World*
—————— "Commonplace Sacrifices" *On Spec*
—————— "Tiny Drops" *Midnight Echo #4*
Richard Harland, "Shakti" *Tales of the Talisman*
—————— "The Fear" *Macabre: A Journey Through Australia's Darkest Fears*
Narrelle M Harris, "The Truth About Brains" *Best New Zombie Tales: Volume 2*
Robert Hood, "Wasting Matilda" *The Mammoth Book Of The Zombie Apocalypse*

George Ivanoff, "Trees" *Short & Scary*
Trent Jamieson, "The Driver's Assistant" *Ticon4*
Pete Kempshall, "Dead Letter Drop" *Close Encounters of the Urban Kind*
——— "Signature Walk" *Sprawl*
Martin Livings, "Lollo" *Close Encounters of the Urban Kind*
Penelope Love, "Border Crossing" *Belong*
Geoffrey Maloney & Andrew Bakery, "Sleeping Dogs" *Midnight Echo #4*
Tracie McBride, "Lest We Forget" (audio) *Spectrum Collection*
Kirstyn McDermott, "Monsters Among Us" *Macabre: A Journey Through Australia's Darkest Fears*
Andrew J McKiernan, "All The Clowns In Clown Town" *Macabre: A Journey Through Australia's Darkest Fears*
Simon Petrie, "Running Lizard" *Rare Unsigned Copy: tales of Rocketry, Ineptitude, and Giant Mutant Vegetables*
Michael Radburn, "They Own The Night" *Festive Fear*
Janeen Samuel, "My Brother Quentin" *Andromeda Spaceways Inflight Magazine #44*
Angela Slatter, "A Porcelain Soul" *Sourdough and other stories*
——— "Gallowberries" *Sourdough and other stories*
——— "The Dead Ones Don't Hurt You" *The Girl With No Hands and other tales*
Cat Sparks, "All the Love in the World" *Sprawl*
Grant Stone, "Dead Air" (poem) *Andromeda Spaceways Inflight Magazine #46*
Lucy Sussex, "Albert & Victoria/Slow Dreams" *Baggage*
Anna Tambour, "Gnawer Of The Moon Seeks Summit Of Paradise" *Sprawl*
Kaaron Warren, "Sins Of The Ancestors" *Dead Sea Fruit*
——— "The Coral Gatherer" *Dead Sea Fruit*
——— "Hive Of Glass" *Baggage*
David Witteveen, "Perfect Skin" *Cthulhu's Dark Cults*

AUSTRALIAN & NEW ZEALAND FANTASY & HORROR AWARDS

THE AUSTRALIAN SF "DITMAR" AWARDS

BEST NOVEL

Power and Majesty by Tansy Rayner Roberts (HarperVoyager)
NOMINEES
Death Most Definite by Trent Jamieson (Hachette)
Madigan Mine by Kirstyn McDermott (Pan Macmillan)
Stormlord Rising by Glenda Larke (HarperVoyager)
Walking the Tree by Kaaron Warren (Angry Robot Books)

BEST NOVELLA OR NOVELETTE:

"The Company Articles of Edward Teach" by Thoraiya Dyer (Twelfth Planet Press)
NOMINEES
"Acception" by Tessa Kum (*Baggage*, Eneit Press)
"All the Clowns in Clowntown" by Andrew J McKiernan (*Macabre: A Journey Through Australia's Darkest Fears*, Brimstone Press)
"Bleed" by Peter M Ball (Twelfth Planet Press)
"Her Gallant Needs" by Paul Haines (*Sprawl*, Twelfth Planet Press)

BEST SHORT STORY

"All the Love in the World" by Cat Sparks (*Sprawl*, Twelfth Planet Press)
"She Said" by Kirstyn McDermott (*Scenes from the Second Storey*, Morrigan Books)
NOMINEES
"Bread and Circuses" by Felicity Dowker (*Scary Kisses*, Ticonderoga Publications)
"One Saturday Night With Angel" by Peter M Ball (*Sprawl*, Twelfth Planet Press)

"The House of the Nameless" by Jason Fischer (*Writers of the Future XXVI*, Galaxy Press)
"The February Dragon" by Angela Slatter & Lisa L Hannett (*Scary Kisses*, Ticonderoga Publications)

BEST COLLECTED WORK

Sprawl edited by Alisa Krasnostein (Twelfth Planet Press)
NOMINEES
Baggage edited by Gillian Polack (Eneit Press)
Macabre: A Journey through Australia's Darkest Fears edited by Angela Challis & Dr Marty Young (Brimstone Press)
Scenes from the Second Storey edited by Amanda Pillar and Pete Kempshall (Morrigan Books)
Worlds Next Door edited by Tehani Wessely (FableCroft Publishing)

BEST ARTWORK

"The Lost Thing" short film, Andrew Ruhemann and Shaun Tan (Passion Pictures)
NOMINEES
Cover art *The Angælien Apocalypse/The Company Articles of Edward Teach* Dion Hamill (Twelfth Planet Press)
Cover art *Australis Imaginarium* Shaun Tan (FableCroft Publishing)
Cover art *Dead Sea Fruit* Olga Read (Ticonderoga Publications)
Cover art *Savage Menace and Other Poems of Horror* Andrew J McKiernan (P'rea Press)

BEST NEW TALENT

Thoraiya Dyer
NOMINEES
Lisa L Hannett
Patty Jansen
Kathleen Jennings
Pete Kempshall

AUREALIS AWARDS

FANTASY NOVEL

Power and Majesty by Tansy Rayner Roberts (HarperVoyager)
NOMINEES
The Silence of Medair by Andrea K. Höst (self-published)
Death Most Definite by Trent Jamieson (Orbit/Hachette)
Stormlord Rising by Glenda Larke (HarperVoyager)
Heart's Blood by Juliet Marillier (Pan Macmillan)

FANTASY SHORT STORY

"Yowie" by Thoraiya Dyer (*Sprawl*, Twelfth Planet Press)
"The February Dragon" by Lisa L Hannett & Angela Slatter (*Scary Kisses*, Ticonderoga Publications)

NOMINEES

"The Duke of Vertumn's Fingerling" by Elizabeth Carroll (*Strange Horizons*)
"All the Clowns in Clowntown" by Andrew J McKiernan (*Macabre: A Journey Through Australia's Darkest Fears*, Brimstone Press)
"Sister, Sister" by Angela Slatter (*Strange Tales III*, Tartarus Press)

BEST HORROR SHORT STORY

"The Fear" by Richard Harland (*Macabre: A Journey Through Australia's Darkest Fears*, Brimstone Press)

NOMINEES

"Take the Free Tour" by Bob Franklin (*Under Stones*, Affirm Press)
"Her Gallant Needs" by Paul Haines (*Sprawl*, Twelfth Planet Press)
"Wasting Matilda" by Robert Hood (*Zombie Apocalypse!*, Running Press)
"Lollo" by Martin Livings (*Close Encounters of the Urban Kind*, Apex Publishing)

BEST HORROR NOVEL

Madigan Mine by Kirstyn McDermott (Pan Macmillan)

NOMINEES

After the World: Gravesend by Jason Fischer (Black House Comics)
Death Most Definite by Trent Jamieson (Orbit)

BEST COLLECTION

The Girl With No Hands and other tales by Angela Slatter (Ticonderoga Publications)

NOMINEES

The Library of Forgotten Books by Rjurik Davidson (PS Publishing)
Under Stones by Bob Franklin (Affirm Press)
Sourdough and Other Stories by Angela Slatter (Tartarus Press)
Dead Sea Fruit by Kaaron Warren (Ticonderoga Publications)

BEST ANTHOLOGY

Wings of Fire edited by Jonathan Strahan & Marianne S Jablon (Night Shade Books)

NOMINEES

Macabre: A Journey Through Australia's Darkest Fears edited by Angela Challis & Dr Marty Young (Brimstone Press)
Sprawl edited by Alisa Krasnostein (Twelfth Planet Press)
Scenes from the Second Storey edited by Amanda Pillar & Pete Kempshall (Morrigan Books)
Godlike Machines edited by Jonathan Strahan (SF Book Club)

BEST CHILDREN'S FICTION (TOLD PRIMARILY THROUGH WORDS)

The Keepers by Lian Tanner (Allen & Unwin)
NOMINEES
Grimsdon by Deborah Abela (Random House)
Ranger's Apprentice #9: Halt's Peril by John Flanagan (Random House)
The Vulture of Sommerset, by Stephen M Giles (Pan Macmillan)
Haggis MacGregor and the Night of the Skull by Jen Storer & Gug Gordon (Penguin/Aussie Nibbles)

BEST CHILDREN'S FICTION (TOLD PRIMARILY THROUGH PICTURES)

The Boy and the Toy by Sonya Hartnett & Lucia Masciullo (Viking)
NOMINEES
Night School by Isobelle Carmody & Anne Spudvilas (Viking)
Magpie by Luke Davies & Inari Kiuru (ABC Books)
Precious Little by Julie Hunt, Sue Moss & Gaye Chapman (Allen & Unwin)
The Cloudchasers by David Richardson & Steven Hunt (ABC Books)

YOUNG ADULT SHORT STORY

"A Thousand Flowers" by Margo Lanagan (*Zombies Vs Unicorns*, Allen & Unwin)
NOMINEES
"Inksucker" by Aidan Doyle (*Worlds Next Door*, Fablecroft Press)
"One Story, No Refunds" by Dirk Flinthart (*Shiny #6*, Twelfth Planet Press)
"Nine Times" by Kaia Landelius & Tansy Rayner Roberts (*Worlds Next Door*, Fablecroft Press)
"An Ordinary Boy" by Jen White (*The Tangled Bank: Love, Wonder, & Evolution*, The Tangled Bank Press)

BEST YOUNG ADULT NOVEL

Guardian of the Dead by Karen Healey (Allen & Unwin)
NOMINEES
Merrow by Ananda Braxton-Smith (black dog books)
The Midnight Zoo by Sonya Hartnett (Penguin)
The Life of a Teenage Body-Snatcher by Doug MacLeod (Penguin)
Behemoth by Scott Westerfeld (Penguin)

BEST ILLUSTRATED BOOK/GRAPHIC NOVEL

Changing Ways Book 1 by Justin Randall (Gestalt)
NOMINEES
Shakespeare's Hamlet by Nicki Greenberg (Allen & Unwin)
EEEK! Weird Australian Tales of Suspense by Jason Paulos et al (Black House Comics)
Five Wounds: An Illustrated Novel by Jonathan Walker & Dan Hallett (Allen & Unwin)
Horrors: Great Stories of Fear and Their Creators by Rocky Wood & Glenn Chadbourne (McFarlane & Co.)

BEST SCIENCE FICTION SHORT STORY

"The Heart of a Mouse" by KJ Bishop (*Subterranean Online* Winter 2010)
NOMINEES
"The Angælian Apocalypse" by Matthew Chrulew (*The Company Articles Of Edward Teach/The Angælian Apocalypse*, Twelfth Planet Press)
"Border Crossing" by Penelope Love (*Belong*, Ticonderoga Publications)
"Interloper" by Ian McHugh (*Asimov's* January 2011)
"Relentless Adaptations" by Tansy Rayner Roberts (*Sprawl*, Twelfth Planet Press)

BEST SCIENCE FICTION NOVEL

Transformation Space, by Marianne de Pierres (Orbit)
NOMINEES
Song of Scarabaeus, by Sara Creasy (EOS)
Mirror Space, by Marianne de Pierres (Orbit)

PETER MCNAMARA CONVENORS' AWARD

Helen Merrick

AUSTRALIAN SHADOWS AWARDS

LONG FICTION

Under Stones by Bob Franklin (Affirm Press)
NOMINEES
Madigan Mine by Kirstyn McDermott (Picador Australia)
The Girl With No Hands and other tales by Angela Slatter (Ticonderoga Publications)
Guardian of the Dead by Karen Healy (Allen & Unwin)
Bleed by Peter M Ball (Twelfth Planet Press)

EDITED PUBLICATION

Macabre: A Journey Through Australia's Darkest Fears edited by Angela Challis & Dr Marty Young (Brimstone Press)
NOMINEES
Scenes From The Second Storey, edited by Amanda Pillar & Pete Kempshall (Morrigan Books)
Dark Pages 1, edited by Brenton Tomlinson (Blade Red Press)
Scary Kisses, edited by Liz Grzyb (Ticonderoga Publications)
Midnight Echo #4, edited by Lee Battersby (AHWA)

SHORT FICTION

"She Said" by Kirstyn McDermott (*Scenes from the Second Storey*, Morrigan Books)

NOMINEES
"Bread and Circuses" by Felicity Dowker (*Scary Kisses*, Ticonderoga Publications)
"Brisneyland by Night" by Angela Slatter (*Sprawl*, Twelfth Planet Press)
"All The Clowns In Clowntown" by Andrew J McKiernan (*Macabre: A Journey through Australia's Darkest Fears*, Brimstone Press)
"Dream Machine" by David Conyers (*Scenes from the Second Storey*, Morrigan Books)

SIR JULIUS VOGEL AWARDS

BEST NOVEL
The Heir Of Night by Helen Lowe (Orbit)
The Questing Road by Lyn McConchie (Tor Books)
NOMINEES
Barking Death Squirels by Douglas A. Van Belle (Random Static)
Tymon's Flight by Mary Victoria (HarperCollins Publishers Australia)
Geist by Philippa Ballantine (Ace Books)

BEST NOVELLA / NOVELETTE
"A Tale Of The Interferers: Hunger For Forbidden Flesh" by Paul Haines (*Andromeda Spaceways Inflight Magazine* #46)
NOMINEES
"L" by Bill Direen (*A Foreign Country: New Zealand Speculative Fiction*, Random Static)
"Her Gallant Needs" by Paul Haines (*Sprawl*, Twelfth Planet Press)

BEST SHORT STORY
"High Tide At Hot Water Beach" by Paul Haines (*A Foreign Country: New Zealand Speculative Fiction*, Random Static)
NOMINEES
"Consumed" by Lee Murray (*A Foreign Country: New Zealand Speculative Fiction*, Random Static)
"The Future Of The Sky" by Ripley Patton (*A Foreign Country: New Zealand Speculative Fiction*, Random Static)
"The Interview" by Darian Smith (*Andromeda Spaceways Inflight Magazine* #49)
"I've Seen This Man" by Paul Haines (*Scenes From The Second Storey*, Morrigan Books)

BEST COLLECTED WORK
A Foreign Country: New Zealand Speculative Fiction edited by Anna Caro and Juliet Buchanan (Random Static)

NOMINEES
The Care And Feeding Of Your Lunatic Mage by Douglas A. Van Belle
(Andomeda Spaceways Special Project)
2010 Semaphore Anthology edited by Marie Hodgkinson
Rare Unsigned Copy by Simon Petrie (Peggy Bright Books)

BEST PRODUCTION / PUBLICATION
White Cloud Worlds Anthology edited by Paul Tobin
NOMINEES
Semaphore Magazine edited by Marie Hodgkinson
The Art Of District 9: Weta Workshop edited by Daniel Falconer
White Cloud Worlds Art Exhibition: The New Dowse Art Gallery
curated by Leanne Wickham

OTHER AWARDS AND ACHIEVEMENTS

The 2010 AHWA Short Story and Flash Fiction competition winner for short story was "Letters of Love from the Once and Newly Dead" by Christopher Green, with Honourable Mentions to Aaron Ashley Garrison and Felicity Dowker. The flash fiction category winner was "Goggy" by Jason Fischer, with Honourable Mentions to Aaron Ashley Garrison and Eugene Gramelis.

Tansy Rayner Roberts won the Washington SF Association Small Press Short Fiction Award for *Siren Beat.*

Marianne de Pierres, under the nom de plume Marianne Delacourt, won a Davitt award for *Sharp Shooter,* book 1 in the Tara Sharp series of paranormal crime novels.

Shaun Tan was recognised as the Artist Guest of Honour at the World Science Fiction Convention and won the Hugo Award for Best Artist. Jonathan Strahan was nominated for the Best Editor (Short Form), and Helen Merrick was nominated for Best Related Work for *The Secret Feminist Cabal: A Cultural History of SF Feminisms.* Lezli Robyn was a nominee for the John W Campbell Award for Best New Writer.

Shaun Tan also won the Adelaide Festival Awards for Literature, both the Children's Literature Award and the Premier's Award, for his *Tales From Outer Suburbia.*

Margo Lanagan won the World Fantasy Award for the novella "Sea Hearts" (X6, couer de lion). Jonathan Strahan's anthology *Eclipse Three* (Night Shade Books) was nominated and Strahan won the Special— Professional World Fantasy Award.

Lucy Sussex was presented with the Peter McNamara Achievement Award, recognising lifetime achievement.

The Bram Stoker awards featured two nominations of work by Australians. Kirstyn McDermott in the category of Superior Achievement In Long Fiction for "Monsters Among Us" (*Macabre: A Journey Through Australia's Darkest Fears*), and in the category of Superior Achievement

In An Anthology, *Macabre: A Journey Through Australia's Darkest Fears* edited by Angela Challis and Marty Young (Brimstone Press).

Scott Westerfeld was nominated for the Andre Norton Award for Young Adult SF and Fantasy for *Behemoth* (Simon and Schuster).

The Western Australian Premier's Book Awards shortlists include Isobel Carmody's *The Red Wind* (Penguin) and Sonya Hartnett's *The Midnight Zoo* ((Penguin).

Tansy Rayner Roberts and Gary Kemble both received Australia Council grants to write novels.

The Horseman (2008) dominated the A Night Of Horror Film Festival Awards, taking out the following categories: Best Australian Film, Best Australian Director (Steven Kastrissios), Best Female Performance (Caroline Marohasy), and Best Male Performance (Peter Marshall). The A Night Of Horror Film Festival Awards Audience Choice Award from the Australian short showcase was a tie between *The Clothes* (directed by Toby Morris) and *Mr Pin* (directed by Andrew Daley). The award for Best Special Effects went to *The Dark Lurking* (directed by Gregory Connors).

The 2010 Ned Kelly Awards for Australian crime writing were presented at the Melbourne Writers Festival. Garry Disher won best fiction book for *Wyatt* (Text), best first fiction went to Mark Dapin for *King Of The Cross* (MacMillan), the true crime award went to Kathy Marks for *Pitcairn: Paradise Lost* (HarperCollins) and Zane Lovitt won the SD Harvey Short Story Award for "Leaving The Fountainhead" and Lucy Sussex took out second prize with "The Fountain Of Justice". The lifetime achievement award was presented to Peter Doyle.

Patty Jansen won first place, and Brett Mann won second place, in the second quarter of the Writers of the Future contest.

The winner of the long-running Nameless competition organised by Stephen Studach and Felicity Dowker to raise money for author Paul Haines' medical treatment was decided by guest judge Ramsey Campbell. The winner was Robert N Stephenson, with finalists Tim Martain and Martin Livings.

ACKNOWLEDGEMENTS

"After the Jump" copyright © 2010 Felicity Dowker. First published in *Aurealis #43*, July 2010.

"L'esprit de L'escalier" copyright © 2010 Peter M Ball. First published in *Apex Magazine #16*, September 2010.

"That Girl" copyright © 2010 Kaaron Warren. First published in *Haunted Legends* (Tor, 2010).

"Walker" copyright © 2010 Dirk Flinthart. First published in *Sprawl* (Twelfth Planet Press, 2010).

"The Bone Mother" copyright © 2010 Angela Slatter. First published in *The Girl With No Hands and other tales* (Ticonderoga Publications 2010).

"Children's Story" copyright © 2010 Bob Franklin. First published in *Under Stones* (Affirm Press, 2010).

"Night Shift" copyright © 2010 Dale Elvy. First published in *A Foreign Country* (Random Static Press, 2010).

"Manifest Destiny", copyright © 2010 Janeen Webb. First published in *Baggage* (Eneit Press, 2010).

"Hive" copyright © 2010 Stephen M Irwin. First published in *Macabre: A Journey Through Australia's Darkest Fears* (Brimstone Press, 2010).

"Acception" copyright © 2010 Tessa Kum. First published in *Baggage* (Eneit Press, 2010).

"Brave Face" copyright © 2010 Pete Kempshall. First published in *Andromeda Spaceways Inflight Magazine #46*, 2010.

"Home" copyright © 2010 Martin Livings. First published in *Scenes from the Second Storey* (Morrigan Books, 2010).

"Soil From My Fingers" copyright © 2010 Lisa L Hannett. First published in *Tesseracts 14* (Hades Publications, 2010).

"Feast or Famine" copyright © 2010 Gary Kemble. First published in *Macabre: A Journey Through Australia's Darkest Fears* (Brimstone Press, 2010).

"Johnny and Babushka" copyright © 2010 RJ Astruc. First published in *Electric Spec* vol 5 issue 4, November 2010.

"Schubert by Candlelight" copyright © 2010 Matthew Chrulew. First published in *Macabre: A Journey Through Australia's Darkest Fears* (Brimstone Press, 2010).

"Slow Cookin'" copyright © 2010 Angela Rega. First published in *Belong* (Ticonderoga Publications, 2010).

"The School Bus" copyright © 2010 Jason Fischer. First published in *Andromeda Spaceways Inflight Magazine #46* 2010.

"The King's Accord" copyright © 2010 Alan Baxter. First published in *Flesh & Bone: Rise of the Necromancers* (Pill Hill Publishers, 2010).

AVAILABLE FROM TICONDEROGA PUBLICATIONS

WWW.TICONDEROGAPUBLICATIONS.COM

THANK YOU

The publisher would sincerely like to thank:

Elizabeth Grzyb, Talie Helene, RJ Astruc, Peter M Ball, Alan
Baxter, Jenny Blackford, Gitte Christensen, Matthew Chrulew,
Bill Congreve, Rjurik Davidson, Felicity Dowker, Dale Elvy,
Jason Fischer, Dirk Flinthart, Bob Franklin, Christopher Green,
Paul Haines, Lisa L Hannett, Stephen Irwin, Gary Kemble, Pete
Kempshall, Tessa Kum, Martin Livings, Maxine McArthur,
Kirstyn McDermott, Andrew McKiernan, Ben Peek, Simon
Petrie, Lezli Robyn, Angela Rega, Angela Slatter, Grant Stone
(NZ), Kaaron Warren, Janeen Webb, Simon Brown, Jonathan
Strahan, Peter McNamara, Ellen Datlow, Grant Stone,
Jeremy G. Byrne, Lucy Sussex, Sean Williams, Garth Nix,
David Cake, Simon Oxwell, Grant Watson, Sue Manning,
Steven Utley, Bill Congreve, Jack Dann, Stephen Dedman,
the Mt Lawley Mafia, the Nedlands Yakuza, Amanda Pillar,
Shane Jiraiya Cummings, Angela Challis, Donna Maree Hanson,
Kate Williams, Kathryn Linge, Andrew Williams, Al Chan,
Alisa and Tehani, Mel & Phil, Hayley Lane, Georgina Walpole,
everyone we've missed . . .

. . . and you.

In memory of Eve Johnson (1945–2011)

www.ingramcontent.com/pod-product-compliance
Lightning Source LLC
Chambersburg PA
CBHW022237020726
47496CB00004B/941